Secrets

Books by Jude Deveraux

The Velvet Promise
Highland Velvet
Velvet Song
Velvet Angel
Sweetbriar
Counterfeit Lady
Lost Lady
River Lady
Twin of Fire
Twin of Ice
The Temptress
The Raider
The Princess
The Awakening
The Maiden
The Taming
The Conquest
A Knight in Shining Armor
Holly
Wishes

JUDE DEVERAUX

Secrets

ATRIA BOOKS
New York London Toronto Sydney

ATRIA BOOKS

A Division of Simon & Schuster, Inc.
1230 Avenue of the Americas
New York, NY 10020

This Atria Books export edition May 2008

ATRIA BOOKS and colophon are trademarks of Simon & Schuster, Inc.

For information about special discounts for bulk purchases,
please contact Simon & Schuster Special Sales
at 1-800-456-6798 or business@simonandschuster.com.

Designed by Davina Mock-Maniscalco

Manufactured in the United States of America

1   3   5   7   9   10   8   6   4   2

ISBN-13: 978-1-4165-7708-9
ISBN-10:   1-4165-7708-4

Secrets

Prologue

CASSIE HAD HEARD that drowning was the easiest form of death. She had no idea how anyone could know that, since whoever said it had lived, but as she drifted down in the deep end of the pool, she decided they were right. She could feel her long hair floating upward, and all weight left her twelve-year-old body. She wasn't trying to kill herself. No, she was just waiting for *him* to rescue her. But dying was interesting to think about. What if this really were the end? Smiling, she let her body relax into her thoughts. Never again would she have to hear her mother declare how easy Cassie's life had been while her mother's had been so difficult. "We stopped a war!" her mother, Margaret Madden, loved to say, referring to Vietnam. "No one else in history has ever done that!" Until she was ten, Cassie believed that her mother had single-handedly made the president of the United States remove the troops from the war that was never declared to be a war.

But when Cassie was ten, an old college friend of her mother had visited them, and when she'd heard Margaret bawling out her daughter, the friend started laughing. "Maggie," she said, and Cassie looked up in wonder because no one ever dared to call her mother "Maggie." "You never left your classes and you told us all that we were idiots to sit around on the grass smoking pot and protesting."

Needless to say, that was the end of that friendship, but it had been an enlightening experience for Cassie. That was when she found out that not every word that came out of her mother's mouth was the truth. She learned that just because someone delivered a statement with force and volume, didn't make it a fact. From that time on, she began to see her mother for what she was: a bully and a tyrant who believed that there was only one way to do anything, and that was the way *she* had done everything. To her mind, if her daughter wanted to grow up to be a successful person, then she had to conduct herself exactly as Margaret Madden had. That meant going to a top school, getting the best grades, then working her way up to the head of some mega corporation.

One time Cassie asked, "What about a husband and children?"

"Don't get me started," Margaret said, then said nothing else. But she had piqued Cassie's curiosity, so she began to secretly listen in on her mother's conversations. Most of the discussions revealed nothing of interest, but one day Cassie had the horror of hearing her mother say that her daughter had been conceived from a one-night stand with a man she hardly knew while she was on a business trip to Hong Kong. "Defective condom," Margaret had said without a hint of sentimentality. She was so disciplined that she hadn't realized she was pregnant until she was nearly five months along and it was too late for an abortion. Margaret said she'd done her best to ignore the pregnancy, and that she'd meant to turn the baby over to a childless colleague, but then her boss—the person she most admired—had said he was glad Margaret was going to be raising a child. It made her seem more human.

When he gave her a sterling silver rattle from Tiffany, she decided to keep the kid.

As she did with all things, Margaret planned it carefully. She bought a house in upstate New York, hired a live-in housekeeper and a nanny, then turned the child over to them while she stayed in the city and clawed her way to the top.

Cassie saw her mother only on alternate weekends, and had spent most of her life terrified of her.

It was when her mother had been invited to a weeklong seminar at Kingsmill Resort in Williamsburg, Virginia, that Cassie's life changed. She knew about her mother's career because Margaret Madden thought it was her duty to inform her daughter how to get ahead in the world. Margaret loved to tell how she had been raised in a middle-class household full of "morons" but that she had "risen above" them. She'd put herself through college, studying business administration, then got a job as a junior manager with a big office supply chain. In her sixth year there, the company was bought by a fledgling computer business, and Margaret was one of only three upper-employees kept. Within four years she was at the top of that company.

By the time she'd been out of college for fifteen years, she'd been in five corporations and had moved near the head of each one. She was creative and dedicated, and every waking second of her life was given to the company where she worked.

The trip to Williamsburg was to be pivotal. The company where she was second in command was about to be bought by an enormous conglomerate, and at the end of the week she was either going to be jobless or made executive vice president.

The only problem had been that Cassie's latest nanny had broken her ankle and the housekeeper was on vacation, so there was no one to take care of the child. Margaret had used the inconvenience to her advantage when she'd called her boss and said she so rarely got to see her beloved daughter, could she please take the child with her? The man had been pleasantly impressed and agreed readily.

Cassie and her mother were given one of the many pretty, two-bedroom guest condos, and Cassie had been left on her own. Her mother was busy "making contacts" as she called it, never friends, never anything just for pleasure, so she was unaware of where her daughter was.

It was the first time Cassie had really seen her mother's colleagues, and for a whole day she'd been fascinated. There were over three hundred people at the conference and within hours they had assembled themselves into little groups where they put their heads together and whispered. When Cassie got near them, she heard "Madden," then they broke apart. It was as if they thought the girl had been brought there to spy for her mother.

Cassie spent her time wandering about the beautiful resort and watching and listening, something she was good at.

By the second day, she saw that there was one person who seemed to be different from the others. He was a tall young man with blue eyes, black hair, and a tiny cleft in his chin. She didn't know who he was or what he did, but he seemed to run the place. The CEOs of the two merging corporations both talked to him. He'd listen, then go away, and later he'd nod toward someone that something had been done.

Cassie thought he was the quiet in the eye of the storm. Tempers were high that week. There were big negotiations of who was going to stay and in what position, and who was leaving. Little cliques of men and women were everywhere, plotting and planning.

In the midst of it all was this young man, who was very calm. She watched him step into the middle of angry people, and within seconds, whatever he said to them made them quit shouting. Maybe it was a re-action to her hyper mother, who was always living in the future, constantly scheming about the next product that would sell millions, the next takeover, the next position up the ladder, but Cassie really liked this quiet man who could settle others down.

By the third day, Cassie began to study the young man. As much as possible, wherever he went, whatever he did, she was there. When he spoke, she put herself close enough to listen. Several times he turned quickly and winked at her, but he never once addressed her directly, and she was glad. She had no idea what she'd say if he did speak to her. What she liked the most was that he seemed to be at peace with himself and the world. She never once heard him talk about a "five-year plan."

By the fourth day, she knew she was in love with him, and as a result, her watching of him became more secretive. She hid in bushes as he played tennis and laughed with the other guests. On Saturday when he went sailing, she was nearby when he left and watching when he returned. She saw that every morning he went swimming before it was quite daylight, so early on Sunday, the last day, she waited for him by the pool. The fact that she couldn't swim very well was, to her mind, an asset. If she did begin to sink, he could save her.

Six came and went but he didn't show up. Cassie was in the deep end and she was getting tired. She hadn't had much sleep in the last few days because she'd been keeping vigil over him.

By six thirty, she knew she should get out of the pool. She'd decided he wasn't going to come, but then she heard voices from the direction of the house and she relaxed. He'd be there soon. She smiled in anticipation as she let her muscles go limp and sunk toward the bottom.

It was never her intention to actually drown, but as she waited for him to come, as she thought about her mother, she forgot about time and place.

The next thing she knew, she opened her eyes and she was being kissed by . . . him. His lips, his eyes, his chin, his body were all near hers and he was kissing her. Or giving her mouth-to-mouth, which was very nearly the same thing.

"She's alive!" Cassie heard a woman say, but she couldn't concentrate because she began coughing up a lot of water.

"Are you all right?" he asked, his hands on her shoulders, holding her as she choked and spit.

Cassie managed to nod that she was fine. As long as he was near her, she was sure that she'd always be all right.

Someone put a towel around her, and she looked up to see a pretty woman kneeling beside her. "You shouldn't go swimming alone," she said softly, tenderness in her eyes.

The man looked across Cassie to the woman. It didn't take much to figure out that they were together, a couple. If Cassie hadn't still been choking she would have burst into tears. She wanted to shout at the woman that he was *hers*! Hadn't she nearly died to prove that?

But Cassie said nothing of what she really thought. Life with her mother had taught her to keep her true feelings and emotions to herself. If people didn't agree with her mother, there were punishments.

"Don't tell my mother," Cassie managed to say at last, looking at him and avoiding the eyes of the woman.

Puzzled, the woman glanced at him.

"Margaret Madden," he said.

The woman let out her breath in a sympathetic sigh. "I didn't know ol' Maggie could have—" She cut off her sentence. "We won't tell," she reassured Cassie. "But maybe we should have a doctor look at you."

"No!" Cassie said, then jumped up to show them that she was all right. But she got dizzy and would have fallen if he hadn't caught her. For a moment she had the divine pleasure of feeling his arms around her. She was glad she hadn't died in the pool because if she had, she wouldn't have felt his lips on hers and his hands on her body.

The woman cleared her throat and he released Cassie.

She backed away, looking at them. They were a beautiful couple, the woman tall like he was, with her dark hair cut short and close to her head. She had on a swimsuit that showed off her long, lean, athletic body. She also probably played tennis and swam. *She* would never drown, Cassie thought, backing away from them. She was embarrassed now and afraid they'd ask why she was in the pool alone if she couldn't swim very well.

"I, uh . . . I have to go," she mumbled, then turned and ran toward the house. Behind her, she heard the man's baritone voice say something. The woman said, "Hush! She obviously has a crush on you and she deserves respect." Cassie heard the man say, "She's just a kid. She can't—"

Cassie heard no more. She wanted to die from the humiliation and embarrassment. She couldn't will herself to die, but she could stay in her room for the rest of the day.

She and her mother left the resort that evening, but while her mother said her farewells, Cassie had skulked in the corners, fearful of running into him again, afraid he and his girlfriend would laugh at her. She didn't see them. But as soon as she and her mother got into the company car, her mother launched into a lecture about how she'd been embarrassed by Cassie's rudeness. "You'll never achieve anything if you don't put yourself forward," Margaret said. "Lurking about in the shadows will achieve nothing. It's possible, even probable, that someday you'll be asking one of those people for a job. You should see that they remember you."

Cassie kept her head turned away. Her heart nearly stopped when she saw *them* strolling across the lawn, hand in hand. She was sure they'd already forgotten the child who had nearly drowned just that morning.

"Him!" Margaret said, looking at the handsome young couple. "He's part of the security hired for this meeting and he stuck his nose in where it didn't belong!" she said, a look of disgust on her face. "He told a senior VP that if he didn't contain his anger, he'd have to leave. I don't know who he thinks he is, but—"

"Shut up," Cassie said, her voice calm and quiet, but fierce. It was the first time in her life that she'd stood up to her overbearing mother. Cassie had survived because she'd figured out the meaning of "passive-aggressive" when she was three. But now she couldn't bear for her mother to say something against *him*.

As they drove by, he raised his hand to her and smiled. Cassie smiled back and lifted her hand in return. Then the car turned a curve in the road and they were out of sight.

Margaret started with, "How dare you—" but when she caught the look on Cassie's young face, she stopped talking and picked up her briefcase from the floor.

When Cassie glanced up, the driver was looking at her in the rearview mirror and smiling. He was proud of her for telling Margaret Madden to back off.

Cassie turned to look out the window, and she smiled too. She wasn't sure what had happened but she knew that the week had changed her life.

1

"CASSIE! CASSIE!"

She opened her eyes to see her boss, Jefferson Ames, standing over her. He was wearing a pair of loose swim trunks and had a towel over his shoulders. Behind him was the ever-present Skylar. As always, she was smiling in that cold, I'm-gonna-get-you way that Cassie was too familiar with. And Skylar was letting Cassie know that when she and Jeff were married, Cassie would be fired. "Like I'd stay," she'd muttered to herself many times.

"Sorry," Cassie said, putting her hand up to shield her eyes from the sun. "I was lost in thought."

He looked down at her with amusement. Everyone else beside the pool was in swim attire, but Cassie had on big, army green shorts, an oversize T-shirt, and sandals. She was lying on a chaise, every inch of her body covered with beach towels. It was as though she'd die if a drop of sunlight touched her skin. "You are a dermatologist's dream," he said.

"I aim to please," she answered, looking past him and smiling at Skylar, who was narrowing her eyes at Cassie. Skylar had on a tiny bikini and her skin had been tanned to the color of walnuts.

Skylar stepped forward, all starved and honed five feet ten of her, her skin glistening with expensive oil. "I think Elsbeth has had enough sun for the day so I want you to take her home."

Cassie didn't lose her smile as she looked at Jeff for confirmation. They weren't married yet, so she refused to take orders from anyone but him.

Jeff's face didn't change. If he was aware of the war between his daughter's nanny and his girlfriend, he didn't give it away. But when he turned to look at his daughter, his face nearly melted with love. Whatever other problems he had, Jeff's love for his daughter was obvious to all. "She looks sleepy, and she's probably hungry. You know how she is. She'd stay in the water all day if she weren't dragged out."

Cassie looked out at Elsbeth in the kiddie pool. In her opinion, the five-year-old girl was the most beautiful child on the planet. She was sitting in the water wearing a suit of white eyelet, a matching hat, and most of a bottle of sunscreen. "Sure," Cassie said, throwing back one of the three towels covering her. "Will you be home for dinner tonight?"

She stood up and stretched. Cassie was several inches shorter than Skylar, but there was nothing on Cassie that wasn't real. Her mother spent many hours in a gym fighting against her natural curves, but Cassie loved hers. She'd once heard Jeff's father call her "a 1950s blonde bombshell with dark hair." It was all Cassie could do not to giggle and let them know she'd heard.

Skylar clutched Jeff's arm to her artificially enhanced breasts. "No, we're going out tonight. Just the two of us." She paused. "He'll have some real food for a change."

"Ah, right," Cassie said. "Home cooking isn't real food. I'll have to tell that to Thomas."

Jeff coughed to cover his laugh. Jeff's father, Thomas, lived with him, and just weeks after Cassie took the job of being Elsbeth's nanny, he'd asked to have some of what Cassie was cooking for herself and the child. From there it had gone to Cassie preparing dinner for the three of them. At first she'd left Thomas a plate in the warming oven while she and Elsbeth went upstairs to the playroom to eat, but he'd asked them to eat with him in the breakfast nook. From there it had gone to Thomas moving them into the dining room and setting the big mahogany table with candles and silver. "No use letting these dishes sit in the cabinet," he'd said as he put out the best china for them to use. If Cassie could use any term to describe Thomas, it would be "Old World gentleman."

Jeff spent the weekends with his daughter. Even if he had to work, he took her with him. Elsbeth was a quiet child who had no interest in rowdy group activities. Cassie would fill a backpack full of art supplies and Elsbeth would hold her father's hand and go with him wherever he led. There were times when Cassie could hardly hold back the tears at the sight of the widower and the motherless child together, clinging to each other.

The weekdays were different though because Jeff worked long, hard hours. But one night he'd come home from work to get a file he'd left behind and seen the three of them sitting at the dining table eating by candlelight and he'd joined them. By the end of the week it had become a regular event that they'd eat together. Because of Elsbeth's age, and Thomas's weak heart, they ate at six thirty, but Jeff didn't seem to mind. He said it beat calling the Chinese place and eating at the drawing board in his office. Sometimes he'd go back to his office afterward, and sometimes Cassie would hear him in the big library off his bedroom. But even if he had to work, it was nice that he got to spend more time with his daughter and father.

As for Cassie, when it had started that she was cooking three meals a day for four people, part of her wanted to protest. It wasn't her job to be a nanny *and* a cook, but she'd said nothing. Instead, she began to study cookbooks as though she were taking a graduate degree in the subject.

The best part was that cooking and eating meals together changed the household. Thomas put his name in for one of the plots that the gated community, Hamilton Hundred, had set aside for gardens, and he'd begun raising heirloom vegetables. They had purple tomatoes and blue potatoes for dinner. He began replacing the landscaper-chosen shrubs around the house with gooseberry bushes and rosemary. He planted raspberries along the back fence, and there was a blackberry bush growing smack in the middle of the front lawn.

"You've changed us, my dear," Thomas said as Cassie sautéed yellow squash and zucchini in a skillet.

Cassie just smiled. She felt that they had changed her more than she them. On the day she'd left her mother's house to go to college, she was as happy as a prisoner being released. The freedom at college had been wonderful, and she'd enjoyed every minute of it. It was after she graduated with what her mother called "a useless degree" in American history that the problems began. All during college she'd only had two boyfriends and she thought she was going to marry the last one. But when he'd proposed, she'd surprised both of them by saying no. With his pride irreparably wounded, he'd refused to so much as speak to her again. After Cassie graduated, she found herself a bit bewildered. For three years she'd thought that when she left school she was going to get married, have kids, and become a soccer mom, something that her mother hated but that Cassie thought would suit her.

Instead, after graduation, she found herself at loose ends, not sure where to go or what to do. Her mother had sold the house Cassie had grown up in, so the only home she had was Margaret's pristine, austere apartment on Fifth Avenue—and most anything was preferable to *that*.

After a few weeks of stoically listening to her mother tell her what she should do with her life, Cassie's love of American history led her to Williamsburg to see if she could find a job there. Williamsburg, with its gorgeous eighteenth-century buildings, seemed to call to her.

For two years Cassie worked in various jobs about town. She answered telephones for lawyers, and for a while became a gofer for a famous photographer. Then she got a job as an assistant in a preschool. "I must say that you are wildly overqualified," the woman who ran the school said, "but we'd be glad to have you."

It was at the school that Cassie met Elsbeth and her father, and when the nanny had been fired—for forgetting to pick up her charge for the third time—Cassie took the job. That had been a year ago. Since then, she'd managed to form a family out of the widower, his lovely young daughter, and his ailing father, and she'd been happier than she ever had been.

But things had changed three months ago when Jeff announced that he'd "met someone." Thomas, Cassie, and Elsbeth had looked at one another over the dining table as though to say, We aren't "someone"?

The tall, very thin, magnificently self-assured Skylar Beaumont had entered their lives, and nothing had been the same since. Skylar was the friend of the husband of a woman Cassie had met at the club at Hamilton Hundred, a woman Cassie had never liked. From the first day, Skylar entered the quiet, peaceful house as though she owned it. Laughing, she'd told Jeff how she planned to redecorate every inch of the place.

Thomas and Cassie had stood there in stunned silence. Jeff's beloved late wife, Lillian, had decorated the house, and therefore it was sacrosanct. Cassie knew better than to so much as move a flower vase because Lillian had put the vase there and that's where it would stay.

But when this woman came into their comfortable lives and began talking of changing everything, Jeff had just stood there smiling.

Cassie hated the woman. She told herself she had no right to hate her, that she probably loved Jeff, but she still hated her. On her third visit to the house, Skylar had handed Cassie her expensive silk jacket and asked her to "give it a little bit of a press, would you?" Cassie had smiled, taken the jacket to the laundry room, and set the hot iron on the back of it and burned a hole through it. Afterward, she'd apologized profusely and even offered to buy a replacement. She said she'd seen that very jacket at Marshalls just last week. That had sent Skylar into a rage, insisting that she'd bought the jacket at Saks, not at a discount store.

Cassie was sure she wouldn't have been as bad as she was if Thomas hadn't been standing in the doorway and covering his laughter with his hand. They had never spoken of it, but she was sure he disliked the woman as much as Cassie did.

As for Jeff, he was clueless. He kept saying that Cassie was usually so good at what she did, so he was sure that the ruined jacket was an honest mistake.

The result was that Skylar never again tried to establish her authority over Cassie, but war had been declared. If Skylar did marry Jeff, Cassie would be out of a job, out of a home, out of a family.

But worse, she'd be sent away from the man she'd loved since she was twelve years old.

2

"I HATE HER," Skylar said. "I don't mean I dislike her. I mean that I hate her right down to my bone marrow. With every molecule I possess. I stay awake at night planning ways to *kill* her. At first I thought of putting her in her place with some witty remark that would reduce her to tears, but now I think of blood. You want to hear the latest thing I've come up with?"

Dana wanted to say that she'd rather do most anything than hear yet another method Skylar had come up with for killing Jefferson Ames's nanny. But Dana knew she had to be nice, if for no other reason than because Skylar was her husband Roger's friend. And, more importantly, because Skylar came from four generations of money and Roger's law firm was handling all the business of Skylar's father's company. "I lose that account and I might as well kiss my job good-bye," Roger had said the morning after she'd met Skylar. "I know she can be a bit hard to take sometimes, but her family is rich and I need the business. Do it for me, will you?"

As always, Dana had agreed.

"What did you come up with?" Dana asked, trying to smile at Skylar, but she wanted to ask if she'd yet wheedled a marriage proposal out of Jefferson Ames. Why oh why didn't Jeff just go ahead and *marry* Skylar?

"You're not afraid that if she doesn't marry him she'll go after Roger, are you?" her mother had asked last week.

"No, of course not. That's absurd," Dana quickly said, but it had sounded false even to her. That's exactly what she was afraid of.

Her husband and Skylar had been "old friends" since college. However, Dana's idea of friends and theirs didn't seem to be the same. Roger and Skylar hadn't been study buddies, nor had they run around together in a group. No, they had been lovers, "almost engaged" was the way Skylar put it. They had met on the first day they entered Princeton and had been inseparable for almost two years. "We taught each other everything we know about anything," Skylar said the first time Dana met her, howling with laughter over the double entendre. The first time she'd met Skylar, Dana worked for a day and a half preparing a meal that Roger would declare fit for his old "friend." At the time, Dana'd had no idea what kind of friendship they'd had.

"Remember the time we went out with Beth and Andy and the car broke down?" Skylar asked, waving a piece of roast about on her fork. "There we were, stuck in the middle of nowhere, and it began to rain." She took a sip of her wine, barely able to hold in her laughter. "But there was a motel down the road so we—" She broke off, sliding her eyes sideways at Dana. "Oops, better not tell *that* story."

"More potatoes?" Dana asked, holding out the bowl even though Skylar hadn't touched what she'd already taken. In Dana's eyes, Skylar was a walking ad for "eating disorder."

"No thanks," Skylar said, seeming to be oblivious to Dana's discomfort. Or was she? Dana wondered. Could she be as unaware of other people as she pretended to be?

"You have to forgive me," Skylar said. "It's just that we had such great times in college. Roger must have told you all about me."

"No," Dana said, smiling. "Roger never said a word about you."

She'd meant for Skylar to see how unimportant she was to her husband's life, but Skylar took it differently. "Roger, darling, you dog! Keeping me a secret. Really!"

Roger was sitting at the head of the polished, antique table and smiling. He wore an air of contentment, as though everything he wanted was sitting at the table with him. And maybe it was, Dana thought as she excused herself to go to the kitchen to get more rolls.

She got the bread but she didn't go back into the dining room. Instead, she went into the sunroom and looked out the back window. It was summer now and the leaves blocked her view, but sometimes in the winter she could see the water of the James River.

When Roger had first shown her the site he'd purchased, Dana had been ecstatic. Most of the plots in Hamilton Hundred were fat little squares, but there were a few that were on the curves of the new streets, and they were long and narrow. That meant that she and Roger could put in a long driveway and the house would be at the back of the property. Instead of having houses on each side of them, they would be nestled in the trees. Over 40 percent of the subdivision was to be left as conservation area, never to be built on. All Dana could think of was what would be good for the children they would have. She'd been an only child, but Roger had come from a family with eight children. It was both their dreams to have at least four.

Those had been happy days, Dana thought as she looked out at the woods that she knew led down to the water. The house they would build would have room for all the children and they'd have a wonderful place to play. Through the woods to the east were lots of little houses, but next door, to the west, was the only true mansion in Hamilton Hundred. As soon as plans for the new gated community were announced, someone had bought six plots and started building an enormous house. It wasn't until nearly two years later that they found out the resident was to be Althea Fairmont.

Dana heard her husband and Skylar laughing in the dining room and dreaded going back in there. She and Roger had never had wild weekends in a motel before they were married. But then, to be fair, she'd refused to go to bed with him until after they were married—which she was sure was why he did marry her.

Sometimes at night she could see lights from the Fairmont mansion, but no one ever saw the Great Lady herself. She had employees to run her errands, and when she did go out, she rode in a black limo with darkened windows.

Years ago, Dana had dreams of her polite, courteous children befriending the old woman and . . . She hadn't thought much past that, but she had imagined mentioning to people that "Althea and I . . ."

But none of it ever happened. Not the children and certainly not meeting the woman who had been called "the greatest actress who ever lived."

Instead, she and Roger had walked through the woods and they'd met Jefferson Ames there. Like them, he'd built a house on one of the few long, skinny pieces of land. His house was on the other side of the Fairmont mansion.

But there the similarities between the families ended. Jeff's wife died less than a year after they moved in, just months after she gave birth to their daughter. When they met Jeff, he was so overtaken with grief that he was just a shell of a human being. Even when he was with his daughter, his eyes were empty, dead.

It had been as natural as breathing that Dana had taken over baby

Elsbeth's weekday care after Lillian died. Dana had helped Jeff hire nannies, but they had been glad to turn the child over to Dana. Gradually, as the years passed and Dana had no children of her own, her weekdays had begun to revolve around Elsbeth.

Roger saw what his wife was feeling and warned her not to get too attached. "Some woman will go after Jeff and he won't stand a chance," he said, his dark eyes sparkling. "Like you did to me."

As always, Dana had protested that she'd done nothing to "catch him," as he liked to say.

Roger had rolled his eyes and smiled. "Red silk. Black lace. Skirts cut up to here, but 'no touch.' You make torturers of the Spanish Inquisition seem tame."

Sometimes she loved his teasing; sometimes she hated it.

He'd been right about little Elsbeth, but right in a different way. It wasn't a wife who came in and took over, but a shy young woman with big brown eyes, lots of thick chestnut hair, and a way of looking at Jeff that was embarrassing to everyone who saw it. She was named Cassandra, and she seemed to love Elsbeth with all her heart.

The first time Dana saw her was when she'd heard voices at the tiny strip of beach that was at the bottom of the Fairmont property. By rights, it was private property, but no one ever went to the bit of sand except Roger and her, and Jeff and his daughter.

But one day, there was Elsbeth with a young woman Dana had never seen before, and they were laughing and playing as though they'd known each other all their lives. As Dana stayed hidden in the trees and watched, she felt such a sense of loss that it was as though something inside her had broken. Pretty, quiet, motherless Elsbeth was the closest thing she had to having her own child. And now she'd been taken away as completely as though she'd moved to another country.

That day, Dana had walked back to her house, made herself a gin and tonic, then got on her hands and knees and scrubbed the kitchen floor. Three days later, when Jeff introduced her to Elsbeth's new nanny, Dana tried to be polite, but she felt such anger at the young woman for stealing what should have been hers that she couldn't keep her upper lip from curling.

Since then, Dana had been polite to the woman, but she couldn't bring herself to be nice to her. And the truth was that the reason she put up with Skylar without a protest was because if Jeff and Skylar married, that girl, Cassandra, would go, and maybe Elsbeth would be given back to Dana. Heaven knew that Skylar wouldn't want the day-to-day care of a child.

In the months after that first dinner, Dana had helped Skylar tone down her way of dressing and the way she said whatever came into her head. She didn't want Skylar to offend Jeff. For all that it had been years since his wife's death, Jeff was still a man in grief, and he wasn't ready for a woman who liked to tell stories about how she and a boyfriend had tried to do all the positions in the Kama Sutra.

So, now, Dana smiled and listened to Skylar rant about Cassie.

3

"SO WHAT'S FOR BREAKFAST?" Jeff asked, looking over Cassie's shoulder at the big griddle on the stove.

"Harvest grain pancakes," she said, stepping away from him. Once again, he was shirtless. It was Saturday, so he was in jeans, with a T-shirt slung over his shoulder, exposing his magnificent torso. No matter how busy he was, he always found time to work out.

"Daddy!" Elsbeth squealed as she ran to him and threw herself into his arms. She snuggled her face into his neck. "You smell good."

"It's called aftershave and it's guaranteed to drive women wild." He nuzzled her face. "Do you feel wild?"

Elsbeth giggled. "Not me, grown-up women. Like Cassie."

Cassie waited a moment, but when Jeff made no comment, she said, "Here, sit down and eat." She put a tall stack of pancakes at Jeff's place on the breakfast table. The room had a huge bay window, and outside were a dozen bird feeders that she and Elsbeth kept filled with everything from peanut butter to suet.

"You're going to make me fat," Jeff said after he'd seated his daughter.

"Not with all the exercise you get," his father said from the doorway.

As always, Cassie "inspected" the older man when she first saw him in the morning. Her eyes swept up and down him to see if there were any changes in his health. He'd had two heart attacks before she met him, and she lived in fear that another one would take him away from them. He'd told her that when he first moved in with Jeff, after Lillian's death, Jeff had wanted his father to take the downstairs master bedroom, but Thomas wouldn't hear of it. They had compromised by making one of the walk-in closets into an elevator.

"I'm perfectly all right," Thomas said, looking from Jeff to Cassie then back again. "You two can stop undressing me with your eyes."

Smiling at his remark, she turned back to the stove. "How many pancakes do you want?"

"A dozen at least," Thomas said as he kissed his granddaughter then sat down beside her. He raised an eyebrow at his son. "Aren't you a bit cool without a shirt on?"

Jeff started to say something, but then grinned and pulled his T-shirt over his head. "So what do we have planned for today?"

The "we" in that made the three of them stop in midmotion. Jeff ate dinner with them and he spent time with Elsbeth on weekends, but he rarely went anywhere with all of them.

Thomas recovered first. "*We* are going to do what we always do on Saturday morning and that's go to the farmers' market."

"Sounds like fun," Jeff said, cutting into his pancakes. "When do we leave?"

Thomas leaned back in his chair and stared at his son. "You're about to drop some really bad news on us, aren't you? You're trying to get into our good graces before you bomb us."

Jeff smiled. "Actually, I'm celebrating. I finished the Newcombe project."

"That's wonderful!" Cassie said. Jeff was a structural engineer, and his firm had been working on a huge building project in Virginia Beach for over two years. Jeff had been in charge of it, and the responsibility had nearly killed him. When Cassie moved into the room upstairs, Jeff had been in the middle of the task. She'd never been around him when he wasn't working long, hard hours. And for the last months, when he did have some time off, if he wasn't with Elsbeth, he was with Skylar.

"Does this mean we'll be seeing more of you?" Thomas asked. "Or will your Somebody Skylar be taking *all* your time?"

"Dad, don't start on me," Jeff said. "It's too early in the morning and it's my first day off in . . . I don't know how long it's been. Just let me enjoy it."

"All right," Thomas said slowly. "Elsbeth and I are going to go work in my garden, so why don't you go to the farmers' market with Cassie?"

"Sure," Jeff said, "but isn't Cassie supposed to have days off? Maybe she'd like to do something other than bum around with me."

"I don't mind," Cassie said quickly. "I'd love the company. I want to get some oysters and scallops, and I need—"

"Did I hear 'oysters'?" came a voice from the doorway. It was Skylar, and she was holding up a bag of something. "Hope you don't mind but the door was unlocked. I let myself in."

"Like the cat," Cassie said under her breath. She lifted the last pancake off the griddle and put it on a plate, then untied her apron and draped it over the big handle on the stove. Skylar was already at the table and pulling out some greasy croissants and coffee in paper cups. It was as though Cassie was seeing the future. When Jeff married Skylar, this is the way it would be. Only Cassie wouldn't be there to witness it.

Quietly, she left the kitchen and went up the back stairs to go to her room.

Jeff caught her on the second-floor landing. "Cassie," he said. "I'm sorry about this. I didn't know she was coming. Maybe we can go together another time."

Cassie's pride wouldn't let her disappointment show. For a few moments it had been exciting to think of being alone with Jeff. "Are you kidding?" she said. "You're right. I *should* take the day off. Sounds wonderful! I can't imagine what I'll do with all that time to myself."

"Oh," Jeff said and stepped back from her. "You're welcome to go with us. Skylar's been invited to go on Roger Craig's boat, and we're going with them. It'll be fun."

"I'm sure it'll be lovely," she said, "but I really do have my own things to do. Thanks for the invitation, though." Turning away, she went into her bedroom and shut the door.

Once inside, she wanted to kick herself. She should have gone with them. She should have accepted his invitation and gone and . . . And what? she thought. Stand up against beautiful Skylar? Cassie had had her chance with Jeff. She'd spent a year in his house, taking care of his child, looking after his father, cooking for him, making sure his clothes were clean and put away where they belonged. When Jeff couldn't find something, he asked Cassie. When he wanted an opinion about a structure he was designing, he asked Cassie.

He was always courteous. There were many times when Cassie had stared at him, willing him to look at her with lust. She daydreamed about his putting his arms around her and kissing her neck. But he never came close.

Cassie wasn't the sort of person to push herself onto a man, so she kept her distance and was as respectful toward him as he was to her. But on a few occasions in the last year she made what she thought of as subtle advances toward him. Each time had been the same. She'd heard him downstairs in the kitchen late at night and she'd gone down. The first two times she'd pretended that it was an accidental meeting; by the third time, she didn't bother. They'd spread out his latest drawings on the big dining table and he'd explained them to her. She didn't understand a lot of it, but she liked his enthusiasm and his love of his work. She'd made a pot of tea and they'd drunk it all. It wasn't until the wee hours that they'd parted and gone to bed—without so much as even a tiny impropriety.

However, in that year there'd been a few embarrassing encounters. One morning she'd walked into his bathroom with a load of clean linens and been shocked to see him standing outside the shower with just a towel wrapped around him. Last summer he'd brushed up against some poison ivy and Cassie had twice coated his sore back with calamine lotion.

But in all that time, Jeff had never come close to making a pass at her. He'd never so much as brushed her hand with his. He'd never looked at her in any way except as a . . . If she had to label it, it would be as a kid sister. He was eleven years older than she was, and while it didn't bother her, it seemed to mean a lot to Jeff—or else he just plain wasn't attracted to her.

And since seeing Skylar, Cassie was sure she wasn't Jeff's type. His wife, Lillian, had been thin and athletic. Skylar was also thin, although not from athletics. But, like Lillian, Skylar was tall and sure of herself and . . .

Skylar was all the things that Cassie wasn't, she thought. Cassie was short and curvy, and she wore whatever was comfortable and could be washed in the machine. Skylar was sophisticated, a woman who had been places and seen things, whereas Cassie had done little in her life.

Whatever the reason, it was obvious that, as a woman, Cassie was of no interest to Jeff.

Cassie stayed in her room for over an hour, waiting until after they'd left and she could go downstairs and not be seen. Thomas had cleared the breakfast dishes off the table, but the kitchen still needed to be cleaned. Cassie started on it, then threw down her cloth. It was only a matter of time before Jeff would marry Skylar and Cassie would be out of a job, so why was she still trying to be a "pretend wife" to a family that would soon be gone from her life?

She went through the mudroom and out the back door, then through the trees of the conservation area. She was almost to the beach before she saw that Dana Craig was there. Cassie's impulse was to turn around and leave, but Dana had already seen her. Dana was exactly the kind of woman Cassie'd always heartily disliked. Dana was the woman who ran every charity event, who organized every happening at the club's recreation center. She was the woman who never made a mistake. Her husband was perfect; her home was perfect. Women like Dana had no visible flaws. Cassie thought that Dana was the suburban equivalent of her mother.

Cassie gave a weak smile and a little lift of her hand. It took all her strength not to turn around and go back to the house. Jeff kept a car, a yellow MINI Cooper, just for Cassie's use. She should go to the farmers' market and buy what they needed for the coming week. She should wander around Colonial Williamsburg—there was always something interesting going on there. Or maybe she could call her mother. Most anything was preferable to spending time with the perfect Dana.

Cassie drew in her breath and sucked in her stomach. What she should really do is go to the gym. "Hello," she said.

"I didn't think anyone would be here today," Dana said. "If you and Elsbeth want the place, I'll leave."

Cassie motioned behind her. "It's just me. All of them went sailing."

"Ah, yes, of course. They went with Skylar on Roger's boat."

Cassie looked at Dana, with her hair neatly arranged in a short, flattering style, in her pressed chinos, and her tasteful knit shirt, and again resisted the urge to run away. "You didn't want to go with them?"

"No. I'm not good on boats. And you? I mean, that is, if . . ."

When Dana hesitated, the hairs on the back of Cassie's neck stood up. What Dana meant was that maybe Cassie hadn't been invited. After all, she was just a paid employee. Not family. "I was invited," Cassie said and tried to unclench her teeth. "But I wanted Jeff and Elsbeth to have time together."

"Yes, of course. And Skylar too. She'll soon be part of the family. I was wondering if they've announced their engagement yet."

"No," Cassie said softly. "At least I haven't been told of it."

"But you think it'll be soon?"

"I don't know," Cassie said, and wanted to throw sand at the woman. "I just came out here for some air. I have a lot to do today, so I'd better go."

"I didn't mean to offend you," Dana said. "I know how it is between you and Skylar, but I'm sure you'll find another job right away. I'm sure Jeff's reference will lavish praise on you."

"I know," Cassie said as she looked out at the river. With each day she was coming closer to the time when she'd have to leave a house she'd come to love, leave a community she loved. And worst, leave people she had come to love.

She was about to start back to the house when a sound from the mansion that was just visible through the trees made her jump.

Dana looked at Cassie, her eyes wide. "Was that a shot?"

There were two more explosions, sounding like two more shots.

"Do you have a phone with you?" Dana asked. "I think we should call the police."

Cassie thought the same thing, but she wasn't going to tell Dana that. After all, she was a nanny who deserved "lavish praise"—who used such a term nowadays?—so she wasn't going to turn chicken and run away. She put her shoulders back. "I'm sure it's nothing, but maybe I should check." The last thing in the world she wanted to do was walk toward a house where she'd heard shots being fired, but she didn't want the snooty Miss Perfect Dana Craig to know that.

"Maybe I should go home and call from there," Dana said.

"Yes, of course, you do that," Cassie said, her head held high as she started walking faster. "I'm just worried that if nothing is wrong, Miss Fairmont might not like the police intruding on her."

"Certainly not," Dana said, keeping pace with Cassie and not veering off toward her house. In front of them loomed the huge Fairmont mansion. It was a new house, but during the two years it had taken to build, no expense had been spared in making it a grand estate. There wasn't a corbel or a post that wasn't decorated in a tasteful, expensive way.

"How big do you think that place is?" Dana asked quietly.

"Twenty-one thousand, two hundred and ten square feet," Cassie said quickly.

"With only five bedrooms but twelve bathrooms," Dana said.

"And a screening room that seats thirty, and the house has its own generators."

"In case the power goes out, the movie won't be interrupted," Dana said, then for a brief second she and Cassie almost exchanged smiles.

"It's all on the Internet," Cassie said as they reached the back of the formal garden that surrounded the house. "Anyone can read about it."

"If you spend hours searching," Dana said.

"Exactly," Cassie answered.

When they reached the garden with its manicured lawn, and the boxwood-edged shapes that were filled with pink begonias, they began to walk more slowly. The house loomed over them, with its huge windows seeming to look down on them. They were in the sacred territory of a woman who was a legend. She had been famous when Cassie's mother was a child. There were few people on earth who could remem-

ber a time when Althea Fairmont wasn't famous—at least it seemed that
way. She'd been a child star before talking movies, looking up with big
eyes, begging the villain not to throw her and her mother out into the
street. The 1930s came, and along with them, Shirley Temple with her
singing and dancing. Althea could do neither of those, but she could
act. By the time Althea was fourteen, the studio was lying about her age
and casting her with the Barrymores. When she reached thirty, the studio began lying about her age the other way.

All that had been done had worked. Althea had starred in every
type of movie and stage production. Whether she played a comedy, a
tragedy, or did a guest appearance on a talk show, the viewer was
guaranteed a great show. Althea Fairmont could play any part and had
proven it many times over. Still, at her age—whatever it was, as the
bios disagreed—whenever she appeared, there was a line waiting to
see her.

Now, Dana and Cassie walked through the garden, uninvited, trespassing, and they slowed with each step.

"Maybe it wasn't a shot," Dana said.

"It could have been a car. Or something falling."

"Exactly. Maybe we should leave."

"Yes, I think maybe we should," Cassie agreed, then turned to head
back out of the garden. But they had taken only one step when they
heard what sounded like a moan.

Dana and Cassie turned to look at each other, then they looked
back toward the house. The ground floor had an enormous, deep veranda that was divided in the middle by a conservatory. They could see
orchids and tropical ferns inside it. A short flight of steps led up one
side of the veranda, but they didn't dare climb them. All they could do
was stare. The furniture on the slate-floored area looked as though it
had been made for the house. It was all oversize and padded in a cream-
colored linen, with pillows with palm leaves printed on them. In the

back was a stone-topped table and beneath it, on the slate-paved floor, was what looked to be a shoe.

It took them a moment to realize that the shoe was attached to a foot. The women rushed up the stairs and across the veranda. Lying on the stone, her eyes closed, her beautiful pantsuit in disarray, was Althea Fairmont, her perfectly preserved features recognizable to every adult in the United States.

For a moment Dana and Cassie just stood there looking at her, unable to breathe. For Cassie, she remembered one movie after another that she'd watched as a child, then all the movies she'd gone to as an adult. If Miss Fairmont was in it, Cassie went to see it. There had been a three-day retrospective on her at college, and Cassie had attended every lecture and movie. She still had the binder that had Althea's photo on the front.

As for Dana, she saw a woman who had achieved everything that life could give. Althea Fairmont was a legend, true, but she was also a woman of great personal success.

Althea opened her eyes and looked at the two young women staring down at her, neither of them moving. After a few moments, she made an attempt to get up by herself.

Cassie was the first to recover. "Oh, my gosh!" she said. "Let me help you."

"That would be kind," Althea said, extending her arm toward Cassie.

Dana took the woman's other arm. When she was standing between them, the women stood still, not knowing what to do with their famous charge.

"Perhaps you could help me inside, to sit somewhere comfortable," Althea said in a voice that was almost as familiar to them as their own.

Cassie lifted her chin to look at Dana over Althea's blonde head. Inside? *Inside* the mansion? her eyes asked. The place that all Hamilton

Hundred had been dying to see since it was built? For the year after Althea moved in, everyone who lived in the resort community—the women anyway—had talked of nothing but seeing the inside of that house. They'd left business cards of services for interior decorating, floral arrangements, even private nursing. But the Great Althea had called on none of them. They speculated on whether she was going to give herself a housewarming party. One of the women had even written Miss Fairmont a letter stating her qualifications as a party planner—but there was no response.

Years had passed and no one who lived in Hamilton Hundred had ever seen the interior of Althea's house. But now Dana and Cassie were being told to help Althea Herself inside.

Since the woman was leaning on Cassie more heavily, Dana stepped forward to open one of the doors. Even as she did so, her mouth opened and wouldn't seem to close. The door was of some exotic wood that had swirls of black and deep red. There were little round whorls of brass on the door, making it look like the entrance to a fortress. But it swung open easily on its enormous hinges.

They walked into a high-ceilinged sitting room that looked like something out of a Jane Austen movie, and it was the prettiest room either of the women had ever seen. It was done in peach and a pale, mossy green. There were two big sofas facing each other, with an inlaid coffee table in the center. Elegant tables of mahogany were along the walls, with pretty Chinese lamps on them. The walls had oil paintings of what looked to be Althea's ancestors, but upon closer inspection were of Althea in her many roles on stage and screen.

Cassie helped the woman to sit on one of the sofas. The chintz curtains were open, and the windows showed straight through the trees to the little beach where she and Elsbeth played so often. With a sick feeling, Cassie realized that every time they'd been trespassing, they'd been seen.

"Can I get you something?" Cassie asked. "Call someone?"

Althea leaned back against the sofa and smiled. "No, thank you. It's just my housekeeper and me here. And Brent outside. Just the three of us."

Dana was looking at the ornaments on the mantelpiece. She wasn't sure but she thought one of the two eggs was genuine Fabergé. "But surely it takes more than just three people to run this place," she said.

Althea smiled at Dana. "Now and then I need more people, but for day-to-day living, it's just the three of us. Would you be so good as to push that button on the wall? I hope that you two will stay for a mid-morning tea. Or are you too busy on this lovely Saturday morning to share a bite with an old woman?"

"No, of course not," Cassie said quickly. "Our families have run off together on a boat and we're absolutely free."

"Families?" Althea said, looking at Cassie. "I thought you were the nanny for that beautiful little girl. Don't you work for a widower and his father? Have they become your family?"

Cassie stood up straight, blinking at the woman. What she'd said was true, but Cassie didn't want to hear it put so bluntly. No, they weren't her family. "I . . . I . . . ," Cassie began, but she could think of nothing else to say.

"She's been there so long that they seem like family," Dana said. "I can attest that Cassie loves little Elsbeth very much."

"Ah," Althea said, looking at Cassie in speculation. "But isn't Jefferson Ames about to marry David Beaumont's daughter? I met the girl when she was a child and I found her to be the most spoiled creature I'd ever met. Has she changed much?"

Dana smiled. "Not at all. But how in the world do you know so much about what's going on in Hamilton Hundred? Names, marital stats. You seem to know everything about us."

"Won't you sit down, both of you?" Althea said, smiling. "Let's just say that I have a spy. I can't, of course, tell you who it is, but I'm kept informed of whatever is thought to interest me. I'd love to go to your country club and hear the gossip myself, but did you know that I did that once?"

Dana and Cassie sat by each other on the couch on the opposite side of the pretty coffee table and smiled. Of course they knew that. Within ten minutes of Althea's arrival at the club, the parking lot had been full and the manager had had to ask that no one bother her while she ate. But afterward, graciously, Althea had signed autographs. They could understand why she'd not returned.

"We heard what we thought were shots," Dana said.

"Yes," Althea said, giving a sigh. "He was here again. I think Kenneth waited until he saw my young Brent drive away, then he walked around the fence to the house."

Both Cassie and Dana blinked at her. Althea's second husband had been the great Shakespearean actor, Kenneth Ridgeway. He was the sort who thought that only Broadway was worth an actor's time, and during the years he was married to Althea, he had been publically disdainful of her film work. In spite of his nasty little remarks, their marriage had lasted for over twenty years. It was when Althea had taken a role on Broadway and been heralded as "magnificent" that the marriage died. The day after the fabulous reviews came out, Kenneth Ridgeway filed for divorce. But the joke was on him. His career never recovered from his so-obvious jealousy. He became a national joke, the butt of talk show hosts' monologues.

"Kenneth Ridgeway was shooting at you?" Cassie asked, wide-eyed.

Althea smoothed her perfect hair, pulled back from her exquisite face, the cheekbones nearly as perfect today as they had been in the 1920s, and nodded. "I assume it was a stage pistol that uses blanks. Kenneth always did love drama over substance. But, yes, there were shots fired."

"At you?" Cassie asked quietly.

"Of course," Althea said, smiling. "He wants more money. But then he always wants more money. I told him I'd pay him if I just didn't have to hear that speech again about how he made me what I am and how I owe him everything. But this time I think I said too much because he pulled out a pistol and shot at me."

Cassie and Dana just looked at her, too astonished to say anything, when the door opened and in came a woman with a wheeled cart covered with a pretty porcelain tea set, and dishes with tiny sandwiches and cakes. The woman was short, dark skinned, and probably as old as Althea was—except that she looked her age.

"Just put it there, Rosalie," Althea said. "I'll serve."

"What have you done this time?" the woman asked as she shoved the cart to the side of the couch. She stood with her hands on her hips, glaring at Althea.

"This is not the time . . . ," Althea began. "I have guests."

"It ain't never the time," Rosalie muttered as she went toward the door, then turned back to look at the two young women. "If somebody shot at you, maybe you should call the police."

Cassie and Dana nodded in agreement.

"I don't think so," Althea said. "Not now."

"Just what I thought," Rosalie said, then left the room, closing the door loudly behind her.

Althea turned back to the two women. "Do you take milk or lemon?"

"Let me do that," Dana said, at last beginning to recover from the awe of being in Althea Fairmont's presence. She got up and began to expertly pour and serve the tea.

Cassie took her cup after Dana had served Miss Fairmont. "What do you plan to do about this man?" she asked sternly.

"Nothing," Althea said, sipping her tea. "He loves the excitement and it makes him feel manly, rather like a pirate come here at gunpoint to demand that I give him money."

"But this morning it was more than excitement, wasn't it?" Dana said, sitting down by Cassie, her cup in her hand. "When we found you, you were passed out on the floor. If we hadn't found you, who would have helped you?" She didn't say the words, but it hung in the air that it was a big house and it was peopled by only two elderly women. For all that Althea—thanks to modern surgery—looked like a well-preserved fifty, she was still an older woman. And Rosalie wasn't any younger.

Dana's eyes said it all as she looked at Althea.

"Yes, well," Althea said, looking away from Dana's stare. "I know I should do something about it, but I did make Kenneth a laughingstock of the country, and I carry some responsibility for that."

"He made himself a laughingstock," Cassie said firmly. "You beat him at his own game by showing him up on stage. He was the idiot who filed for divorce right after the reviews came out."

Althea smiled warmly at Cassie. "Oh, my, you do have a passionate nature, don't you? Thank you for championing me, but I do feel guilty in a lot of ways. Kenneth had to work for what he had, but I . . ." She gave a little shrug.

"You had raw, natural talent," Dana said.

"I had hunger," Althea answered.

Dana and Cassie nodded. They knew Althea's story, as did most of the United States, thanks to the movie that had won Althea her first Academy Award. She was born to a beautiful, ambitious, husbandless mother who wanted to be in the movies, so she'd dragged her infant to Hollywood when the place was mostly desert. The problem had come when the woman was found to have no talent whatever. But that hadn't stopped her from trying to push her way in front of the camera. She'd been unable to afford child care so she'd dragged her daughter to the sets and left her to fend for herself. One day, a director needed a child to play a small part, he'd seen Althea sitting in the shade with a coloring book, and he'd put her in the role.

As they say, the rest was history. Althea had all the talent her mother yearned for but didn't have. From the time she was three Althea lived on movie sets, and as her fame and wealth grew, her mother's extravagant lifestyle increased. The woman died when Althea was twenty-eight. Everyone said it was a good thing because Althea found herself not only broke but also deeply in debt. Her mother had not only spent all that Althea had earned, but also had borrowed heavily on her daughter's talent. Biographies and the resulting movie—in which Althea played herself—told of the hardship she'd gone through to pay off the debts and to keep her dignity while doing it. The movie ended when her husband filed for divorce the day after he read the reviews of her stage performance. In one of the all-time greatest scenes, Althea vowed that she'd not only survive, but she'd triumph.

"Here, have one of these raspberry tarts," Althea said, holding out the plate. "The young man who works for me has a stand of raspberry bushes somewhere about the place. Perhaps you could bring the young lady over here sometime and pick them," Althea said to Cassie.

Cassie took another tart, but Dana didn't. "Skylar?" Cassie asked. "I don't think she'd like to— Oh, sorry, you meant Elsbeth."

"Skylar. That's David Beaumont's daughter's name, isn't it?"

At even the thought of Skylar and the rapidly approaching end of her time with Jeff and Thomas and dear little Elsbeth, Cassie's eyes teared up. "Yes, that's her name," she said softly. "I think she'll soon be Elsbeth's mother."

Althea looked from one woman to the other, Cassie with her head down, staring at her half-eaten tart on the pretty porcelain plate, and Dana sitting ramrod straight, with all emotion erased from her face, as though she dared anyone to know what was really inside her. "Men are fools, aren't they?" Althea said, putting down her teacup. "I am the only thing other than the theater that Kenneth Ridgeway has ever loved, but he'd die before he admitted that. So what does he do but come here every six weeks and put on a grand performance in order to get money from me. The poor dear doesn't have a cent."

"He probably thinks his performance is worth your money," Dana said.

"I'm sure he does," Althea answered. "In fact—"

She broke off when the door was loudly pushed open and in came a divinely handsome young man. He had a beautiful face, dark blond hair that looked as though the breeze had just ruffled it, and he wore jeans and a knit shirt that showed off his well-sculpted body.

"You were *shot* at?" the young man said in anger, glaring down at Althea. "How did he get through? Rosalie said it was your ex-husband again."

"Brent, dear, I'll talk to you later, but I'm sure it was just a prop pistol, not real at all. And these two young ladies saved me."

He ignored the women on the opposite couch. "Those so-called prop pistols can kill!"

"He isn't going to harm me," Althea said, smiling up at the beautiful young man. "I have the money and I've made sure he knows that my will does not include him. If I die, the money will stop. He'd have to go out and earn a living." She gave a delicate shudder.

"I've met him and I know the old ham is nearly blind and that he's too vain to wear glasses. He could shoot you without even seeing you."

Cassie couldn't help herself as she gave a giggle at that image.

The young man turned on her, his face full of anger. "You think this is funny?" He didn't give her time to answer. "You're the one who trespasses all the time. And you!" he said, turning his icy blue eyes to Dana. "I've seen all of you down there. Don't you realize that this is private property? Miss Fairmont has paid for the privacy that comes with this place. She doesn't need you and your entourage sneaking onto her private beach."

"That's enough, Brent," Althea said. Her stage-trained voice was quiet but it probably could have been heard above a hurricane.

Immediately, the young man straightened up and looked back at Althea. "I apologize. It's just that when Rosalie told me what happened, I was worried. Did you know he was coming? Is that why you sent me out today?"

Reaching out, she patted his hand, which was clenched in a fist at his side. "We'll talk about this later. Right now, I have guests." Her voice was purring, placating, soothing.

Cassie and Dana looked from one to the other, then back again.

With a smile, Althea introduced him to Cassie and Dana. His name was Brent Goodwin and Althea described him as a gardener, but added that he also "looked out" for her. "Go on, now," Althea said. "I'll talk to you later. I had Rosalie bake that lemon cake you like so much. Go and have some."

After a mumbled "Nice to meet you" Brent left the room and closed the door behind him.

"I think we should leave," Dana said stiffly. "And I can assure you that we won't trespass again."

Althea gave a laugh. "If you don't continue to use the beach, I'll nominate Skylar Beaumont to be president of the social activities committee for Hamilton Hundred."

It took Cassie and Dana a full minute to realize she was kidding. They laughed politely.

"That young man seemed adamant that we stay away, and he's right. It is your private property," Dana said.

"Let me handle him." Althea's green eyes twinkled, then she looked at Cassie. "Actually, I've been wanting to talk to you. I've heard nothing but good about you, about how you run Jefferson's household. I've heard that you look after his father as well as his daughter."

"It's a pleasure," Cassie said hesitantly. It was disconcerting to have this very famous woman know so much about her.

Smiling, Dana looked at Althea. "Cassie is very good at her job. It will be a shame when she has to leave, but I'm sure she'll get another job right away."

Althea turned unsmiling eyes on Dana. "And if Jefferson marries the very rich Skylar Beaumont, that would leave a place for a mother for pretty little Elsbeth, wouldn't it? I hear you practically adopted the child after Lillian Ames died."

Dana's face turned red, but she said nothing. She just kept her back rigid.

Cassie looked at Dana in wonder as she began to understand some things. "You want Elsbeth."

"Absolutely not," Dana said. "Roger and I plan to have our own children." She looked straight ahead, avoiding the eyes of both women.

"That's neither here nor there," Althea said, looking at Cassie. "My point is that if Jefferson marries Skylar, you're going to need a job. I wonder if I could persuade you to work for me as a sort of social secretary and a researcher."

"I don't know," Cassie said slowly. The truth was that she couldn't actually imagine a time when she wasn't living with Elsbeth and Jeff and Thomas. To go from living with them to being at the beck and call of this woman . . . She just couldn't conceive of it. "I'll have to think about it."

"Of course. But remember that if you work here you'll be near the child." Althea leaned forward. "Or is it Jefferson who you want to be near?"

Cassie also leaned forward. "If he was interested in me, he wouldn't be marrying Skylar, now would he?"

Althea laughed. "You've got some backbone, don't you?"

Dana started to say something, but suddenly there were noises from behind the door that led into the main part of the house. When a man's voice sounded, Althea listened, then stood up. Moments before, she'd been nearly helpless, an old woman in distress, but she stood up with the energy of a woman a third her age.

"I apologize, but I have something I must take care of," she said quickly, then went to the door that led out to the veranda and opened it. "Perhaps you wouldn't mind going out this way."

"Of course," Dana murmured and went to the door, Cassie beside her.

"Could I presume to ask that you tell no one of this?" Althea said. "You know how gossip is in this place. I wouldn't want the tabloids writing something about Kenneth."

"We won't tell anyone," Cassie said. "It'll be our secret. We'll—"

She broke off because Althea nearly shoved her out the door, Dana in front of her, and shut the door firmly behind them. In the next second, they heard muffled voices, but when they turned to look, the curtains had already been drawn.

"Well," Dana said as they walked through the garden and back toward the little beach.

"Yes, well," Cassie said. Had Dana been her friend, she would have suggested that they go to the club for lunch and talk about what had just happened. But Dana wasn't a friend, so she didn't. "I'm glad we were around to help," Cassie said at last, but then she looked at the beach with longing. Never again would she feel that she could use the beach, and she and Elsbeth were going to miss it. "Well, uh . . ." Cassie wasn't sure what to say to Dana. She'd learned a lot in the last hour, and none of it was particularly good.

"Yes," was all Dana said, then they parted at the end of the garden, each of them going in opposite directions to their houses that flanked the Fairmont mansion.

But when Cassie got home—no, correction, to Jeff's house—she couldn't bear being in the house alone, so she went downtown to the farmers' market. When people first moved to Williamsburg they were shocked that "downtown" meant Colonial Williamsburg. They assumed that the beautiful, restored city of eighteenth-century houses was for tourists and that the residents had somewhere else to do their shopping. There were lots of stores in Williamsburg, even an outlet mall that could make one dizzy with the variety and quality of goods for sale, but where was the downtown? The confusion between tourist and resident led to the building of New Town, a pristine, modern—but Colonial-looking—town not far from William and Mary College. New Town was a place where people could get a haircut or sit at a sidewalk café to eat. There was a to-die-for bookstore, and the courthouse, and a huge movie theater. And all of it was beautiful.

But the farmers' market, with vendors from all over eastern Virginia, was still held in the exquisite Colonial Williamsburg. Cassie parked the MINI Cooper in the lot near the cemetery, walked to the booths, and browsed through stands selling herbs in pots, seafood caught that morning, and homemade jams. She purchased bags full of goods, making three trips to the car to put her purchases inside. Cassie believed in supporting local merchants and growers, so she bought as much as she could from people who grew their own.

After she finished shopping, she drove back to Hamilton Hundred and put the food in the refrigerator.

Through all her activities, her mind was only half on her tasks. She kept thinking about meeting Althea Fairmont and all that had been said. When she was away from the presence of the famous woman, Cassie could think more clearly. And the more she thought, the more confused she became. It seemed that Miss Fairmont knew an extraordinary amount about both her and Dana Craig. Had Althea really guessed, on the spur of the moment, that Dana wanted Elsbeth? Jeff had said that he owed a lot to Dana for taking care of Elsbeth after his wife died, but Cassie had never thought about how Dana must have felt when the child was taken away from her.

And Cassie had been the one to take the child. Jeff had hired three other nannies before Cassie, but Thomas said they were all incompetent and lazy—which meant that Dana had Elsbeth most of the time during the week.

It was when Cassie was hired that things changed. She paused as she pulled the scallops out of the bag. Who had hired the three nannies that were so incompetent? she wondered. Instantly, she knew without a doubt that it was the let-me-take-care-of-that-for-you Dana. Cassie could almost hear her asking Jeff to let her help him find a nanny. She could imagine Dana saying that she felt "responsible" for the bad nannies, so she'd make up for it by taking over little Elsbeth.

But Cassie had foiled her. Cassie had nearly thrown herself at Jeff. But then, hadn't she been throwing herself at him for years? Not that it had done any good, but she'd done it. She'd come to Williamsburg because she knew he was here. She got a job at Elsbeth's nursery school because she knew that Jeff's daughter went there. And she was the one who'd called Jeff several times to tell him that the nanny had screwed up yet again.

It was Cassie who'd been there the day when Jeff arrived to pick up his daughter. It said on Elsbeth's card that Dana Craig was to be called if there were any problems, but Cassie ignored that and called Jeff's cell number. He'd arrived right away. But then, Cassie had made it sound like an emergency.

She'd listened to him complain that this was the third nanny he would have to fire and he couldn't understand why he couldn't find competent child care. When he paused, Cassie said she'd love to have the job. She said that she never got to know the children in the nursery school and it was too much to take care of so many. She'd love to work with just one child. Jeff asked her when she could start.

She gave a week's notice to the school and moved into Jeff's lovely house the day after.

Did I mess up Dana's plans? she wondered.

More importantly, was Elsbeth the reason Dana was pushing to get Skylar and Jeff married? Skylar looked at Elsbeth as though she were an annoying insect that she wished would go away. Cassie was sure that Skylar would love to turn Elsbeth over to Dana.

Cassie took a pot of basil out of its bag and went outside to plant it in the raised brick beds that Thomas had had made for the herb garden. She went to the little shed to get a hand shovel and, with her mind elsewhere, began to replace the basil that she'd cut down to the stems.

Wasn't it odd that Althea Fairmont had figured this out, but Cassie, who was involved in it, hadn't? And wasn't it strange that Althea had asked Cassie if she was after Jeff? She'd lived in his house for a year, and only in the first few weeks had people at the club made little innuendos about them. But they'd soon stopped. But here was Althea bringing it all up again. It was almost as though she knew things that other people didn't.

Or was being told some rather hurtful gossip, Cassie thought. Who in the world was her spy? Had she not been with Dana today, Cassie would have thought it was her. But Dana had been as surprised as she had been. So who in their tight little community was sitting down with Althea Fairmont and spreading what could be considered malicious gossip? Gossip that could cause a lot of problems if it was spread around. What if someone told Jeff that his nanny was "after him"? Cassie was sure he'd laugh about it, but he'd look at her differently.

But then, what did it matter how Jeff looked at her, since Cassie was going to be thrown out of his house soon?

Cassie had thought about going to a movie at the beautiful New Town cinema, but her head was racing so fast that instead she stayed in and baked six batches of cookies. She knew that Jeff loved her sesame seed and apricot bars, so she made a double batch of them. As she baked, a plan was forming in her head. If Althea knew so much about people, maybe she knew of a way to break up Skylar and Jeff. It was a low-down, devious plan, but Cassie couldn't stand by and see Elsbeth have to put up with a mother like Skylar.

Maybe if Cassie could get into Althea's good graces, she could find out more about Skylar's past. Maybe she could find out something she could tell Jeff that would change his mind about the woman he thought he was in love with.

And at the very least, if she did accept a job from Althea, just as she said, Cassie would be right next door.

Smiling, she took a sheet of cookies out of the oven and put another one in.

4

BY SIX THAT EVENING, Cassie had piles of cookies made, but no one to eat them. Thomas, Jeff, and Elsbeth still hadn't returned from the boat, and she didn't like to think what was going on. Maybe Thomas had taken Elsbeth so Jeff and Skylar could have a romantic dinner. But what about Dana's husband? It was his boat. As to that, why had the man bought a big boat if his wife wasn't, as Dana said, "good" on boats? Cassie smiled at the image of perfect Dana heaving over the side. Maybe her husband had bought a boat to get away from his wife.

Cassie took a basket from the pile of them she had stored in the pantry, tied a ribbon around the handle, put a good linen napkin in the bottom, and filled it with cookies. She would take them over to Althea's house as a thank-you gift for the tea she'd served them.

She told herself she wasn't sneaking, but she avoided the path to the beach. She'd seen the way the windows in the house showed any movement on that path. Instead, she made her way through the trees to the side of the Fairmont house.

As she quietly walked toward the house, she thought how oddly secured it was. It almost looked like a fortress. It had a tall iron fence across the front, with a big iron gate that was opened by a security code box. The residents of Hamilton Hundred saw this from their side of the street and assumed the fence went all around the property. But it didn't. It ended about two-thirds of the way down to the water, leaving the end of Althea's property free for walking—and trespassing.

Cassie slipped around the end of the fence and walked into the garden, staying hidden under the trees and between the plants.

Most of the house was dark and she heard nothing. Her soft-soled shoes made no noise on the slate as she went to the door of the room where she and Dana had had tea.

The curtains were still drawn, but she could see light in the room, and she could hear voices. For a moment she stopped, telling herself that she was spying on a woman who had been very nice to her. She should go back the way she'd come and never bother Miss Fairmont again.

But even as she thought it, she couldn't help looking at a gap in the curtains. She could see part of the room through the space. It was as pretty as she remembered, and for a moment she thought about asking Althea who had been her decorator. Maybe she could redo their living room. If Jeff would let her touch it, that is. If Jeff didn't marry Skylar, that is. If Jeff—

Cassie stopped thinking because into her view came Roger Craig, Dana's lawyer-husband. He had a drink in his hand, and he was laughing.

Cassie stepped forward, moving closer to the glass. On the couch she could see two people. One was Althea with her perfectly coiffed head and the other looked to be her gardener-cum-bodyguard, the beautiful Brent Goodwin. The three of them were drinking cocktails and laughing.

When Roger turned his head, Cassie quickly moved to the side. She hoped he hadn't seen her.

She wasted no time as she ran across the terrace, down the steps, then ran back toward Jeff's house. She didn't look back, so she didn't know if anyone had opened the door or not.

Roger! she thought as she ran all the way back as fast as she could. Perfect Dana's perfect husband was the neighborhood spy. What's more, he'd ratted his own wife out, telling an outsider that his wife desperately wanted little Elsbeth Ames for her own. Why? Because Dana was infertile? Had the rat fink told Althea that too?

When Cassie reached Jeff's house, she ran in through the back, into the mudroom, closed the door, then leaned against it to catch her breath. She could hear voices in the breakfast room. They were back. But then, she knew that, didn't she? Ratty Roger must have run straight from the boat to report to Althea about what he'd heard that day. Every secret he'd gleaned from Jeff, Thomas, Elsbeth, and Skylar would be told to Althea Fairmont.

And what would she do with those secrets? Cassie wondered. The woman kept to herself. She didn't see anyone at Hamilton Hundred other than Roger. Her meeting with Cassie and Dana had been an accident. So what harm did it do that Roger Craig was blabbing everything to her? Maybe she was his client and maybe the way he got to handle her multimillions was to entertain her with the happenings about Hamilton Hundred.

"I thought I heard someone," Jeff said, looking at her from the doorway. "Why are you standing in the dark?" He flipped on the light switch, then stared at her. "Are you all right? You look out of breath."

"Jogging," she said, not meeting his eyes. "I've decided to take it up. I need to lose about twenty pounds."

He smiled. "You don't need to lose an ounce, and since when does a person go jogging while carrying a basket of cookies?"

"Since Little Red Riding Hood ran through the forest."

Jeff chuckled. "In that case, I think you should look out for the Big Bad Wolf." He took the basket from her hand and put it on the counter. "The house smells great, but I thought you were going to take the day off and have some fun."

"I did have fun. I like to bake." She still wasn't looking at him.

"Hey," he said softly, taking a step toward her. "What's going on? You look upset. Are you okay?"

"I'm fine," she said, taking a deep breath and straightening her shoulders. "Have you guys had dinner?"

"Nope. We decided to eat with you, so we bought about twenty different Chinese dishes. Dad couldn't make up his mind so we got everything. Come and eat with us."

"Sure," she said. "Just let me change first."

Jeff caught her wrist. "Cassie, you can tell me if something's bothering you."

"Nothing," she said. "I'm just not used to running, that's all. You guys start without me. I may take a quick shower."

Jeff was frowning slightly and watching her. "We'll wait. Hurry and join us."

"I'm sure Skylar—"

"She's not here," he said quickly. "And she won't be here tonight. I sent her off with Roger. They're old friends, and since I came into the picture, they don't get to see each other enough."

"Right," Cassie said. "Roger and Skylar. And Roger's boat."

Jeff frowned deeper, but before he could say anything else, Cassie ran up the stairs to her room. By the time she took a shower and pulled on clean clothes, she was calmer. What did it matter if someone told a famous star the gossip of a small, gated community? Didn't they all sit around the pool and watch the kids swim while they told everything they knew about everyone else? Gossip was as common as SUVs in the community.

But everything she knew and had been told had been harmless. No one was talking about Dana's desire for a child, which was so strong that she'd spent years maneuvering a neighbor's life so she could have his child. But Dana's husband had told that to a stranger. And the stranger had thrown that knowledge in Dana's face.

When Cassie went downstairs, Jeff, Elsbeth, and Thomas were sitting at the table, waiting for her. Elsbeth and Thomas made a great show of digging in just as Cassie appeared. She got extra napkins from the kitchen, and when she returned, Jeff was looking at her intently.

She smiled at him. "So tell me about every second of the day," she said as she heaped her plate full of Chinese food. Immediately, Elsbeth started talking so fast that her grandfather could hardly get a word in.

"Did Mr. Craig have a good time?" Cassie asked after ten minutes of Elsbeth's chattering about the boat and the water and every shell she'd seen.

"He caught two fish," Elsbeth said. "And he cleaned them himself. But he had to clean Skylar's fish for her. She's a silly chicken and afraid of everything."

Cassie waited for Jeff to defend his girlfriend, but he said nothing. In fact, he'd been silent since they sat down.

"But Mr. Craig wasn't afraid?" Cassie asked. "He's good on a boat? No seasickness?"

Thomas looked at her. "What's all this concern for Roger?"

"I saw his wife on the beach today and she wasn't very happy. She didn't say so, but I think it hurt her that her husband went without her."

Jeff frowned. "But Dana throws up if she so much as steps onto a boat. I've seen it. Roger's done everything to get her to go, but she refuses."

"Isn't it interesting that a man would buy a boat when he knows that his wife can't get on it? Sure does allow him lots of private time, doesn't it?"

"Are you implying that Roger is doing something he shouldn't? Like having an affair?" Jeff asked, incredulous.

"What's an affair?" Elsbeth asked.

"It's something that your father has no idea how to conduct," Thomas said. "Ellie, darling, how about if you and I go brush our teeth and get into our jammies?"

"So Daddy and Cassie can talk in private?" Elsbeth whispered loudly.

"Exactly." Thomas took Elsbeth's hand and led her out of the room.

Cassie stood up and began clearing the table.

"You want to tell me what's made you so sulky?" Jeff asked as he closed the tops of the food containers.

"I am not sulky."

"Right, and I don't want a Maserati for my birthday. Okay, so you saw Dana today. I thought you didn't like her."

"What gave you that idea?" Cassie snapped.

"I don't know. Maybe it's the way you can't say her name without sneering. Or maybe it's the way you get upset whenever I suggest that you take Elsbeth to visit her. Dana has been a good friend to me. After Lillian—"

"I know," Cassie said. "Dana was a saint. She took over your daughter as though she were her very own. And I'll bet *she* was the one who hired all your bad nannies."

Jeff gave a crooked smile. "Yeah, she did."

Cassie glared at him. "You *knew* what she was doing, didn't you? You knew it but you let her hire one awful woman after another to look after your precious daughter."

"You make it sound criminal. Yes, I knew that Dana wanted Elsbeth to stay with her. She even told me so. Or at least she said she'd take care of my daughter until I . . ." He turned away and looked out the windows of the breakfast room. It was dark outside, and the windows had no curtains. When he turned back, his face was calmer. "Cassie, it may seem that I don't know what's going on, but I do. Roger and I have talked. I know that Dana is sick with worry that she'll never have her own baby, but they've both had thorough medical exams and nothing is wrong. The doctor thinks her fear is most, if not all, of the problem."

He took a breath. "After Lillian died I couldn't think about anything. It was a year before I could function. I would have left Elsbeth with Dana full-time, but Roger asked me not to. He thought that when I did take my daughter back it would destroy Dana." Jeff smiled. "But Dana had her own way of getting what she wanted. Yes, she hired those rotten nannies, and until you asked for the job, I didn't know what I was going to do. I didn't want to hurt Dana's feelings by telling her that I'd hire my own nanny, but I was getting sick of dealing with those lazy girls she chose."

Cassie was behind the kitchen counter, looking at him. She wanted to tell him about Roger and Althea, but she couldn't bring herself to do it.

"As for Roger and his boat," Jeff said, "I got the idea that Dana loves getting rid of him for a day or two. Roger is pretty hyper, and I think Dana likes the peace and quiet."

"Peace and quiet won't get her pregnant," Cassie muttered, then caught herself. She looked up at Jeff and saw that he was holding in his laughter. "I mean—"

"I know what you meant. I know how babies are made."

Cassie wanted to laugh in a sophisticated way, but instead her face turned red.

"Are you over whatever was eating you?" he asked. "If you're mad at Roger about something, I don't think you should take it out on us."

"You're right," she said, smiling. "Would you like some cookies?"

"You didn't make those apricot ones, did you?"

"A double batch."

Smiling, Jeff went to the kitchen and Cassie nodded toward the refrigerator. He opened it, shifted the plastic wrap, and came out with three fat cookies. "I don't know what we'd do without you," he said, then kissed her on the cheek on his way out of the room.

"Then don't throw me out," Cassie said under her breath as she started cleaning up the kitchen.

5

THE SECOND JEFF was out of Cassie's sight, he practically ran down the hall to his bedroom. As soon as the door was closed, he flipped open his cell phone and speed-dialed Roger's number. "What the hell have you done?" he asked as soon as Roger answered. "Cassie's ready to skin you."

"I don't know what you're talking about. I went fishing with you today, remember?"

"Yeah, and in case you're asked, you caught two fish."

"So who came up with that one?"

"Elsbeth."

"How did *you* create such a dear, smart child?"

"I married well," Jeff said quickly. "Where are you?"

"You know where I am."

Jeff groaned. "Okay, get out of there ASAP. Something's up with the womenfolk."

"No!" said Roger in a voice that was mostly groan. "Anything but women trouble. I can take it all but that."

"You and me both," Jeff said.

"If that were true, you'd ditch Skylar."

"Would that I could, old buddy. I really wish I could. Meet me on the landing in ten minutes."

"Better make it thirty," Roger said. "Her Royal Highness has me, and you know how that is."

Jeff grimaced. He knew that Roger and Althea had a chummy relationship that he'd never developed with the woman—and had never wanted to.

"Okay, thirty minutes," he said, then hung up.

The house was quiet, and he had papers to grade, but he didn't feel like doing it. He had no idea what had happened, but something had agitated Cassie today. He well knew that she and Skylar hated one another, but it seemed to be more than that. Whatever it was, Cassie hadn't been herself.

He felt the vibration of his phone and looked to see who it was. Leo. Or rather, code name 386. None of the people Jeff worked with used their names. He flipped the phone open.

"Hey, old friend," Jeff said. "What's up?"

Leo didn't waste time on preliminaries. "I need a favor."

Jeff smiled at Leo's elegant English accent. Leo could say horrible things and it came out sounding as though he was inviting a person to afternoon tea. "Shoot."

"You remember that cabin you and I had the meeting at about four years ago?"

"Sure. Roger's place."

"Does he still own it?"

"Yes. You want to borrow it?"

"I want you to meet me there the weekend after this coming one.

The twenty-eighth. I need you to take delivery on something for me."

"Me? This is an honor."

"Don't get your knickers in a twist. My contact is an old man, and he only trusts your father. I talked him into handing it off to Thomas's son. Can you do it?"

"I don't see why not. Fax me the details and I'll arrange it all with Roger."

"Great. Thanks a lot. I'll owe you one."

Jeff waited for Leo to say more, but he was silent. "Anything else you need?"

When Leo still said nothing, Jeff understood. Years ago, he and Skylar were an item. "You want me to bring Skylar, don't you?"

"I wouldn't mind seeing her again."

And I wouldn't mind turning her over to you, Jeff thought but didn't say. "So who will you be?"

"Myself," Leo said, laughing. "I look forward to a whole weekend of no disguises and time with my friend and a pretty girl. When we get back from the drop, I'm going to get into swim gear and laze in the water with Sky. Tell her to wear that tiny purple suit of hers."

"Gladly," Jeff said as he hung up.

He looked at his watch. He still had twenty minutes before he was to meet Roger, and since he was with Althea, he'd probably be late. Leaning back in his chair, Jeff closed his eyes for a moment and thought back to the time he'd told his father about Skylar.

The derelict building was roofless and had a thousand bullet holes in the walls. The floor was covered with chopped bark that made footsteps soundless. Four men and one woman, all clad in black and wearing ski masks, slipped about in the shadows. They each carried a handgun held at arm's length. Their breathing was as controlled as they could manage, but their hearts were pounding with anticipation and fear.

Suddenly, a lean, agile form came around the far corner of the building, and in an instant, there were three blasts from his gun. Behind him came another person, but the man spun and shot. They saw the man quickly raise his gun and fire the fifth round, this time at the figure crouched on top of the wall.

"Damn it!" said the man as he jumped to the ground. "I thought I had you that time."

Their teacher, Jefferson Ames, had shot all five of them with the red paint slug, then removed his mask and was now reloading. "I heard you and I saw you." He looked up at them, their masks now removed and their young, eager faces looking at him with wide eyes.

"Have any of you reloaded?" His voice was full of the frustration of having to tell them the same things over and over.

"No, sir," three of them said sheepishly.

"A good agent—" Jeff began, but then he saw the face of the girl. She was good at the book work, but she had a long way to go with the physical aspects of being an agent. Right now her eyes were open wide in astonishment, as though she saw something behind her teacher.

Jeff spun, but not fast enough to shoot first. The intruder's gun went off. Exactly over Jeff's heart, in a perfect shot, a red blob of paint marred his black running suit. In front of him was a man wearing a pair of khaki trousers and a dark brown leather jacket, his face hidden under a black ski mask.

Behind Jeff were his five students, and he could feel that they were standing absolutely still. Who had had the audacity to shoot their teacher? And who had been able to sneak up on him and get that deadly shot off?

Jeff turned to the students. "May I introduce my father? Thomas Ames."

Jeff smiled at the respectful silence that hit his students. His father's name was in the textbooks and on award plaques around the school. Thomas Ames was a legend to those training at the CIA school, the school that the United States government said didn't exist.

Thomas pulled his ski mask off, revealing his handsome face and thick gray hair, and smiled at the students, who still hadn't recovered enough to speak.

"Our guest lecturer for the next hour," Jeff said, and he was pleased to see his father's slight frown. Thomas hated teaching. He was a man who learned by doing and thought others should learn that way too. Jeff knew his father had come to have lunch with him, but the elder man couldn't resist showing off by shooting his own son in front of his students. So his punishment was to have to teach for an hour while Jeff showered and changed.

Thirty minutes later, Jeff went back to the classroom to find his father reading a book, his feet propped on Jeff's old desk.

"What did you do with them?" Jeff asked. "They didn't deserve a holiday."

"You're too hard on them. That blond boy has potential."

"Maybe. He's too impetuous for my taste."

"I seem to remember saying that to someone else."

Jeff smiled. For all that his father said he hated teaching, when Jeff was growing up, they had played endless games of "find the spy"—or whatever name they came up with. By the time he was in the second grade, Jeff was figuring out simple codes. When he was twelve, he started training with weapons.

In their house, what his father did for a living was never spoken about, but Jeff and his mother knew. There were many nights when Jeff had sat by his mother and held her hand while she waited nervously for a call from her husband. Three times the call had come from agents to tell her that Thomas had been injured.

It was an injury to Thomas that had caused Jeff to be at the conference where Margaret Madden and her daughter were. As a favor to an old friend, not on official business, Thomas had agreed to work on security that weekend. Tempers were high over jobs that were being lost and others that were to be gained. Jeff was young and wasn't a CIA agent then, but he'd had a lifetime of training, so when his father was incapacitated, Jeff went in his place, and he'd done an excellent job. Not one argument had gone past the shouting stage.

When Jeff first mentioned Skylar to his father, they had gone to downtown Williamsburg to The Trellis restaurant. Jeff knew that after lunch his father would want to go to the William and Mary bookstore and spend hours browsing.

But the minute their order was placed, Thomas started on his favorite topic: Cassie. As always, he asked Jeff when he was going to ask Cassie out.

"Don't start on me again," Jeff said. "Cassie is wonderful, but if I let her get close to me, she'll find out too much, and you know that she couldn't handle the truth about my life."

"Don't underestimate her," Thomas said. "There's more to that girl than you think."

"Do you forget that I've known her for a very long time?"

"Since you never let me forget it, how could I?"

Jeff paused until the waiter had put his salad down and left. "Look, Dad, Cassie is great. I couldn't like a girl better than I like her, but, face it, she's a quiet, gentle person. She lives in a world that's normal. My world would scare her. Look at the way she's terrified of her own mother."

"I've met Margaret Madden, and she scares everybody."

Jeff ate a few bites before speaking. "Cassie is an innocent and it's better that way. She stays at home with Elsbeth and that's all she needs."

Thomas smiled. "I've seen the way you look at her, and it's not especially 'innocent.'"

Jeff grinned. "Who wouldn't? She's a knockout."

"She's in love with you."

Jeff put his fork down. "She thinks she is, but it's just an old-fashioned crush that she's carried into adulthood. She loves my daughter, and that's what's important."

"Jeff, my son, you're a fool. Someday that beautiful young woman is going to get tired of waiting for you."

"She's not waiting for *me*. If she finds some nice young man, great. I'll walk her down the aisle and give her away."

Thomas looked at his son in astonishment. "I wonder where your mother and I failed in raising you. Or do you think it's a genetic defect? I must brush up on my Mendel to see how two intelligent people could give birth to an idiot."

"Are you finished?"

"No. I'm not going to be finished until you come to your senses about Cassie. If you don't do something soon, someone's going to swoop down and snatch her away from you."

"Good. I hope she finds someone nice and *safe*."

Thomas snorted in derision. "I'd like to see what you'd do if someone went after Cassie."

"You don't know me as well as you think you do. Look, let's forget this. I have a problem. You remember David Beaumont?"

"I remember his money."

"The agency wants him to help—" Jeff broke off and looked away.

"I know. You can't tell me. So what's the problem?"

"They want me to look after his daughter for a while. Get her settled here in Williamsburg."

"Is she too old for Elsbeth?"

Jeff smiled. "I guess so. She's thirty-four and gorgeous."

Thomas was silent as their entrées were placed before them. "And how were *you* chosen to be this woman's escort?"

Jeff shrugged. "I don't know. She and Roger Craig knew each other in college, so—"

"Couldn't he and that lovely wife of his, Dana, show this older woman around?"

Jeff frowned. "What is wrong with you today? I'm going to be spending time with a beautiful woman. Haven't you been complaining that I never go out?"

"No," Thomas said angrily, "I've been complaining that you live with a woman who is equal to both our late wives but you're too stubborn to see it."

Jeff's face was just as angry. "Are you forgetting that the last woman I was in love with was killed because of me?"

Thomas sat back in his seat, his anger leaving him. "No, I haven't forgotten. Do you plan to go through your life without love?"

"Come on, Dad," Jeff said. "How's your fish?"

Thomas sighed. "Excellent, as always." He lowered his voice. "It's true that Cassie is an 'innocent' as you call her, but she's only that way when you're around. When she's alone with Elsbeth and me, she's . . ." Thomas searched for the word. "She's a firecracker. She's funny and smart and creative. It's just when you come into the room that she becomes quiet and subdued."

"You've said all this before," Jeff said, "but it changes nothing. I don't want Cassie to get hurt."

"You're no longer a field agent," Thomas said, "so there wouldn't be the danger that Lillian was in."

Jeff had heard every word before, so he couldn't bring himself to listen. "Dad," Jeff said slowly, "I know you've come to love Cassie and so do I, but not in the way you want me to. Sure, I've had some problems with . . ." He hesitated.

"Raging desire?" Thomas asked.

"I'm a firm believer that parents shouldn't say such things to their children, but, yeah, raging desire. It wouldn't work out between Cassie and me. I really hope that I like this woman, Skylar Beaumont. In spite of being a rich kid, she's been around. Did you know that she used to go with Leo Norton? And she and Roger were nearly engaged when they were in college."

"In my day, we had a name for girls like that," Thomas said quietly.

"I'm not going to argue with you," Jeff said. "I know what I'm doing."

Thomas pushed his empty plate away. "I've never seen anyone who knew less what he was doing than you. Thank you for lunch." He stood up. "By the way, when you saw your students' eyes widen, you should have ducked."

"And let the bullet go over my head and hit one of them?"

Thomas smiled. "Good boy. You look out for the people in your care. Now, if you just applied that to your home life and took care of—"

Jeff cut his father off with a look, and Thomas went away, shaking his head.

On his way to the bookstore, Thomas thought that the real problem was that Cassie made their home life so very easy. It had crossed his mind many times that what would help them all is if something happened to unsettle their lives. Lately, every time Cassie did something nice for Jeff, like buy him a new set of gym clothes or cook his favorite meal, Thomas wanted to tell her not to do it. Sometimes he wanted to shout "Don't make him so damned comfortable!"

But Thomas didn't have the courage to upset their lives. The outcome could be good, but it could also mean that they'd lose Cassie, and he didn't think that he or Elsbeth could stand that.

He needed to think of something that would make his son see sense!

6

IT WAS COOL BY THE WATER, and Jeff hadn't brought a jacket. The little landing where he was to meet Roger was secluded but well lit with tall streetlamps. He shoved his hands in his pockets and waited for Roger, who came with his usual loud movements. "You'd never make an agent," Jeff said, frowning. He wanted to be in his warm house, away from the mosquitoes, but one look at Roger's face made him forget his complaints. "What's happened?"

"After you called, I made Althea tell me what she knew." He grimaced. "Getting information out of that woman is nearly impossible. Dana and Cassie were at the beach this morning and heard shots coming from Althea's house."

Immediately, Jeff flipped open his phone. "I'm going to kill that kid Goodwin. I knew he was too young to be put on a job like that."

Roger put his hand out to stop Jeff from calling. "Althea did it. She put on a little play."

"She did what?"

"After the housekeeper left on a long list of 'errands' that Althea came up with, Althea faked a migraine and sent Brent off to get her some pills. Truth was, she saw the girls on the beach, fired some old prop pistol into the air, then arranged herself on the terrace. They came to rescue her."

"I bet she didn't muss up her hair while she was being rescued," Jeff muttered. "What lie did she tell them?"

"Althea made up some cock-and-bull story about her ex-husband, Kenneth Ridgeway, having fired at her because he wanted money."

"That poor man," Jeff said. "He hasn't been near her in . . ."

"Not since Althea made the whole country laugh at him," Roger said. "Anyway, our ladies showed up, masquerading as angels, and offered to help. Althea served them tea."

Jeff groaned. "And I'm sure they had a lovely time." His head came up. "Could Cassie have seen you at Althea's tonight?"

"No. Not possible. We were in the back most of the time so—" Roger broke off. "Actually, there were about ten minutes when I was with Althea and Brent in the living room. The curtains were closed, but maybe . . . What happened to make you think I was seen?"

"Cassie came running into the house, out of breath, and holding on to a basket of cookies as if her life depended on it. Her face was white, and she looked as though she'd seen something she didn't like."

"Damn!" Roger said. "Think she was taking cookies to Althea?"

"Yeah, that's something she'd do."

"So now what do we do?" Roger asked.

Jeff looked at the river. "It was only a matter of time before Althea broke her promise to stay away from other people."

"Why would she want to do that when you send such fascinating people to visit with her? There's Clyde from Accounting. He comes—what is it?—three times a week? Hoskins from Internal Affairs. And my favorite: Mrs. Simpson from Foreign. What a jolly lot they are."

"And she has Goodwin to mow her grass. I hear he's half in love with her. Maybe she's the grandmother he never had."

"Speaking of which, I think you'd better get a real gardener in there to look after the place. It looks good now, but it won't last. And my Dana knows good gardening."

Jeff gave Roger a hard look. "You can't possibly be thinking of allowing Dana to visit her again."

Roger gave a laugh. "What am I supposed to do? Forbid my wife to visit a woman I'm not supposed to know? Besides, Althea must have asked them to keep their visit a secret because Dana hasn't said a word to me about it. What about you? Did Cassie tell you she spent the morning having tea with the Great Lady?"

"Not a word," Jeff said, "but I'll get it out of her."

"Spoken like an unmarried man."

"I was married," Jeff spat out, "but you know how that ended."

"Yeah," Roger said, his voice lowered. "Listen, I know you just want to protect the women, but I don't know how to do it without telling them too much. I think we should let the three of them have their little secret. After all, what trouble could they get into? Althea is how old now?"

"Not even the United States government is powerful enough to find out *that* information. The woman has four passports that we know of, and each one has a different birth date."

"Okay, but we agree that she's an old woman, so how much bad can she do? Her days of sticking her nose into the governments of foreign countries are over. Besides, maybe meeting a great actress will cheer Dana up."

"Still down, is she?"

Roger rolled his eyes. "Skylar is a real bitch to her. Sometimes I want to . . ."

"Yeah, I know. Strangle her."

Roger laughed. "I wouldn't quite put it that way, but I could see that. Is she really nasty to Cassie?"

"Horrible."

"And Elsbeth?"

Jeff smiled. "Except for one hilarious incident involving a jacket, when Skylar makes one of her remarks meant to draw blood, Cassie just lowers her head and takes it. She's a pouter. She goes into her room and holds on to her wounds. But Elsbeth is like me."

"What does that mean? She's devious, underhanded, and living more than one life?"

"Exactly," Jeff said, smiling. "When Skylar makes a remark that Elsbeth doesn't like, my daughter gets her back. When we went on the trip to DC and had to go to the formal embassy party, Skylar was hysterical because her makeup bag was missing. It was night, we were late, and she didn't have so much as a tube of mascara. When my daughter is around, Skylar refuses to take off her shoes because of all the things she's found in them."

Roger laughed. "With your daughter's ancestry, how can she be anything but devious? Tell me, have you ever *seen* Elsbeth do anything to Skylar's possessions?"

"Not one single thing," Jeff said with pride. "Nor has Dad."

Roger gave a low whistle. "I am impressed. And here I thought she was an ordinary little girl."

"She is, and she's mad about Cassie."

"Who isn't? Last time I saw her at the pool in that red swimsuit, I—" He broke off at the look Jeff gave him. "Just kidding. I'm happy with my wife, even if she is the gloomiest person on the planet right now."

Jeff was frowning. He didn't like the references to Cassie in a swimsuit. She was built like a real woman: big on top, big on the bottom, with a twenty-four-inch waist in the middle. More than once when he'd seen her and his daughter getting ready to go to the club pool he'd had to leave the room and get into a cold shower. "Okay, we'll let the women have their little social mornings, but let's keep an eye on them."

"Aye, aye, captain," Roger said mockingly. He looked at his watch. "I have to go or Dana will think I'm having an affair."

"I think she already does. Cassie hinted that she thinks you're doing something you shouldn't on that boat."

"I am," Roger said, grinning, then he lost his smile. "You don't mean . . . not another woman? Dana couldn't think I'm having—" He shook his head in disbelief. "Anyway, it's a good thing that young Brent didn't believe Althea's story. He did just as you've taught him and checked it out before calling for backup. He showed me tapes from two cameras that clearly show that she fired the shots."

"Thank heaven for hidden cameras."

Roger chuckled. "Hidden? I hope you don't mean you think they're hidden from Althea. She turned to the one that's embedded in the wrought-iron casing of a flowerpot and said, 'I'm ready for my close-up now, Mr. Goodwin.' "

"Why was I given the job of guarding her?" Jeff groaned, running his hand over his face. "I'd rather take on the Mafia."

"We know why you took it on," Roger said quietly.

Jeff looked away for a moment. At the time, he had a pregnant wife, and the agency had offered him a low mortgage on a great house in an outstanding community. The catch was that his new house would be next door to a mansion that would house a living treasure: Althea Fairmont. At the time, all he knew about her was that she'd made some great movies and she'd helped the United States in time of need. He'd felt guilty to be given such a cushy job.

It was months before he found out the truth. An angry agent, embittered by his lack of promotion within the agency, had spent his last years writing a tell-all book. To Jeff's mind the man was the lowest form of scum. He'd betrayed his oath of secrecy. When he died, his will instructed his children to send the book to a publisher. Some smart lawyer for the publishing house, concerned about lawsuits, had called the CIA and e-mailed the manuscript to them. Within three hours, all copies of the book had been destroyed.

But even the government couldn't keep all the information secret. The names of people who had secretly helped the United States government, spies, were leaked. The agency was able to keep the public from knowing, but the inner circle of the espionage world knew. A man who'd helped during World War II was found facedown in his swimming pool. Another man disappeared one night and was never seen again. After the second death, the president of the United States got involved.

One of the names on the list was that of Althea Fairmont, the most beloved actress who had ever lived. There had been no sign of any attempts on her life, no threatening letters or phone calls, but the order came down from the highest offices that she was to be protected. If nothing else, the United States didn't want to bear the humiliation of the public knowing that an actress had helped them in every major war since the 1920s.

But how to protect her? They couldn't put one of the most famous people in the world in witness protection. How could such a famous person be anonymous? In the end, they decided to put her in a gated community near the military bases and the CIA school.

When she was told what needed to be done to protect her, Althea said she'd rather live in the Gulag than in suburbia.

But her desire for life won out. A mansion was built at government expense, with the plan that, later, after Althea passed away, the house would be used for visiting dignitaries.

Jefferson Ames and his well-trained, well-respected father were put in a house on one side of Althea's, and the attorney who'd take over her financial and legal affairs on the other side. Althea's house was liberally sprinkled with concealed buttons. If she pushed one of them, an alarm would go off in both Jeff's and Roger's houses, as well as in agency headquarters. But no alarm had ever sounded.

When Althea was told that a third man had to live in her house with her, she'd protested so loudly that they'd let her choose the man herself. She went through a stack of photographs and chose the rookie Brent Goodwin. He was a pupil of Jeff's and was to report to him by phone every day. Jeff hadn't liked the choice. He thought Goodwin was too young, didn't have enough training, and was too attractive to women. He didn't think the young man would keep his mind on the job.

But in spite of Jeff's worries, in the years since it was set up, it had worked out well.

Jeff had met Althea repeatedly and they'd been cordial, but he'd kept their relationship on a business level. Not so Roger. Brent said Althea kept Roger at her house for hours, and he told her all the gossip of the entire community.

"She knows more about the people who live here than I do," Brent said, making Jeff frown. So far, nothing bad had happened, but Jeff spent his life expecting it to all fall apart. Now, here was the news that Althea had stupidly fired a prop pistol in the air. Why? To get the attention of the women who lived near her?

"I've warned you that something like this would happen," Jeff said. "That woman is smarter than you and me combined. And I don't trust her. You shouldn't—"

Roger cut him off. "Okay, so sue me. I like the woman. Not all of us can have hearts made of steel."

Jeff gave him a sharp look.

"I apologize. You have your father and your beautiful daughter." Roger sighed. "Lucky you."

Jeff's anger left him. He well knew that what Roger wanted most in life was children. Jeff was missing a wife; Roger was missing kids. Put us together and we're one whole person, he thought.

"I'll deal with Althea later," Jeff said. "I need a favor from you. Could I borrow your old cabin for the weekend after next? I, uh, thought I'd take Skylar up there."

Roger gave Jeff a hard look. "The last person you want to be alone with is Skylar. You're meeting someone there, aren't you?"

Jeff hated the way Roger saw things he didn't want seen. Roger had every security clearance that Jeff had, but caution was built into him. "Yeah, I'm meeting an old friend of mine," Jeff said.

"I heard Leo's in town. Couldn't be him, could it?"

Jeff said nothing. It had been instilled in him since he was a child to give out as little information as he could.

"Leo Norton," Roger said thoughtfully. "I've met him. There's something about him. . . . What is it he does?"

Jeff gave a sigh. If he didn't tell, then he had no doubt that Roger would start snooping. Roger's lawyerly curiosity would get the better of him. "Leo is the most brilliant at disguise of any operative we have. What that man can do to change his appearance is fascinating. He'd give Andy Serkis a run for his money."

Roger laughed. Serkis had played Gollum and King Kong. "Fan of his, are you?"

"Yeah."

Roger waited, but when Jeff gave no more information, he asked, "Does he have anything to do with the mystery weekend?"

Jeff groaned. "Don't remind me of that thing. And, no, Leo has no part in it. That's just my burden to bear."

Roger smiled. "Sure wish I could join you."

Jeff grimaced. Next summer, at Althea's request, he was to go to a "mystery weekend" at the house of a man named Charles Faulkener, a man who'd once been a friend of Althea's. As a young man Faulkener had desperately wanted to be an actor, but his lack of talent got him few roles. But Faulkener couldn't face the fact that he didn't have the gift for acting. Instead, he blamed his lack of success on a murder that happened in his house in 1941. Over the decades, he'd become obsessed with the unsolved murder, and every ten years he re-created it. The problem was that since no new evidence had come to light in the ensuing years, the dramas produced nothing new.

Three years ago, Faulkener, who was as good at making money in the international market as he was bad at acting, had accidentally run across some information that the U.S. government wanted. Jeff hadn't been told what it was, but he thought it was a list of names. But Faulkener had refused to turn the info over unless he was told what Althea, who had been there the weekend of the murder, knew.

As always, Althea had her own ideas about how to do things. She said that she wouldn't just tell. Instead, she wanted one of her agents, Jefferson Ames, to play Hinton Landau, the young man who had been accused of the murder. She said she'd tell Jeff what she knew just before the weekend.

"Wasn't this Landau married?" Roger asked.

"Yeah." Jeff grimaced. "And Skylar is to play my wife."

Roger laughed. "You shouldn't worry about her so much. She never stays with any man very long."

"I'm not 'with' her and never have been."

"Does she know that?" Roger asked, then laughed again at Jeff's expression. "Trust me, I've known her for ages. She'll get bored and dump you."

"It wouldn't matter if she did. Althea wants her to play my wife."

"Hmmm, wonder what she's up to?"

"Why don't you ask her?" Jeff said. "You're so good at getting information out of her."

"That's a joke! Althea charms me into telling her every piece of gossip I hear, but she tells me nothing. To find out the truth about the shots I have to work for her for free for the next six weeks." Roger looked at Jeff. "What you ought to do is get Cassie to go up to the cabin with you."

"Cassie? Are you out of your mind? Cassie is—"

"Is what? The babysitter?"

"Whatever she is, I want to keep her that way."

"How fatherly of you."

"Don't you start on me too. I get enough of this from Dad. *Why* did Althea fake a shooting? Other than to meet our women, that is."

"Since when have you had 'a woman'? Other than Skylar, that is." Roger said the last with a derisive laugh.

Jeff looked out at the dark James River. "You know we need Skylar, and Cassie's fine. Except that she thinks I'm about to marry someone she detests and throw her out on that beautiful rear end of hers."

"The way you lead that girl on is horrible to watch," Roger said without animosity. "It's a wonder she doesn't dump cake batter on your head and tell you to go stuff yourself."

Jeff shrugged. "I told you that Cassie's fine. We're all doing well. In my book, everyone is fine except for Goodwin."

"Don't be so hard on the kid. He's up against one of the great espionage brains of the century." Roger smiled. "So you're taking Skylar up to the cabin. Are you sure that you and she are just an act? Maybe you two could get married and—"

"And let her near my daughter?" Jeff asked, his voice fierce with protecting his child.

Roger put his hands up. "Okay, don't take it out on me. I was just asking." He looked at his watch again. "I really do have to go. I better get home and prove to my wife that she's the only woman for me."

They said their good-byes and Jeff watched Roger leave, then he thrust his hands in his pockets, frowned, and started walking, his frown deepening with every step. He shouldn't allow Dana and Cassie to spend time with Althea, he thought. What Althea Fairmont knew was important to the U.S. government and she had to be protected, but he should do everything he could to keep her away from other people. On the other hand, she was an old woman and she'd had a life of being around people. Isolation was the worst form of punishment for her and she didn't deserve to be penalized. And Jeff knew the two women who would be visiting her well. No, he hadn't checked their backgrounds, but Roger had known Dana since they were in elementary school together, and Jeff had known Cassie for almost as long.

His frown was replaced by a smile as he remembered that time when he'd pulled her from a swimming pool and saved her life. He'd been well aware that she'd been following him all that week, and he felt sorry for her. She had a mother who made piranhas seem nice, and Cassie had been the only kid at the convention, which had been fraught with tension and anger. Part of his job had been to know about everything, even about little girls hiding in the bushes.

But on the last morning there, Lillian had arrived the night before, and so he was late for his early morning swim—almost too late. They'd found a half-dead kid floating facedown in the pool. For several minutes it had been touch and go as to whether she was going to make it. But she had, and as soon as she could, she'd run away in embarrassment.

For the next several years, Jeff had kept an eye on Cassandra Madden. Maybe he felt so responsible for her because he'd saved her life. Or maybe it was because her mother seemed so tough. Whatever the reason, he'd had his office check on her whereabouts a couple of times a year, and he'd even had copies of her college grades sent to him.

But after Lillian died, he lost contact with Cassie, and with most of the rest of the world. He stayed close only to his father and daughter. It wasn't until he checked out the credentials of Elsbeth's new nursery school teacher that he saw her name again. For months he'd laughed every time Cassie called him to report on whatever Elsbeth's nannies had neglected to do. And when Cassie told him she wanted the job of nanny, Jeff had had to work hard to keep a straight face.

She'd moved into his house and taken over his life in a way that made everyone comfortable. Her mother was reputed to have no heart, but Cassie had one as big as the moon. She loved Elsbeth and Thomas as though they were her own family. And, yes, Jeff had to admit that she loved him too. As he loved her. It hadn't taken long for him to fall in love with Cassie. She had a quirky sense of humor and . . . Well, there wasn't anything about her that wasn't good.

The problem was that Jeff too often remembered that little girl who had hidden in the bushes and watched him. And he remembered that he'd saved her life. It was as though he now had a lifelong commitment to take care of her, just as he did with Elsbeth.

Living with Cassie caused him a lot of indecision and anxiety. Lusting after her gorgeous twenty-five-year-old body one minute, the next feeling like he wanted to tuck her in bed and kiss her forehead, sometimes made him crazy.

But every time he thought of getting closer to her, he remembered what had happened to Lillian. Happened because of him. Sometimes he thought he should send Elsbeth away so she'd be safe. If it weren't for his father, a man who'd had a lifetime of training in being an agent, living with them, Jeff thought he might do that.

How could he risk taking on another real relationship? he often wondered.

When he reached the house, he quietly opened the door. His bedroom was on the ground floor, but he tiptoed up the main staircase, as he always did, to check on the windows, and the occupants. Elsbeth was asleep in her bed, looking as perfect as an angel. Down the hall was his father's bedroom. Jeff didn't knock but opened the door silently and looked in. His father was propped up in the bed, reading a book, and he didn't look up or acknowledge his son.

Jeff closed the door and smiled. He'd seen the way his father's hand had disappeared under the covers. Jeff didn't know and didn't ask if his father slept with a weapon, but he wouldn't doubt it. Old agents never changed their habits. Every birthday since he was eight, Jeff had given his father a gift that had 007 printed on it.

Down the corridor, at the top of the back stairs, was Cassie's room. The light was on; he could see it under her door. He wanted to knock; he wanted to talk to her. Sometimes what he missed most about marriage was having a confidante. He'd told Lillian all that he could. But, then, what she did or did not know had caused her death.

He didn't knock on Cassie's door but silently went down the back stairs to his own bedroom.

7

CASSIE RAN THE RAZOR up her leg, then slid back in the tub and closed her eyes. Both Dana and Althea said that waxing was the way to go. She hadn't done that yet, but she planned to. Next week she had an appointment at a salon on Richmond Road where she was to get waxed and massaged, and her skin was to be made luminous. Or at least that's what the ad promised.

It had been a week since she and Dana had met Althea Fairmont, and it had been an exciting time. There had been no more talk of Cassie becoming Althea's employee, but somehow, the woman had maneuvered both Dana and Cassie into working for her—without pay.

But the work had been good for Cassie. For months she'd thought that if she had to leave Jeff's house, had to leave Elsbeth, her life would be over. But in the last week she'd begun to see possibilities of a future without Jefferson Ames. Since she'd lived for over half her life with the idea that he was the only man for her, it hadn't been an easy transition.

But Althea's energy and enthusiasm were helping her. On Monday morning, she and Elsbeth had met Dana at the end of the garden, ready to go to Althea's house. Dana worried that they would tire Miss Fairmont. "After all, she is a woman of a certain age," Dana said as they walked toward the house.

"I dare you to say that to her face," Cassie said.

"No, I think I'll continue to live for a while."

It had been at Althea's invitation that they visited. She'd called Cassie on Sunday and asked if she and Dana would like to look at some memorabilia she'd saved from her many years in show business. "I have a few things that need to be cataloged," she'd said on that first Monday as she'd climbed two flights of stairs, Cassie, Dana, and Elsbeth behind her, to a walk-in attic that covered the entire house. When she opened the door, the two women gasped. It was an Aladdin's cave of treasure. There were hundreds of boxes and trunks, and what looked to be thousands of the most extraordinary items. Costumes, props, and printed matter from every play and movie that Althea had done were piled on top of one another.

"This should be in a museum," Cassie said in awe, looking inside a carton labeled *Moments in the Sun*. It had been the movie Althea had won her second Oscar for. "Is this . . . ?" Cassie asked, lifting a silver cup from the bottom. At the end of the movie, Althea, as the heroine, had drunk poison and died in a futile attempt to take the blame for a murder the man she loved had committed.

"The very one," Althea said.

Gently, with reverence, Cassie put the cup back, then stood up. There was furniture, posters, and bound scripts; costumes peeped out of big cloth bags. It was all gorgeous, and she wanted to go through every piece of it.

"Now you're seeing my dream," Althea said. "I want to open a library for the study of film. It would not only be a repository of artifacts, but also a place where students can see films and learn."

"In L.A.?" Dana asked as she picked up a dress that was covered with silver beads.

Elsbeth stuck her little feet into a pair of red shoes from the 1940s. Cassie recognized them as from *Shadow of a Woman*. She wondered if the matching dress was there.

"I plan to leave everything, including my money, to the establishment of the library," Althea said, ignoring Dana's question. "But I do wish I could leave it all in better order than it is now."

"And that's why you want to hire Cassie," Dana said, sounding as though she'd solved a mystery.

"Actually, I think there's more than enough work here for two people," Althea said, smiling and looking at Dana. "If that husband of yours can spare you from . . ." She waved her hand. "From whatever women who are supported by their husbands do all day."

Cassie saw Dana stiffen, so she stepped between them. "I don't know how much I can do," Cassie said. "I have Elsbeth to care for until . . ." She hesitated.

"Until Skylar takes over your home and throws you out?" Althea asked. She looked at Elsbeth. "Think you could stand giving up your little playdates to spend time with me?"

Most children wouldn't want to spend time with an older woman, but Elsbeth wasn't like other children. "Oh, yes," she said, her eyes wide as she looked at a pile of hats that covered the centuries from the 1700s to the 1970s.

"I think Elsbeth will do quite well here," Althea said, eyeing the child with approval.

"But I don't know if Jeff will like this," Cassie began.

"And does he disagree with you often?" Althea asked.

"No, not usually. Actually, not ever. But Thomas . . . I make lunch for him."

Althea smiled. "Do you think I've forgotten Jefferson's handsome father? Rosalie is already working on a rather splendid lunch for him."

Dana and Cassie looked at each other in wonder. It seemed that everything had already been settled—and settled the way Althea wanted it, which they soon learned was always the way with her. Within two hours of arriving, Dana and Cassie were hard at work. By Tuesday afternoon, they had established a routine. And while Dana and Cassie worked like drudges upstairs, Althea and Thomas and Elsbeth spent the day downstairs, their laughter floating up to the women in the attic. From the second day on, the three of them went out to lunch together and didn't return until evening. Cassie and Dana ate a sandwich while continuing to work.

When Cassie put Elsbeth in the tub at night, she'd ask, "Where did you go today? What did you do?" but the child never told anything except uttered vague phrases. "To a restaurant," she'd say. Or "to look at some old buildings." That about covered every inch of Williamsburg, Cassie thought, frustrated that she couldn't get much out of Elsbeth.

She got no more out of Thomas. "Sightseeing," he said.

At dinner with Jeff, which had been cooked by Althea's housekeeper, Rosalie, and carried home, Elsbeth and Thomas wouldn't so much as mention what they'd done during the day. So Cassie followed suit. It wasn't as though they were keeping a secret from Jeff; they just left out Althea from their talk.

As for Cassie and Dana, they were loosening in their attitudes toward each other. It started on Tuesday when they were both sweating and dirty, and they heard more laughter from downstairs.

"So how much are we being paid to do this?" Dana asked, standing up and stretching her aching back.

"I think it's four million an hour," Cassie said, deadpan.

"We should ask for a raise." Dana held up a green velvet dress. "Do you remember this one?"

"*Watching You*," Cassie said. "It's when she sees him off at the pier."

"Wasn't that movie made in the 1940s? And wasn't it in black-and-white?"

"Yes." Cassie looked at her in question.

"So how do you recognize a *green* dress and how do you remember which movie, even which scene it was in?"

"Chalk it up to a boring childhood spent alone with my very own video player and an account at a local video store."

"Rich kid," Dana said, holding up a pair of black and white shoes. "Please tell me that you don't remember these shoes."

"*The Last Night.* She leaves one behind when he pushes her out the window of the stone tower."

There was another burst of laughter from downstairs. "I can understand why he did it," Dana said, putting the shoes back in the trunk. "I think she should get a professional in here. I really don't understand how *I* got rooked into doing this."

Cassie was sitting on a chair that looked as though it had been used in a play about Cleopatra, with a clipboard on her lap. "It must be nice to have the choice of not taking a job," Cassie said, "but I need one. I'm about to be out of employment and a place to live, remember? Doing this beats sitting in an office and answering telephones."

"Sorry," Dana said, ducking her head. "I'm complaining too much. Maybe I'm just jealous. I had an image of spending fascinating afternoons with the Great Althea, but instead, I've spent two days in her attic."

"She'd rather be with Thomas," Cassie said, looking down at her clipboard.

"I don't blame her. He's a very handsome man." Dana hesitated. "Like his son. Jeff will look just like him when he's that age."

Cassie put her head closer to the clipboard.

Dana sat down on a purple stool. "On Saturday when we met Althea she suggested that you . . . well, that you liked Jeff."

"He's a great guy," Cassie said quickly. "Is there anything more in that box?" She was recording every item, then putting a number on the container. After they were done, it would be easy to see what Althea had and where it was.

"Look," Dana began, "I think you and I got off on the wrong foot."

"No," Cassie said. "I understand. You were taking care of Elsbeth and I took her away from you. If I were you, I wouldn't like me either."

"Damn!" Dana said. "Why do you have to be so blasted *nice*?"

"I grew up with a mother who doesn't know the meaning of the word. I figured I had to be the opposite of her to balance the world."

Dana dug into the bottom of a hatbox and pulled out a silk scarf. "This important?"

Cassie's eyes widened. "*Wednesday's Child*," she said. "Althea was about sixteen—give or take twenty years—and she murdered a little girl with that scarf."

Grimacing, Dana dropped it back into the box. "Do you have any idea why Jeff wants to marry Skylar?"

Cassie looked up. "None whatever."

"Maybe she knows some fabulous tricks in bed," Dana said as she lifted the lid of an old wooden crate. "She likes to tell a disgusting story about how she had a boyfriend in college that she went through the entire Kama Sutra with. Sometimes I have nightmares that she's actually talking about Roger. I—" She broke off at a noise from Cassie.

"Sorry," Cassie said. "Pen broke."

Dana looked at the ink on the page on the clipboard. It wasn't just the tip of the roller ballpoint pen that had broken but the barrel.

"I, uh, better wash my hands," Cassie said and got up.

It was on Wednesday, at about 10 A.M., that everything changed. Althea sent Elsbeth up to the attic to ask that Dana come downstairs.

"I wonder what I did to be so honored?" Dana asked sarcastically. Her enthusiasm for getting to know Althea had petered out on Tuesday afternoon when an old trunk lid had just missed slamming on her hand. She'd had to cancel three meetings at the Hamilton Hundred country club to be able to spend so much time at Althea's house, but now all she wanted was to get out of the dusty attic.

But Cassie was more than content. To her, every item was a piece of wonderment, something she remembered from her lonely childhood. Althea's movies had been a close friend to her when she was growing up.

Somehow, Althea had known exactly what was happening in the attic and who had done what. She lavished praise on Cassie, thanking her profusely. "You're too good for Jefferson," she'd said. "I don't think he appreciates you."

Cassie smiled her thanks, but Dana stepped forward and said that she also thought Cassie was doing a great job. "Maybe we should talk about her salary and when she's to start working for you officially."

Althea wasn't about to be bullied by someone a third her age. "I think that's a wonderful idea. Just as soon as Cassie quits her other job we can talk about terms. Now, who'd like tea? Or would you like a nice gin and tonic?"

After four tries, Dana gave up trying to pin Althea down to hours and wages. She showed up at the mansion on Wednesday, but she didn't want to stay. Seeming to be oblivious, Althea had bustled her up the stairs, but at ten she'd called Dana down again.

Cassie didn't know what happened, but Dana didn't return. But then, she was quite happy to work alone. She and Dana had cleared a path back to an old wardrobe that stood against a back wall. She couldn't remember for sure but she thought the wardrobe had been in a movie. It wasn't the one where Althea hid from a couple of murderers, she was sure of that, but it did seem familiar.

"*The Twenty-sixth of December*," came a voice and she looked up to see Brent in the doorway. Immediately, Cassie knew what he was talking about.

"Of course. She kept her journal in the back, under a loose board."

"And after she was killed, the journal was what told the detective who'd murdered her."

Cassie smiled. "But she wasn't dead. She was hiding."

Brent walked around three chairs and a steamer trunk to move closer to her. "And she was waiting."

"For the detective to find her."

Brent stopped by the wardrobe, put his hand on top of the door, and glanced inside, his head close to hers. "She said that—"

"If he was smart enough to figure out the mystery, then she was interested, but if he wasn't . . ."

With their eyes locked, Brent and Cassie imitated Althea's famous shrug of indifference.

Together, they laughed.

"So you're a fan too," Cassie said as she knelt to look into the bottom of the wardrobe and search for the panel that would move. A moment later, she said, "It's empty." She stood up again. "No journal."

"Of course not," Brent said. "Reed, the detective, took it."

"Oh, yes, of course. How silly of me."

Brent leaned back against the wardrobe and looked about the huge room with all its paraphernalia. "Making much progress?"

"A little. It's slow. I keep stopping to look at things and think about them. How is everyone?" She nodded toward the doorway.

"Great. Althea hasn't been this happy in . . . Well, I've never known her to be this happy. She's charming Thomas and he's loving it."

"Two lonely people," Cassie said and felt guilty that she'd never before realized how lonely Thomas probably was. He'd tried to make her and Elsbeth into the sophisticated company he liked, but they weren't Althea. "He isn't overdoing it, is he? His heart isn't strong."

"His heart?" Brent said, then smiled. "Oh, right. His heart. The only danger there is that Althea might break it. She likes to do that."

"I think her heart has been broken a few times," Cassie said more stiffly than she meant to.

"I doubt that," Brent said. "I think her heart is made of iron."

Cassie couldn't keep from frowning. "She doesn't seem to please you, does she?"

Brent smiled at her, his handsome face lighting up, and Cassie couldn't keep her frown. "She pleases me so much that I'm damned jealous of Thomas. I work myself to death to try to keep her safe, but she's never once flirted with me as she does with him."

Cassie laughed. What he was saying was ridiculous, since he was young enough to be Althea's great-grandson.

"Can I help you with this?" he asked, motioning toward the packed attic.

"Dana—"

"Has been sent away. Althea said something about the world's committee women needing her."

"Yeow!" Cassie said. "That sounds nasty."

"Althea's middle name." Brent took a knife from his pocket, flipped out the blade, and cut open a big cardboard box and looked inside. "When she wants to be, that is. And when she wants to be nice, she can make people melt. I've decided that she's not so much an actress as a wizard who puts spells on people."

Cassie walked around a 1930s ashtray on a stand to peer into the box beside him. "My goodness."

"Yes," Brent said softly, reverently. "*Queen of the Morning.*"

Inside were three of the magnificent costumes from the historical drama in which Althea played a doomed queen of a fictional country. The critics had ridiculed it because the character was an amalgamation of Mary, Queen of Scots, Anne Boleyn, and Lady Jane Grey. But the audiences loved the movie.

"Every time I saw it, I cried when they beheaded her," Cassie said.

"Me too," Brent said, then smiled at her. "More or less, anyway."

She reached in and began to pull out one of the heavy dresses. It was burgundy velvet on top, burgundy silk on bottom, with a quilted gold skirt underneath. "It's beautiful," she breathed.

"I think that would fit you," Brent said.

"And what have you been smoking?"

"No, really. Don't you remember that Althea was pregnant during that movie?"

"Pregnant? Are you saying that to be as fat as I am she had to be pregnant?"

"I think you look like one of those Victorian women with their hourglass figures," Brent said. "But that's beside the point. In case you haven't noticed, Althea doesn't have much on top. You'd never be able to button most of her clothes, but this one might fit."

Cassie blinked at him. Did all men everywhere look at the figures of all women? And how could he tell about her? Every day she'd worn loose, baggy clothes.

"Try it on," he said.

"I wouldn't dare," Cassie said, but she couldn't keep the desire out of her voice. Try on a costume that Althea Fairmont had worn?

"Come on, she and Thomas and the kid left an hour ago. I think they were going plantation visiting, so they won't be back before evening. Let's go down to her bedroom and you can try it on. I'll get my camera, then we can go somewhere and take photos."

The idea of seeing Althea's bedroom, plus putting on the famous dress, was too tempting to pass up. "You're on," she said.

"Isn't there a hat with that thing?"

"Yes," she said. "A little velvet cap with a net that goes over the hair."

He looked in the tall box but didn't see it. "Why don't you go down and I'll see if I can find it. I think there are some shoes on the bottom."

Cassie was holding the dress draped across both arms. "Where is her bedroom?"

"See that door there? It leads to the ground floor. Her bedroom is at the bottom." He looked up. "Rosalie went to the grocery, so we're alone in the house, so look around if you want to."

Cassie didn't know if she was brave enough to go snooping. Trying on a dress without permission was more than she could handle in one day. At the far end of the attic was a door she hadn't noticed before and she went down two flights until she came to the bottom. Quietly, she opened the door and listened. Not a sound in the house. Even though she was alone, she tiptoed across the corridor, then cautiously opened the door into Althea's bedroom.

It was as romantic as she'd hoped. The room was mostly white—as for a virgin, Cassie thought—but had splashes of red and green here and there. The bed, as big as a small stage, was draped in gauzy white silk. The bed skirt was white and embroidered with a border of red rosebuds, the leaves entwining with one another. The coverlet was white with red buttons, and there were tiny red silk pillows among the many white pillows.

She walked carefully across the pristine white carpet to the open door into the white marble bathroom. As soon as she saw it, Cassie smiled. It was an exact copy of the bathroom in the 1936 classic *To One and All*. Art Deco to its core.

Feeling like a criminal—and maybe she was, since she was trespassing—she stripped off her ugly, modern clothes and slid the big costume over her head. It wasn't easy to get into, and it caught, with something hanging on to her hair and not letting go. When she heard the soft knock on the door, her heart nearly stopped.

"It's me," Brent said.

"I'm stuck," Cassie called out, and in the next moment she felt Brent's hands on the dress. Part of her was aware that she was just in her underwear, but then, didn't she show as much at the pool?

"Be still," he said. "There! I got it. Now careful." He helped her slide the dress downward over her body.

The dress had been heavy in her arms, but when it was on her body, it seemed even heavier.

"Suck in," Brent said, "and I'll get this hooked."

As Cassie stared at herself in the wall-to-wall mirror over the gold sink, she could see herself transforming with every hook that Brent fastened in the back. Her waist was going in, hips out, and breasts up. Cassie's neat French braid had come undone, and now her thick dark hair was cascading around her face and over her shoulders.

He moved her hair to the front, over one shoulder, as he fastened the last hook. "There. I told you it would fit. Perfect."

He looked at her in the mirror, his hands on her shoulders. He was a foot taller than she was, and his blond hair was as thick as Cassie's. "Beautiful," he said. "Really beautiful."

Cassie ran her hands down the sides of the dress. It was uncomfortable and it was cutting off her breathing, but a girl could put up with a little discomfort to look like this, she thought.

Suddenly, Brent's head came up and he turned toward the door. "Houston, we have a problem."

Cassie heard the voices and especially heard the distinctive voice that was heading toward the bathroom. It was Althea, and she was about thirty seconds away from finding them. Cassie was petrified, too scared to move.

But not so Brent. He scooped her clothes off the floor as he grabbed her arm and pulled her toward the door on the right-hand side of the bathroom. They were in an enormous walk-in closet, and she could see that it held winter clothes. There was a glass-doored area that was full of furs, and incongruously, Cassie wondered if it was a refrigerated room.

Brent didn't let her stand in the middle of the room but opened a white, louvered door and pulled her inside, then shut the door behind them. They were slammed together in the tiny room-within-a-room, chest to chest. She could feel his heart beating against her own.

Part of her thought the whole thing was funny. After all, what would happen if they were caught? Cassie couldn't be fired from a job she didn't really have. And she was sure that if Brent were fired he could get a better job than being a gardener/bodyguard.

But common sense had nothing to do with reality. They waited, their bodies pressed together, and listened for the quiet sounds of Althea's heels on the marble bathroom floor. When she came close to the door to the closet, they held their breaths, then let them out when she moved away.

For a moment they heard nothing. Had she left? Or was she in the bedroom? Cassie looked up at Brent, and he put his finger to his lips. Silently, he opened the door and looked out. Nothing and no one.

But just as he started to step out, the door to the closet opened and Brent stepped back inside with Cassie. His arms went around her and he pressed her face to his chest as they listened to Althea's footsteps on the carpet. They could hear drawers being opened and closed, then a door was opened. Cassie hadn't had much time to look about, but there were at least three doors inside the closet. The area they were in now had floor-to-ceiling shelves filled with what seemed to be cashmere sweaters. If what Althea was looking for was a sweater and she opened the door, they would be exposed.

They heard her just outside the door and Brent held Cassie tightly, as though to protect her from something, but Althea didn't open the door. Instead, they heard her call out in answer to someone that she was ready to go. Seconds later, they heard her heels on the marble floor, then the bedroom door was closed and all was silent.

"I think it's safe now," Cassie said several minutes later. Her voice was muffled because her face was pressed against Brent's chest—his beautifully sculpted chest, that is.

"Mmmm," was all Brent said as he put his cheek against the top of her head.

Cassie's arms were around him, the two of them holding on to each other as though they were under siege, but she dropped her arms. His grip on her didn't loosen. "Brent!" she said. "I think it's safe to leave now."

"Do we have to?"

It wasn't easy, but she managed to step back from him about two inches. "Yes, we have to," she said. She put her hand on the door to open it. It was dark in the little room, but she could still see his eyes gleaming.

He put his hand over hers. "Will you go out with me? On a date?"

"I'm not sure this is the time to—"

"This is the perfect time. How about Saturday? I'll pick you up at eleven and we'll have lunch, then we can . . . I don't know. I'll think of something. How about it?"

"And what if I say no?" she asked, teasing.

"I won't unfasten the back of that dress."

"Is that extortion or blackmail?"

"It's the plea of a desperate man."

His words were, of course, absurd, but they made her feel good. Maybe it was the dress that made her feel as though she were beautiful, but she could almost believe he was sincere. "Saturday at eleven it is," she said. "I'll meet you at—"

"Oh, no, you don't," Brent said, his voice changing from seductive to firm. "I am not to be denied the pleasure of picking you up at Jefferson Ames's house. He'll be there, won't he?"

"I assume so," Cassie said as Brent opened the door and looked around. Why was it that so many people seemed to know Jeff? Was it from his work? He worked on commercial buildings and bridges, anything that had a superstructure of iron and steel. Maybe he'd calculated where the I-beams for Althea's house had been placed.

Brent took Cassie's hand as she stepped out of the tiny room. "Don't tell him I'm going to pick you up," he said. "I want to surprise him."

"Do you want to take out Jeff or me?"

"You. Definitely you."

They walked out of the closet, through the bathroom, and into the bedroom. Brent opened the door of the bedroom and looked in the hallway, but saw no one. He turned back to Cassie. "Promise?"

"That I won't tell Jeff that I have a date?" She was confused. "Why would he care if I have a date or not? He's about to get engaged to Skylar Beaumont."

"Think so?" Brent asked, turning to look at her. "I think we should take your photo in the conservatory. With the orchids."

"I need to brush my hair."

For a moment, Brent put his hand on Cassie's long, dark hair. "It's perfect as it is. Don't touch it. Stay here and let me have a look, but I think the cars are gone."

She didn't ask how he knew that, but then she was still thinking too hard about what he'd meant about Jeff to think of anything else. There was no reason why Jeff would care if Cassie dated or whom she went out with, but it was nice to think that he would.

The house was empty, and when Brent returned, they went to the beautiful conservatory and spent over an hour taking photos of Cassie in the heavy dress. It seemed that Brent's hobby was photography and he showed up with a big tripod and a professional-quality digital Nikon. Under his direction, Cassie was able to laugh and enjoy herself, and not worry that Althea was going to return at any moment.

"Isn't that the dress the queen wore to beg for her life?" Brent asked as he looked at her over the camera.

"Yes," Cassie said. "But the king wouldn't listen to her."

"Remember any lines?" he asked.

Before Cassie knew what she was doing, she was performing. As a lonely child, she'd often replayed the roles she'd seen in old movies, and she had a good memory for even lengthy scenes. With Brent's subtle urgings, Cassie soon found herself on her knees, her hands clasped, and she was begging a selfish king to spare her life. She put herself so deeply into the role that when the tears came, they were real. She felt as though she was there in the moment and that she was actually begging for her life.

When she finished the scene, she came back to the present and heaved herself up, the weight of the dress making it difficult to stand. Brent was staring at her in an odd way. "What?" she asked.

"I think you're the daughter Althea wanted."

Cassie knew he was just being nice, but the compliment pleased her so much that she blushed. Anyone who knew much about Althea had read that the great disappointment of her life was her daughter, her only child. The girl had left her mother's house when she was eighteen, and refused to have anything more to do with her. As far as Cassie knew she was still alive, but she had no idea what had happened to her.

"Okay," he said as he began to pack up his equipment. "It's time to get back upstairs and pretend we've been hard at work these last hours."

A minute later, they heard voices. This time there was no hesitation as they grabbed the equipment and began running. They stopped to pick up Cassie's clothes from the bathroom, then scurried up the back stairs to the attic. Quickly, he unfastened the hundred or so heavy-duty hooks and eyes at the back of her dress. She stepped behind a wooden screen and put her own clothes back on.

When Elsbeth came upstairs to see them, Brent and Cassie were on opposite sides of the attic, quietly cataloging.

Now, in the bathtub, Cassie thought about the whole week with fondness. Most of the time she'd spent alone in the attic, going through the artifacts, but sometimes Brent joined her. He called her "Houston," from when he'd said that they had a problem. She'd never had a nickname before and she liked it.

And now it was Saturday and she had a date. An old-fashioned, ordinary date. Like she'd had in college, she thought. She told herself not to be so excited, but she was. This is good for me, she thought. It was good to get away from Jeff—and even from Thomas and Elsbeth. As much as she loved them, they weren't her family. She wasn't Elsbeth's mother and she wasn't Jeff's wife and she wasn't Thomas's daughter.

For a moment those thoughts made her heart lurch, but she took a breath, got out of the tub, and began to dry herself. Yes, indeed, this was good. She would go out with Brent, and later, she'd make an effort to meet other men and go out with them as well. She had foolishly thought she was "in love" with some guy she'd met when she was a kid, and even more foolishly, she'd pursued him. And look where it had got her, she thought. She was twenty-five years old and had nothing. She had no home, no family—her mother didn't count—and soon she'd have no job.

By the time she dressed, she was feeling much better. She'd get over Jeff. In fact, after days around a gorgeous hunk like Brent, she thought she might get over Jeff rather quickly.

Downstairs, Thomas and Elsbeth were sitting on the couch in the big living room, watching a DVD. Or, rather, Elsbeth was watching and Thomas was dozing. Cassie put her finger to her lips for Elsbeth to say nothing and let the man sleep. Althea had worn him out in the last week.

Jeff was in the library, sitting at his desk and looking at his laptop. He didn't look up when she entered.

"I don't mean to bother you," she said quietly, "but I'm going out, so you'll have to do something about lunch."

"Sure," he said distractedly. "What do you want?"

"Nothing. I'm going out."

"Okay, then you pick up something." Obviously, his mind was on whatever was on his computer.

She stepped farther into the library. "*I* am going out, so *you* must get lunch. And maybe dinner. Elsbeth is too young to make lunch, and your father is too tired."

He looked up, blinking at her. "If you're going to the grocery, you can get something there. I really need to—"

"I'm not going to the grocery," she said, looking at him hard. "I am going *out*."

It was then that he looked her up and down and saw that she wasn't in her usual big cotton clothes. She had on nice linen trousers and a pretty blouse. She was also wearing makeup and jewelry. "Where are you going?" he blurted.

"On a date," she said, then turned to leave the room.

But Jeff bounded across the room in a few steps and stood in front of her. "You're going on a date?"

"Yes," she said and took a step to walk around him.

He blocked her way. "Why are you going on a date?"

She looked at him in disbelief. "Because I want to. Because I need to get out of this house. Because I want to have some fun. Why does anyone go on a date? *You* go on dates all the time."

"Me? Oh, yeah, Skylar."

"Yeah, Skylar." Again, she started to step around him, but he wouldn't let her.

"So who are you going with? Albert?" He was grinning in a smirking way.

Albert was the man who came once a month to trim the hedges. He was about ninety. Cassie glared at Jeff. "Yes, I'm going out with Albert. We're going to spend the afternoon having wild sex. Would you please move?"

He stepped aside with a flamboyant gesture, but he followed her into the kitchen. As Cassie straightened up the room, Jeff sat down on a bar stool at the island. "So if it's not Albert, who is it?"

She started to tell him that she was going out with Brent Goodwin, but she'd promised she wouldn't tell. She said nothing.

"Okay, so don't tell me," Jeff said, "but I think you should leave a number where you can be reached. In case of an emergency. You never know what could happen. To Elsbeth, I mean."

"If anything bad happens to Elsbeth, call a hospital, not *me*."

"Yeah, of course I would, but she'll want you. It would be horrible if she were in a hospital and crying for you and you were out with some stranger having a good time."

Cassie looked at him in disbelief. She really couldn't believe he was saying these things. "You're her father. If she was crying for anyone, it would be for you. I'm the paid employee, remember?"

"Come on, Cassie, you know that you're a great deal more to Elsbeth than just an employee."

Cassie threw up her hands. "I don't believe this! You're about to discharge me in . . . however long it is until you get married, but you're dumping guilt on me for going on a date. I need a life. A real life. One of my own. I need something to do besides fold your socks and take care of your house."

Jeff's eyes widened. "Discharge you? Why would I do that? You know that Elsbeth loves you."

She leaned across the island so her face was close to his. "But Skylar hates me."

"Oh, well," he said. "She's one of those women who hates all women. It's nothing personal." He smiled at her.

Cassie wanted to throw something at him, but the ringing of the doorbell made her straighten. She took a couple of deep breaths and straightened her shoulders. "That's probably my date."

Turning her back on him, she walked to the entrance hall. She opened the door to a smiling Brent; he was holding a large bouquet of flowers.

"For you," he said. "Hope you like them."

Before she could say anything, Jeff—who was about three inches behind her—said, "What the hell are *you* doing here?"

Cassie grimaced before turning around. "He is my date!" she almost shouted. "Not that it is any of your business."

"Is something wrong?" Thomas asked from the doorway.

Cassie glared at Jeff. "Are you happy now? You woke your father and he needs his rest."

"I wasn't the one who was shouting, you were."

"Brent," Thomas said, smiling as he held out his hand to shake. "Are you taking our Cassie out?"

"Yes," Brent said, grinning. "I thought we'd go to lunch, then see a plantation or two. If that's all right with you, Houston," he said to Cassie.

"It sounds wonderful." She started to say that she needed to put the flowers in water, but she didn't want to take the time. From the way Jeff was acting, he might do something to make her stay home.

"Could I take those for you?" Thomas asked, holding out his hands for the flowers. "You young people go and have a good time. Take all day. Stay out until tomorrow. Elsbeth and I can handle things here."

"Houston!" Jeff said, as though coming out of a trance. "Why are you calling Cassie Houston?"

"An inside joke," Brent said as he and Cassie exchanged smiles.

She picked her bag up off the table by the door. "I don't know how long we'll be," she said and thought how ridiculous it all was. You would have thought she was leaving on a two-year-long trip around the world.

"I need to speak to you, Goodwin," Jeff said, his jaw rigid and his voice serious.

Cassie put her arm through Brent's. "I think we'll be off now." She looked at Jeff. "You can talk to him later. Bye."

As quickly as she could, she went outside and closed the door behind her.

8

WHEN CASSIE UNLOCKED THE DOOR to Jeff's house, she made sure she made no noise. The lamp on the hall table was on so she could see the stairs. She silently put her purse down and the big tote bag of things she'd bought that day—mostly gifts for Thomas and Elsbeth—and tiptoed toward the stairs. When Jeff's shadowy form appeared at the entrance into the family room, she jumped, her heart pounding.

"It's after midnight," she said, her hand to her heart. "What are you doing up?"

He didn't smile. "Come with me," he said seriously, then turned and walked back toward the kitchen.

Cassie was tired and wanted to go to bed, but she followed him. Truthfully, Jeff's attitude that morning had stayed with her all day. Why had he acted so . . . well, jealous?

She followed him into the kitchen, and there, sitting on the counter, was a tall glass of milk and a plate of the cookies she'd baked.

"I thought you might be hungry," Jeff said, his face still solemn.

Cassie went into the kitchen, got a roll of plastic wrap, covered the cookies and milk, put them in the refrigerator, then poured herself a cold glass of white wine. At last, she turned to look at him. "I'm not hungry, and even if I were, I'd want something besides cookies and milk. Could you please tell me what's bothering you?"

He sat down at the breakfast table, his hands folded in front of him. "First of all, I want to apologize for the way I acted this morning. It was just a shock that you were going out, that's all."

She took the seat across from him, then leaned back in the chair, sipped her wine, and waited for him to continue.

"Elsbeth missed you today. We all missed you."

"Last Saturday all of you went out without me and I didn't hear any talk of missing me." She narrowed her eyes at him. "Has something happened?"

"I guess so," he said and gave her a half smile. "I think that today it hit me that maybe you could leave us."

Cassie couldn't help it, but she drew in her breath and clutched the stem of the wineglass so hard it almost snapped in two. She put the glass on the table. Was this it? she wondered. Was this every dream she'd had since she was twelve? Was he going to say that the thought of her leaving had made him realize that he loved her?

"I didn't mean to shock anyone," Cassie said softly.

"You only shocked me, no one else."

He has a disarming way of smiling, she thought. It was dark in the room except for the kitchen lights. There was a light over the breakfast table, but neither of them had turned it on.

"So how was your date?" he asked.

"Great," she answered. "We had a wonderful time. Brent and I—"

"Cassie," Jeff said slowly, interrupting her, "I can honestly say this with affection, as I have come to honor and esteem you greatly in this past year, but I think you should be cautious about that young man."

Honor and esteem me? Cassie thought. "Do you know something bad about him?" she asked.

"A little." He paused. "Okay, I know more than I'm letting on. I don't think he's what he seems, and I feel that I must warn you to be cautious with him."

"Could you be more specific?"

"I really can't," Jeff said. "I'm not at liberty to tell what I know, but I do feel the need to warn you."

Cassie took a deep swallow of the wine. Maybe she should be grateful that Jeff was trying to admonish her about a young man she hardly knew, but she didn't feel gratitude. "I guess I should take your advice and call off any future dates," she said quietly.

"I think that would be best," Jeff said, giving her a look that said she was a very smart girl.

"I guess that, all in all, it would be better for me to stay at home, meaning here in your house, and take care of your child and your father, to cook your food, wash your clothes, and run your errands."

Jeff's face lost its look of helpfulness. "That's not what I meant! It's just Goodwin who I object to."

"Why?" she asked, leaning across the table toward him. "Because he's young and handsome and because he likes me? He does things *for me*. Can you imagine that? He takes me places and buys me lunch. He laughs at my jokes. He—" She picked up the wineglass and drained it. "He does *not* treat me as though I'm his eleven-year-old daughter and feed me milk and cookies." She stood up and glared down at him. "For months now, I've been dreading the moment when you would tell me I was going to have to leave your house. I'm sick of the way I wake up and wonder if this is the day I'll be fired."

"Cassie, I—"

She put her hand up. "I can't take it anymore. In the last week I've had fun. I've had freedom from—" She couldn't say any more or she'd say that she'd had freedom from thinking that he was the only man in the world for her. "Let's just say that in this last week I've been awakened from a dreamworld and I've seen reality. Jefferson Ames, I hereby give you my two weeks' notice."

Blinking in disbelief, Jeff stood up. "Cassie, what are you saying? You can't quit. Elsbeth loves you. You're like a—"

"So help me, if you say that I'm like a mother to her, I'll deck you. Really, I will." Say something about *us*, Cassie wanted to shout at him. Tell me you were jealous of Brent because you love me.

But Jeff just stood there, looking at her, seeming not to know what to say. "We all need you," he said at last. "You can't quit."

What little hope Cassie had escaped her in a great gust of air. One moment she was so angry she could have entered a boxing ring, and the next she just wanted to go to bed.

"Yes, I can," she said tiredly. "I'll put it in writing tomorrow. Good night." She turned toward the back stairs. Ten minutes later, she was in bed, and in spite of all the emotion of the last few minutes, she went to sleep at once.

Jeff wasn't surprised when he heard his father's voice. He'd sat back down at the table, his head in his hands.

"You really blew it this time," Thomas said as he handed his son a glass with a shot of single malt whiskey and kept one for himself. He sat down across from Jeff.

"Completely. Totally. What am I going to tell Elsbeth?"

"I think Elsbeth may leave with Cassie."

Jeff looked up at his father, questioning.

"Althea offered Cassie a job cataloguing that mess she has in the attic, and being her assistant."

"What? Fetch her slippers and make her tea?"

"It's an easier job than she has here."

Jeff took a gulp of his whiskey. "What did you find out this week?"

"Not much. For all that she talks nonstop, Althea Fairmont tells very little."

"You don't like her," Jeff said—a statement, not a question.

"On the contrary. I've never met a more charming woman. If I didn't know all I do about her, I'd be half in love with her."

"You and a million other men," Jeff said.

"Maybe so, but I imagine that a lot of men are happy just to have known her. So what are you going to do about Cassie?"

"What can I do?"

"Tell her you love her. Ask her to marry you."

"Funny," Jeff said. "You should go on the stage. I did that once, remember? I was madly in love, got married, had a baby, then my wife was murdered because of me."

"Lillian's death was a tragedy, I agree, but it doesn't always happen that way. Your mother and I were married for thirty-eight years and nothing bad happened."

Jeff looked at his father with his eyes wide. "What about Munich? Barcelona?"

Thomas waved his hand in dismissal. "Close calls, that's all. The difference was that your mother knew what was going on. You kept Lillian in the dark. She knew nothing about you. Not the truth anyway. If Lillian had known the truth, she wouldn't have believed those men so easily. She wouldn't have stepped into their car with them. She wouldn't have—"

"Died," Jeff said. "If she'd known the truth, it wouldn't have made any difference. They would have found her anyway. No matter what, I couldn't prevent it. I couldn't protect her."

"And that's why you teach now," Thomas said. "You're not in the field anymore."

"Not in the field?" Jeff said. "Then what do you call living next door to Althea Fairmont and that time bomb mind of hers? And Roger Craig was put on the other side of her. As long as I could keep things quiet, everyone was safe, but now I think Cassie saw Roger at Althea's house, and Cassie is dating Goodwin."

"He seems like a nice enough young man."

"He's trained to kill people," Jeff said, glaring at his father.

"So are you. So am I."

"Yeah, well, I don't want Cassie involved in this. She's a sweet kid. I've known her—"

"Yeah, yeah, I know. Since she was in diapers. Or thereabouts. But she's grown up now, and she deserves to have a life of her own, a home of her own, and children of her own."

"And I can't give her any of those things," Jeff said glumly.

"You've given all of them to her for the past year except without the glorious sex you could have been having."

"'Glorious sex'? Althea's getting to you, isn't she?"

"She's certainly made me remember some things. But you're the problem now. What are you going to do about Cassie? And how are you going to deal with Elsbeth when she's told that you've made Cassie leave? Are you going to tell her that Skylar will be her new mother?"

"Give me a break! That woman is driving me crazy. Another month and we'll be finished and I can get away from her."

"Then what will you do? Cassie plans to leave in two weeks. By then she'll probably be engaged."

"Engaged?" Jeff said, horror in his voice.

"All she'd have to do is make those French doughnuts with that almond custard filling and any man in his right mind would propose."

Jeff snorted. "It's not her cooking that drives me insane."

"When I was your age I didn't think about almond custard either. All I'm saying is that you need to think very hard about what you're doing."

"I have thought about it. I've not thought about anything else all day." He looked at his father with a sheepish expression. "I made a fool of myself this morning when Goodwin picked her up. A class-A jerk. My only excuse is that Cassie caught me off guard. One day she's dedicated to us, and the next day she's going out with one of my students—and not a very good student at that. It was a jolt to my system, and I handled it poorly."

"So how do you plan on handling this situation? She said she was going to quit."

"I think I'll talk to her and say anything I can short of telling her that Skylar is the last woman on earth that I'd marry."

"If you were already married, you wouldn't have had her dumped on you," Thomas said sternly.

"Hindsight is great, but I can't afford that now. People must believe that Skylar and I are an item or her father won't come through."

"And the United States government needs the man," Thomas said, his voice dripping sarcasm.

"It seemed a simple task when I agreed. I just didn't think Skylar . . ." Jeff trailed off and took another drink of his whiskey.

"You were told she was a flibbertigibbet who only wanted a man if he drove a race car. But she wants to settle down."

"No," Jeff said slowly, "I'm a conquest to her, and she likes to conquer. I'm not entranced by her father's money or her beauty."

"Okay, so that takes care of Skylar. What are you going to do about Cassie?"

"The honorable thing."

Thomas groaned so loudly he glanced at the doorway to make sure he hadn't woken anybody. "I hope that doesn't mean what I think it does."

"I'm going to step back and let Cassie have her life. She's young. She deserves happiness. I'd rather she wasn't dating Goodwin—did I tell you what he made on his last weapons test?—but if that's her choice, I won't stand in her way."

Thomas couldn't seem to think of anything else to say, so he stood up. "Do what you think is best, son. I trust you and I think you have the intelligence and wisdom to figure this out on your own."

"Thanks, Dad, I appreciate that." Jeff looked down at his whiskey glass and didn't move. He knew his father was waiting for him to say he was going to bed too. It was after 1 A.M. and he had to get up at six, but Jeff knew he wouldn't be able to sleep. "Use the elevator," he mumbled as his father headed toward the stairs.

"I think I will," Thomas said, then went down the hall toward the library.

But he didn't get on the elevator. Instead, he went into the library, picked up the land telephone, and called Althea. She answered on the first ring. "Did I wake you?"

"You know I never sleep," she said. "I'm still on Broadway time."

Thomas chuckled. "I guess it gets in your blood."

"So what can I do for you at this hour?"

"I'd like you to throw a temper tantrum. Think you can?"

"I believe I could manage." There was laughter in her voice.

He waited for her to say something else, maybe to ask why, but she didn't. "You don't need a motivation?"

"I'm being held prisoner by my own government. I need no more motivation than that. Just give me a time and a place and a few lines of dialogue and I'll take it from there."

"You're a true lady, Althea."

"I can be if the part calls for it. But I can also be a woman."

"Ah, yes," Thomas said, smiling. "*Not Enough*. Did I ever tell you that was my favorite film of yours?"

Althea laughed. "On Monday you told me it was *The Last Good-bye*. On Tuesday you said it was *First and Always*. On Wednesday, you said—"

His laugh cut her off. "And every word of it was true. I'll see you tomorrow morning and tell you everything."

"I love that idea."

"Yes, I've noticed that you are quite good at getting 'everything' out of people while giving 'nothing' in return."

"Not vertically, anyway," she said, then hung up the phone.

Thomas smiled all the way up in the elevator.

9

"I PROMISE THAT we'll have separate rooms," Brent said, his eyes pleading. "I swear it. On my honor as a knight."

Cassie smiled. Brent was promising that if she spent the weekend after next with him in a cabin on a lake he wouldn't make a pass at her. It was certainly an honorable promise, but a big part of her wished he was saying that he couldn't wait to get in bed with her. But then, if he did that, she knew she'd refuse to go with him. A true dichotomy, she thought.

"Althea wants me to go up there and check on the place," Brent said. "She had a dream that it was infested with mice and bad men, so I have to go take a look at it."

They were in Althea's attic, Cassie with the clipboard on her lap, and he had interrupted her cataloguing to do whatever he could to persuade her to go with him to the cabin. She had her head down, so he lifted her chin to force her to look at him. Althea wasn't the only one who can act, he thought.

The truth was that Althea had hinted that she wanted Brent to do a little spying. When she'd asked him, she'd given a little pout that made Brent feel good. What she was really saying was that he was doing his job of guarding her so well that she'd come to depend on him.

It hadn't taken much for him to agree to go. To do some *real* work! he thought. He was still reeling from the bawling out he'd received from Ames, so he was anxious to show that he would someday make a good agent.

Althea gave him directions and the keys to a lakefront cabin and told him that he needed to watch what a Mr. Norton was doing. Brent was told to arouse no suspicion, so if he had a girlfriend he should take her with him. Since he was given just twenty-four hours' notice, there was no way his long-term girlfriend could get down from Massachusetts in time to go with him, so that left Cassie. He didn't want to screw up his first real assignment—other than the job of guarding Althea, that is—so he *had* to get Cassie to go with him.

"It's just overnight. Two nights if we're having a good time. I have the whole weekend off, and so do you. Please," Brent said, reaching for Cassie's hands.

She hesitated. She felt like she should stay with Elsbeth. She'd told the child on Monday that she was leaving, and Elsbeth had hardly reacted. In fact, her silence had been almost eerie. But three hours later, she threw a plate across the room. Cassie had done everything to get Elsbeth to talk to her, but the child had just sat there with glazed eyes and stared.

As for Thomas, she didn't have to tell him. Somehow, he already knew. He didn't say anything, but he looked at Cassie with eyes full of sadness. It seemed that every time she looked up, there was Thomas with his big, sorrowful eyes.

Between Elsbeth and Thomas, Cassie had spent the week on the verge of tears.

It was only Jeff who was unaffected by any of it. He was as oblivious to the turmoil inside the house as he was to Skylar's spitefulness. Jeff left the house early, came home late, but when they saw him, he was cheerful and smiling. He didn't say a word about Cassie's leaving, and when she mentioned—four times—that she was going out with Brent again, Jeff said he hoped she had a good time.

By Friday, Cassie didn't know if she wanted to run out of the house and never return, or tell them she'd never leave. She did know that every time she thought of never seeing Elsbeth and Thomas again, she had to reach for a tissue.

As for Jeff, she hoped he would fall into a vat of oil and be fried.

"Please," Brent said again. "I've seen the place, and it's a very nice cabin."

"All right," she said at last. Maybe it would strengthen her for the coming final week if she got away from the tears and guilt for two days. What she couldn't understand was why Thomas and Elsbeth were upset with *her*. Why weren't they lashing out at Jeff? "What should I take?"

"Hiking clothes," he said, grinning broadly as he stepped back from her and looked about the attic. "Don't worry about anything else. There's a grocery just down the road from the cabin. We'll stop there and get everything we need. I can't tell you how much I appreciate this. I was dreading going by myself." He waited a moment, then said, "Is everything set then?" He looked anxious to leave the attic, and Cassie was glad for him to go. She wanted some time alone to think. After he left, she went back to cataloguing the contents of Althea's attic.

At noon, she called Dana and told her most of the story. "I thought I'd just go ahead and resign before I was fired. I've told them I'm leaving and that I've accepted Althea's job. I'm going to get my own place, but for now I'm going to be living in her house." She didn't tell Dana how she'd told Elsbeth over and over that she'd be "just next door." Her words hadn't made a dent in the child's cold anger. I've never betrayed anyone before, Cassie thought, and I start with a five-year-old.

On the phone, Cassie could hear Dana's breathing. This is what she's waited for, Cassie thought. Jeff is going to marry Skylar, and Dana will get to take care of Elsbeth on a regular basis. Would she decorate one of the many bedrooms in her house for a fairy princess? If she did, Elsbeth would hate it.

But that was no longer Cassie's problem or concern. "Could you take care of Elsbeth this week?" she asked Dana. "I'm at Althea's all the time, and I think she'd like to be alone with Thomas."

"Of course. I'd be happy to," Dana said, and Cassie could hear that she was trying to keep the excitement out of her voice.

"Unless you have other plans," Cassie said, knowing she was being a brat. But the last week had been so bad that she couldn't find it in herself to be nice to anyone.

"No, nothing," Dana said quickly. "I'll see what's going on in Colonial Williamsburg and maybe Elsbeth and I will go. No! Wait! Busch Gardens. Or maybe Presidential Park."

"Or Yorktown or Jamestown," Cassie said tiredly, trying to stamp down her jealousy. She'd taken Elsbeth to all those places and many more and they'd always had a great time. Such a great time, that even the thought of going on a semi-romantic weekend with a man she liked wasn't cheering her up.

"Dana?" Cassie said.

"Yes?" she asked cautiously.

"Did you ever think about putting all the men in the world into a great big hole and covering it up?"

Dana took a moment before answering, as though she were considering her response carefully. "My husband has a wife who gets seasick just looking at a boat, yet he bought a forty-footer and spends three weekends a month on it. What do you think?"

"I think you'd make a great backhoe driver."

They laughed together, then set a time for Dana to pick up Elsbeth.

It was Althea who brought Cassie back to life. Thomas had begged off from another week of going and doing with the indefatigable Althea, and Cassie knew that it was her fault. Her leaving had made Thomas too depressed to go out.

Cassie tried to keep her mind on the cataloguing, but she couldn't. She found a box of clippings from the murder of a starlet back in 1941, but Cassie wasn't interested. She made a note about it on her list, then closed the box.

Even when she found a big box containing photo albums of a very young Althea with her daughter, Cassie couldn't work up any interest. The world had always been curious about Althea's child and so was Cassie, but her own personal problems overrode everything else.

On Monday Cassie reported to work at Althea's with a packed bag containing the extras she'd accumulated in the last year. She'd spent the weekend alone in Jeff's house. Jeff, Thomas, and Elsbeth had gone somewhere, and they didn't tell Cassie where they were going or invite her to go with them. For the first time since she arrived, she was treated as an employee, not a member of the family. All weekend, she'd packed her belongings and tried to keep from crying as she told herself that she was just moving next door and she'd see all of them often.

Althea met her at the door on Monday morning. "You look awful," she said. "So what torture has Jefferson been putting you through?"

"None," Cassie mumbled. "They've all been very nice. Which room is to be mine?"

"Any you want," Althea said, shutting the door.

Cassie started toward the stairs, but Althea caught her arm. "Let Brent take that upstairs. I want you to come with me."

Listlessly, Cassie followed Althea down the hall toward her bedroom and into a small room that she hadn't seen before. It was long and narrow, and from the look of it, it was Althea's private office. "I want to know everything that's going on," she said when they were seated. "I don't want you to skip a word."

When Cassie didn't answer right away, Althea pushed a full box of tissues toward her. "Now start!" she ordered, and Cassie obeyed as the words came tumbling out of her.

Althea listened without comment until Cassie had finished. "Since you were twelve years old?" she said at last.

"I know," Cassie said, sniffing. "It's stupid. How could anyone fall in love at twelve? Or if they do, they have the good sense to fall in love with a movie star. My mother once told me that when she was a girl, she was mad for James MacArthur. Did you know him?"

A noncommittal "Mmmm" was all that Althea said as she leaned back in a leather chair that looked as though it had been made for her. "You can't help love," she said. "Try as you might, you can't control it. I once lived with a man who was the perfect match for me, but I never could love him. The man I loved was the one I shouldn't have, the forbidden man."

"Mr. Ridgeway?" Cassie asked as she blew her nose.

Althea gave a snort of laughter. "I never came close to loving him. No, I loved the father of my daughter."

That statement made Cassie look up with wide eyes. Never in any interview had Althea talked of her daughter. When she was asked questions about her, she just smiled and said nothing. If it was done on live TV, it was called "dead air" and it made the interviewer frantic.

"Have you seen the photo albums?" Althea asked, and Cassie knew which ones she meant. She nodded. "Then go and get them and meet me in my bedroom."

Cassie ran up the stairs to the attic, grabbed the box, and hurried down the back stairs to Althea's bedroom. Even as she ran, it went through her mind that Althea knew that Cassie had made a lifelong study of Althea's life and career, and as a true fan, the prospect of revelations about Althea's only child would take Cassie from her own problems.

In the bedroom, Althea was sitting in the middle of her bed, and for a moment Cassie didn't know where to go. If she sat on a chair, she'd be too far away for both of them to see the albums. But Althea patted the bed beside her and Cassie climbed up next to her.

"This is me when I was pregnant," Althea began. "Wasn't I the fattest thing you ever saw?"

"Yeah, but you looked great in the Elizabethan dresses."

"And why do you think I agreed to wear them all through my pregnancy?"

Cassie and Althea laughed together.

"What happened?" Cassie asked softly, and they both knew what she meant. What had happened between Althea and her daughter?

Althea took a while to answer. A lifetime of keeping quiet about the subject was ingrained in her. "She didn't like me. My daughter just plain didn't like me or my life or what she grew up with. But I understood. It was the same with me. When I was a child I never fit in with my mother's relatives. They loved routine. Their idea of excitement was having lemon pie on Sunday after church. My mother and I were born wanting endless excitement."

While Althea said this, Cassie could hardly breathe. She was being told things that no one else knew about this famous woman.

"I think we do reap what we sow," Althea said, "because my daughter was like them. All she wanted was a middle-class life. Nothing I did impressed her. No one I introduced her to impressed her. She didn't want fabulous clothes or a house with marble bathrooms. She wanted . . ." Althea waved her hand in dismissal. "I never figured out what she wanted. Growing up with me, she was like a nun living in Las Vegas, and she couldn't wait to get away from me."

Cassie turned a page of an album and looked at the little girl in the photo. It was of Althea with Cary Grant. The adults were laughing and clowning for the camera, but the little girl in the background had a serious face, unsmiling. Cassie thought it was what Elsbeth would look like if she had been born into a rowdy family of children who liked to run and yell and tumble all over one another.

"Where is she now?" Cassie asked.

Althea closed the album and got off the bed. "Midwest. One of those states I've never wanted to visit. I have great-grandchildren, but I've never seen them. I have a private detective who sends me photos of all of them every six months, but my daughter is the only one of them I've ever seen in person."

"Have you contacted them?"

"I used to write my daughter letters," Althea said. "But not anymore. A person can only take so much rejection. Isn't that right?" she asked, her eyes boring into Cassie's. She knew what Althea meant. Cassie had been rejected by her mother since the day she was born, and somewhere along the way, she'd stopped trying to please the woman. There was never going to be a time when her mother liked who she was or what she did.

"Maybe now that I'm on my own I should try to become the president of some company," Cassie said jokingly.

But Althea didn't laugh. "If you'd like to open a business around here, I'd back you. Spending a week with a house full of people has made me realize how bored I am."

"A business?" Cassie said. "What kind of business could I open?"

"I wouldn't recommend dress designing," Althea said in a way that made Cassie laugh.

"Come on," Althea said, "let's go upstairs and start cataloguing. Or do you want to be alone with your misery?"

"I've spent too much of my life alone," Cassie said.

"Me too," Althea said, but when Cassie looked at her in disbelief, she shrugged. "Okay, so I've only spent the last few years alone, but that's more than I can stand." She put her arm through Cassie's as they went up the stairs. "There's a young man who's been writing me every month for about ten years now. He wants to write my biography."

"I think that sounds like a good idea," Cassie said.

"Maybe. It has run through my mind. Do you think anyone out there would be interested in the life of an old movie star?"

"I think that if you told the truth about everything, it might be a shock, and shocking stories sell well, don't they?"

"My thoughts exactly."

They were at the attic door and Cassie opened it and let Althea go in before her. "Why don't you tell *me* the truth and I'll help you decide."

"Only if you tell me the truth about yourself," Althea said.

"But I just did," Cassie said. "I told you everything."

"Then I guess it'll just be me on the stage. Oh, darn," Althea said, and they laughed together.

Cassie spent all that week with Althea. They were two lonely women, and even though Althea's life experience was much longer than Cassie's, there were similarities. They had both grown up as misfits in their families. Cassie was nothing like her mother, and Althea had been nothing like her relatives. In spite of the unhappiness of her leaving Jeff's family,

Cassie had a good week. She was Althea's audience and she loved every minute of it. She loved every story Althea told about her life onstage, and when Cassie suggested that they start recording the anecdotes, Althea had agreed readily. Althea talked into a microphone while Cassie catalogued, and they helped each other with their loneliness.

But most of all, they developed a friendship. While Althea talked about herself and her extraordinary life, she bossed Cassie around about everything, starting with how she needed to lose weight and exercise. "The concept of 'hard bodies' wasn't invented by your mother's generation," Althea said as she put on a mink stole she'd worn in *First of the Days*. "I think that young man of yours could be won with a little old-fashioned sex appeal, what we used to call the 'it factor.' "

"Like Skylar," Cassie said with a sigh. Althea made no reply, but she looked at Cassie in speculation. Sometimes she thought that Althea looked as though she was planning something for Cassie, but there was never a hint as to what it was.

By Friday, Cassie felt a great deal better. She was almost looking forward to her weekend with Brent.

At 3 P.M. on Friday Cassie was in Jeff's house when Dana appeared at the back door with a basket full of home-baked muffins and cookies.

"They're in there," Cassie said, pointing toward the big living room. There was a DVD showing on the TV, and Thomas and Elsbeth were looking at it, but Cassie was willing to bet they weren't seeing it.

Cassie could do no more than nod toward them, then she scurried out of the room, leaving Dana to cope on her own.

"I am going to be happy and have a good time this weekend," Cassie told herself as she put on her jacket and got her duffel bag. She remembered how she and Brent had had a good time on their all-day date. True, he had a wandering eye and three times she'd seen him staring at some other female. But that was normal, wasn't it?

They'd had lunch on Richmond Road, then went to see the five James River Plantations: Sherwood Forest, Westover (divine garden!), Shirley, Evelynton, and Berkeley. Cassie had loved them, and Brent said that he did, but sometimes she got the impression that he'd have much rather gone to Busch Gardens and ridden the big roller coaster. Cassie would have liked that too, so why had he chosen something historical instead? Was he trying to impress her? But as the day progressed and they came close to running out of things to talk about, she had the oddest idea that Brent was trying to impress not her but Jeff. Now and then, as though it were of no consequence, Brent asked a question about Jeff. What was he like at home? Did he have any hobbies? What had he told her about his job?

Cassie answered all the questions with a lot of words, but she didn't tell much. It wasn't as though Jeff ever did anything that called for secrecy, after all, he was just a normal, hardworking father. But there was something about the way Brent slyly slipped the questions in as he was doing something else, like reading a guidebook to a plantation's history, as though the questions didn't matter, that bothered her.

What did Brent and Jeff have to do with each other? she wondered. When she got home that night and Jeff started warning her against Brent, Cassie wanted to scream at both of them. She felt as though she'd been caught in some Shakespearean drama. Her instincts told her the men weren't fighting over her, but that there was a deeper issue between them. It was just that she had no idea what it was.

When she left the house, she didn't exactly tiptoe and sneak out, but she certainly didn't make any noise. She was almost to the road when Brent arrived in his little red sports car.

"You're here," he said, and she could hear the disappointment in his voice.

"Jeff isn't home," she said as she tossed her bag in the back and got in the passenger seat.

"I know. He's—" Brent cut himself off as he backed out of the driveway. "I think I saw him on 199."

"What is it with you two?" Cassie blurted out. "Are you two in love with each other?"

"In—?" Brent began, then laughed. "Of course not. Baby, I'm pure heterosexual. Maybe your boss swings the other way, but . . ." He glanced at her. "Does he?"

"I know nothing whatever about Jefferson Ames's sexual preferences, so you can stop that line of questioning this minute."

"I had no intention of asking about him," Brent said stiffly. "You're the one who brought it up. Boy! You're in a bad mood, aren't you?"

Cassie took a moment to calm herself. "Sorry. I guess I am. Thomas and Elsbeth are really angry at me for quitting my job. But then, I'm the one who takes care of them, so they'll miss what I do."

"I think it's more than that," Brent said softly. "I think they love you."

It was more than Cassie could take. All Althea's attempts at distracting her flew out the window. She put her face in her hands and began to cry. Brent opened the center console, pulled out a pack of tissues, and handed her a bunch of them.

"I'm sorry," Cassie said, blowing her nose. "I didn't mean to do this. I love them too. They've become my family, and I don't want to leave them, but I have to."

"Because of Ames?"

"He's going to get married and his girlfriend hates me. It's either now or later, so what's the difference? It's just that I'd think Thomas and Elsbeth would have some sympathy for me, but they look at me as though I'm the cruelest person on earth."

"Maybe they think you should stay and fight."

"I thought about it, but how do I do that? I burned a hole in an expensive jacket of Skylar's just to show her I wasn't going to be bossed around by her. But if she married Jeff, she'd be my employer. Would I have to burn up all her clothes?"

"She'd complain about anything you cooked, so you'd better burn that too," Brent said without a hint of a smile.

It took Cassie a moment to get his joke. She didn't laugh but she quit crying.

"Look, I'm sorry I made you think I was prying about you and Ames," he said. "It's just that I wanted to know about my competition. You see, Jeff and I know each other from way back, and there's always been some rivalry between us." He glanced at her. "I know what you're going to say, that Ames is old enough to be my father, but women seem to like him, so there have been some, uh, problems."

"You and Jeff fought over a woman?" Cassie asked, wiping the tears from her eyes. "When was this? He married Lillian when he was very young, and since then there've been no women except Skylar."

"Is that what he told you?" Brent asked, smiling as he turned onto Highway 64.

"I live with the man. I should know," she said, then stopped. "I mean, I don't really *live* with him, not in the old-fashioned way."

"No, you just take care of his life so he has time to do whatever he wants. You don't think that all the time he's away from home that he's actually working, do you?"

"Yes," she said hesitantly. "I think so. Thought so. He isn't?"

"I have no right to tell anyone's secrets. Let's just say that I know some things about Jefferson Ames and he's not what he seems to be."

Cassie opened her mouth to say that that's just what Jeff had said about him, but she didn't. Her mother once told her that it was better to take in information, file it, and put it all together later. Margaret said that keeping her mouth shut and listening was half of why she'd been such a success.

Turning away from him, Cassie looked out the window at the beautiful Virginia scenery and at last began to realize that she had two whole days away from the turmoil of the Ames household. Between days working for Althea and evenings with an angry child, Cassie hadn't slept much in the last week. Before long she found herself nodding off. It was a four-hour drive to the cabin, and the next thing she knew, the car had stopped.

She awoke with a jolt, sitting up straight and looking about her in confusion.

"You okay?" Brent asked as he turned off the engine.

Cassie rubbed her eyes. "I think I must have dozed off."

"You slept soundly enough that horns and motorcycles didn't even make you move." He was smiling at her.

"I'm sorry," she said, embarrassed.

"You slept like a very pretty baby." He nodded out the window to the little store in front of them. "We're here and this is it," he said.

They were in the gravel parking lot of a grocery store, with two gas pumps in the front. Next door was a shop that seemed to do everything from rent DVDs to pack and ship. It also seemed to have a tiny café.

"Want some coffee?" he asked. "Or a Coke? Ice cream bar? Marijuana?"

She was still sleep befuddled and could only look at him.

"Local gossip says that they grow it in the backyard where they keep the dog, but that may only be a rumor. But they do serve a spaghetti that has some very suspicious-looking green flakes in it."

Cassie smiled.

"That's better. Wanna help me get groceries?"

"Sure," she said, opening the car door.

He held open the screen door to allow her to enter before him, and she smiled when she saw the interior. It was the kind of place she loved. The wooden floor was so warped it looked as though it had been through a flood. Along the back wall was a glass-doored refrigerator case that contained lots of different drinks in bottles. To her left was a glass butcher's case with meats that probably came from a local farmer's herd. To the right was a cash register on a cabinet that was so piled with things to sell there was almost no room to put purchases.

But Cassie's smile soon left her because standing in the back, near the ice cream chest, was Jefferson Ames. Ten feet away from him was Skylar Beaumont.

"What the hell are *you* doing here?" Brent said loud enough that the butcher and the woman behind the register stopped to look at them.

Jeff had a red plastic basket over his arm with three bottles of wine sticking out of it. For an instant there was shock on his face, but he got himself under control. "I think I should ask you the same thing, Goodwin."

Cassie stood silent, still in the doorway, and looked at Skylar, who was now glowering at her. Cassie remembered that Brent said Jeff had been out with lots of women in the years since his wife's death, but Cassie had defended him. She'd said Jeff worked long, hard hours. But did he? Right now he was supposed to be at work or with his daughter, but he wasn't. How many other times had he let them think he was working when he wasn't?

Cassie couldn't bear to listen to whatever Jeff and Brent were saying to each other, so she left the store. Outside, it was that beautiful time of twilight and she leaned against Brent's car to look at the trees across the road.

"Cassie?"

It was Jeff, but she didn't turn to look at him.

"It seems that Althea has played a joke on all of us. She asked Goodwin to check on her cabin and asked me, through my father, to do the same thing. I have no idea what she had in her devious little mind, but here we all are together."

"I thought you were working," Cassie said, still looking straight ahead.

"I am," he answered, then glanced back at the store. "Oh, I see. You think I was lying. For your information, I called Dad and told him that I'd be away for the weekend."

"Away for the weekend," she said as she looked at him. She really had no right to be angry at him. He'd made no secret that he was nearly engaged to Skylar, so of course they wanted to spend time alone. At least he was considerate enough not to parade a string of women in front of his daughter, she thought. No, he'd waited until he found the right one, Skylar, then brought her home.

Jeff leaned on Brent's car beside her. "So now what do we do? It's too late for you two to drive back to Williamsburg."

"Us? Why not you and Skylar? You two could spend the weekend at her house. Neither Brent nor I have private homes. He lives over Althea's garage, and I live with you. Sort of, anyway. Until Monday."

Jeff moved away from the car to stand in front of her. "You came up here to spend the weekend with a man you just met a few days ago?"

Cassie smiled at him. She really hated it when he put on his avuncular attitude and set himself up as her guardian. "Of course. It is the twenty-first century, you know. Or did you think that women today need to have a yearlong courtship before—" She wiggled her eyebrows. "Before, you know."

He glared at her. "I told you that Brent Goodwin is not who he seems to be and that you'd be better off staying away from him."

She came away from the car and glared back at him. "At least Brent tells the *truth*. He told me about you, and he understands what you've been putting your whole family through, all because of your lust for some spiteful—"

"What has that kid told you about *me*?" Jeff asked, his eyes angry.

"That a lot of times when you say you're at work you aren't."

Jeff looked as though she'd slapped him. "Where does he say I am?" he whispered.

She leaned toward him. "With women. Lots of women."

To her consternation, Jeff laughed. All the anger left his body and he relaxed. He put his hands in his pockets and smiled. "That's right. When I say I'm working late I'm actually having candlelight dinners with gorgeous women. Did he tell you about the diamond bracelets I give them? Or about the nights in four-star hotel rooms with wanton sex? Hot, steamy sex that goes on until sunrise. Sometimes it's with two women. Even three. Sometimes—"

"I get the picture," Cassie said, but she didn't. Jeff's sarcasm made her doubt what Brent had told her. But then, maybe Brent had assumed that that's where Jeff was when he stayed out late.

She and Jeff looked at each other for a while, neither saying anything, then the door to the store opened and Brent and Skylar came out carrying bags of groceries. They were smiling and laughing.

"We've decided that we'll all stay at the cabin for the weekend," Brent said cheerfully. "There are two bedrooms, so there's plenty of room for all of us. In the morning we'll go fishing or something."

When Cassie heard "two bedrooms" she nearly panicked. She had no intention of going to bed with Brent.

"Good try, Goodwin," Jeff said, pulling his car keys out of his pocket. "But the girls go in one room and the boys in the other. I don't participate in orgies and I don't listen to them."

Cassie felt such relief that she could have kissed Jeff. Instead, she avoided his eyes. After all, she'd just told him that she and Brent had come to the cabin to be together. "I hope you two got some decent groceries," she said loudly, as though it didn't matter to her what the sleeping arrangements were.

"Pasta and jars of sauce," Skylar said, her smile gone. "What else do you need?"

"Little green flakes would be nice," Cassie said, looking at Brent, and he laughed as though she'd made the greatest joke in the world. As she got into the car, she glanced at Jeff and saw that he was frowning, and that made Cassie smile more.

When they got to the cabin, Jeff said he wanted to talk to Brent. Alone.

The second they were out of earshot of the women, Jeff turned to his student, his face showing his anger. "What the hell are you really doing here and why did you bring Cassie?"

Brent gave a smug little smile. "I have an assignment."

"An assignment?" Jeff asked. His voice was cold. "And who gave you this assignment and what is it?"

"I—" Brent opened his mouth to say that he couldn't tell, but he knew that Jeff had the highest security clearance there was. "To find out what a Mr. Norton is doing."

For a moment, Jeff just stared at him, but the anger in his eyes made Brent take a step back. "And who told you to spy on Norton?"

"Althea said . . ." Brent's face changed as he realized that he'd been duped—just as he had been when Althea sent him after medicine so she could shoot a pistol and get the attention of Cassie and Dana.

"Althea." Jeff's voice was very calm. "Althea told you to come up here with Cassie and do a little spying and you believed her? You believed a woman who has spent over sixty years wheedling secrets out of the minds of the heads of foreign governments?"

"Yes, sir." Brent was standing at attention, trying not to let his feelings show.

"Now what do I do?" Jeff said, turning away. "No matter what I say,

I'm going to look like a jealous fool." He looked back at Brent. "What did you tell Cassie to get her to come up here with you?"

Brent looked surprised. "I told her I had to come up here to check on the place for Althea and would she go with me?"

"So you *were* planning to return tonight."

"No, sir. We brought bags and I thought we'd get food here. Althea said— I mean . . ."

"Are you trying to tell me that all you did was ask Cassie, young, sweet, Cassie, to spend an entire weekend alone in a remote cabin with you and she agreed?"

Brent glanced around at the other cabins. "It's hardly remote, sir." After the bawling out that Jeff had given him, he wasn't about to tell him that he had sworn not to touch Cassie if she went with him.

Jeff looked at Brent.

"Yes, sir, I did. I asked and she accepted."

Jeff stared at him, his mouth slightly open. "But you hardly know her," he said at last.

Brent couldn't resist a grin. "We had a good time on our other date, so—" He broke off at Jeff's look, then took a step back.

"I want you to remember, Goodwin, that Cassandra works for *me*, in *my* house. She is to be treated with the utmost respect. Do I make myself clear?"

"Yes, sir."

"Get out of here," Jeff said.

Obediently, Brent walked away, but the moment his back was to his boss, he smiled big enough to crack his face.

10

It was during the dinner of overcooked pasta and tasteless store-bought tomato sauce that Cassie began to feel like a third wheel. For all of Jeff's and Brent's hostility to each other, they seemed to know each other well. And Skylar seemed to know both of them. Jeff and Brent disappeared as soon as they got there, and Cassie was sure that something awful would result, but it hadn't. Brent returned first and he'd been laughing. When Jeff came back, he'd spent a few minutes saying nothing, then he seemed to have made up his mind to let go of whatever was bothering him. During dinner, both he and Brent joked with each other in a way that seemed to come from years of . . . Cassie wasn't sure what it was. It wasn't exactly friendship, but it was a camaraderie that she wasn't part of.

Three times Jeff stopped the other two from whatever it was they were hinting at, and Cassie knew that if she weren't there their talk would be a lot different. Would they reminisce about places they'd been together?

Once, she tried to enter into their laughter and asked a question about something Brent said about Gibraltar. "Have you been there?" she asked. "What's it like?"

Immediately, Brent and Skylar stopped talking and looked down at their plates.

Earlier, Cassie had gone to the kitchen with the intention of helping prepare dinner, but Jeff caught her arm. "You go in there now and you won't be allowed to leave all weekend. They'll make you into their private chef."

She'd nodded in understanding and stayed out of the kitchen, letting Brent and Skylar prepare the meal.

The cabin was nice enough, but Cassie couldn't imagine Althea in it, as it wasn't elegant, or even very interesting. It had a living room in front, a kitchen in one end, then a hall leading to two bedrooms with a shared bathroom. Across the front was a deep porch that looked out onto the lake.

While Brent and Skylar overboiled the pasta, Cassie sat in the living room and looked at a three-year-old issue of *Field & Stream*. She'd been puzzled by the low voices of Brent and Skylar in the kitchen. They certainly seemed to have a lot to say to each other.

After a while, she went out to the porch, where Jeff was sitting in a big Adirondack chair, looking out at the lake, seeming to be content to do or say nothing. "Sorry about accusing you of lying," she said.

"Think nothing of it. Goodwin must like you a lot if he's trying to discredit every man around you." He turned to look at her. "I understand his actions. All's fair, that sort of thing, but what I don't understand is why you believe a man you've only recently met over me. What have I done to lose your trust?"

Nothing, Cassie wanted to shout. You've done *nothing* and that's the problem. But she didn't say that. "I apologize. It's just me. It's difficult leaving Elsbeth and Thomas."

"Oh, that," he said. "There's really no reason you have to leave, and I don't think you should."

Cassie opened her mouth to ask him questions. She wanted to blurt out about his coming marriage to Skylar. Had something happened that was making him rethink marrying her?

But she didn't ask that. "I think it's better that I do leave," she said softly. "I've become too attached and that's not good. I have other things I want to do in my life and I need to do them."

She stopped talking and waited. What would he say? If he begged her to stay, if he told her that they needed her, if he promised to never marry anyone, could she hold out?

But Jeff said nothing. He just looked out at the lake in silence and listened to the night.

A few minutes later they were called to dinner and went inside.

An hour later, everyone except Cassie was yawning. It had been a long day and she was the only one who'd had a nap. But she faked exhaustion and said she was ready to go to sleep. Right, she thought. She was dying to climb into bed with Skylar. Ha-ha.

It took over an hour for everyone to get settled, mainly because Skylar hogged the bathroom. It seemed that she had a beauty routine that took forty-five minutes and involved using most of the hot water.

Once they were in the room alone, Cassie made no comment to Skylar's orders of which side of the bed would be hers, and how Cassie wasn't to spend the night reading and keep the light on. With a fake smile, Cassie turned out the light and got under the covers. Skylar kept to her side of the bed, and within minutes she was asleep. Obviously, there was nothing troubling Skylar to keep her awake.

But Cassie was awake—awake and jittery. There was too much in her head, too many questions rambling about inside it. With every passing hour, she was beginning to think that there was something going on that she knew nothing about. Since the day she and Dana heard the shots at Althea's house, nothing had been the same. Her quiet, orderly life had been turned upside down, but she wasn't sure how it had been changed—and certainly not why.

She looked at the clock at midnight, then again at one. Beside her, Skylar was sleeping deeply, her left arm flung out over the floor, her mouth open a bit. At least she didn't snore.

At one thirty, Cassie came alert. She'd just heard the front door open. Quietly, she got out of bed and looked out the window. It wasn't a full moon but close enough for her to catch a glimpse of a body she knew well hurrying through the trees. For some reason, Jeff was dressed all in black and was running through the woods as though he needed to put out a fire.

Cassie didn't hesitate. After a quick glance at Skylar, she went to her duffel bag and withdrew a black turtleneck shirt and black trousers. She pulled them on, then hurriedly put on dark socks and slipped her feet into black running shoes. She made no noise as she left the bedroom, tiptoed down the hall, through the living room, and out the front door.

There were cabins all around the lake, each one hidden from the other by tall trees, but the one next to their cabin had a porch light. Between the lights on some of the cabins and the moonlight, Cassie could see fairly well. Twice, she saw Jeff ahead of her, and she practically ran to catch up with him.

When she got six cabins down from Althea's, she lost him. She stopped and looked about her. There was only the sound of the water and a few animals scurrying about in the underbrush. She turned around slowly, looking and listening, but she neither saw nor heard Jeff. What was he doing out in the middle of the night?

With a grimace she thought that maybe he hadn't been able to sleep without Skylar beside him so he'd taken a nighttime jog to tire himself out. Maybe he—

She sat down on the ground under a tree, hidden in deep shadow. There was no way that Jeff could get back to the cabin without her seeing him. Unless he entered from the other side, she thought, but she didn't think that was likely. She leaned back against the tree and waited.

"What is this?" Leo Norton said in a low voice. "A convention? Bloody hell! I thought it was going to be just you and Sky, but you show up with half the agency."

"Calm down," Jeff said, looking about them in the dark. "I saw you by the boat. That's why I took Goodwin out there to let him have it."

"Goodwin?"

"One of my students. Althea picked him out of a bunch of photos to be her bodyguard. He's an idiot."

Leo smiled. "Althea. How is she?"

"As wily and conniving as ever. I don't know what she's up to now, but she sent young Goodwin up here to . . . she said to 'check on' you."

"How'd she know I was going to be here?"

"That's the first question I wanted to know the answer to, but I wasn't about to ask Goodwin that."

"So what do we do now that the entire world knows about this drop?"

"If you find out how that woman finds out things, please let me know. For all I know, she called the president and asked him. She can wheedle anything out of anybody. The question is *why* she wanted Goodwin to come up here. I've already called Dad, and he's got two men with her this weekend, so she's as safe as we can make her."

"Who's the doll with Goodwin?"

"Cassie. She's nobody. Just a cover."

"Some cover! She's a beauty. She's—"

"Cut it out! She's a kid!"

"Kid? She looks old enough to me." Leo looked at Jeff in speculation. "What's she to you?"

"She's my daughter's nanny."

"Your what?" Leo smiled. "She didn't come up here as a date with young Goodwin, did she?"

Jeff clenched his teeth. "Yes, she did."

Leo laughed at Jeff's expression. "Okay, send those two home, leave Sky in the cabin, then you and I can meet this guy tomorrow by ourselves."

"No," Jeff said. "I don't want Cassie alone with Goodwin."

Leo frowned. "If she stays, then Goodwin will stay. Do you think we should give out name tags and convention binders?"

"Can it, will you?" Jeff said. "The four of us will go out on a boat tomorrow and we'll meet the man near the house where we're supposed to. Nothing will change."

Leo stared thoughtfully at Jeff. "I'm curious. Is that cute little nanny of yours live-in or live-out?"

"In." Jeff's voice was terse. "Would you get your mind off Cassie? This is between you and me."

"You and me? You and young Goodwin have made this into date night. How the hell are we to escape your entourage long enough to pick up a package?"

Jeff put his hand on Leo's shoulder and smiled. "I trust you, old friend, to make yourself so repulsive that Cassie won't want to be near you. Think you can do that?"

"Make myself unlikeable to the ladies? How can I do that?" Leo said, but his eyes were sparkling at the challenge. "That's an impossible disguise."

"I believe in you," Jeff said as he started to walk away.

"You just want to get rid of the competition with your buxom little nanny, don't you? You better watch Goodwin. He's not a bad-looking chap."

Smiling, Jeff walked away.

As Jeff left Leo, he was feeling pretty good. When he'd first seen Goodwin with Cassie, he'd thought there was no way he could pick up the package that Leo's man was to give him. Leo had e-mailed Jeff a map of where they were to go, to a house Jeff's father knew that was so far up the coast that it was in Maryland. Jeff got further directions from his father so he knew exactly where to go.

When Goodwin told his story about Althea sending him to the cabin "to find out what a Mr. Norton is doing" it had run through Jeff's mind that his father had been the one to tell Althea that Norton was to be at the cabin this weekend. But Jeff had quickly dismissed the idea. That would mean that his father had betrayed a secret. Couldn't happen.

Jeff knew that when he got back to Williamsburg, he'd find out the truth, but now he just had to deal with it. Tomorrow he'd take the lot of them up the coast, pick up the package, then they'd have the rest of the weekend to . . . He wasn't sure what they'd do, but it could be nice. Maybe he could tell Cassie some of the truth about Skylar, enough to make her give up her idea of leaving them. Maybe he could appeal to her—

He broke off because he heard something. Silently, he circled around the back of the trees, out of the lights from the cabins. There, leaning against a tree, was Cassie. He had no doubt that she was waiting for him and he was sure that what she planned to do was ask him what the heck he was doing there.

Damn, damn, damn! he thought. Now what should he do? One minute he was thinking about telling her that he was going to break up with Skylar, and the next he had to explain why he was at a lakeside cabin with her. Damn Leo! he thought. He's the one who wanted to see Skylar. Jeff certainly didn't want to be alone with her.

He closed his eyes for a moment. He had to give Cassie a reason for why he was here. Quick, think! Suddenly, he remembered a story his father told him years ago when he was a kid. It was about robbers and a woman who had spent many years tracking them down. Thomas had said that with a bit of embellishment, the story could be made into a screenplay and sold to Hollywood. Jeff always thought that if he ever retired, he might write the story. Could he use it now? Maybe he could make Althea the protagonist. But the important question was, would Cassie believe him?

He glanced at her, sitting so still. Whatever he said, he rather liked the idea of spending a little time in the moonlight with her. She stood up and looked around. If she'd heard him, he was losing his edge.

Cassie was standing upright and in the next second, she was flat on her back, a heavy body straddling her. A hand was over her mouth.

"What do you want?" Jeff said in a growl such as she'd never heard him use before.

At first she couldn't say anything because she hadn't recovered her breath from being knocked down. She managed to make a sound against the man's hand.

"Oh, good Lord," Jeff said. "Cassie! What the hell are you doing out here?"

Removing his hand, he got off of her, and she struggled to sit upright. "Saw you," she managed to say after a few moments of trying to get her breath. "Followed you."

Jeff looked down at her. "Come on, get up, and I'll take you back."

Cassie didn't move. She drew her legs up and put her arms around her knees. "What were you doing out here?"

"I couldn't sleep," he said as he offered her his hand.

But she still didn't move. She looked past his legs to the lake with the moonlight shining on it. "Would you mind telling me what's going on?"

"What do you mean?"

"Maybe I'm just the nanny but I have ears and eyes. First of all, I don't think Althea Fairmont has ever been near that cabin. There isn't a single closet outfitted to hold her Manolos." She didn't look up at Jeff hovering over her, but she could almost feel his smile.

"Second, I don't think she's the kind of woman who would worry herself about some cabin and whether or not it's being robbed."

"Is that what Goodwin told you the problem was?"

"He said Althea'd had a dream that the cabin was full of . . . Let me see, I think he said 'mice and bad men.' Now, tell me, does that sound like something Althea would be afraid of?"

Jeff sat down on the leaves about three feet from her. "I think that if Althea thought there were 'bad men' up here she'd be here herself in ten minutes."

"Exactly," Cassie said, then looked at him. "So you want to tell me the truth?"

He looked straight out at the lake and took a while before he answered. "Remember those shots you heard recently?"

"Yes," she answered. "Althea said they were fired by her ex-husband and that they were from a prop pistol."

"Not quite true. In fact, every word of it was a lie."

"Just for a change, I'd like someone to be honest with me. Just to be a little different."

Smiling, he leaned toward her, picked up her hand, and kissed the back of it. In the next moment, he seemed to realize what he'd done and put her hand back on her knee. "Too much moonlight to do that," he said.

"Yeah, mustn't touch the nanny," Cassie said under her breath.

"Anybody but the nanny," Jeff said cheerfully. "Okay, I'll tell you the story that Althea told to my father and he told me. The truth is that the shots were real and they were fired by a man who's been dead for over twenty years."

Cassie looked behind her to see how far the nearest tree was, then she scooted back so she could lean against it. "Just wanted to get comfortable," she said. "I love a good story."

Jeff moved back too, but he stretched out on the ground beside her, his head near her. With all her might she wanted to tell him to put his head on her lap, but she couldn't make herself do it.

"Of course the man wasn't really dead," Jeff said, looking up at the dark leaves above them. "What Althea said is that years ago he raided her safe of all her jewelry, then faked his death."

"Does that mean he's now been seen and he's trying to kill her?" Cassie asked.

"Exactly right. You should write mysteries."

"Why write them when I'm living in the middle of one? So how did you and Brent get involved?"

"I don't know anything about him. Maybe Althea told him the same story she told Dad. Anyway, Althea managed to keep the robbery quiet. The public didn't hear about it."

He rolled onto his side to face her. "Between you and me, I don't think Althea cared that her public knew about the robbery. I think there was something else going on with the man that Althea didn't want the world to know about."

"Such as?"

"I have no idea. I'm just an ordinary guy with an ordinary job. What do I know of the underworld?"

When he looked up at Cassie, for a moment it flashed through her mind that what Brent had told her was right: Jefferson Ames was not the man she thought he was. The very last thing he was was "ordinary." But maybe just she felt that way. "So Althea kept the robbery out of the media."

"Better than that, she didn't even tell the police. She hired her own squad of PIs to try to find the man and her missing jewels."

"But they found out he was dead."

"Yes. His boat blew up with him and the jewels on it."

"A great actress like Althea would never believe that story. She's seen too many movie sets to not know that everything is fake."

"Right."

"So if I can figure this out, why couldn't the private detectives?"

Jeff turned onto his back, smiling. "Althea thinks they were paid off. The investigators knew they had her where they wanted her. She couldn't go to the police or her secret would be out. She told Dad that in the end it was either lose the jewels or have whatever it was that she was hiding exposed."

"If you think about all that's known about her life, I can't imagine what could be so awful that she'd need to hide it," Cassie said. "She laughs and talks about her 'hundreds' of lovers. What could she want to hide?"

"I don't know. My guess is that she wants to protect someone."

"That's an interesting thought. So, anyway, how did she find out that this man was still alive?"

"She's had someone looking for him for the last twenty-one years."

"Not Brent?" Cassie asked in astonishment.

Jeff looked at her in disbelief. "He's just a kid."

"You?"

"How old do you think I am?"

Cassie smiled. "I think you can't possibly be as old as you act toward me," she said sweetly.

Jeff looked puzzled for a moment, then smiled and looked back up at the trees. "A whole year of living with you and I never knew you had such a smart-aleck mouth."

Cassie couldn't help the little thrill that went through her. His words were titillating. Sexy. It was night, the moon was bright. . . .

"Where was I?" Jeff asked.

"On my mouth."

Jeff chuckled. "No, this is about Althea. She paid some detective for over twenty years to find the man who'd robbed her, and about six months ago he did. That's the good part. The bad part is that the idiot detective was so glad to have found the robber that he asked him if he was . . ." Jeff waved his hand. "Whatever the man's name is."

"So then the robber knew that Althea was still searching for him and that she'd found him. So what happened next?"

"It's bad. Are you sure you want to hear?"

"Yes."

"The private detective called Althea, told her he'd found the robber, and gave her all the facts on the man. The next morning he was found dead in his hotel room."

Cassie didn't say anything for a while. "And he was the one who shot at Althea?"

"Yes. You and Dana saved her life. You can see the beach from the house and when he saw you two, he fled."

"Althea never gave a hint that she had just faced death."

Jeff smiled. "She told Dad that she'd rather face a loaded gun than the critics' reviews of her movies."

Cassie smiled. "That sounds like her." Her head came up. "So why are we here? What does this place have to do with Althea and the robber?"

Jeff took a while to answer, as though debating what to tell her. "Dad has a friend in the CIA," he said at last, "and he did a bit of digging and found out that the robber used to own a cabin up here."

Cassie had been leaning back against the tree, but she sat upright. "Are you telling me that Althea asked her gardener and the son of her latest boyfriend to find out about a *murderer*?"

"'Fraid so," Jeff said. "That dear woman set this whole thing up. Dad said she had a major meltdown and asked him to help her because she was afraid for her life."

"Interesting," Cassie said, thinking about the last week. Althea had never given a hint that she was living in fear. "Dana and I saw her right after she'd been shot at and she wasn't the least bit upset. Not that I could see anyway. But she finds out about some cabin and she has a fit?"

"That's pretty much exactly what I said to Dad, but he asked me to come up here and have a look around."

"And it was a good excuse to get to spend the weekend with the woman you love, so you came."

"Cassie," Jeff said slowly, "there's something you should know about Skylar. Her father—"

"So help me, if you tell me that you're spending time with her just to get her father's money, I'll hate you forever. That's despicable."

Jeff closed his lips into a tight line and said nothing.

"So what were you going to tell me?"

"I think I'd better say nothing. Tomorrow we're going to be covered in mosquito bites."

"Are you planning to marry Skylar or not?" Cassie asked point-blank. "Since my job future depends on your answer, I think you should tell me."

For a moment Jeff looked as though he wanted to be anywhere but where he was. "I . . . ," he began. "You . . . I mean, we . . ." He took a breath. "Cassie, sometimes a person's life doesn't belong to himself. Sometimes there are bigger things out there than just us. Sometimes—"

He broke off because they heard a car moving slowly down the gravel road that curved around the lake and led to all the cabins. It was two o'clock in the morning. Who was arriving at this hour?

Jeff was instantly on his feet. "Stay here," he whispered, then he disappeared into the trees.

He'd certainly moved quickly, hadn't he? she thought in disgust. Ask a man a point-blank question and he'll do whatever he can to squirm out of answering it. In this case Jeff had run from her question to see if an approaching car might possibly contain a murderer. Better to be shot at than to answer a question about marriage.

She stood up, her back against the tree, and looked about her. He certainly seemed able to see his way in the dark. And if he could see so well and move so quietly, maybe he'd seen her standing by the tree. Which meant that when he'd knocked her to the ground and straddled her, he'd known exactly what he was doing and to whom.

Yet again, Cassie had the feeling that she was in the middle of a play, and it was as though everyone except her had a script.

After what seemed a long time, Jeff suddenly appeared beside her, and again she marveled at how he managed to travel about in the woods in silence.

"It was nothing," he said quietly, "just some tourists. We'd better go in and get some sleep before morning."

As they started walking, she said, "Which cabin is it that belonged to the robber?"

This question seemed to catch Jeff off guard, but he recovered in seconds. "That one," he said, pointing behind them. "The one with the yellow porch light. But someone else owns it now." He shrugged. "I never had any hope we'd find anything."

"Too bad. I would have liked to pull up the floorboards and find a hoard of jewels. Do you know exactly what was stolen?"

"Historic pieces, I think. Some things that used to belong to Lillie Langtry."

"Nice," Cassie said. "Did you look inside the cabin?"

"Break and enter, you mean? No, I didn't." He sounded almost prudish, as though he'd never think of doing something illegal. He paused for a moment, then said, "But I did make some plans for us, though."

"And what are they?"

"The reason I agreed to come on this wild-goose chase was because an old friend of mine is here this weekend, Leo Norton. I invited him to go on a boat with us tomorrow morning. Can you water-ski?"

"Never been on them in my life."

"Good," he said. "I'll teach you."

He said it in such a lascivious way that she laughed. She started to reply, but he put his finger to his lips. Their cabin was in front of them and the windows were open. He motioned that he'd go ahead of her. No doubt he thought she couldn't open a door without making noise. She was tempted to yell out that she and Jeff were back and see what would happen, but she didn't.

Minutes later they were inside the cabin and Jeff was mouthing good night to her as he slipped into the bedroom he was sharing with Brent. At least they had twin beds. Cassie quietly went back to the bedroom she shared with Skylar, put on her nightgown, and went back to bed. She was asleep in seconds.

11

IT WAS ONLY 9 A.M. and already Cassie had thought of a thousand ways to murder the obnoxious Leo Norton. She couldn't believe he was friends with Jeff. In his fifties, with a big belly, and a loud voice, all he did was leer—and his leering was directed solely at Cassie.

"What's a little honey like you doin' with this bunch?" he demanded when he saw her at the boat. She had on a one-piece swimsuit under a loose pair of trousers and a big cotton shirt. It wasn't exactly what would inspire lust in a man. On the other hand, Skylar was wearing something straight out of *Vogue*. It was a microscopically tiny bikini, barely covered by a big, semitransparent white jacket that just reached to midthigh. Her big straw hat had a band of the same fabric around it.

When Skylar walked down to the dock where the boat that Jeff had rented was waiting, she gave Cassie a look up and down, then smiled as she let Brent help her onto the boat.

Cassie was looking after the huge cooler that held drinks, sandwiches, and fruit. She'd gone to the grocery at seven—it was open for fishermen—and bought lunch for all of them. No more watery pasta.

Jeff was waiting for her when she returned from the grocery. "You should have told me where you were going," he said, frowning.

"I was sneaking off to meet my lover, so I couldn't tell you," she said as she handed him a bag of groceries. "Are they up yet?"

"Yeah," Jeff said, still frowning. "You look awfully chipper this morning."

"And you look grumpy. Has something happened?"

"No. It's just that when I got up and you weren't here I was worried. You should have at least left a note."

Cassie stared at his back in wonder as he took the bags to the kitchen. Worried? Because she was out of his sight for forty-five minutes? What in the world was wrong with him? In the year she'd lived in his house, he'd never once worried about her. Was it the idea that a murderer used to own a cabin near here? Was that what was bothering him? Whatever his problem, she was quite happy as she put the groceries away and made sandwiches for the day's outing. Even when Skylar came into the kitchen, perfectly made up and wearing her beautiful outfit, she didn't stop smiling.

But she did stop smiling when she met Leo Norton. He walked onto the porch, pounded on the screen door, and bellowed, asking if anyone was there. Cassie was the only one in the house. She had no idea where Skylar was, but Jeff and Brent had gone to pack the boat.

"Anybody home?" he asked in an accent that could only be called "redneck." "I'm a-comin' in, so get your clothes on," he said as he entered.

Cassie put the last of the sandwiches in the cooler with a pack of hot dogs, and went into the living room. He was tall, older, with hair that was one long strand combed over his nearly bald head. His shirt

was half out of his trousers. When he saw Cassie, his eyes widened.
"Who are you?" he asked in astonishment, then seemed to recover
himself quickly. "Well, little lady, who are you? You're the prettiest
thing I've seen in a month of Sundays. Do you belong to Jeff or
Brent?"

"I don't belong to anyone," she said, trying not to frown. "Are you
Mr. Norton?"

"Sure am, honey, but you gotta call me Leo. All my best friends do.
They say I remind them of a lion, so the name fits." With that, he
turned his head to the side and gave a little growl.

Cassie managed to give him a tiny smile, but she began thinking of
excuses as to why she couldn't go on the boat with them. Spend a whole
day with this man? Her stomach turned at the thought.

"I work for Jeff," she said. "I'm his daughter's nanny."

"Are ya, now, honey? You can be my nanny any time you want." He
took a step toward her and Cassie backed toward the kitchen.

"Mr. Norton," she began, "I don't think—"

Jeff opened the door and came into the living room. "Leo, I see
you've met Cassie. She's—"

"Your nanny. She told me."

Something that Cassie didn't understand passed between the dreadful man and Jeff.

"I was just gettin' to know this little honey. Why don't you leave us
alone for a while?"

Jeff moved so his body was between Leo's and Cassie's. "Why don't
you go down to the boat and I'll help Cassie get ready here. Goodwin
and Skylar are already on it. I'll be there in seconds."

The man hesitated, but after one more glance at Cassie, he left.

"That man is a *friend* of yours?" Cassie asked when she was alone
with Jeff.

"He hasn't always been that bad," Jeff said as he went into the kitchen. "Once you get to know him, he's . . ." He trailed off. "Is this cooler ready to go?"

"I don't like the way he looked at me or the things he said," Cassie said. "I don't want to go. You three go without me."

"You can't stay here alone," Jeff said. "I can't leave you here."

"Then let Brent and Skylar go boating with him, and you can stay here with me."

Jeff's face softened. "I'd love to do that, but I can't. I mean, Leo is my friend, not theirs. Come on, Cassie. We'll have fun, I promise."

Cassie was torn between wanting time with Jeff and not wanting time with that lecherous, greasy Leo Norton. She looked at Jeff, trying to decide.

"Please," he said. "For me."

His eyes, looking so full of need, won her over. "Okay," she said at last, "but if that creep touches me I'll hit him with the gas can."

"I'll beat you to it," Jeff said. "Just stay close to me and I'll protect you."

With a reluctant heart, she'd added more bottles of juice to the cooler, and Jeff carried it to the boat. Leo Norton was already sitting on one of the padded seats at the back. Brent was in the front at the steering wheel and Skylar was perfectly posed in the middle. When Leo saw Cassie, his eyes lit up. "Oh, boy, honey, you are a sight for sore eyes. I'm gonna love this trip from just lookin' at you."

Cassie took Jeff's hand as she stepped onto the boat. "Mr. Norton," she said firmly, "my name is not 'honey' and I don't like your innuendos."

"Cool it," Jeff said, giving Norton a warning look.

Leo put his hands up, as though Jeff was going to hit him. "I meant no offense. What's wrong with women today that they don't want to be told they're pretty? Now Skylar here, she loves to be told she's pretty. Don't you, pretty lady?"

"How would I know?" Skylar said, smiling broadly at the man, as though she liked him very much. "Why don't we stay here all day and let me find out what I like and don't like that you do?"

Leo gave a laugh that rang out across the lake, and Cassie looked from one to the other in wonder. She would have thought that Skylar would look down her nose at a man who was as fat and greasy as Leo was. His big belly alone was enough to turn a person off. But his loudness, his leering, and his generally obnoxious behavior didn't seem to matter to Skylar.

Brent started the big fiberglass boat with a key, and they set off. There was a bimini across the middle, and Cassie and Jeff stayed under it, but Brent, Leo, and Skylar were never out of the sun.

After a while, Cassie was able to ignore Leo, and she enjoyed the wind on her face and the water spraying onto her. They didn't waterski. Instead, they just rode in the boat for over two hours. The lake by the cabin was fed by a river that led out into the Atlantic Ocean. In theory, they could travel up the coast to Maine and into Canada, she thought. She asked Jeff if they were headed somewhere specific. He nodded but didn't tell her where.

Everyone and their damned secrets! she thought, looking up at Brent and Skylar standing by the helm, their heads often close together. She glanced at Jeff sitting across from her, then at Leo in the back. He was staring off into the distance, and for a moment he didn't look as stupid as he seemed. But when he turned and saw her looking at him, his expression changed to a lascivious one, and she looked away, puzzled. It was almost as though he was trying to keep her from looking at him.

She wondered why Jeff wasn't with Skylar. If they were in love, wouldn't this be the perfect time to be together? Instead, Skylar was with Brent, occasionally taking the wheel, then laughing when they hit a wave. It seemed to Cassie that if Jeff were in love with Skylar he'd be jealous and stop what was going on.

But Jeff didn't seem to notice. Once, he went to the front and talked quietly to Brent, who nodded often. Jeff seemed to be giving directions. As far as she could tell, Jeff was in charge of everyone and everything—and no one disputed his authority.

After Jeff left Brent, he returned to the middle of the boat, sat down by Cassie, and asked if she was having a good time. She honestly told him yes and again asked where they were going.

"To a little cove where I've been before," he said, leaning close to her ear so she could hear him. "I thought we'd have lunch there. Sorry about the water-skiing, but Leo couldn't go so I thought—" He shrugged to finish his sentence, then leaned closer to her. "Besides, the sight of you in a swimsuit is more than ol' Leo's heart could stand. It's too nice a day to have to deal with a dead body."

Cassie laughed, then turned to him, their faces close together.

"Hey!" Leo yelled from the back. "You two gonna do it on the floor? Get away from her, Ames, I got dibs on that baby."

"Your fantasy life is only exceeded by your girth," Jeff yelled back at him, but his voice was full of humor. "You want a beer?"

"I thought you'd never ask."

Jeff winked at Cassie as he got up and went to the drinks cooler and tossed a can of beer to Leo and took one for himself, then he threw cans to Brent and Skylar. He asked Cassie if she wanted one, but she declined. He then went to the back of the boat, where he sat with Leo for nearly half an hour, their heads close together as they talked in low tones. Cassie tried to hear what they were saying, but she could only catch bits now and then. She heard the name "Althea" three times. And two times she heard Leo say that he "didn't know." Jeff seemed to be the one asking all the questions and Leo did all the answering. Every time Cassie turned her ear toward them so she could hear better, Leo would look at her in a way that made her turn back to the front of the boat. Again, she felt he was doing it on purpose.

By the time she heard Jeff tell Brent that they were to pull into the coast, Cassie's mind was full of unanswered questions. For months her life had been ruled by her belief that Jeff was going to marry Skylar Beaumont and that she was going to lose her home as well as her job. Skylar had often appeared at Jeff's house and he'd often left with her, and other times, he'd said that he was going out with her. But when Cassie thought back on it, she knew she'd never seen the two of them locked in an embrace, never stumbled on them in a passionate hug.

And today, Jeff had never so much as asked Skylar if she was all right. He seemed not to care that she had spent the whole trip laughing with Brent.

And as for Brent, wasn't Cassie supposed to be *his* date? So why was he ignoring her? Not that she minded, but it was odd, wasn't it?

Jeff directed Brent to pull the boat into an opening in the coastline that couldn't be seen from the water. To Cassie, it looked like just rocks and trees, but as they got closer she could see a narrow inlet that led back in toward land. Brent cut the engine to an idle and slowly made his way into the narrow waterway. When they got past the shallow water, they hit wider, deeper water. A river.

It was eerily quiet as they moved along the river, with tall trees looming over them. She felt as though she was an early explorer, seeing the North American continent for the first time.

"Where are we?" she whispered to Jeff when he moved to stand beside her. She could smell the beer on his breath and she wondered if his lips were cool on this hot day.

"Maryland," he said. "Private property. Dad knows the owner." He pointed ahead. "There's a little cove up there with a big rock overhang. I thought we'd have a picnic there. You like the idea?"

"Very much," she said, and wished she could make the other three people disappear. What would happen if it were just she and Jeff on the boat and they landed in a secluded cove?

When she gave a great sigh, Jeff asked if she was feeling all right. "Not seasick, are you?"

"There's some sickness about her, but it ain't from the sea," Leo said. He'd left his perch at the back of the boat and was standing across from them, holding on to the poles of the bimini. "Ain't that so, little missy?" he said, looking Cassie up and down.

Her shirt was unbuttoned so the top of her suit was exposed, as well as some skin. She pulled her shirt closed.

"Cut it out!" Jeff said to the man as he moved away from Cassie, but there was no anger in his voice.

Brent turned the engine off and they floated toward a pretty little rocky beach. As Jeff had said, there was a deep overhanging rock, enough to shelter them if it started to rain. Jeff jumped over the side into the water and soon had the boat tied securely to a tree. Brent helped Skylar down, then Jeff held his arms up and Cassie fell into them. She hoped he'd fall into the water with her on top of him, but he held her securely and they didn't fall.

Behind her, she heard Leo laugh, as though he knew Cassie's thoughts. She ignored him. He made his way up to the front of the boat and climbed down the ladder, as though he didn't want to get wet.

Brent started gathering wood to make a fire and Skylar stretched out on a rock in a pose straight out of a magazine. Jeff was unloading the cooler, so that left Cassie and Leo on their own. Behind her was a narrow trail and she stepped toward it. She'd really like to walk some after being on the boat. But first she looked at Jeff askance and he nodded. His eyes said that he'd keep Leo away from her.

Turning, she walked up the path and soon realized that it probably led to a house, maybe to Jeff's father's friend who owned the property. The last thing Cassie wanted was to meet people. She didn't want to have to explain who she was or why she was there, so she turned off the path and headed to the left. By her calculations, she was going over the rock outcropping below her. When she smelled smoke from the camp-fire, she knew she was right. She turned left again and thought about calling out to the others from the top of the cliff, but just as she got to the edge, she heard a sound behind her that made her stop. She stood still. Her first thought was that it was a large animal and she was in trouble, but the next moment she heard, "Damned rocks!" and knew that Leo Norton was coming toward her.

Was the creep following her? Maybe, maybe not. Cassie had turned off the path. With a sudden feeling of panic, she looked about for a hiding place and found one near a rotten log. In normal circumstances she would have been repulsed by the bugs that inhabit old wood, but as far as she was concerned, Leo was a bigger insect than any of the six-legged kind. She went onto her stomach behind the log and lay absolutely still. There were holes in the wood and she could see the area of forest where she'd just been.

Within seconds, she saw Leo's legs come into view. Please go on, she thought, closing her eyes and wishing with all her might. Please, please, please just keep going. But he didn't move. He stopped where she had been. Had he seen her tracks? she wondered. Is that why he was stopping? Did he know that she was near?

In the next second she heard a familiar sound. He was using a cell phone.

"At last," she heard him say, and the way he said it almost made her forget herself and sit up, but she didn't move except to lift her head a bit so she could see through a higher hole in the log.

"Yes, I'm here," he said into the phone. "It's been a bit of a push but I made it."

Cassie's eyes widened. Leo Norton had an English accent! And not one of those accents that leaves off the beginning and end of every word, but an upper-class accent that sounded to her of the BBC and the British royal family.

She moved her body upward so she could see him. He had his back to her, his phone to his ear, and he was listening. "I'm here with him now, but Jefferson brought a crowd with him. One of them I don't know. I think maybe she's an innocent, but check her out anyway. Better yet, start a file on her. Her name's Cassandra Madden."

He paused and listened. "No, Jeff is smarter than that. Yes, I already made the pickup. The little man slipped out of the rocks as soon as we got here. Easy as could be."

He paused again. "No, go ahead and pick me up today. Yes, I know I was going to stay for the weekend, but that was changed. Five o'clock at the usual place. Yes, I can be there. I'll make them leave soon."

He closed his phone and stood where he was. Cassie was tempted to step out of hiding and confront him—but not too tempted. The man wasn't obnoxious as much as he was secretive, she thought. He'd met someone here and received something, but she couldn't figure out if Jeff knew about it or not. Besides that, what was it that he'd received? Something to do with Althea's jewel robbery?

Okay, so he'd made his call, so why wasn't he leaving? To her left she heard a whistle and knew it was Jeff. She'd heard him whistle like that before and knew that he was telling her lunch was ready. When she didn't come quickly, he'd start searching for her, and she had no doubt that he'd find her. He'd found her last night in the dark, so of course he could find her now. And if he did, Leo would know that she'd heard him on the telephone.

She didn't move, just kept watching Leo. What was he doing now? she wondered. He was unbuttoning his shirt! She felt panic rising in her throat. He must know she was there and he was planning— No, she couldn't think that. Jeff was too near. Leo wouldn't do anything like that. He—

She drew in her breath when she saw him open his shirt and lift a thick pad off his stomach and scratch under it. She heard him sigh in ecstasy as he scratched his belly—his flat, muscular, hard belly.

Astonishment froze her in place. The man was disguised to look fat and out of shape, but underneath, he had a stomach any bodybuilder would envy. She glanced at his bald head and wondered if that was a disguise too. The truth was that the man had so repulsed her from the first moment she saw him that he could have been wearing a latex mask and she wouldn't have noticed.

Very clever, she thought.

She heard the whistle again, heard Leo mutter under his breath, then he hurriedly put the pad back in place and rounded his shoulders so he looked saggy and old and out of shape. Turning, he quickly headed back into the woods on the opposite side from the one Cassie had come up.

The second he was out of sight, she got up and nearly ran down the path on the other side.

"There you are," Jeff said. "I was about to send the cavalry after you. Hungry?"

"Famished," she said. Leo was on the opposite side of the camp and she couldn't help but look at him. As usual, his face instantly changed to a leer, but this time she didn't look away. For a split second, she saw something else in his eyes and she made herself look away. She didn't want to give it away that she knew more than he wanted her to.

"Did you see the house?" Jeff asked.

"No, I missed it. I went that way," she said, pointing in the opposite direction of where she'd actually gone. "Beautiful view."

Jeff looked at her sharply but said nothing. He knew this place, so had she said something wrong?

The five of them ate lunch together, but only Skylar and Brent made conversation. Cassie was quiet in her thoughts, and Leo seemed to be thinking about something too. Jeff ate and watched them all.

12

"HE'S NOT WHO HE SEEMS TO BE," Cassie whispered to Jeff as they put the cooler back in the boat.

"Do you mean Leo?"

"Of course I do."

"Is anyone who they seem to be? I can't figure out why Althea hired Goodwin, since he can hardly drive a riding mower. What kind of gardener is that?"

"He looks great with his shirt off," Cassie said quickly, "and stop trying to change the subject. Leo is not who he seems to be."

They were alone on the boat, the others still on the shore. Jeff glanced at them. "I've known Leo a long time, and I'm sorry he's been so obnoxious to you. He's not usually like that. Would you like to take a hike? We could go up to the house. Dad says the owners are away now, so we could look around. I hear she's a fantastic gardener."

"No," Cassie said, "we have to go back right away." It was obvious that Jeff didn't want to hear what she had to say.

"No, we don't. It's early yet, so we have time. Unless you have to be somewhere." He was joking with her, but she didn't smile.

"I don't have to be anywhere," she said, "but that man has to meet someone at five, so we need to leave soon." She was watching Jeff and realized that he was purposefully changing the subject and pretending that he didn't understand what she was saying. She knew from experience that he was a good listener, but now he was refusing to understand what she was trying to tell him.

"Leo didn't say anything to me about leaving early," Jeff said.

"That's because he doesn't want you to know what he's doing," she said quietly.

Jeff stopped moving the cooler around and turned to look at her. "I think maybe you should tell me what it is that you know. Or is it just intuition?"

Cassie's first impulse was to tell him every word she'd heard Leo Norton say on the phone, but something stopped her. For one thing, lately, she'd caught Jeff in too many "stretches of the truth." And for days his attitude had been odd, as though he was trying to hide something. All in all, Cassie was sure that there was a great deal more to why Jeff had come to the cabin than just a twenty-one-year-old jewel robbery.

"Intuition," she said with a sigh and a fluttering of her lashes that she hoped made her look innocent. "Leo doesn't wear a ring but I think he's married."

Jeff smiled in a fatherly way—and with more than a little relief, she thought. "Probably. I know he's been divorced several times. After our hike, I'll have a talk with him. I haven't liked his behavior today at all."

Cassie started to reply but turned when they heard a yelp of pain come from Leo. When they looked, they saw him holding the side of his calf, and there was blood on his khaki trousers.

Jeff turned to Cassie and lifted his eyebrows.

She shrugged and said, "Intuition," then she went to the front of the boat and asked Brent what was wrong.

"Leo's hurt his leg. I think we better go back," Brent called out. "There's a lot of blood."

"I bet there is," Cassie said under her breath, then turned to smile at Jeff. He was frowning at her in a way that made her wish she hadn't told him as much as she had.

Part of her wanted to tell Jeff everything, but she didn't think he'd listen to her. What she needed was some proof, then she'd be able to back up whatever she said about Leo Norton. If she had proof that he wasn't what he seemed, then maybe Jeff would believe her—and tell her the truth about what was going on.

Cassie stepped back and watched the others quickly load the boat. Once they were in open water again, heading back to the cabin, she turned to look at Leo. He'd wrapped a towel around his leg and it was bloody, but he was sitting there quietly looking at the water and didn't seem to be in pain.

She was willing to bet that there was no wound under the bandage. On impulse, Cassie got up and went to him. He was so astonished that he didn't say a word until Cassie bent down to put her hands on the towel.

"What're you doin'?" he yelled.

"I thought I'd look at your cut," she said.

"Look, baby, I want you to take off my clothes, but not now, not in front of ever'body. Unless that's the way you like it."

Cassie again bent to go to his bandage. "Just let me look at the wound. It's still bleeding, so maybe it needs pressure on it. Maybe you cut a vein."

"I didn't cut no bleedin' vein," he snapped, then clamped his mouth shut as he glared at her.

"All right," she said sweetly, then returned to her seat. He'd said "bleeding." A person couldn't get more English than that.

As Cassie took her seat, she saw that the other three were looking at her in surprise. They know, she thought. That's why Jeff wouldn't listen to her. All of them know that Leo isn't who he seems to be. Only she was in the dark, and not privy to their secrets.

It was a quiet trip back to the cabin dock, and the silence gave Cassie time to think. It was as though all of them thought of her as a child. She knew that was Jeff's problem. He thought because he was eleven years older than she was, that she was a kid. Hardly older than his daughter.

As they pulled into the dock, she made a vow to herself that she was going to show the lot of them that she was an adult as much as they were, and that she could keep secrets as well as they could.

Cassie looked up at the cabin window and was sure she could squeeze through it. It was the cabin that Jeff had pointed out as being the one the robber had once owned. There were signs of recent occupation around it, including a fresh oil spot on the gravel drive, so she had an idea that this was where Leo had been staying. She'd waited until after five, when she knew he'd be gone. She didn't know what she'd find inside, but she was going to have a look. The sun was low in the sky, and all around the lake was quiet. There was a curtain in front of the window, and if she broke the glass it would be hidden from the inside. He wouldn't know it was broken until he felt the breeze. That is, if he ever returned.

Okay, she told herself, time to stop thinking about it and *do* it. She'd found a short ladder in the little shed behind the cabin where they were staying, so she leaned it against the wall and climbed up. She wrapped her shirttail around her hand, then with her head turned, she hit the glass. It took two times before the window broke. The sound seemed loud to her, but she looked around and saw no one.

It was easy to reach through the window, unfasten the latch, and push it up. Minutes later, she was inside the cabin. It was smaller than theirs, one of those one-room houses that was open space, with only a tiny bathroom closed off. The bed was in one corner, the kitchen in another, the living room in the other half of the house.

When she looked around and saw nothing out of the ordinary, her first impulse was to climb back out the window and leave. No, she told herself, she needed to do this. She needed to have some proof to show Jeff when she told him what she'd heard Leo say, and she needed to show him that she could be part of whatever he and Brent and Skylar were into. If there was any proof, her only hope of finding it was inside the cabin.

By the bed was a huge, beat-up, old wardrobe, with one door crooked on its hinges. She opened the door and looked inside. It was filled with a man's clothes, all well worn and uninteresting. They looked to be Leo's size, the one that included the huge pad he wore, that is. She started going through the clothes, checking each pocket for anything she could find.

After they'd returned from the cove today, Leo had scurried off in the direction of the cabin that Jeff had told her was the one the robber used to own. Cassie didn't see him enter it, but then she didn't want to rouse suspicion by staring. She'd tried to act the same as she always did, but she knew she was being too quiet.

"Would you mind telling me what's wrong with you?" Jeff asked as he carried the cooler back to the house.

"Nothing is wrong," she said. "I'm just tired. The sun must have worn me out. I think I'll take a nap."

"That's a good idea," Jeff said quickly. "And I think I'll take a run.

Too much sitting for me. I wish we could have gone skiing today. I need the exercise."

Cassie knew he was lying. Her guess was that he meant to go after Leo and ask him more questions. Let him, she thought. She had her own ideas about what she was going to do.

She looked back at Brent and Skylar, and they seemed lost in each other. If Cassie really were Brent's date, she would have been furious. Wasn't it enough that Skylar had Jeff? Or did she? Cassie thought, and made yet another vow to do some investigating on that matter too.

As soon as Jeff left to go running, Cassie told Skylar and Brent that she was going for a walk. They didn't seem to notice her one way or the other. They were in the living room, and she could feel the tension between them. Sexual tension. Good, she thought, that should keep them busy.

It had been easy to get the ladder from the shed and carry it to the cabin that Jeff had told her had belonged to the thief. And now she was inside it and searching for . . . For what? That was the big question. Did she think she would find a treasure trove of jewels?

There was nothing, not even a grocery list, in the pockets of the clothes in the wardrobe, and Cassie thought that was odd. Who had empty pockets? Turning away, she began to search inside cabinets and drawers, but after half an hour, she'd found nothing. It looked as though Leo had made an effort to leave nothing of himself behind. Except dirt, she thought as she looked at the kitchen, which was filthy.

She was in the kitchen, searching through the cabinets, when she heard the key in the front door. She hadn't heard a car drive up, hadn't heard any noise at all, but now someone was coming into the cabin. Her first thought was that it was Jeff, and he was at last "breaking and entering." But what if it wasn't him? She wouldn't like to be caught alone by Leo.

Frantically, she looked around for a hiding place. The iron bed frame was two feet off the floor and the bedspread didn't reach down far enough to offer cover. The only place she could see to hide was in the clothes cabinet. She ran to the wardrobe, opened it, and stepped inside.

A second later, the front door opened and she heard footsteps. She could see out through a half-inch space along the back of the door. Across from the cabinet was a mirror over an old dresser. A man she'd never seen before had entered the cabin, and he was carrying a bag of groceries. He was tall and so thin she wondered when he'd last had a meal. He wore old blue jeans and a red flannel shirt over a stained white T-shirt. They weren't his clothes in the wardrobe.

"What a mess!" she heard him mutter as he put the bag on the kitchen counter. "Damn Lester! Never cleans up anything."

She watched him in the mirror as he unloaded the groceries and put them in the refrigerator. He cursed some more when he saw that the fridge had been unplugged. She waited for him to start cleaning the kitchen, but he didn't. Instead, he went into the living room and sat down on the dusty couch with a beer in his hand and turned on the TV.

Cassie leaned back against the cabinet and had to stifle a groan. There was no way she could get out without being seen. With a sigh, she thought that her best hope was that he'd fall asleep and she could sneak out.

When the TV came on loud, she jumped. Within seconds he was watching something that seemed to have one car chase after the other. While it was good for covering sounds, it wasn't good for making him fall asleep.

A few minutes later, she thought maybe he was interested in his movie enough that he wouldn't notice the wardrobe door opening. Maybe she could slip out of the cabinet, go into the bathroom, then climb out that window—if it was big enough, that is.

But she moved the door a mere inch and he saw the motion in the mirror. When he got up, Cassie held her breath. He went straight to the window and saw that it had been broken. She was glad she'd closed it after she entered. She tried to make herself small in the back of the wardrobe, but she was sure he'd open it and see her. He was only a few feet from her and she could see his face more clearly. He had a scraggly mustache and a bit of a beard, and acne scars on his neck. He didn't look like a man who'd be nice about finding someone inside his house.

The man cursed at "kids," then slammed the door on the wardrobe hard. It looked like he thought the breeze from the broken window had made the door move. Cassie could still see him through a tiny hole in the paneling and she watched as he got a roll of tape from the kitchen and covered the broken glass. She heard him mutter that "the damned place oughta be burned to the ground."

After the hole in the window had been patched, he got another beer and went back to the TV, and Cassie almost cried in relief. But she was still trapped inside the wardrobe; she still had no way out.

She'd been standing up, but now, slowly, silently, she sat down. There was nothing she could do but wait.

What seemed like days went by, but it was probably only an hour. The car chase movie went off and the man found a karate movie to watch. She lost count of the number of beers he had. It was at least six.

She'd spent the first half hour thinking about being put in jail and how for the rest of her life she'd have a criminal record. By the second half hour she knew she was falling asleep, which meant that if an opportunity to escape did present itself, she wouldn't see it.

To keep herself awake in the stuffy closet, she thought back over the last few weeks since she and Dana had heard the shots from Althea's house. Now, that seemed so long ago, and she wished she were back in Althea's attic, with her clipboard on her lap, and cataloguing. That thought made her remember one of Althea's movies in which she'd hidden in a closet with the murderer just outside. How did she get out of that? Cassie wondered—then remembered that Althea's character had been found and strangled to death by the man.

That thought made her wake up! She checked on the man on the couch, and he seemed to look sleepy. He'd made a trip to the bathroom, but other than that, he hadn't moved, so maybe he'd fall asleep and Cassie . . . She didn't know if she'd push out the taped window she'd used to get in, or run for the front door.

Her leg was going to sleep, so she quietly changed her position and pushed the sleeve of a flannel shirt out of her face. When she moved her foot, the heel of her shoe scraped across a board that protruded from the floor of the wardrobe. Smiling, Cassie remembered the time she and Brent had been excited about seeing the armoire used in Althea's movie about the detective. *The Twenty-sixth of December*, she thought. The all-important journal had been hidden under the boards.

More to keep herself awake than because she thought something would be there, Cassie squashed herself into a corner and pulled at the loose board. She got a splinter in her fingertip when she tried to lift it, but she kept pulling.

When it came up, she smiled in accomplishment, then started to put it back, but on impulse, she cautiously put her hand into the dark hole. She was ready to snatch it back out if she felt anything slimy or moving.

But the hole was just a big empty space and seemed to have nothing in it. She was about to give up when her hand touched something. It felt like stiff paper. It wasn't easy to maneuver herself so she could get hold of it, but she did. She pulled it out and knew what it was as soon as she had her hand fully around it. It was a computer CD in a white paper sleeve. It was her guess that someone had once used the hole as a hiding place, but when they'd cleaned it out, this disk had stuck and been left behind. Smiling, and feeling a sense of achievement, she tucked the disk into her bra. Reaching her trouser pocket would entail standing up, and she couldn't risk the noise.

Cassie sat back against the wall of the wardrobe and didn't know whether to be happy or terrified. Of course the disk could just contain some ordinary files, but if so, why hide? She leaned forward to peer in the mirror to see the man. He looked wide awake, fascinated by whatever show was on TV.

Cassie was so absorbed in looking at the man that when she saw the hand at the window, she almost screamed. It took her several seconds to calm down. She knew the hand well. It was Jeff's.

He had cut away the tape the man had put over the window and was trying to get her attention. But how did he know she was in the closet? she wondered, but then she knew. He'd seen the ladder that was still outside, and which he was standing on, then he'd looked inside the cabin and seen that, other than the bathroom, the only place she could hide was inside the wardrobe.

She desperately wanted to signal to him, but she couldn't open the door even an inch or the man would see the movement. But if she didn't signal Jeff she was afraid he'd leave and she'd be caught. And sent to jail. Or worse!

When the man got up to go to the kitchen to get yet another beer, Cassie nearly burst into tears of happiness. She opened the door a few inches and put her face to it so Jeff could see her, then she closed the door again. She did *not* want to think about the expression Jeff had been wearing.

It was less than a minute before she heard a car alarm go off, and then the man jumped up and ran out the door. Cassie was out of the wardrobe and at the window in a split second. Jeff had the window open, and he wasn't gentle when he pulled her through it. He grabbed the waistline of her trousers and hauled her out, catching her in his arms as he stood her on the ground. The man's car alarm was still going off so loudly that she knew that if she said anything, she'd have to shout, so she stood in silence as Jeff angrily tore off strips of tape from the roll he held and covered up the hole in the window. If the man looked at it he'd see that this tape had been put on from the outside, but Cassie guessed that as long as wind and mosquitoes didn't come into the room, the man wouldn't look behind the curtain.

When he finished, Jeff picked up the ladder in one hand and grabbed Cassie's arm in the other, then they took off running toward their cabin.

13

"Do YOU HAVE ANY IDEA what you put me through?" Jeff said. He was so angry that veins were standing out on his temples. They were back in their cabin. Cassie was sitting on the couch, Jeff was looming over her, pacing, and telling her in loud detail what he thought of her escapade. "Cassie, I have always thought of you as a sane and sensible person. If I didn't think you were, I wouldn't have let you take care of my child."

She wanted to remind him of the idiot nannies he'd hired before her, but she thought better of it and kept her mouth closed. Even from her limited experience she knew that angry men recovered more quickly when they were allowed to blow off steam.

She and Jeff were alone, and she wondered where Brent and Skylar were, and if he'd sent them away.

"I guessed where you were," he said. "I remembered that you suggested that I break into that man's cabin, so it came to my mind that

that's what you'd done. But I thought no, that couldn't be possible. Not sweet little Cassie. Not the cookie-baking Cassie who everyone depends on. Not the Cassie who takes care of everyone, who is reliable and trust-worthy. Not that Cassie breaking and entering into some man's house, hiding in a wardrobe and spying on him."

Cassie put her arms over her chest and she couldn't help it, as her bottom lip stuck out. He certainly made her sound boring. Cookie-baking? Trustworthy? Reliable? Is that how he saw her? No wonder he was taken in by someone like Skylar. No wonder he'd never made a pass at Cassie.

"Would you mind telling me what you were doing in there? What did you think you would find? A bundle of jewels from a robbery that happened over twenty years ago?"

"Leo," she said.

"What?"

"Leo," she said louder. "I thought Leo was staying there and I thought I could find out something about him. I told you he wasn't who he seemed to be."

Jeff's face drained of color. "You thought Leo Norton was a person who was . . . What was it you said? Bad? You thought he was a *bad* per-son, yet you went snooping around where you thought he was and searching through his belongings?"

Jeff seemed to be so overcome with the enormity of it all that he sat down on a chair as though he weighed hundreds of pounds.

"I told you that Leo said he was leaving at five P.M., so I thought I was safe in searching his cabin," Cassie said.

"For your information—which I would have told you if you'd asked—Leo wasn't staying in any of the cabins. I don't know where he was staying. He just came in for the day."

"Oh," she said. "I thought that since you'd told me about the cabin and Leo was here that that's where he was staying."

"And where he was hiding the jewels, I guess." Jeff wiped his hand across his face. "Cassie, you don't seem to realize how dangerous what you did was. If I hadn't found you, what would have happened?"

"That man was on his seventh or eighth beer, and eventually, he would have fallen asleep and I would have climbed back out the window." She knew that Jeff was running down. It was funny, she thought, how one person could bawl you out and you'd be terrified, but another person could do it and you'd just have to wait for him to finish. With Jeff, she didn't have the least bit of fear. But then, Cassie knew she had an advantage over other people: she'd been terrorized by the best. All her life, her mother had told her that whatever she'd done was wrong. In the rare times that Margaret Madden visited her daughter in the country house, there was nothing that escaped the woman's attention and nothing that she didn't find fault with.

And every word out of her mother's mouth had terrified Cassie. Right now, Cassie realized that the difference between her mother and Jeff was that he wasn't going to hurt her. Jeff cared. He was a man who loved people very, very hard. He wasn't a man who punished and ridiculed, as Margaret Madden did.

Cassie hung her head and let Jeff say what he wanted to, but she wasn't upset that he was yelling at her. She could tell that most of his anger was relief that she was all right. He'd told her in detail how he'd been upset when she'd "disappeared." "I knew that you'd done something you shouldn't have. A voice in my head told me that you were where you shouldn't be," he'd said.

Now, he finally seemed to have run down a bit. "Would you like to see what I found?" she asked softly.

"Found? What do you mean, 'found'?"

"In the cabin. I found something in the cabin."

He gave her a hard look. "Cassie, that cabin is occupied by a man neither you nor I know, and he has a right to hide anything he wants in there. It's none of your business or mine. I think we should return whatever it is that you found."

"But what if it's from the robbery?"

He opened his mouth to speak, then closed it again. "Okay, I'll bite. What did you find?"

"A disk." As she removed the disk from inside her bra, she couldn't help herself, but she made her movements rather slow and she hoped sexy as she unbuttoned her shirt—one button lower than necessary— and withdrew the disk. When she looked up at Jeff she was happy to see that his face was a shade paler than it had been.

It was a moment before he spoke. "If you think that's from the jewel robbery, it couldn't be. You're not old enough to know that twenty years ago they didn't have disks like that."

"I'm old enough to know that information can be transferred," she said, smiling. "Did you bring your computer? We could look at this."

"I don't think we should," Jeff said. "It's private property and—"

"Fine," Cassie said as she started to put the disk back into her bra. "I'll look at it when we get home. By the way, when are we leaving?"

"Not soon enough," Jeff said, then got up. "Stay here. Don't move. Don't break into anyone's house, and don't go sneaking around and listening in on anyone's conversations."

"When did I do that?"

"I don't know, but I think you may have done many things that you shouldn't have." He paused at the door. "Cassie, I'm beginning to wonder if you're the girl I thought I knew."

After he left the cabin, Cassie broke into a smile. She was sure he'd meant his statement as a put-down, but she couldn't take it as such. She liked that she was changing his mind about her.

Minutes later, he returned with his laptop and power cord in his hand. She couldn't help teasing him. "I don't think you should look at this disk," she said seriously as he put the computer on the table and turned it on. "What if it has something illegal on it? You'd be an accessory then. No, it's better that I take full responsibility onto myself and leave you out of it." With that, she started to shove the disk back into her bra.

But Jeff caught her hand. "Would you please stop doing that?" he said in a way that made Cassie laugh.

He put the disk into the drive and opened the file.

It was disappointing, just a list of places in and around Washington, DC, and dates from the 1980s. A dress shop, and a date in 1981, then a house and a date in 1982. There were six house addresses in '83, and a jewelry store in 1984.

"It looks like someone's address book," Cassie said. She'd hoped she'd found something interesting, but it obviously wasn't.

"Why do you think I wouldn't go into that house?" Jeff asked. "How could there be anything in there after twenty-plus years? What did you think you'd find? Did you—"

He broke off because as he scrolled down the screen, one address caught their attention at the same time. It was the last entry on the page, and it was the name of a small bank that had been robbed in 1994 and had been in the news for many days. Cassie was a teenager then, but she still remembered the story. The robbers hadn't taken any money, but they'd killed two tellers and the bank president before they'd run out the back and jumped into a car with the license plate covered. They'd never been caught.

Cassie and Jeff looked at each other, their eyes wide. "Let me do it," Cassie said. "I can type faster than you." Jeff moved to the chair beside her to let her take over the computer. She reduced the word-processing screen to half size, then connected to the wireless Internet that the computer kept saying had been found. Minutes later she'd typed in the name of the dress shop. Robbed in 1981. She found newspaper articles about four of the houses listed, all robbed in the year that was on the disk. The jewelry store had been robbed of nearly a million dollars in 1984.

"Well," Jeff said, looking at her.

"Yes, well," Cassie said, smiling. "So what do we do now?"

"I'm glad you said 'we,'" he said, smiling back at her. "I feel like I'm making progress." He nodded toward the computer. "Mind if I take over now?" Five minutes later he had e-mailed the contents of the disk to someone.

"Who did you send that to?"

"Dad, of course," Jeff said, then looked as though he wished he hadn't said that.

Cassie jumped on his words. "We find a list of robberies and you send the information to your father? The one whose heart is so bad that he can't even walk up a flight of stairs? Why didn't you send it to the police?"

"Why would they believe me?" Jeff asked. "Are you hungry? I'm starving. Why don't we go to that little café by the grocery and get something to eat? If you can refrain from breaking anybody's windows, that is."

"You didn't answer me."

Jeff pushed the button on the side of the computer, took the disk out, and put it in its sleeve. "You want to put it back in the safe?" he asked, looking pointedly at the front of her still-open shirt.

"You're not going to distract me. Why did you send this information to your father?"

Jeff got up from the table. "He knows people. He'll know what to do with the information. Have you seen Goodwin or Skylar? They were supposed to be back by now. Of course I was so busy finding you that they could have come and gone again."

"Did you check the bedrooms?" Cassie asked, glaring at him. "How does your father 'know people'? He's a retired accountant. How would he know people who have knowledge of criminals?"

Jeff picked up the laptop, turned it off, and waited for it to shut down. "You know him, he's charming, something that I, unfortunately, didn't inherit. He charms his way into people's lives, like Althea's. Dad said that in other circumstances, he'd ask her to marry him. Wouldn't that be something? My new mother would be the greatest living actress."

"She's much older than your father."

"Who cares about age where love is concerned?"

"That is a question I'd *really* like to have answered," Cassie said, her eyes boring into his.

Jeff looked at her and laughed. "This is a whole new Cassie. So, are you ready to go?"

"Go where?"

"To get something to eat, of course. Or would you rather cook?"

"I'm beginning to want to tie you to a chair and make you answer questions," she said.

"I can take the chair and the tying part, but not the questions," he said, smiling. "Do you want to change clothes or go as you are?"

"She's driving me insane," Jeff said into his cell phone. "Dad, stop laughing. This is serious. No, I had no idea she was going to break into somebody's house. Who would have thought Cassie would do something like that? Cassie is predictable. You could set your clock by her. She picks up Elsbeth exactly on time. She goes to the farmers' market every Saturday morning. She makes an appointment for her next haircut when she's still at the shop."

Jeff listened to his father. "Yeah, I know she's been under duress with Skylar lately, but what can I do? I promised Sky's father I'd look after her. I had no choice. Yes! Of course I knew the pirate thought he could buy me for his daughter."

He paused. "Yes, Cassie is fine. A little too fine, if you ask me. Too curious, too observant, too inquisitive. I don't know what Leo did wrong, but she didn't believe his act. But then, you should have seen him! He put on an accent that made my ears turn red. Do we really sound like that to the English? What was it he majored in at Oxford? Some obscure English playwright, wasn't it?

"Oh, right. Chaucer. Only the English . . .

"No, I'm not jealous. Cassie hated him. Skylar? She flirted with him, but then she knows him. She almost gave it away in front of Cassie. I'm going to kill Goodwin for bringing Cassie here in the first place.

"Yes, I did question him. I'll tell you all about it when I get home. When? Tomorrow, late. How's Elsbeth? Good, good. I guess she's in bed. I miss her."

Jeff paused again. "Skylar? She's fine. She's out with Goodwin. He's more her type than I am. I don't know what Cassie suspects. I'm still too shocked by her comments about Leo, and about her breaking into the cabin of some guy who turns out to be a murderer. What are the chances of that, right? Who could have guessed?"

Jeff listened to his father. "I guess I'm the one who made her do it," he said softly. "Remember that story you told me about that man who stole the Nazi documents, then he disappeared for twenty years? Yeah, that one. I changed it around and made it into jewels and said they were stolen from Althea and that she'd been looking for them all these years."

Jeff rolled his eyes. "Dad! Stop shouting. It's not good for you. How was I to know that a story about a murderer would intrigue Cassie so much that she'd break into some guy's cabin? No, none of this is *my* fault."

He waited, listening. "Okay, you got me. Yes, maybe I made a big mistake in pointing the place out to her. But before today I would have thought that the worst she would have done is bake the owner some cookies.

"All right, I better go. Send that info to the right people, will you? I put a device on the man's car so he won't be able to lose us."

He paused. "I already told you. Cassie is fine. She's inside the diner waiting to have dinner with me. No, I don't know where Goodwin and Skylar are and I don't care. It's good to get away from them for a while. Yes, I'm having dinner alone with Cassie. Look, I have to go. I'm afraid to leave her by herself for long. Heaven only knows what she'll do."

Jeff grimaced. "Very funny, Dad. She's not going to run off with another man. Even if she finds one who is—what did you say? 'Honest and forthright.' Cassie is fine with the way things are and so am I."

He paused. "Yes, I'm meeting Leo's little man again tonight. This time, it'll be in secret. Cassie will *not* meet him. When we get back, I'm going to write a report on Goodwin's stupidity for bringing her here. No, I do not sound like an overprotective father! It's just that Cassie needs to be looked after, and I'm going to do it. When Goodwin gets back I plan to tell him a few things."

He listened. "Okay, give Elsbeth a hundred kisses from me and tell her I miss her. I'll see you both on Monday."

Jeff shut the phone and looked at the woods across the road. Cassie was waiting for him inside. In spite of what he'd told his father, he was more worried than he'd let on about the way she'd been behaving. Protecting Althea Fairmont had been a priority in his life for years now, but it had fallen apart recently. He'd been stunned that Cassie had become involved in it, and even more shocked when she'd told him nothing about hearing gunshots and seeing the famous woman lying on the terrace.

The Cassie Jeff had known for so long would have run to him and told him everything. So what was happening to change her? Was it, as his father said, Skylar? But from the beginning, Jeff had planned that when the time came, he'd tell Cassie that it was over between him and Skylar. He hadn't planned to tell her that it had all been a made-up job, but he'd often thought that there would be a nice, sympathetic scene between him and Cassie, and she would, of course, call off this idiot scheme of hers to move out of his house. But everything had taken too long, and the time for Cassie to leave was approaching too fast.

On top of his other problems, Cassie said she was planning to move into Althea's house. He hadn't yet figured out how to forbid her to do that, all while, of course, seeming to not forbid her to do anything. But Cassie was fascinated with Althea's very interesting life—even though she knew only half of it—so any attempts Jeff made at telling her she shouldn't live in Althea's huge house were met with blank looks.

And then there was Goodwin. Jeff hadn't figured out how to tell Cassie to get away from him without sounding as though he were jealous. Which, of course, he wasn't. How could he be jealous of a kid like that? On the other hand, Jeff planned to tell him that from now on, when he mowed the lawn, he was to wear his shirt.

Inside the café, Cassie watched Jeff talk on his cell phone, then after he hung up, he stared at the trees as though he might get some answers from them. It made her feel good that he seemed to be upset about her. She was still smarting at all the things he'd called her. "Trustworthy." How disgusting!

The waitress handed her a couple of menus. "You and your boyfriend know what you wanta eat?" she asked, pencil poised above the pad.

Cassie wasn't tempted to say that Jeff wasn't her boyfriend. "Iced tea for both of us," she said. "No sugar, no lemon." She glanced at the menu, and it struck her that she knew everything about Jeff's eating habits. "Crab cakes for him, with coleslaw, no beans. I'll have the fish of the day with the yellow squash."

"How about a margarita?" came Skylar's voice from behind the waitress, and Cassie wanted to groan.

"We only have beer."

"Then bring us four of them." Skylar looked at Cassie. "Or are you too young to drink?"

The waitress didn't look up from her pad as she said, "Right, I'll have to check her ID, but not yours." When she turned away, she smiled at Cassie, who had to suppress a giggle.

"So where have you two been all day?" Cassie asked as Skylar slid into the seat on the opposite side of the booth.

"Wouldn't you like to know?"

"Not really," Cassie said.

"Brent and I were out," Skylar said. "Doing things. Together. What did you do? Did you see Jeff?"

"All day," Cassie said sweetly. "Every minute."

"But I thought he was going to be busy."

"He was." Cassie tried to put as much suggestion into her tone as possible. She looked around Skylar's head out the window and saw that Jeff and Brent were outside in the parking lot and seemed to be deep in conversation. If she kept up this cattiness, she'd never find out anything from Skylar. Besides, when it came to cattiness, Skylar was sure to win. "So, have you chosen your dress yet?" she asked Skylar.

"Dress?"

"Your wedding dress."

The waitress put four glasses and four beers on the table, then left. "Do you know something I don't?"

"I'm sure Jeff told you that I gave notice. I'm leaving."

Skylar took a drink of her beer from the bottle. "Oh, yeah, of course he told me. We don't have secrets from each other." She picked up the menu and looked at it. "Tell me again when you're leaving."

"On Monday he's all yours. He'll need a babysitter right away, so maybe that'll help things move faster. I know Jeff has been . . ." Cassie waved her hand, as though searching for the right word. "Slow to make decisions lately."

"Yeah. Rocks move faster than Jeff. What's good to eat in a place like this?"

"Seafood," Cassie said, then lowered her voice. "So tell me, what kind of lover is he?"

Skylar's head came up. "Who?"

"Jeff, of course. Who else would I mean?"

Skylar put down the menu and narrowed her eyes at Cassie. "What are you up to? Why all these girly questions?"

Cassie smiled. "I just thought that now that I won't be employed by Jeff any longer, we might be friends. The truth is that I was hoping to lead up to asking you to give me some advice about clothes, that sort of thing."

Skylar looked at Cassie's wrinkled shirt, which was now buttoned to just below her collarbone. "You could use some advice. But you're around that Fairmont dame all day, so what do you want *me* to help you with?"

Cassie had to think for a moment. Of course she didn't want any help with clothes from Skylar. Only if she planned to take up pole dancing for a second career would she ask Skylar for help, but she did want to find out the truth about her and Jeff. She needed to get Skylar back on course. "The truth is that I thought maybe you could help me win Brent."

Skylar sat upright against the wooden bench. "So now it's Brent that you want?"

"I think so. He's been very nice to me. He took some photos of me. . . ." Cassie did her best to blush and insinuate that the photos were something that they weren't.

"You know, don't you, that Brent doesn't have a dime?" Skylar said coldly.

For a second, Cassie looked at Skylar in disbelief. She had Jeff, yet she'd been flirting with Brent for a whole day. And now she was acting like Cassie was stepping onto her territory with Brent. Cassie wanted to tell the woman that she couldn't have both men. "I can't say that I ever gave his income a thought. He has a good job working for Althea."

"Cutting the lawn?" Skylar said with a sneer. "Is that all you want from a man? Somebody's gardener? If that's true, honey, you need more work than just some new clothes. Besides, how can *you* afford good clothes? I don't shop at Wal-Mart."

Cassie had to work to keep the smile on her face. "I know that you're a woman of the world."

"And what is that crack supposed to mean?"

"Nothing bad," Cassie said. "I just meant that you've traveled and seen things and met people."

Skylar was quiet for a moment as she looked at Cassie. "So what exactly is it that you want?"

"I just want some tips on winning a man, that's all. After all, you've won a catch like Jeff, so you must be an expert."

Smiling, Skylar took a deep drink of her beer. "He is good, isn't he?"

"So how did you win him? I mean, all the women at the country club have been after him for the last year, but they got nowhere. What's your secret?"

"Just, you know, natural attraction." Skylar wouldn't meet Cassie's eyes.

"So when did he first tell you that he loved you?"

"After the first night," Skylar said quickly.

"After the first night you made love?"

"Right. Not that it's any of your business. Why this third degree, anyway?"

"This is what girlfriends do," Cassie said, smiling broadly. "Anyway, I'll have to make out a list for you about all that Elsbeth needs—her foods, her schoolwork. Everything. And then there's Thomas. He takes quite a bit of care because of his heart. You have to watch him because he'll cheat on his diet, so you'll catch him eating fried chicken. I'll get that list to you as soon as I can. I'm sure you're anxious to see it so you can start taking care of things."

Skylar looked at Cassie as though she'd lost her mind. "I don't change diapers."

Cassie laughed. "I can assure you that Elsbeth was potty trained years ago. But she is only five, so she needs a lot of attention. In the winter she has school, but in the summer she has quite a few lessons during the week. She has ballet and swimming and riding. She loves horses, and Jeff is thinking about getting her one. You'd hardly ever have to clean the stables, though."

Skylar was staring at Cassie in horror as the plates of food were placed on the table. The waitress looked at Skylar and said, "You decided what you want?"

"Freedom," Skylar muttered and looked back at the menu.

The waitress turned and left, and the next minute, Jeff and Brent came into the café. Brent was smiling; Jeff was frowning.

"Come and have your food while it's hot," Cassie said to Jeff. He took the seat beside her and quietly began to eat.

"What pictures did you take?" Skylar asked Brent as soon as he'd sat down beside her and given his order to the hovering waitress.

"Funny you should ask," Brent said as he got up. "I ran them off last night and I have a set of prints in the car. I'll go get them."

"How's Elsbeth?" Cassie asked Jeff after Brent left.

"Great," Jeff said. "And Dad will get the info to the right people."

"What information?" Skylar asked.

"Nothing," Cassie said, and for the first time she felt that she was part of the in-group, not the one who was on the outside. "Your dad okay?"

"Everyone is fine," Jeff snapped, still looking down at his plate. "Life is just great."

"What's your problem?" Skylar asked, taking a drink of her beer.

"Where did you and Goodwin go?" Jeff asked, ignoring her question.

"Just walking," Skylar said, then said nothing else.

Brent returned with an envelope and tossed it toward Cassie as he took his seat beside Skylar.

She was a bit leery of what she was about to see, so she took the photos out slowly. But her eyes widened when she saw them. They were excellent. Even if they were of her, she knew they were very good.

The light from the outside, streaming through the conservatory windows, put an ethereal shine on one side of her face, while the one toward the camera was in deep shadow. The contrast was arresting.

The dress Cassie had on was magnificent, true, but it was the expression she was wearing that made the photos so good. It was as though every thought that was in Cassie's mind could be seen on her face. In the first pictures, she was a lovely young woman who was thrilled to be in such a beautiful dress, but after Brent told her to become the character who'd worn the dress, Cassie's face changed. She was an innocent young woman who was about to be executed, and she was begging for her life.

"Scary," Skylar said, tossing the photos onto the table, but she seemed to look at Cassie differently.

"Houston," Brent said, "you should be a model. I can see terror in your eyes, real fear. Looking at these, you'd think an axe was hanging over your head."

Cassie was pleased by his compliments, but Jeff said nothing. She turned to him. "What do you think?"

"You look great," he said, holding up one where she was on her knees and looking up into the light. Jeff looked at Brent. "So when did you take these? And what did you say to Althea to get her to let you use her dress for these pictures?"

"Well," Brent said, his eyes sparkling as he looked at Cassie, "we didn't really ask. In fact, I think we are guilty of . . . What were our crimes?"

"Trespassing," Cassie said. "And stealing. Or maybe not stealing, since we didn't take the dress out of her house, but I'm sure that what we did was illegal."

"Not to mention what we did in the closet," Brent said.

At that Cassie started to laugh and Brent joined her. In the next second, they were telling the story of what happened the day he took the photos and how they'd had to hide in the closet, smashed together, while Althea was in the bedroom.

"I don't know what would have happened if we'd been caught," Cassie said, laughing. "I don't know if Althea would have forgiven us or called the police."

"She would have called someone, but not the police," Jeff said, looking at Brent like he wanted to strangle him. "I really don't think your job includes pilfering your employer's possessions."

"Oh, come on, Jeff, lighten up," Skylar said, much to Cassie's surprise. "It sounds like fun. Does that old woman have anything in her attic that a real person could wear?"

"Wonderful things," Cassie said and launched into telling Skylar about the glorious items in Althea's attic.

They laughed about what Althea would say if she saw the photos and knew her dress had been used without her permission.

"She'll come around," Brent said. "Let me handle Althea."

At that, Skylar and Cassie made hissing noises so loud that Brent put his arms up as though to protect himself. "Help me!" he said to Jeff.

But Jeff wasn't laughing. He stood up. "I think we should go."

"Why?" Skylar asked. "It's all of what? Eight o'clock?"

"Cassie's used to going to bed early," Jeff said, "and I think we should think of her."

She looked up at him in consternation, but when he held out his hand to her, she couldn't resist. At the car he opened the door for her, then got in beside her. She couldn't help that her heart was pounding hard as she thought, This is it. He's going to say something. After all this time, Jeff is going to at last say something.

But he didn't. He didn't say a word on the short drive to the cabin, and when they got back, he opened the screen door and let her go in before him. "Look," he said, "I have some things I need to do, so I'd appreciate it if you'd stay here where you'll be safe."

"Sure," Cassie said cautiously, "but, Jeff . . ." She hesitated. "I think it's time you and I talked."

"Yeah," he said impatiently and looked at his watch. "I know you've been acting oddly ever since we got here, but your explanation is going to have to wait. I really do have something I have to do right now."

"Me acting oddly?" she said. "You're the one who's been strange. Everything I've said, you've—"

"We're going to have to have this discussion some other time," he said. "Right now I have to meet someone." He narrowed his eyes at her. "And I don't want you to do anything stupid like you did today. You understand me?"

So many emotions went through Cassie that she couldn't think clearly. They all jumbled about in her head, so tangled that she couldn't say anything. Maybe what she'd done today was stupid, but the result had been great, hadn't it? It's possible that through her a murderer would be caught.

"I've got to go," he said, then he put his hands on her upper arms and gave her a kiss on the forehead as though she were twelve. "We'll talk when I get back. I promise."

With that, he walked into the night, silently disappearing into the trees, leaving Cassie standing on the porch of the cabin. "Don't do me any favors," she mumbled. "'We'll talk when I get back,'" she said mockingly. And what did he plan to tell her? That what she'd done that day had been dangerous and foolhardy? Or was he going to tell her that she was too trustworthy to do something like that?

She slapped at a mosquito on her neck and turned back to the cabin. Right now, Brent and Skylar were probably laughing together. Maybe they'd even gone to a bar and were drinking and dancing. Cassie was sure that wherever Skylar was, she was having a good time.

"She's practically engaged to Jeff, but she doesn't let him keep her from having fun," Cassie said under her breath.

Inside the cabin, it seemed lonelier and emptier than she could have imagined. She glanced at the ancient TV and thought of turning it on, but didn't want to. "Alone on a Saturday night," she said. "Story of my life."

She looked out the kitchen window and wondered when the others would be back. Probably not before morning. As for Jeff—

If someone had asked her a month ago if Jeff was a "mysterious" person, she would have laughed—he had a regular job, a home, and a family—but in the last weeks, it seemed that everything she knew about him was false.

When she turned toward the river, she saw a light on a boat that was slowly pulling into a dock. Were they night fishing? she wondered.

Suddenly, it hit her that whoever was in that boat was the person Jeff was meeting—and Cassie wanted to know who it was.

She ran out of the cabin, being careful to close the door silently, then ran in front of the four cabins between her and the boat. She slipped behind a tree and watched as the boat pulled into a dock. It was dark and the light from the nearest cabin was far away, but she'd recognize Jeff's silhouette anywhere. He went onto the dock, tied the motorboat onto a cleat, then stepped back as a man got out.

She leaned forward to try to hear what they were saying, but beyond a murmur of two male voices, she could hear nothing. After a few minutes, they walked away from the boat and disappeared into the trees. Cassie ran after them, trying to see where they were going, but they seemed to have vanished. There were three cabins close together, and each one had lights on inside it, so they could have gone into any of them. She wondered if they were meeting other people.

"A hotbed of activity," she murmured. It was just that she had no idea what kind of activity. If it was serious, why didn't Jeff go to the police? Why didn't he call someone to help him with whatever he was doing that made him sneak about during the night?

She waited awhile but heard or saw nothing, so she walked to the boat and looked inside it. It was just an ordinary outboard boat, but it had a big pile of canvas-covered boxes in the back. She looked around again and saw no one. Cautiously, she walked to the edge of the dock and leaned toward the boat, wondering what was under the canvas.

She couldn't reach it. She looked behind her again. Nothing. Cautiously, she stepped into the boat and lifted the corner of the canvas. All she saw were wooden crates. They were nailed shut, but there was writing on the far side. She lifted the canvas higher and leaned in closer to see the words, but she couldn't make them out in the dark.

In the next minute, she heard a noise and figured it was Jeff returning. Her first instinct was to run back to the cabin so he wouldn't catch her there, but she was tired of hiding. She sat down on the side of the boat and waited.

14

"WHAT THE HELL—!" Jeff said when he saw her sitting there. "I told you I wanted you to stay in the cabin."

"But I didn't want to stay in the cabin. Would you mind telling me what you're up to?"

"It's just some private business. Boring stuff."

"All right," she said, her back stiff as she got up and started walking toward the cabin.

"Okay," he said and caught her arm. "I apologize. I know I'm being rude, but there are things—"

"That I know nothing about," Cassie said with a sigh. "I bet your friend Leo is glad he no longer has to wear that big pad over his stomach. By the way, how old is he really?"

There was a flash of shock across Jeff's face. "You're certainly clever, aren't you?"

"I have lots of hidden talents."

Jeff laughed. "Leo is fine. In fact, before he left, he asked me if you were dating anyone. You can add him to the string of men you've been attracting lately."

"I'll see if I can fit him into my schedule. No, wait! My schedule is full of taking care of *your* father and *your* daughter and *your* house and *your*—"

"I get the picture. Come on and I'll walk you back to the cabin."

"Then you'll dump me there and leave me? If you were going to get rid of me why didn't you leave me with Brent and Skylar?"

"To be eaten alive by her?"

Cassie glared at him.

"Okay, so maybe you can hold your own against her. By the way, she still mentions that jacket you burned a hole in."

"It served its purpose. So why did you *really* drag me away from them?"

"Because Goodwin was sure to take off his shirt," he said as he gave her a crooked grin that made her laugh. "All right, you win. I have to go across the lake to meet someone. Would you like to go with me?"

Cassie had to work to keep from jumping up and down and yelling Yes, yes, yes! Be cool, she told herself. "Sure, why not? I got cheated out of a party with Brent and Skylar so you owe me."

"You don't want to go to any party that those two attend," he said as he stepped into the boat, then helped her into it.

"You think I wouldn't like a night of drinking and dancing?"

"Maybe you would," he said as he pulled the cord to start the motor, "but I don't want to see you that way."

The motor started and was so loud that their conversation was drowned out, but Cassie was content. Jeff had come close to telling her that he was jealous and didn't want to see her with other men.

It was cool on the lake, and in the middle it was quite dark. She had fantasies that he'd turn off the engine and take her in his arms. But when she looked at him, he just smiled, then glanced out at the lake.

When they got closer to the shore, she saw that one of the cabins along that side was lit up and she could hear music. She kept her eyes on it as they motored in. The dock was full of boats and there were cars all around the cabin, which was blasting with dance music. People were spilling out of the house and onto the beach, and they could hear laughter mixed with the music. It looked as though every person on that side of the lake was at the party.

Jeff cut the engine and they coasted into shore three cabins away. He jumped out and tied the boat to the dock. There were four other boats tied there as well.

"Why don't you go and join the party?" Jeff asked as he helped Cassie onto the dock.

"I wasn't invited."

"I don't think the butler is checking invitations," he said.

She stood just inches from him. "In other words, you want me out of your way for a while. You want to keep me busy until you finish doing whatever it is that you're doing."

"Exactly," he said.

"What if I say no?"

"Then I'd have to drug you, wrap you in canvas, and put you in the bottom of the boat. You'd wake up in Shanghai."

When Cassie started to speak, he said, "Alone."

"Rats! Okay, I'll meet you at the party. Don't take too long," she said, then ran her fingertip down the front of his shirt. When she walked away, she was sure he was watching her.

When she got to the party, she felt great. For the first time since she was twelve years old, she thought she was making real progress with Jeff. At last he was beginning to see her as a woman. But what kind of woman? she wondered.

Whatever was happening, she liked it. When she got closer to the cabin where all the music and people were, she hesitated.

"Wanta beer?" a young man asked, holding out a bottle to her.

"I wasn't invited," she shouted above the music.

"Who was?"

Laughing, she took the beer, thanked him, and went inside. She'd just stepped in when a young man grabbed her about the waist, pulled her close, and began dancing. It was the right time and the right circumstances, and she gave herself over to the music and the good-looking young people who had turned the whole house into a dance floor. All the furniture had been moved against the wall, and the big room that had a kitchen in one corner was being used for dancing. There was a fabulous-looking couple dancing on the wooden countertop of the kitchen. She wore a tiny black skirt, and a blue tank top, while he wore just jeans.

Cassie gyrated to the music with the blond man and saw that his eyes were on the girl on the bar—as were everyone else's. She looked at the other girls there and saw that they were wearing either very few clothes or garments that were so tight they left little to the imagination. But Cassie had on a baggy sweatshirt jacket over a bulky pair of sweatpants. When she'd dressed to go to the café with Jeff, she hadn't wanted him to think that she had any thoughts that they were going out on a date, so she'd covered herself well. But she knew that underneath she was wearing a tank top as tiny as any of them at the party, and she had on a pair of short shorts. When she'd dressed she'd had a fantasy that maybe after they ate she and Jeff might . . . She hadn't thought about what exactly, but she had prepared for whatever might happen.

Maybe it was the night, maybe it was the fact that the man she loved had dumped her at someone else's party, but whatever it was, Cassie felt as though she wanted some of the attention that the girl on the bar was getting.

She moved her hips toward the boy with her, and when he didn't notice, she put her hands on the front zipper of her sweatshirt and began to pull it down slowly. The boy with her didn't notice. But the boy next to her did.

"Don't stop!" he yelled, and Cassie grinned at him.

She circled her hips and began to pull the zipper down, and three boys began to yell. A girl began to clap. It didn't take long before Cassie was unzipping and thrusting her shoulder out of the heavy shirt.

The couple on the bar stopped dancing, then the boy got down and helped the girl down. They were laughing, and the girl shouted, "It's your turn."

Two tall young men grabbed Cassie's arms and hoisted her up to the bar. She was shocked for a moment, but she recovered herself. The music was throbbing, and what is more, she had a year's sexual frustration inside her. She thought about Jeff and imagined that she was undressing for him, and in the next moment she was doing a strip on the kitchen countertop. Everyone was clapping and Cassie was moving. The jacket came off slowly, and she twirled it over her head, then threw it out to the crowd to the sound of wild cheering. Her tank top was small and tight and Cassie's large breasts threatened to spill out. The cheering was deafening.

Next came the pants as she pulled down one side over her hip. Someone yelled, "What's your name?"

"Cassandra," she said, and in the next moment the room started chanting, "Cassandra! Cassandra! Cassandra!"

When she began to push her sweatpants down her legs, she nearly bent double, her ample rear end sticking out prominently. And when she bent, that's when she saw Jeff standing in the doorway. He was frowning, but that didn't bother Cassie. She stuck out her leg for two boys to pull the pant leg over her shoe. And when it was off, she had two other young men remove the other pant leg.

She had danced herself out of the pants amid great shouts and cheering. "More! More!" they yelled, and Cassie ran her thumbs under the straps of her tank top, as though she might remove it.

"No more," Jeff said, then held up his arms to help Cassie off the counter.

There was a groan through the crowd as their fun was over. But Cassie was hardly on the floor before there was another girl on the counter.

"Come on," Jeff shouted. "Let's go. Do you know where your clothes are?"

"I have no idea," she shouted back. "You'll have to take me as I am."

"Don't leave," said a very good-looking young man as he caught her arm, pulling her away from Jeff. "Ask your dad to let you stay."

"I am not her father," Jeff said, glaring at the boy.

"Sorry," the young man said. "But can she stay? I'll look after her."

"I saw how you looked after her," Jeff said.

Cassie didn't like the way it was assumed that Jeff had the right to give permission for her to stay or not. "I'm staying across the lake," she said to the young man. "Could you take me back later?"

"Sure," he said, his eyes alight. "Glad to."

"I'm not leaving," she said to Jeff.

"You could stay too, sir," the boy said, looking at Jeff. "My mom—"

"I'm not old enough to be her—" Jeff began, then stopped. The music changed to an old, funky blues song, the bass guitar thumping out a rhythm as primitive as native drums. Jeff took a moment as he seemed to make a decision, then he grabbed Cassie by the wrist and pulled her into the middle of the room.

She'd never seen Jeff dance. In fact, she had no idea if he could dance, but within a second, she saw that he couldn't just dance, he was a master at it. Before she could take a breath, he grabbed her about her waist, tossed her in the air, then caught her as she came down.

The three girls on the countertop stopped dancing and looked at Cassie and Jeff—and within a minute, the whole room had stopped dancing, moved back, and cleared the floor for them.

There are times, Cassie thought, when everything in your life works. She had taken a lot of dance classes when she was a child—so her mother could list the lessons to others—but she'd never had a reason to use what she'd learned. But when she was faced with an empty floor, some great music, and the man she craved, everything she'd ever learned came back to her.

She had on about eight ounces of clothing, a tank top, tiny shorts, and a pair of flexible sneakers. When she came down from Jeff, she moved away from him, put her arms up and did a perfect ballet pirouette. When the cheers went up, she was energized.

She began to dance with Jeff in the way that she'd always dreamed of: sexy, lusty, wanton. It was just the two of them. The audience that was cheering and clapping faded away. She was dancing for and with Jeff.

Arms, legs, hips were together, apart, sliding, raised, lowered. The music urged them on. She threw her body at his, then lifted her leg until it rested on his hip. He ran his hand up her leg until his fingertips were just under the band of her shorts. The crowd yelled in appreciation.

Jeff held her hand as he pushed her away from him, then after a moment's pause, he pulled her back. Just as she reached him, anticipating the touch of their bodies, he grabbed her waist and lifted her upward so that her hips were level with his face.

As the song ended, Jeff let her come down slowly, inch by inch, as her body ran the length of his.

The music stopped, and for a moment no one put on another CD.

In the quiet, the audience erupted, yelling, cheering, whistling, shouting. Jeff held Cassie to him, his hands about her waist, her body close to his.

"Not bad for an old man," a boy said as he slapped Jeff on his shoulder, then stepped toward Cassie. "But you can go rest now. I'll take over from here."

"In your dreams, kid," Jeff said as he took Cassie's hand and led her out the door.

Her heart was pounding, her breath still not calm. She was exhilarated but also shocked that she'd found out this new thing about Jeff.

He kept hold of her hand as they left the cabin. As they crossed the porch a girl handed Cassie her pants and jacket. "But I don't think you're gonna need these tonight," she said, laughing, nodding toward Jeff, and Cassie smiled back.

Jeff said nothing, just led her to the boat, then waited for her to put her sweats on over her top and shorts.

So now what happens? she wondered as she stepped into the boat. Would confessions of love come? Would they carry their erotic dance into the bedroom in the cabin? Whatever happened, she knew she was ready for it.

The boat ride across the lake was in silence, and she was glad. All she wanted to do was remember their dance. She felt that her body and Jeff's had said it all tonight. The way he'd danced with her told her that he felt the same way about her as she did about him. She looked at the water, felt it spray against her, and thought how silly they'd been all this time that they hadn't declared their love for each other. They could have been together as a family. They could have shared their lives this past year. They could have been so much more than they had been.

By the time they reached the cabin, Cassie was having to work to keep from grinning. For so very long, this is what she'd wanted and waited for. She was pleased to see that Brent and Skylar weren't there.

We'll just use the big bed in our room, she thought, then, when they return, Brent and Skylar can take the twin beds.

By the time they got out of the boat and Jeff tied it up, Cassie was wondering if he'd carry her over the threshold.

But he didn't. They walked up the steps to the porch and inside in silence. But she didn't mind. She knew where they were headed. She paused at the door to the bedroom with the double bed and turned back to look at Jeff, but he wasn't behind her. He was standing in the living room and seemed to be waiting for her.

"Is something wrong?" she asked.

"I think we have to talk."

Cassie smiled, then turned away so he wouldn't see her. Jeff was the kind of man who'd ask a woman to marry him before he went to bed with her. She imagined going to a jewelry store with him and choosing a ring.

He motioned for her to sit down on the couch, while he stood. So he can more easily get down on one knee? she wondered.

"Cassie," he began, "you and I have known each other a long time."

Longer than you know, she thought, but didn't say anything.

"I know what you feel about me, about us, and I want to reassure you that everything you've, uh, worked for will happen, but it can't be right now."

She looked at him in puzzlement. "What do you mean?"

He sat down beside her and took her hands in his. "I mean that I know that you . . . You are a person of goals and I know that you follow through on those goals, and that's a good thing. It's just that I'm involved in something right now and I can't help you in your goals."

"I have no idea what you're talking about," she said.

"Goals," he said, then looked down at her hands. "I wonder if you know that you're more like your mother than you think."

She pulled her hands away from his. "I don't know what you're talking about, but I can assure you that I'm not like my mother."

"I don't mean to insult you. I know what your mother's like. She's ferocious in the business world. You're not like that, but in a way, you are. She decides what she wants, then she goes after it, and so do you."

"I have never wanted to be the CEO of a corporation."

"No, of course not," he said, reaching for her hands again and pulling them toward him. "But you did set yourself a goal and you went after it. And I want you to know that you've attained it. That's not a problem. I do love you."

He paused when Cassie drew in her breath. Smiling, he squeezed her hands. "How could I not love you? You're the sweetest person in the world, and my father loves you and my daughter thinks you hung the moon."

"Jeff," Cassie said, "pardon me for being stupid, but I think I'm missing the point to what you're saying. If you love me, shouldn't we . . ." Breaking off, she looked down at their hands together. This wasn't how she'd imagined that he'd tell her that he loved her. Why wasn't he pulling her into his arms and kissing her?

"When I get this thing with Althea finished, then maybe you and I can be together, but not now. And I know that's not right because you've waited so very long."

"Waited so long for Althea?"

"No, of course not. Waited so long for *me*. Sometimes I think about it and I marvel that a little girl could make up her mind and never deviate from it. I could see it if you were born with a talent—say, to play the piano—and you grew up to be a concert pianist, but to see some man and set your heart on him and never let up even when you were an adult . . ." He looked at her with admiration in his eyes.

At last, at long, horrible last, Cassie was beginning to understand what he was saying. "When did you and I first meet?" she whispered.

Jeff squeezed her hands and smiled. "When you were twelve. It was just before Lillian and I got married and we found you facedown in a swimming pool. Do you know that you almost died?"

Cassie pulled her hands out of his. "And you've always known that I was that girl? Ever since you hired me?"

"Yes," he said, but the smile left him. "Cassie, I kept track of you after that day at the pool. It was like I was responsible for you, so I kept in touch. Well, not in touch, exactly, but I kept tabs on you. I even had a copy of your grades in college sent to me."

"My grades sent to you," she said softly.

"Is something wrong? You don't look so good."

"I'm fine. So you had my grades sent to you, then what?"

"Nothing. After Lillian . . . died, I lost touch with you for a while, but then you started calling me about the nannies."

"I called you about the nannies?"

"Sure," he said, smiling again. "When they didn't show up, that sort of thing. I can tell you that I was impressed that you'd managed to get a job at Elsbeth's nursery school. You have a degree in American history but there you were, wiping snotty noses."

"But you knew that I'd done it to be near you," Cassie said quietly.

"Yeah," Jeff said. "I knew it and I was pleased by it. It was good of you. But I didn't know why you'd done it until you asked me for the job of taking care of my daughter."

"Then you understood everything."

"Yeah. Cassie? Are you sure you're okay?"

"Yes. Tell me about the part where you love me."

Again, he took her hands. "Of course I fell in love with you right away. How could any man not love you? You're—"

"Trustworthy and sweet," Cassie said.

"Yes," he said hesitantly. "But you make it sound as though those are bad traits. I think they're wonderful."

"But of course you'd want someone trustworthy and sweet to take care of your daughter and your father. Tell me, I'm just curious: Why didn't you tell me that you loved me when you decided you did?"

"The time wasn't right."

"I see," Cassie said, moving just a bit away from him. "And why should you tell me? You had a great life as it was. I was taking care of your home, your daughter, your father, and Skylar was taking care of your body. What more could you want in life?"

"Ah, I see. You're angry about Skylar. There's more to that than I can tell you about."

"I know. Something about her father. But then, you didn't have to explain things to me, did you? I was just good ol' Cassie, quietly living in your home, baking myself into a stupor to take care of your life and your family. Why should you have to explain anything to me? Sweet, trustworthy Cassie, who had been in love with you since she was twelve years old. Tell me, Jeff, now, when you told me you were in love with me, what did you expect me to do?"

"Cassie, you're taking this wrong. What was I supposed to do when I first saw you at Elsbeth's school? Embarrass you by telling you that I knew you were the girl who'd hidden in the bushes and followed me around when she was a kid? I couldn't do that to you."

"So, instead, you let me call you, not Dana, as it was on Elsbeth's cards, and tell you about the nannies. Then you let me ask you to give me a job that entailed living in your house. And you let me move in and take care of every aspect of your life. Tell me, Jeff, how hard did you laugh on those nights when I went downstairs when I knew you were down there alone?"

"Cassie, it wasn't like that. If you knew how much I wanted to take you in my arms and tell you what I felt—"

"But you didn't, did you? You let me do your laundry. You even let me mend your clothes. You let me do everything for you, all while you knew what I had done. I made you my lifelong goal, isn't that what you said? I was like my mother and set myself out a goal, then I went after it. I'll have to call her and tell her that I am just like her. I'm sure she'll be so proud. She may not agree with my goal, but she'll certainly understand that I went after it without so much as a thought about my dignity or my self-respect. The truth is that I never thought about myself at all."

"Cassie," Jeff said, reaching for her as she got up. He stood up and tried to take her arm, but she pulled back. "Let's talk about this. We'll talk this through and maybe we can work things out."

"What does that mean?" she asked, glaring at him. "That in order to keep your maid, nanny, and cook, you'll what? Decide that you *can* find time for me? Or maybe you're going to tell me that you aren't in love with Skylar after all, that you were just hinting that you were going to marry her for some reason that has to do with her father?"

"It's a great deal bigger than that," Jeff said, his hands at his side. "There are things in my life that you know nothing about. Cassie, you can be angry with me all you want, but I've done nothing to be ashamed of."

"Okay, so tell me all about your life," she said.

"I can't. I can't tell you anything. I made a mistake in allowing you to get involved with Althea, and I made a mistake allowing you to come here."

"'Allowing me?' Is that what you said? Oh, I see. You think that since you've known me since I was a kid that you need to take care of me. But then you said that, didn't you? What was it you said? You're responsible for me."

"Cassie, please don't do this. There are things that I can't tell you. Things about Lillian's death that influence every decision in my life."

"I'm willing to listen," she said.

"I'm sorry, but I can't."

"Well, that's that, then," she said.

"Cassie . . . ," he began as he reached for her. "I think I made a mess of everything. I've hurt you when I never meant to. I've worked hard to keep it light between us. I can't begin to tell you how difficult it's been to have you in my house and not be able to touch you. I wanted to do things like tonight."

"Dance?"

"Yes. That and more. You've been good to all of us. You've made our lives pleasant and easy. You've—"

"Saint Cassandra who does a strip on the countertop."

"I could have done without that," Jeff said, grinning, but she didn't smile back.

"This has been a lot of information," Cassie said. "I'm going to have to think about it all."

"Yeah, sure," Jeff said. "Cassie—"

She put up her hand. "I've heard more than I can process tonight," she said, then went into the bedroom, shut the door, and began to quietly pack her bag.

Thirty minutes later, she heard the shower running. She picked up her bag, tiptoed out of the room, and took Jeff's keys off the top of the dresser in his bedroom. She slipped the car key off the ring and left the others. Silently, she left the cabin, got into his car, and drove away into the night. There was only one place and one person who she knew to go to: Althea.

15

CASSIE STEPPED OFF THE TREADMILL and mopped the sweat off her face.

"One hour?" her trainer, Xavier, said, and she nodded, then made a face at his back. He was a man who was very aware of his clients. If they ate a muffin, he could tell. When Cassie first enrolled in his program, he'd been very polite and had listened to all her likes and dislikes about exercising. She'd told him the truth, that she was a woman who would much rather spend the afternoon baking than doing lunges. She told him the exercises she hated and the ones she enjoyed.

What she didn't understand was that he was asking her so he knew what to give her to do. If she hated an exercise or was afraid of something, then that's what he assigned her to do. She was afraid of heights, so he spent six weeks making her climb a rock face. When she'd managed to make it up the side of his plastic mountain in five minutes, he took her to a bigger rock.

For six months she'd done little but work out. She'd started with two thirty-minute sessions a week with Xavier, and alone on the treadmill three times a week, feeling like she was going to faint after a mere ten minutes. After a month, she was able to increase her sessions to three times a week and spend forty-five minutes at a time running. By six weeks, she'd added a yoga class and kickboxing.

After three months, Cassie started taking advantage of Fort Lauderdale's divine weather and going outside. A man from the gym asked her on a date, and she spent a day on a boat with six other people and had a great time. She took along some cupcakes she'd baked, and the others raved about them so much that she enrolled in a cooking course.

After four months, Cassie had lost a lot of weight and her body was toned and hard. And she was beginning to think that she could have a life without Jefferson Ames.

But she still thought about him. And she thought about Thomas and, most of all, Elsbeth. Althea kept Cassie informed about what was happening in Williamsburg, and she was now able to look at it from a distance.

That hadn't been so on the night she'd fled the cabin in Jeff's car. She'd driven straight to Althea's house, arriving there just as the sun was coming up. On the long drive, she blasted the radio and sang along with it, trying to be loud enough to hold off crying. If she cried, she wouldn't be able to see where she was going, and she didn't relish having a car wreck.

Althea was in bed, but Rosalie, the housekeeper, took one look at Cassie and led her back to her mistress's bedroom. Althea was wearing a gorgeous gown of champagne silk. Without makeup, she looked years older, but infinitely sweeter than Cassie had ever seen her—like everyone's image of the perfect grandmother. Althea pulled back the comforter, and said, "Tell me what he's done." There seemed to be no question that a "he" was the cause of all the problems.

Cassie climbed into the bed and told Althea everything, from the beginning to the end, all while crying and blowing her nose on Althea's scented tissues.

"I want to make sure I understand what you're telling me," Althea said. She had put on her makeup while Cassie unburdened herself, and now she was again the Great Lady. "Let me see if I have this correct. You tried to get a man by dedicating your life to him?"

"Sort of," Cassie said, sniffing.

"And of course you've spent a long time trying to show him how good you are by being a dutiful wife and mother. And you were always there when he came home."

"Yes."

"And you were completely reliable?"

"Jeff called me trustworthy." Cassie blew her nose loudly.

Althea shook her head in disbelief. "Truly horrible. You know, don't you, that you went about everything in exactly the wrong way."

"I don't know any other way," Cassie said.

Althea leaned toward her. "Don't you know that men haven't moved on from the cave? Oh, they may wear tuxedos and pretend they're civilized, but they're not. In their minds, they still live in caves and eat meat all day and love to fight. Only now they watch it on TV."

Cassie gave a little smile.

"You think I'm joking, but I'm not. Men are still hunters. No matter that they say they're tree huggers, they aren't. What you did to Jeff was a horrible thing."

"Me? What did I do? I took care of his home. I—"

"I know all that," Althea said. "You took away Jeff's right to hunt. Men want to stalk their prey. They want their prey to put up a fight so they can sit around the campfire and brag about what they had to do to kill it."

"You're saying I made it too easy for him," Cassie said.

"You were a doe that walked into his cave, sat down on his lap, and offered up your throat to be cut."

"That's an ugly image."

"You know what I think?" Althea said. "I think that your imagined love for Jeff got you through a loveless childhood."

"But the real Jeff is a nice guy. Or I thought he was. But all this time he knew that I was . . . that I was . . ." Cassie's tears began again.

"What he knew was that he didn't have to fight for you. Do you know anything about his late wife?"

"According to Jeff, she was a saint."

"No, not that. What about her circumstances in life?"

"She was rich. My mother said she was a class above Jeff."

"There you go," Althea said. "Getting her was a struggle. A hunt. A fight."

"So you're saying that I need to make Jeff fight for me?"

"I'm saying that you need to dump that idiot man and find one who wants to slay dragons to win you."

"I think you're right," Cassie said slowly. "I know that if I ever have to see him again, I'll die of embarrassment. But what about Thomas and Elsbeth? I can't bear to think of not seeing them ever again."

"Cassie, you need to think about *you*."

"I'm not very good at that," she said.

"Obviously," Althea said under her breath. "I'm going to outline a new plan for you and you're going to follow it."

"I'm going to need a new job. I can't stay here." The thought of being far away from Thomas and Elsbeth made Cassie start crying again. "It's so unfair. All I did was fall in love and—"

"Do stop whining," Althea said. "It's beginning to give me a headache. Do you have any money?"

"I have about four thousand in the bank."

"That's nothing. Tell me, this mother of yours, does she earn a lot of money?"

"I read in *Forbes* that last year she got a bonus of three million."

"And how much of that did she share with you?"

"None. But then I wouldn't dream of asking her for money."

"Well, start dreaming, girl. Or in your case, stop dreaming and *do* something. You're going to go to your mother and—"

"Oh, no, I'm not," Cassie said firmly. "I would rather live on the streets than ask my mother for anything. I'd rather—"

"I'm going to give you some things to do and you need the freedom to do them. You can't be trapped in a nine-to-five job."

Cassie looked at her suspiciously. "What kinds of things do you want me to do?"

"A little acting, that's all, but you need time to prepare for the role."

"I can't act."

"Oh? And what have you been doing for the last year? Haven't you been acting like you weren't crazy in love with Jefferson Ames?"

"I guess so," Cassie said, then looked at Althea. "If I'm to do work for you, then maybe I could get a salary from you. I could—"

"No, it doesn't work that way. I'm no therapist, but I think it's necessary for you to face that mother of yours."

"I can do that, it's just asking her for money that I hate."

"Cassie, as far as I can tell, you never ask anyone for anything. And unless you want to spend the rest of your life being the girl everyone takes advantage of and no one loves, then you *are* going to your mother. And you're going to do exactly what I tell you to."

"What's the difference?" Cassie mumbled. "I'm being bullied by you or her."

Althea took Cassie's hands in her own. "There comes a time in every girl's life when she must deal with her mother. You may not think so, but you need her."

"Like you need your daughter?"

Althea tried to pull away, but Cassie held on.

"I'll make you a deal," Cassie said. "I'll meet with my mother, I'll even hit her up for money, but only if you agree to contact your daughter. And you have to invite the whole family here for Christmas."

Althea pulled her hands away and stiffened. "I can't do that. There are things you know nothing about and they—"

"Such as whatever part Roger Craig plays in your life? And Leo Norton? And of course there's Brent, who has to be the worst gardener in the world."

Althea laughed. "Keep your eyes open, don't you? All right, I'll do it. Rosalie will like having lots of kids to cook for—if they come, that is."

"Even if your daughter isn't interested in you, I bet her daughters are. "

"What a good idea!" Althea said. "I'll send invitations to each one of them, not just my daughter. She can stay home and sulk if she wants to."

Cassie laughed. "Okay, so now what do we do? Do I go groveling to my mother and beg?"

"Not by a long shot," Althea said. "When I get through with you, your bully of a mother will grovel to you."

"That would be something I'd like to see."

In the end, Cassie did fly to New York and did meet with her mother. And she dealt with her in a way that Althea had made her rehearse. "There isn't a personality type that I haven't played or played against," she said, obviously enjoying herself immensely. They went to the attic and Althea had Cassie dress as close to her mother as possible.

The wool suit wouldn't button over her chest, but it was enough that she felt as though she looked like Margaret Madden. Cassie pulled her thick hair back from her face and tied it in a severe bun.

For over an hour, she and Althea took turns playing the roles of Margaret and Cassie. Althea was a better bully than Margaret was in person, but Cassie was finally able to stare her down, to sit up and not be intimidated by her mother's aggression.

"It's all in how you handle it," Althea said. "If it weren't, there'd be no need for divorce and the hope that the next spouse will be a better one."

Althea sent Cassie into Richmond to Saks and instructed her stylist to dress Cassie as though for a corporate meeting. Although Althea organized it all by telling Cassie exactly what to do, she didn't offer to help with the finances. By the time Cassie got the plane tickets and the clothes, she had less than a hundred dollars in her account and the bank was calling her.

During the few days she spent at Althea's house, Cassie stayed hidden. Not even Brent knew she was there. He was outside mowing the lawn, and a couple of times Cassie heard his voice, but she stayed in her room. The only time she came close to giving herself away was when she saw Thomas and Elsbeth walking away from the house. They were holding hands and they both looked downcast.

Cassie wanted to throw open the window and call out to them. Elsbeth had lost her mother before she knew her, and Thomas had lost a beloved daughter-in-law. They had given Cassie their love, but she too had left them.

But when she thought of Jeff and how he had known all about her for all those years, Cassie turned away from the window.

Althea had pointed out that Cassie should have told Jeff when he hired her that she was the girl he'd saved years before. The words made her feel worse. No wonder Jeff had never thought of her as a mature woman.

On the flight to New York, Cassie had searched her brain for what to tell her mother about why she wanted money. In the end, Cassie told the truth, that something bad had happened in her life and she needed time to recover from it, so she needed some money to live on. Margaret had looked so relieved that her daughter wasn't asking for something emotional that she'd written a check then and there. "Will that be enough?" she'd asked.

Cassie gulped at the amount. "More than enough," she said, then smiled at her.

"Cassandra," Margaret began, "I've rented a house on Martha's Vineyard for this summer. Maybe you'd like to visit me there."

It took Cassie a moment to recover herself. Her mother had rented a house? For a vacation? For time off? She remembered something Althea said: "The problem with setting goals is, What do you do when you reach them?" Cassie answered that you set new ones and went after them, but Althea had said it didn't work that way. And Cassie was seeing the truth in that. Since she was twelve, her goal had been to have Jefferson Ames tell her he loved her. He'd done it, but it hadn't made her feel good. So maybe her mother was feeling some of the same thing. She'd devoted her life to reaching the top and now that she was there, what did she do? She was a naturally frugal woman, so she wasn't about to go out and pay six grand for a shower curtain, as other CEOs had done. So what did she do with her life now that all her goals had been achieved?

As for Cassie, in her time with Althea, she'd begun to think about what she'd do with her life other than be at the beck and call of Jefferson Ames.

"I'd love to visit," Cassie said, smiling at her mother. "Actually, I'd like to talk to you about a business I'm thinking about starting."

Margaret's eyes lit up. "What kind of business?"

"Mail order nursery plants of heritage varieties."

"I've read about that," Margaret said. "It's a business that's generating a lot of interest. I could do some research and look into it for you."

Cassie leaned back in her chair and listened to her mother's ideas. On the plane she'd read an article about the growing interest in old-fashioned varieties of fruits and vegetables. Smiling, she'd thought of Thomas's purple potatoes, and how he'd said that there were lots of varieties of berries and tree fruits that you could buy in England but couldn't get in the United States. "Their country is smaller so the fruits can be shipped without a lot of expense. In the United States you have to have hard skins on the fruits so they can travel in a truck across thousands of miles."

The memory of Thomas's words filled her with pain. Her memories of days with Thomas and Elsbeth were vivid and the agony of not seeing them filled her. If she ever did open a business, it wouldn't be with Thomas.

But when she was having lunch with her mother, Thomas's potatoes and the article all came together, and she began to talk about her thoughts. For the first time in their lives, she and her mother talked on an equal level. Margaret didn't bludgeon her daughter because she hadn't chosen the same path she had. But instead, she talked of Cassie's new business with enthusiasm.

It was later that night, in Margaret's pristine apartment, that Cassie asked her what was wrong. There was something in her mother's eyes that Cassie had never seen before. "They want me to retire," was all Margaret would say, but in that sentence, she said it all. All Margaret had in her life was her work. She had no hobbies, and her only family was Cassie, a daughter who she rarely saw. Without work, Margaret had nothing.

For the first time, Cassie saw life from her mother's viewpoint. Smiling, she told her mother that, yes, she'd like her to see what she could find out about opening a mail-order business.

From New York, Cassie flew to Fort Lauderdale. It's where Althea recommended she go, and since Cassie had no other ideas, she did as she was told. As she'd said to her mother, she needed time to heal. It was as though her whole life had been geared toward one thing—a life with Jefferson Ames—and in one horrible night, everything had ended, and Cassie didn't know where she was going.

Cassie figured that Althea had seen enough life that she knew what she was doing, certainly that she knew what a woman needed when her heart was broken, so she followed her instructions to the letter. The first thing that Althea said Cassie needed was exercise. "You can't use your mind if your body is in bad shape," Althea said. "I haven't stayed thin by the grace of God. I've done it through hard, even brutal, work. Your modern movie stars have nothing on us. Did you ever notice Barbara Stanwyck's arms?"

"I can't say that I did."

"Rent a movie," Althea said. "We knew about training. Keep your body strong and your mind will follow."

Althea hadn't left anything to chance. By the time Cassie got to Fort Lauderdale and rented a small apartment with a view of the Intracoastal Waterway and had logged online, an e-mail was waiting for her with the information that Althea had signed Cassie up for six weeks with a personal trainer.

Over the following weeks, there were e-mails with the name of the best stylist at the local Saks, the name of the best organic grocery store, and even a list of old, classic movies that Cassie needed to see. "For your education," Althea wrote.

By the end of four months, Cassie had changed so much that she hardly recognized herself. Her curvy body had been stretched, pummeled, and had resisted so much weight that it was lean and firm. Her hourglass figure was still there, but not so exaggerated.

And as Althea had said, with a better body, she had a better mind.

Of course it hadn't hurt that Althea had sent four handsome young actors to meet Cassie. At first, she'd been angry. How dare Althea do such a thing! Was she saying that Cassie was too backward to get her own dates?

Grudgingly, Cassie had gone on the dates, but, to her surprise, she'd had a good time. Neither she nor the actors wanted anything serious to happen between them, so they'd been free to have fun. All four of them were planning to become great stars someday, but in the meantime they were working in bars and surfing during the day. They auditioned at local theaters, and Cassie helped them memorize their lines. She enjoyed playing the part of the girl and acting with them. They complimented her extravagantly, but she was sure they were just being polite.

By the end of five months, she was close to having a life. She went out; she had things to do. Her mother and she had reached, if not a friendship, at least a relationship. Margaret sent her a six-inch-thick envelope of research about opening an organic nursery. And she'd found one for sale near Seattle. A couple had started it in the 1970s and were now wanting to sell it. Margaret said that if Cassie was interested, she'd buy it and they could run it together.

Cassie had been torn between the positive aspect of going into business with her mother—and the horror of going into business with her mother. She put the letter and information aside. She needed time to think about the whole idea.

It was at night, when she was alone in her apartment, that she felt bad. She still missed Elsbeth and Thomas. And, yes, she missed Jeff too, but that feeling was easily stamped down when she thought of their last night together. Sometimes she remembered their erotic dance and thought how he'd known he was dancing with a girl who'd been in love with him since she was a child. Over the months since that dance, she'd gone over every minute of the time she'd lived in his house. The nights when she slipped downstairs just to be with him. The way she'd cooked just for him. The way—

She always made herself stop thinking about that year. She'd now been away from all of them half as long as she'd been with them. Her mother was pushing about the Seattle nursery. She'd talked to the owners, and they'd agreed to let Cassie work for them for a year in a managerial position so she could learn about the business.

"It will take me a year to wrap up here," Margaret had written, "so that will be about right. I'll move to Seattle and buy us a house and we can start expanding the business right away."

Every time Cassie read the letter, her stomach started hurting. Cassie's idea of a nursery was a few acres near Williamsburg. It would be open to the public only two times a year, and the rest of the time all sales would be done over the Internet. Done that way, she'd be able to work when she wanted to, whether it was all night or for days in a row. And she'd be able to take off when she wanted to. In case one of her children was ill, she thought.

Margaret's letter conjured up loading semis with a thousand fruit trees and selling only to wholesalers. She imagined hundreds of employees, and a selling arena that covered at least twenty acres. She saw her mother calling her fifty times a day with some crises that had to be taken care of *now*!

Cassie thought of calling Althea and talking to her about this problem, but Cassie was tired of asking other people to solve her problems. If she was ever going to grow up fully, she was going to have to learn to deal with her mother—and to stand up for herself.

So, now, as Cassie stepped off the treadmill, she checked her cell phone and saw that she had seven calls from Althea, but no messages had been left. Cassie felt a tightening in her heart. Had something bad happened? To Thomas? Elsbeth? Or was someone calling from Althea's phone with bad news?

She went outside the gym and pushed the buttons to dial Althea's number. When the older woman answered, Cassie let out a sigh of relief. "Are you all right?"

"Perfectly fine," Althea said briskly. "Better than fine. Remember that I said I wanted you to do some acting for me? I just arranged it all."

Cassie smiled into the phone. Every time she talked to Althea, the aliveness in her voice made her feel good. At Christmas, Althea's daughter, husband, three grandchildren, and twelve great-grandchildren had come to visit her for two days.

Althea had told Cassie she'd loved every minute of it. Althea called in favors from young actors. "They'd do anything for a free meal," she'd said. "And to meet you," Cassie said. They'd waited tables, kept kids from jumping into the river, and poured endless drinks for the adults. On Christmas morning, screaming, hysterical children had torn into the many gifts that Althea had ordered over the Internet.

"And what about your daughter?" Cassie asked.

There was a pause on the line, then Althea said, "She and her husband are coming for a week this summer. I do hope I can get her to talk to my plastic surgeon. She looks older than I do."

Cassie had burst out laughing.

So now Cassie asked what the greatly anticipated acting job was.

"I want you to go on a mystery weekend at the house of an old friend of mine."

"Of course," Cassie said. "It sounds like fun."

"His name is Charles Faulkener, and he's massively wealthy. He likes to tell people that his wealth is part inherited and part self-made. He has a huge estate that was built—he says—by his grandfather. He also says that his ancestor was George Washington's best friend. The truth is that he bought the place back in '38 when it was derelict and over the years he's plowed masses of money into it. He made up the

story about having inherited money, and he bought the portraits in an-
tiques shops."

"And you want me to spend a weekend at this man's house and
solve a mystery?"

"Yes," Althea said.

"Is he an actor?"

"Honey, I go onstage, then get off. Charles never gets off the stage.
His whole life is lived as a drama. You'd do well to remember that."

By now Cassie knew Althea well enough to know that, with her,
nothing was simple. "So what's the real reason you want me to do this?"

Althea chuckled. "I want you to get something that I hid in his
house years ago."

"And you think it's still there?"

"If the house hasn't burned down, which it hasn't, then it's there.
The problem is that it's been so long that I'm not sure which room it's
in. One of the bedrooms, that's all I remember. I hid it under a loose
floorboard under a window."

"You hid what?" Cassie asked.

"A diamond necklace that once belonged to the czarina of Russia."

"Good heavens!" Cassie said. "Do these jewels have anything to do
with the ones that were stolen by the robber twenty years ago?"

Althea hesitated. "Yes. The necklace was all I had left from what was
stolen from me, and after the robbery I didn't trust anyone. I was staying at Charles's house and I didn't trust any safe so I hid it under a
floorboard."

Cassie was frowning. "Why didn't you get it when you left?"

"Because Charles and I were lovers and that weekend he found out I
had spent the afternoon in bed with another man, so he threw me out.
Under the circumstances, I couldn't very well ask Charles that I be allowed to go back upstairs to get the necklace the other man had given
me, now could I?"

"No, of course you couldn't," Cassie said, her eyes wide. "So now you want me to go there, find the bedroom, locate the loose floorboard, and dig out the necklace?"

"Exactly," Althea said. "Charles is an old man now, but he still hates me, so I can't go, nor can anyone who is known to have any connection to me. It was only through someone who knows someone else that I was able to get this invitation for you. It's one of those mystery weekends where someone pretends to be murdered, then the guests have to figure out who killed him. I was told that the prize for winning is a rather nice sapphire ring."

"All right," Cassie said slowly. "When do I go and where?"

"I'll write it all out for you and e-mail it. You'll need some clothes, but I've taken care of that. Just keep your calendar clear for this coming weekend," Althea said, then hung up.

Cassie looked at the phone in disbelief and was tempted to call her back. But, knowing Althea, she knew she wouldn't answer. She'd told Cassie all that she meant to. This weekend, Cassie thought. Today was Monday. That didn't give her a lot of time.

Althea put down the phone and smiled at Thomas. They were in her sitting room, a pot of tea before them, surrounded by plates covered with tiny sandwiches, scones, and little cakes frosted with pastel icing, a tiny rose on each one.

"Well?" he asked. "Will she do it?"

"Yes, but then I've taken months to set this up. I had to be careful what I said, though, as she has a habit of seeing what she shouldn't."

Thomas sighed. "Oh, how I miss her and long to have her back! Our house, which was once a haven, a refuge for the weary, is now like a ship on a storm-tossed sea."

"Mmmm," Althea said, "I do so love when you talk poetry."

"More truth than poetry. If Jeff weren't my son, I'd never speak to him again."

"He's still angry?"

"I had no idea he was capable of such anger—and I can't figure out what is the cause of his anger. Is he angry at himself? I can't see that it could be Cassie. After Lillian died—"

"Was murdered," Althea corrected.

"Yes, after Lillian was murdered, Jeff had grief to numb his anger. And he had the work of finding who killed her."

"Which he did," Althea added.

"Yes," Thomas said. "He found them and . . ."

"We don't have to speak of that," Althea said. "But they won't be hurting anyone ever again. And your son was so fed up with his job that he would have gone into the civilian world if they hadn't offered him a teaching position."

"Yes," Thomas said, taking a sip of his tea. "Cassie brought him back to life. It was her love for all of us and her constant cheerfulness that brought Jeff back to this world."

Althea made an unladylike grunt of a noise. "I can't understand why that idiot son of yours didn't just tell her he loved her."

"I think he thought it would betray Lillian, or maybe he was afraid that if he married again, someone would kill Cassie. I'm not sure even Jeff knows why he didn't declare his love. Truthfully, I think he thought he had all the time in the world. Cassie had been part of his life since she was a kid, and I think my son thought she would wait for him forever."

"I've heard that that's happened before, but only in the olden days," Althea said.

"If it did, it only happened when the woman was sure of the man's love. Poor Cassie had no idea Jeff was mad about her."

"How could she not know?" Althea said with a sigh. "I remember seeing them together and Jeff hovered over her, as though he'd slay anyone who got too close."

"When did you see them together?"

"I may be held prisoner in this place, but I do own a pair of binoculars. I saw them at the beach often."

"Ah, yes. How I miss those days of the four of us together."

"You miss Cassie's cooking and the way she fluffed your pillows. And you miss the sight of those knockers of hers."

Thomas grinned. "Truly a beautiful girl. I miss all of her. So, tell me, what makes you think that Cassie won't go to Faulkener's, see Jeff, then turn around and walk out?"

"Women's intuition," Althea said. "And besides, the idea of finding a diamond necklace under the floorboards is too much for any woman to resist. How could she not be dazzled by such a prospect?"

"So what happens when she pries up Faulkener's floorboards and sees that there aren't any diamonds there?"

"Oh, but, darling, there are."

Thomas nearly spilled tea as he hastily set his cup down. "You mean there *are* diamonds under this man's floor?"

"Maybe not diamonds. I might have fudged on that a bit. Actually, I hid some letters inside a clock, and I'd like to get them back."

Thomas frowned. "So why did you tell Cassie that there were diamonds under the floorboards?"

"Time," Althea said. "If I told her there were letters—which are much less interesting than diamonds—in a clock in Charles's bedroom, she'd go there directly, get the letters, then leave. And, besides, there *is* something under the floorboards. I just don't know what it is."

"You know, of course, that you're going to have to tell me this entire story."

"It would be my pleasure," she said, snuggling into the cushions of the couch. "Of course I can't tell you everything, because I don't know it all, but I can tell you what Hinton Landau and I saw. Do you remember him?"

"Of course I remember him. And so does all of the United States over a certain age. There was that great scandal over a murder. I even read a book about it a long time ago."

"The dear man was accused of murdering a young woman, but no one could prove it. Hinton went free, but his career was ruined. Three years after the trial, he ran his car into a tree and died. But that was later. On the day of the murder, Hinton and I saw his wife hide something under a floorboard in their bedroom. I'm sure that whatever it was is still under Charles's floorboards."

"Charles Faulkener," Thomas said. "If I remember correctly, he was a no-talent actor, but he was rich."

"Very much no-talent, but he had an almost magical ability to invest in the right stocks on the market. He made money on whatever he touched. But what he really wanted was to be a great actor, but he was too self-conscious, utterly unable to lose himself in a role. He made do by inviting any actor who had any success to his house to spend lavish weekends with him. We could eat our fill and be waited on hand and foot. I think Charles thought he could gain talent by osmosis. Or maybe he thought he could catch it like a disease. As I got to know him better, I thought he had plans for using black magic to steal talent from us."

"So you were at Faulkener's house," Thomas said, "and you saw Hinton Landau's wife hide something under a floorboard. I would think she would have done such a thing in privacy."

"She thought she was alone, but Hinton and I were hiding under the bed."

Thomas chuckled. "Althea, I do believe you are the most wicked woman I have ever met."

"Why, thank you, Thomas, dear. I think that's the nicest thing anyone has ever said to me."

"By the way, how far along are you on your memoirs?"

"I wrote 'I was born,' " she said.

"But that—"

"Yes, I know," she said with a sigh. "Some author stole the line from
me. The story of my life."

Thomas chuckled at the idea that Charles Dickens had stolen from
Althea. "Okay, so what did his wife hide under the floorboard?"

"I have wanted to know since it happened in 1941."

"So you and Hinton were hiding under the bed and his wife came
in and put something under a floorboard. I assume that something happened after that, so you didn't have time to retrieve it."

"That's right. As soon as she left, Hinton pushed me out of the
room and I never went back."

"My goodness," Thomas said. "It's been so long since I read that
book about the murder that I don't remember the details. I assume *this*
is the murder Charles Faulkener is re-creating this weekend, the one
you've arranged for both Cassie and Jeff to attend?"

"And Skylar," Althea said.

"Oh, yes. I can't forget that. Did I tell you that Jeff now refuses to
see her?"

"Yes," Althea said, smiling.

"So tell me about Faulkener and this unsolved murder mystery and
why he's still interested in it after all these years."

"Did you ever read that paperback that came out in the 1960s that
said Charles was the murderer? Badly written, but it gathered enough
believers that Charles has made it a lifelong quest to clear his name. All
in all, it was a very bad weekend for him. You see, Charles and I had
been living together—discreetly, of course, no publicity—for about two
years. He was madly in love with me."

"Aren't we all?"

Althea smiled. "I didn't love Charles and he knew it, but we understood each other. He was fairly good in bed, and of course there was all that money. I was quite poor at the time, and I had what he craved: the ability to act." She shrugged. "The problem was that Charles was insanely jealous of one man."

"May I guess? Hinton Landau."

"Yes. Charles and I often had great, blazing rows over my costar."

"And that was because you and Hinton were lovers?"

"No! The irony is that Hinton and I weren't lovers until the day of the murder."

Thomas frowned. "Was jealousy the reason that poor young woman was killed? What was her name?"

"Florence Myers," Althea said. "I will never forget that name. The truth is that we all had a motive for killing her. She was a slimy little snake of a thing. She had no talent for acting, but a great talent for lying and stealing other women's men. When you get down to it, I had a motive for killing her, since I'd seen her in bed with Charles."

Thomas put his hand on Althea's. "Why don't you tell me all of it in order?"

Althea took a deep breath. "I've had years to go over this and none of it makes sense. It was a Saturday, the second day of the weekend, and there were a lot of people there—as there always were when Charles was at home. Hinton and I had just finished our third movie together, but other than in our scenes, we'd never touched each other, not even kissed in private. Although we'd done a lot of kissing, it was always with a camera aimed at us."

She gave Thomas a crooked grin. "It wasn't because we were so strong and upright, it was because Hinton's vulture of a wife, Ruth, never left his side. He'd married her when he was just a kid, a nobody back in Texas, and he was fairly faithful to her."

"Fairly," Thomas said, smiling.

"What can I say? It was Hollywood. But, anyway, Ruth knew that he and I were in love." Althea sighed. "But it was a chaste love. When we were off the set, we never touched, but she knew how we felt, so she waited until the right moment to get her revenge. That Saturday morning, Ruth came to me and said there was something I should see. She showed me that Charles and that woman, that Florence Myers, were lovers. When I saw what that slut and Charles were doing, I—"

"You *saw* them?"

"Charles's old house has peepholes everywhere. He was, and I'm sure *is*, the quintessential dirty old man. Ruth led me upstairs into the attic where I could look through one of the peepholes. I saw straight into Charles's bedroom, the one he and I often shared, and there he was with that little harlot, going at it like rabbits."

Thomas put his hand on Althea's. Even after all these years she was still angry at the betrayal. "What happened after you saw Charles and Florence together?" Thomas asked quietly.

"Hell hath no fury . . . ," she said, then shrugged. "I have never been so angry in my life. There I was, in love with another man, but denying myself everything out of a sense of loyalty to Charles, and there he was in bed with that dreadful girl. And to add insult, she had on *my* new negligee, the one I'd bought in Paris."

"So you went to Hinton."

"Yes, I did. I'd been holding back out of respect for Charles and Hinton's wife, but after his betrayal and her nasty little trick of making sure that I saw what Charles was doing, I had no more respect for either of them. I went to Hinton, and let's just say that I didn't allow him to say no to me." Althea smiled in memory. "It was the most wonderful afternoon of my life. Sex with love is much better than sex without it."

"Yes, it is," Thomas said, smiling. "So while you were with Hinton, that girl was murdered."

"Yes. It happened sometime during the afternoon while Hinton and I were in the bedroom he shared with his wife. I know," she said, putting up her hand. "That was a stupid thing to do, but neither of us was thinking clearly that day. It was pure, blind passion. Oh! How I miss that!"

"And at one point you and Hinton ended up under the bed."

"We heard noises in the house and had no idea what was going on, but we'd been at it for about four hours, so by then we could hear them. An hour earlier and we wouldn't have been able to hear anything. When we heard the voices outside the bedroom door, we rolled under the bed."

"And that's when Hinton's wife came into the room and put whatever under the floorboard?"

"Yes."

"But she must have seen that the bed was messed up." Thomas raised his eyebrows.

"Well," Althea said slowly, "we didn't actually make it to the bed. It was more floor, desk, wall—"

"I remember those days," Thomas said, smiling. "So you were hiding under the bed when she pried up the floorboard."

"Actually, she lifted the board with her fingernails, so it must have been loose."

"Interesting," Thomas said. "But you didn't see what she put into the hole?"

"No, and after she left the room, Hinton and I got dressed in a hurry. He shoved me out the door that led into the bathroom, and he only had time to get his pants on before the cops burst into the room and put handcuffs on him."

"Ah, yes. There was something of his at the crime scene."

"The murder weapon, the knife, was his. It was a souvenir from the last movie he'd done. The whole country could identify that knife as his."

Thomas was quiet for a moment. "Do you think that if Charles killed the poor girl that he'd put on a mystery weekend to try to find her murderer?"

"Why not? What if they did find out the truth? Do you think the police would believe what a house party guest told them about a very old murder? Besides, only Charles and I are still alive, so there'd be no one to prosecute. His guests are the ages of the original participants, and they wear period clothes."

"And you're sending Cassie into this? Sweet, innocent Cassie?"

"Don't forget that Jeff will be with her," Althea said.

"If she doesn't walk out the minute she sees him."

"She won't," Althea said. "Trust me."

Thomas sipped his tea and thought for a moment. "So Cassie will be in period costume and she'll be . . . Who?"

"Me, of course."

"And my son will be?"

"Hinton."

"Ah, yes, the murderer."

"Hinton is the only person besides me who I'm sure didn't kill anyone. He was in bed with me when the girl was stabbed."

Thomas looked at her. "I don't remember reading about you in the book."

"I wasn't in the book. Back then men were gentlemen and Hinton refused to sully my reputation. Besides, I was the only one who had enough money to pay for his lawyers. Minutes after Hinton was arrested, his wife cleaned out his bank accounts and moved back to Texas. That she didn't attend his trial hurt him a lot in the eyes of the American people. And Charles certainly wasn't going to help with the expenses, even though he used to tell the press that he was Hinton's best friend."

"I can see why Charles wouldn't help. So you paid for everything. It must have cost you a lot."

Althea shrugged. "Everything I had at the time. But Hinton didn't tell on me, so the least I could do was pay his fees. Poor man. He told me—through his lawyer—that he thought the publicity would make him a bigger star. I've always wondered if he actually believed that. No one outside the business knew it, and they somehow managed to keep it out of the papers, but the studio had just fired him."

"I'm almost afraid to ask. Why did they fire him?"

"All I could find out was that Hinton had something in his past that was about to be exposed by a girl from his hometown. Whatever someone knew about him, the studio knew that if it made the press, his reputation as a lead actor would be destroyed."

Thomas was silent for a moment. "And we think that today has all the scandals in it. As far as I can make out, that weekend, everyone was sleeping with everyone else, and an innocent young girl got killed."

"Maybe she was legally innocent, but not morally. But, yes, she was stabbed to death."

"Wasn't it something awful? Like thirty stab wounds?"

"Thereabouts. I don't remember the exact number."

Thomas leaned toward Althea. "Do you know who killed her?"

"No, I honestly don't."

"It really was amazing that Hinton would sit there through that whole, long trial and not tell anyone that you were his alibi."

"That's how he was. He was a kind and generous man, but, still, it's always been my belief that he took the blame for the murder to protect someone. I think he knew he'd be freed, but if the other person was brought to trial, he or she wouldn't get off."

"Do you think he was protecting his wife?"

"That's my guess, but I don't know. Charles re-creates the weekend and challenges his guests to find out the truth of what happened. But no one has found out anything new, so they can't come up with a new solution."

"But then, they don't know what Hinton's wife buried under the floorboards, do they?"

"That's right," Althea said, smiling.

"So what are you up to? Really up to?"

"Matchmaking," Althea said. "I'm sending Cassie to a costumer in Fort Lauderdale, and I'm sending her a dossier of facts that I know that no one else knows. And I'm giving your son some secret knowledge also."

"He will be Hinton," Thomas said quietly. "The man you loved. The man who was tried for murder."

"And acquitted," Althea added.

"But who ended up dead anyway," Thomas said, and Althea nodded. "After he was acquitted, did you ever think of getting together again? But wait! Didn't you get married about then? To a soldier? Wasn't he—?"

"Killed in action in World War Two," Althea said softly. "Poor man. My first husband. The studio arranged it."

"But . . . ," Thomas began, then his eyes widened. "Your daughter."

"Yes, my daughter was born nine months after the afternoon I spent with Hinton. He was taken to jail, and a few weeks later I married a young man I hardly knew, and he thought the child was his."

"The things we used to have to do," Thomas said sadly.

"Yes, but Hinton kept my name out of the whole murder trial."

"A true gentleman," Thomas said.

"The last one," Althea said, then looked at Thomas. "Until I met you, that is."

Thomas laughed. "You never lose your touch. Have you written those dossiers yet? The ones with facts to tell Cassie and Jeff?"

Althea grimaced. "You know how much I love to write."

Thomas smiled politely. "I wonder if I could be so bold as to ask if I might help you with the fact sheets? Maybe we could draw a timeline and tell them where they're to be when."

"I see," Althea said, smiling. "Such as when they're to be snuggled together under a bed?"

"Anything to get Cassie and Jeff together," Thomas said as he got up to get pen and paper. "And maybe I might persuade you to tell Faulkener a few facts that he hasn't known."

"Gladly," Althea said. "I owe Cassie a lot. I owe her my daughter, my grandchildren, and my dear, loud, great-grandchildren."

"Does your daughter know who her real father is?"

"Funny you should mention that. I thought I'd tell her just as soon as Jeff and Cassie prove he's not a murderer."

"What a good idea."

They smiled at each other.

16

CASSIE LOOKED DOWN at her luggage on the marble floor of Charles Faulkener's mansion just outside Palm Beach, and shook her head. She was still dizzy from all that she'd been through in the last few days. Althea had sent her the box she'd seen in the attic that was full of files about the 1941 murder. It had taken Cassie several minutes before she realized that the mystery weekend was based on a real murder. And the reenactment was to take place in the same house where it had happened. Plus, the participants were to wear period clothes.

In an instant, what had seemed like fun turned into something serious. Actors might now be involved, but at one time a real person had been found stabbed to death.

On top of the file box was a large sealed envelope on which Althea had written SECRETS. Inside were typed pages of information that Althea said no one but she knew. There was an hour-by-hour schedule of where Cassie was to be when, and with whom. When she got to the part that said she was to have sex with Hinton Landau for four and a half hours, Cassie's eyebrows nearly disappeared into her hairline. Okay, so she and the man playing Hinton could stay in his room for that time and she'd read a book.

The only troubling part of the instructions was that she was to sneak into Charles Faulkener's bedroom and steal some letters from inside a clock. Cassie thought back to the last time she'd gone sneaking and she dreaded trying to get the letters.

Also in the box was a packet of glossy colored photos and instructions printed by the Charles Faulkener Foundation. Cassie read through them in disbelief. The man's breezy style made the murder of a 1940s starlet sound like a nightclub act. He talked of past re-creations and spoke of the "fun" they'd had. One photo showed the victim's character taking a bow while wearing her bloodstained dress.

There were pages of instructions, such as manners and slang, and what were the hottest crazes of the moment.

"Preparing for a world war," Cassie said under her breath. "That's what took up people's minds in 1941." She was disgusted by the tone of the pages.

She read every word sent to her, and tried to memorize her part.

She'd spent all day Thursday at a vintage dress shop in Fort Lauderdale. Althea had sent detailed instructions to the owner of the store, and she'd even had someone in Hollywood send some period clothes that would fit Cassie.

Whereas Cassie didn't like the premise of re-creating a ghastly murder, she loved the clothes. Althea hadn't just had any old, worn-out vintage items sent to her, but there were gowns by Adrian in Cassie's matching period luggage. There was something about bias-cut silk sliding across a woman's skin that could change her mind about almost anything.

In between reading about the murder, and reading Althea's notes about secrets in the Faulkener mansion, she rented movies from 1941. She was astonished at how many fabulous movies had come out that year: *Dr. Jekyll and Mr. Hyde*, *The Lady Eve*, the original *Mr. & Mrs. Smith*, and *Here Comes Mr. Jordan*. And of course Althea's movie *The Best of Tomorrow*, which many people believed was her best.

Now Cassie had on a form-fitting, lightweight wool suit with a matching hat that tipped down over her left eye. Her shoes had thick soles and a strap around her ankle. Now that she was leaner and more fit, the clothes looked better on her than they would have before, and she loved wearing them. Tonight she was to dress in a clingy pink silk gown with earrings that looked like real diamonds.

"You must be Althea," said a man from behind her.

Cassie turned to see a man who was probably over eighty years old, but the skin on his face was stretched so tight there wasn't a wrinkle in it. His eyebrows were "enhanced" with too much dark powder, and they were so high on his face from the skin having been pulled upward so many times, that he had a constant look of being surprised. His nose was tiny, his lips were slightly pouty, and his teeth were so white the sun caught on them and flashed.

He had on a burgundy velvet jacket and a silk cravat. He was quite overweight, but she felt sure he had on a corset to hold in his big stomach. His skin was as white as porcelain.

It was all Cassie could do to keep from laughing, but she just smiled graciously and held out her hand to him. "That I am," she said and did her best to hold herself upright in the way Althea did. Even when she was in bed with no makeup on, Althea's posture was perfect. Of course it didn't hurt that for the last six months Cassie had done several thousand lat pulldowns with ever-increasing weight. Her back was now so tight that her muscles hurt if she slumped.

"I'm Charles Faulkener," he said, "and do call me Charles."

Cassie laughed in a way she'd heard Althea laugh. It was sexy, provocative, and humble at the same time. "How modest you are," she said. "As if the world hasn't seen you in *The Last Man*."

"Well," Charles said, lowering his eyes to the floor for a few seconds, "not many people your age have seen such an old, worthless movie."

"Not many people my age have seen *Citizen Kane*, but that doesn't stop it from being great, does it?" Cassie wanted to kick herself even as she said it, but Charles didn't protest her comparing his worthless cowboy picture to one of the greats. What an ego! she thought. He was just as Althea had described him. She'd said that Cassie could tell Charles he was the best actor ever to have lived and the man would agree.

"You aren't like Althea at all," Charles said, taking her arm in his. "She had such a sharp tongue on her. Always ready to say the nastiest thing possible to everyone. I could never keep employees when Althea lived with me. You did know, didn't you, that she and I were lovers?"

"Of course I did," Cassie said, smiling as though to say she understood why. But inside she was thinking that she was going to ask Althea how she could abide this awful man. Cassie managed to keep her smile plastered on as they started up the wide marble stairs. Behind them two young men in uniform carried Cassie's four matching suitcases.

"You'll have to tell me everything," Cassie said, leaning against the man in a familiar way.

"There's so much to tell! Althea loves to tell people that I asked her to marry me and live in this . . ." He swept his arm out to indicate the magnificence of the house.

Cassie glanced about her. The house was like a time warp. Movies from the 1930s could be shot in the house and no set dressing would have to be done. There were several huge palms in big Chinese pots, and Art Deco ornaments graced the gilded tables. She wanted to ask him if he'd bought anything in the last fifty years. "I can see why anyone would want to be mistress of this house. It must be one of the last great centers of true taste and refinement."

"Oh, my goodness, you are a dear, aren't you?" He leaned toward her and lowered his voice. "Maybe you and I could have a drink together later. Just the two of us. You and me. Alone."

Cassie swallowed. His fat white hands were moving up her arm, feeling her, moving closer to her breast. Again she had to work to keep from squirming.

"Ah! Hinton! Here you are," Charles said. "I don't think the two of you have met."

"Yes, we have," said a voice that made Cassie's heart nearly stop.

She stopped trying to get away from Charles's grasp and looked up into Jeff's eyes. He had on a suit from the 1940s, the wide lapels and the wide tie suiting him well.

"You forget that Althea and I have been in three movies together," Jeff said calmly.

"Oh, yes, of course you have. But then Althea does so much with so many men that it's difficult for me to keep all of them straight. Did you and your wife find your room all right?"

"Yes, thank you. Ruth is quite happy with the room, but she asks if she might have a few more towels."

"Of course," Charles said, and his voice oozed sympathy. He knew that within twenty-four hours this man was going to be arrested for murder.

All Cassie could do was stare at Jeff, but he wouldn't meet her eyes no matter how hard she glared at him. Whose trick was this? Cassie wondered. Was it Althea's or Jeff's? Which of them had set it up?

"There you are, darling," came another voice that Cassie knew well. She looked up at Skylar, wearing a bright blue dress that clung to her tiny waist and skimmed over the rest of her body in a flattering way. She slipped her arm through Jeff's possessively.

"So who's this?" Skylar asked, holding on tightly to Jeff.

"What a funny creature you are," Charles said. "As if you didn't know this was Althea Fairmont." Charles's voice told that he wasn't displeased by Skylar's dismissal of Althea.

"Of course. She was in one of your movies, wasn't she, darling?" she said to Jeff.

Jeff finally looked into Cassie's eyes. "Yes. She was in my movies. She was in my life," he said softly.

"Yes, I was," Cassie said as breezily as she could manage. "I was in your life for a very long time. Oh, how you must have been amused by me! I hate to think of all the laughter I caused you." She looked at Charles and squeezed his arm. "Show me to my room, darling. I'm dying to freshen up . . . for you," she added.

Charles patted her hand and they turned down the hall to the right. He opened the door to a lovely room that was straight out of a 1930s movie. It was all champagne satin, with blond cabinets with gold handles—just as Althea had described it.

"Charles, darling," Cassie said. "It hasn't changed a bit since I last saw it. You are a dear for keeping it for me."

For a moment Charles frowned, then gave a false smile. "I stand corrected. You are very like her," he said quietly. "And you're making me remember things too well."

Cassie stepped back from him. "Oh, dear, but that sounds ominous."

"I apologize," he said, smiling genuinely. "It's just that these weekends are cathartic for me, but they are difficult as well. There's something about you that takes me back in time. I could swear that I once saw Althea in that very same suit. You don't, by chance, know the woman, do you?"

"Me?" Cassie asked, her hand to her throat as she tried to look innocent. "I'm just a struggling actress like everyone else here is. I thought

I was to be in character so I've spent weeks studying Miss Fairmont's movies. And I bought the clothes in a vintage shop. Maybe I'm too good of an actress."

"No, you did right," Charles said, then brightened. "I do believe that I am in the company of a great actress. Perhaps when you receive an Academy Award you'll thank me for giving you your first serious role."

"Of course I will," Cassie said. "So you won't mind if I'm quite like Althea?"

"No, of course not. That's the whole idea."

Cassie looked about her. "Was I right and this is the room where Althea stayed? I can almost see her in here."

"Yes," Charles said. "She always stayed in this room. She wanted to be near her lover."

There was an underlying anger in his tone that made her want to step away from him, but she held her ground. "But I thought you and she . . ."

"Althea was an adulteress," he said.

Cassie gave him a weak smile. Obviously, time had not made him forgive her, but how could it be adultery? Althea was never married to Charles. Cassie cleared her throat.

Charles reached out to pat Cassie's hand. "Now don't you worry your pretty little self about that. At the time, no one outside my intimate circle knew that Althea and Hinton were lovers, but here in this house we play that weekend the way it *really* happened."

"What does that mean?" Cassie asked quietly.

"You must sit and moon over Hinton, of course. Flirt with him. Make a fool of yourself over him, just as Althea did that weekend. Then when he is arrested for murder, you must abandon him completely, just as she did." He gave her a little smile. "Now I must see to my other guests. Florence will be here shortly."

"Florence?" Cassie asked. "Florence Myers? The . . ."

"Yes, the . . ." He smiled at her, then turned to the door. "We have tea in the conservatory at four, then dinner at eight. I do hope you can join us for both. Unless you're too busy with Hinton, that is." With that, he left the room.

Cassie sat down on the foot of the bed and took a few deep breaths. She felt as though the wind had been knocked out of her. What the hell was Althea up to? she thought. This slimy, awful man gave her the creeps. But that was nothing compared to seeing Jeff in the hallway. With Skylar.

Her first thoughts were to take her bags and leave the house. She had been played for a fool by both Jeff and Althea, and probably Thomas. They all thought that if Cassie and Jeff would just get together . . .

Her thoughts trailed off. No, she wasn't going to leave. She wasn't going to make them all think she was a coward. She was going to stay and play out this awful drama, get the letters from the clock for Althea, then go back to her own life. Maybe she'd take her mother up on opening a nursery in Seattle.

She couldn't help a snort of derision. Jeff was here with Skylar. She hadn't heard any news from them for months, so maybe Jeff was now a married man.

"So much for his great love for *me*," Cassie muttered as she began to unpack her bags. Every article of clothing had a label on it telling her what she was to wear when. When she'd first seen the clothes, she'd thought it was kind of Althea to do that, but now she had an idea that these clothes were replicas—if not the originals—of the garments Althea had worn the weekend of the murder. Was this for the sake of authenticity? Or was Althea's little game meant to drive poor old Charles over the edge?

There was a knock on her door and Cassie opened it without thought. When she saw Jeff, she tried to close it, but he put his foot inside.

"All right," she said as he entered and she closed the door behind him. "What do you want?"

"Who told you to come here?"

Cassie went back to her suitcase and continued hanging her clothes up in the wardrobe. "I did," she said. "I begged Althea to get me back with you, so she set this whole thing up."

"Funny," Jeff said as he moved farther into the room. "I see you have nothing but old clothes too."

"If you can call Adrian gowns 'old,' yes I do."

"Adrian?"

"In his day, he was Balenciaga, de la Renta, and Tom Ford rolled into one."

"I guess those are designers." When Cassie didn't reply, he stepped toward her. "Cassie, I've been through a lot since you walked out on us. I—"

She turned toward him with a coat hanger padded in baby blue satin held in front of her like a weapon. "So help me, if you twist everything around so I look like I abandoned a five-year-old child and a man with heart disease, I'll make sure you never sleep quietly again. Do you understand me?"

Jeff stepped back from her. "Yeah, I understand, but—"

"There're no buts in this! I walked away from *you*, only you and no one else. Is that clear?"

"Very," Jeff said, backing up more.

"I don't know what Althea and probably your father are playing at this weekend, but I can guess. I owe Althea a lot, so I'm going to continue this charade even if it means dealing with that slimy man, but you . . . *you* I don't have to put up with. I'm going to do what I have on my list and that's it. Then I'm going back to my life, which doesn't include washing your socks. Have you got that?"

"Completely," Jeff said, his eyes wide. "Have you done something to your hair? You look different."

Cassie went to the door, opened it, and pointed to the hall. "Out. Get out now and don't come back."

"Yeah, sure," Jeff said and put his hands in his pockets as he went past her. He grinned when the door slammed behind him. He grinned all the way down the hall to his room. He opened his bedside table drawer and pulled out his cell phone. He called his father's number and wasn't surprised when he got voice mail. "You're a coward for not answering," Jeff said cheerfully, "but, Dad, I love you." He closed the phone and kept grinning.

17

"SKYLAR, I'VE BEEN THROUGH THIS a dozen times and I'm not going through it again," Jeff said. They were alone in the room they'd been assigned and getting dressed to go down to tea.

"I'm Ruth, remember? Not Skylar. All I said was that your little Miss Cassandra has certainly gone to a lot of trouble to get you back with her."

"She knows nothing about this," Jeff said, taking a clean shirt out of the wardrobe.

"Yeah, and I'm a virgin."

Jeff gave her a look that made her stop talking. In the months since Cassie had walked out of his life and disappeared completely, he'd had little to do with Skylar. He'd told his office that he was through using his personal life for work. If they wanted to get an escort for Ms. Skylar Beaumont while her father fed them information, they could find someone else. Jeff was ready to resign and get a job in a burger joint rather than continue as he was.

That day when Cassie left the cabin in his car, he'd wanted to go after her, but sheer force of will had stopped him. He told himself it was better that she left, that she would be safer away from him.

But by the next morning he'd begun to realize what it would mean to him to not see Cassie every day. He'd ridden with Brent and Skylar back to Williamsburg, and all the way there, he'd hoped Cassie would be at his house. If she was, he planned to go on his knees and beg her forgiveness. He should have told her everything, he'd say. And he'd defend himself by saying she should have been honest with him too.

But Cassie wasn't in his house. In fact, she was nowhere to be found. His office saw that she'd flown to New York, then had taken a plane to Miami, but there the trail grew cold. She was paying all her living expenses with cash, so there was no paper trail for her. Obviously, someone was helping her disappear. Althea? His own father?

For months he lived his life in silence, talking only when he had to. He was angry at himself for being such a fool for the entire year she'd lived with him. He'd taken her for granted, assumed that she'd always be there.

The only good that had come of Cassie's disappearance had been that Skylar had been removed from his life. For a brief time she and Brent were an item, but they called it off after just a few weeks, and Brent had gone back to overseeing Althea's house and life. He reported that Cassie had not been near Althea since the cabin.

It was Thomas who reminded him of the "mystery weekend" Jeff had committed to over a year before. He handed Jeff a thick envelope. "Get someone else to do it," Jeff had mumbled, but his father had persisted.

"You'll find what you want here," Thomas said, his eyes boring into Jeff's.

"The only thing I want," Jeff began, "is—" He broke off as he looked into his father's eyes. As Jeff looked at his father, a lifetime of communication passed between them. He wasn't sure, but he had an idea that his father and Althea had somehow managed to get Cassie to that weekend. Jeff wouldn't ask his father if this was true for fear he'd say no.

For weeks, Jeff did little but read about Hinton Landau and the murder that ruined his career—even though he was innocent, Althea said. Jeff memorized the timeline of the second day of the weekend, and he opened the sealed envelope that contained a paper with some facts that were known only to Althea.

Four days before he was to leave, he went to dinner at Althea's. It was difficult to get over his anger at her because he knew that Cassie's involvement with the woman was what had caused the end of his comfortable life. And, indirectly, it was because of Althea that Cassie had left him.

But if Althea knew anything, it was about men. It didn't matter that she could be Jeff's grandmother, she knew how to get 'round his anger, his sullenness, and his lack of conversation. After dinner, she had him in her attic trying on clothes that Dana Andrews could have worn in the movie *Laura*. By the end of the evening, Jeff was smiling and looking forward to the weekend—and although no one had come out and said it, he was sure Cassie would be there.

In the first hour after he arrived at Charles Faulkener's house, Jeff wished he hadn't come. Faulkener was a jerk, and, worse, Skylar was there and had been assigned the role of Jeff's wife, Ruth. He wanted to call his father and Althea to tell them what he thought of them, but he didn't.

It had been a month since he'd even seen Skylar, but she kept making innuendoes that said she thought Jeff was trying to get them back together.

"We never were together, and you know it," he said, but she just smiled.

When Jeff saw Cassie on the stairs, he wanted to grab her, hug her, and kiss her face. But the look she gave him almost singed his hair. Obviously, she hadn't known he was going to be there.

But later, when he'd seen her in her room, she'd given him hope. No one could be that angry and not still have feelings about a person, could they?

Now, if he could just keep from doing anything to make her hate him, he'd do fine. He promised himself that this time, he wouldn't screw it up. This time he was going to . . . He wasn't yet sure what he'd do, but he hoped to win Cassie back.

"Would you please stop following me?" Cassie said, turning around to glare at Jeff. It was night, after dinner, and they were outside. She'd wanted to get away from Jeff's eyes, which always seemed to be on her, but he'd followed her.

"Cassie . . ."

"I'm Althea," she said. "For two whole days, until you're dragged off for murder, I am Althea Fairmont, the world's greatest actress, and I have no idea who Cassie is."

"All right," Jeff said, moving to stand before her. Around them were flowers lining the paths of Faulkener's lush garden. The scent wafted around them. "You're Althea and I'm Hinton, and we're in love with each other, remember?"

"Vaguely. I do remember that in spite of what Charles says, you and I never touched one another off the set."

"Would you like to rehearse our next movie now?"

"No, I would not. I think I see your wife's face at the window. You'd better go in."

"She can wait. Cass— I mean, Althea, I'd like to talk to you. I think it's time I tell you the truth."

"That would make for a change."

"I'm . . ." He cleared his throat. "This is difficult for me to say. I'm not a structural engineer."

She blinked at him. "But I've seen the plans you've drawn. You love bridges."

"I hardly know one end of them from the other. Those drawings were found by the department and my name put on them. I brought them home because I wanted to impress you."

"Me? Why would you want to impress me? And if you aren't an engineer, what are you?"

"I've been involved in the CIA since before I finished college."

Cassie took a step back from him. Her mind was whirling with the significance of what he was saying. "You're saying that the entire year I lived in your house was a lie?"

"No, not at all," he said as he reached out to touch her, but she pulled back. "Cassie."

She took another step away from him. "I don't know how to make myself more clear. I don't want to have anything to do with you. Every time you open your mouth, you make things worse. I promised Althea that I'd participate in this weekend, so I'll do it. And you can be sure that I'll tell her what I think of her inviting *you*. Now, your wife is watching and I think you should go to her. There's supposed to be only one murder here this weekend and I don't want it to be mine." With that, she turned away from him and walked quickly back into the house and went to her room, where she locked the door.

CIA agent indeed, she said to herself as she showered and got ready for bed. Really! The things men come up with to try to impress a woman. "Does he think that I am a little girl and need the excitement of a CIA agent to turn me on? A plain ol' structural engineer isn't enough for me?"

By the time she got into bed, she was glad she'd run away from Jefferson Ames. She might have thought she knew him because she'd lived in his house for a year, but she was finding out that she didn't know him at all.

She spent thirty minutes going over the notes she'd made from Althea's packet about what had actually happened that weekend so long ago. Tomorrow morning Jeff's—Hinton's—wife, Ruth, was to tell Althea that she had something to show her, then she was to look through a peephole and see Charles in bed with Florence Myers.

Cassie wondered if Althea had given Skylar a set of instructions. If she hadn't, it didn't matter because Althea had sent a diagram of the house that showed how to find the peephole. Of course there would be nothing to see, as she doubted if old, fat Charles would be in bed with anyone, but Cassie planned to look through the hole anyway.

18

CASSIE WASN'T SURE what happened during the night, but it was as though everyone in the house had been coached except her. The evening before, people had been themselves, but today, they were fully in character.

That morning she had checked her notes and read that she was to wear a pale pink charmeuse outfit that had trousers that fit tightly over her newly firm rear end, then flowed out until they were wide around the ankles. When she walked, the slinky fabric clung to her body, exposing every line of it. On top was a matching belted jacket that covered but showed everything.

She looked at herself in the full-length mirror inside the wardrobe door and her eyes widened. Six months ago she wouldn't have fit into the sexy outfit, but now she did. She couldn't help smiling. Skylar had always made nasty little comments about Cassie's weight, but she couldn't now.

When she went down the main staircase, she felt as though she were floating. The silk pajama set made her feel like Carole Lombard. Her hair was smooth about her head, styled in a way that Althea had had a hairdresser teach her to do, even down to two Chinese pins stuck in it. Her earrings were little pink pearls, and her shoes were white kidskin.

When Cassie walked into the dining room, she was happy to see that everyone, six men and four women, paused, plate in hand. Only Charles was missing. She pretended not to notice that they were staring and went to the buffet to pick up a plate.

"Get a load of those gams," one man said.

"Must be a hoofer," said another one.

"A spiffy Sheba," said a third.

Skylar looked over her plate. "A Dumb Dora, if you ask me."

"Someone's been studying the slang list," Jeff whispered into Cassie's ear, and she tried not to laugh.

Cassie took her plate of scrambled eggs to the table and sat down. Jeff as Hinton sat down across from her. He wore an open-throated shirt that clung to his muscular chest. Beside him sat Skylar as his wife, Ruth Landau, and she had a sour look on her face. Cassie didn't know if she was acting or if the look was sincere. And she wondered what Skylar had been told about her part in the coming drama.

The person Cassie was most interested in was the young woman who was playing Florence Myers. Althea had written that Charles always cast this woman himself, and he prided himself on finding girls who looked a great deal like Miss Myers. She had enclosed a studio portrait of Florence, which showed a rather ordinary-looking woman. She was pretty, yes, but not beautiful, and she had the kind of face that wouldn't age well. She would only be pretty when she was young. Her face was too flat to have any lasting beauty. And there was a look in her eyes that seemed to be desperate—or maybe Cassie was reading that into them, since she knew the fate of the young woman.

The actress Charles had chosen to play Florence was the same type as the original, in that she was pretty, but not especially so. Her blond hair was a bit thin and her neck too short. She looked like someone who had just got off the bus from the Midwest and thought she wanted to become an actress, but was now wishing she was back home with her family. Cassie had an idea that this was her first role, and it was upsetting her that she knew that in just a few hours she was to pretend to die a horrible death.

Cassie ate in silence as she listened to the others around her chattering in what they assumed was correct speech from the 1940s. It was mostly colloquial, and they seemed to work to make up sentences that contained as many slang words as possible. She heard "giggle-water," meaning an alcoholic beverage, at least six times.

Jeff sat across from her and kept looking at her. She wanted to avoid his eyes, but the script of the day called for her to "steal passionate glances at him across the breakfast table." How could you look at someone with passion when all you wanted to do was get away from him? she wondered.

Twice, she tried to look at Jeff, but each time, Skylar was glowering at her. Cassie wondered what Skylar's script said. That she was to glare at Cassie/Althea with hatred?

When Jeff finished breakfast, he walked around the table to Cassie, lifted her hand and kissed it. "You are indeed a star," he said in a voice loud enough for everyone to hear. What they didn't know was that he slipped a piece of paper into her hand.

She didn't watch him and Skylar leave the dining room arm in arm. As soon as breakfast was finished, she looked at the paper. *Meet me in the conservatory at ten*, she read.

Upstairs, she crumpled the note and threw it in her bedroom trash bin. Her first impulse was to not meet him. As far as she could tell, this wasn't part of the script. In Cassie's version, Althea had written that after breakfast, she had read a magazine for thirty minutes, grown bored, then gone downstairs, and that's when Ruth, Hinton's wife, told her she had something she wanted her to see.

But maybe Jeff had been told things she hadn't. Sighing, she left the room. When she got to the conservatory, she didn't see anyone.

"Here," Jeff said from behind one of the potted palms, then reached out, grabbed her arm, and pulled her into hiding with him.

"I'm supposed to meet your wife," Cassie said, trying to pull away.

"Change in plans." Jeff held her to him loosely, his hands behind her back. "You really do look different. What have you done to yourself?"

"I had sex and lots of it. Now let me go." With one quick yank, she got out of his grasp, but because they were pressed between the glass and the plants, she was still only a few inches from his body. "Althea and Hinton didn't meet before she saw Ruth—"

"Ssssh," Jeff said as he peered through the palms, then looked back at her. "I thought I heard someone."

"It's probably your CIA training," she said, dripping sarcasm. "No doubt it's made you suspicious."

"You don't believe me, do you?"

"Is there any reason I should?"

Jeff's face lost its humor. "Would you like me to tell you how Elsbeth cried after you left?"

"No," Cassie whispered, her own eyes filling with tears. "I'm sorry for that, but you . . ."

"Yeah, I know. I was a jerk. An idiot. You can't say anything to me that I haven't already said to myself."

"I'd certainly like to take a stab at adding to whatever you said," Cassie said sweetly.

Jeff smiled. "When we get this stupid weekend over, I'd like to give you the opportunity to do anything you want to me, but now we have to get this over with."

"I guess you're here on CIA business. So, are you the spy or is someone else?"

"For your information, I was assigned to attend this weekend over a year ago. Charles Faulkener is—"

"So help me, if you tell me that dirty old man is a spy, I'll never speak to you again."

"Okay, I won't. I'm not allowed to tell you anything, but that old man has been involved in some horrible things in his life, and he still knows some people who are doing things they shouldn't."

"You are truly disgusting, you know that? Next you'll be telling me Althea is a spy."

"One of the best."

At that absurdity, Cassie turned and took a step away from him, but he caught her arm.

"Okay, believe what you want to, but I was told to meet you here." Reaching into his pocket, he pulled out a piece of paper that was folded in the middle. "Look at this. It says, 'Ten A.M., secretly meet Althea behind the plants in the conservatory.' "

She took the paper from him and read about his kissing her hand at breakfast, then giving her the note. When she started to unfold the paper to read what came after the conservatory, Jeff took it from her.

"No, you don't," he said. "The rest of it's just for me to know. But I can tell you that it's been changed in that I'm to go with you when you sneak around Faulkener's bedroom."

"I guess that's because you're more practiced as a spy. Tell me, is Skylar in the CIA too?"

Jeff gritted his teeth. "One of my assignments was to keep Dave Beaumont's spoiled daughter happy while he fed information to a department that I can't even name. And I moved into Hamilton Hundred to watch over Althea."

"Oh, yes, Althea the spy. But why does she need guarding, other than for her ex-husband shooting at her? And to protect her from ancient jewel thieves, of course."

Jeff opened his mouth to speak, then shut it. "Come on," he said as he glanced at his watch, "let's go to the peephole. It's time."

She followed him out of the conservatory. He looked up and down the halls, but saw no one, then they ran up the stairs and took a right.

"I think this is it," Jeff said in front of a door.

"To the right and fourth one from the stairs," she said from memory. "At least that's what it says on my script. I have no idea what yours says, since we seem to have been given completely different stories. Isn't that amazing? Life imitates fiction. I have no idea what you're doing in your life, and I have no idea what is supposed to happen in this old mystery. A truly astonishing similarity."

Jeff rolled his eyes as he opened the door and looked inside. It was a linen closet, both sides of it lined with shelves full of folded sheets. He went in first, waited as she got in, then closed the door. It was very dark in the closet. Jeff flicked open then lit a cigarette lighter.

"I guess you've taken up smoking now," Cassie said. "Or have you always smoked but I didn't know about it?"

"Neither." He was looking up at the ceiling. "A lighter is more in keeping with the period." In the next second, he reached behind a shelf, flipped a switch, and a light came on.

"So much for secrecy," Cassie said, and Jeff grinned.

But in the next second he said, "Oh, applesauce!" as he looked up at the ceiling.

She smiled at his slang. Obviously, he too had read the slang list. "What is it?"

"The string to pull down the stairs is looped up high. I'm going to have to climb up to get it." But when he put his foot on the wooden shelves that held the linen, they wobbled. "Damn things aren't fastened to the wall!" Turning, he looked at Cassie.

She backed against the door. "Oh, no, you don't."

Jeff made his hands into a step. "Put your cute little foot in here and I'll give you a boost up. You get the string, then I'll pull the stairs down. Simple."

She didn't see any other way, so with a grimace, she put her foot in his hands and he launched her upward. She grabbed the string and he let her down—slowly, her body moving against his.

"That wasn't so bad, was it?" Jeff said as he pulled the stairs down. "Let me go first. These things probably haven't been used since the last time Althea went snooping up there, so let me see if they're safe."

"With your wife."

"What?" Jeff asked as he started up.

"Althea went up these stairs with your wife."

"Yeah, and she saw the man she was living with in bed with Florence Myers."

"Poor kid," Cassie said under her breath as she went up the stairs behind Jeff. She could hear him walking around.

When she got to the top of the ladder, she stood still for a moment. Before her was the huge, empty attic to the house. It was dirty, filled with cobwebs, and not a place where she wanted to go.

"Look at this," Jeff said, his voice barely above a whisper. "I was wrong about no one having been here. Someone's been here recently. Look at these prints."

"It was probably Skylar. I'm sure she got some instructions from Althea."

"No, she didn't," Jeff said, looking about him with the cigarette lighter. On the floor was a candle on a plate, and he lit it. "Not a good idea to have an open flame up here." He moved the candle about and looked at the floor. "I don't see evidence of anyone having been here in years, but these prints are brand-new."

Cassie climbed fully into the attic, trying to keep the beautiful charmeuse of her trousers out of the dust. She rolled them up to the knee as Jeff pulled up the stairs behind her. "Why did you do that?"

"I don't know," he said. "Just habit, I guess."

"Oh, right, you're a spy."

"No, I'm not. I never had the nerve for it. If you want to know about spying, you'll have to ask Althea."

Jeff began to slowly walk into the blackness they were now in. With him went the light. Cassie looked about her as the darkness closed in, then she hurried after Jeff, staying close behind him.

"I don't like this place," she whispered.

"Neither do I. Look."

She looked where he held the candle and saw the footprints. "Do you think Charles knows that you and I are plants? He asked me if I knew Althea, but I skirted the question."

"Nice to know that you can lie when necessary."

"What does that mean?"

"That you know that sometimes a person needs to have secrets," he said.

"I don't have any secrets as big as yours."

"Oh? What about the fact that you arranged for me to hire you and that you were living under my roof under false pretenses?"

"Under—" She didn't like what he was saying and she would have turned around and left if they weren't surrounded by utter blackness. "Nothing I have ever done is as bad as what you did to me."

"I'm not so sure of that." He held up his hand. "Do you hear that?"

"Voices," she whispered.

Jeff started walking again, then motioned for her to follow. They had come to a wall. "That peephole should be around here someplace. See if you can find it."

After a grimace of distaste at putting her hands on anything in the dirty old attic, Cassie reached out and started feeling along the wall.

"What I don't understand is how Hinton's wife knew about this peep-hole. I hadn't thought about it before, but now that I see this place, I could imagine that not even Charles knew of the holes. Althea said he bought the house when it was nearly derelict, but it had once been a great estate. I wonder what he changed when he remodeled it? Did Charles put the peepholes in or were they already here?"

"Interesting thought," Jeff said, moving the candle and his hand along the wall. "Charles bought the house a couple of years before this party, so I doubt if all of it was finished then. I wonder if Ruth knew the owner before Charles bought it?"

"Humph!" Cassie said. "From what Althea wrote of her, I can't imagine she came from money. It's more likely that her relatives worked on the place. Besides, wasn't she from Texas?"

"You're not only a gorgeous dame, you have a brain too."

"I found it!" Cassie said, her hand on the wall.

"Good girl!" Jeff moved close to her as he examined the hole in the wall. "There's something blocking it."

"Great," Cassie said. "He's hung a picture over it."

"I don't think so," Jeff said. He was digging at the hole with his finger, but he couldn't reach whatever was obstructing it.

"Wait a minute," Cassie said, then removed one of the long, decorative pins from her hair. "Althea gave me detailed instructions of what I was to wear this weekend, and today I was to stick two of these things in my hair. I almost didn't do it." She motioned for him to move aside. "Let me try."

She stuck the pin into the two-inch-wide hole, wiggled it around, and it slipped into a little indentation of whatever was blocking the opening. Cassie moved the pin to one side and the space opened. "*Voilà!*" she said, then leaned forward to look into the light.

"Let me check it out first."

"No, thank you, Mr. CIA, I opened it, so I get to look through it first. I can—" She paused. "Oh, no. This is too much!" She moved away from the little opening and gave Jeff a look of disgust. "I think Charles knows about us and has prepared for our spying on him."

Jeff didn't say anything but bent to look through the hole. He saw a round vision of what he assumed was Charles Faulkener's bedroom, all of it draped in red damask that looked to be fifty years old. He'd been told that Althea had seen Charles having sex with Florence Myers and he'd half expected to see the two of them on the bed together. But that wasn't what he saw.

Charles Faulkener lay sprawled across the bed and his throat looked as though it had been cut.

Cassie told herself that what she'd seen wasn't real, but it certainly looked real enough that she felt the blood draining from her. Dizzy, she put her hand to her head.

19

"CASSIE," JEFF SAID as he stood up and put his hands on her shoulders. "This is probably a trick. Look at me! I'm sure you're right and this is just some actor's idea of a joke. My guess is that Althea arranged it all."

She raised her eyes to his. "Althea said she no longer had anything to do with Charles Faulkener. She couldn't have done it."

"Althea lies. She's a liar the size of the earth."

Cassie jerked away from his grasp. "I don't want to hear any of this. Althea's been a friend to me."

"To you, yes, and to the U.S. government, but there are a lot of people who haven't been pleased by what she's told about them."

"I don't know what you're talking about," Cassie said, her hand to her throat. She couldn't get the image of that man out of her mind. "Maybe we should call the police and let them handle this."

"Not yet," Jeff said. "First, we have to go down there and see if it's real."

"You mean, see if he's really dead? You mean that you want us to go down there into that room and see if he's really been murdered?"

"Yes, that's exactly what I mean."

She moved away from him. "No, thank you. I'll wait for you in my bedroom behind bolted doors."

"No," Jeff said. "You're going with me. If Faulkener has been murdered, then that means there's a murderer in the house and I don't want you unguarded."

"Good idea," she said. "I'll just get my car keys and leave this place."

"Come on," he said, putting his arm through hers. "Think of this as an adventure. Besides, I really do think it's all part of the game. You saw the footprints. Someone has been up here recently, so they knew about the peephole. It was probably Charles. He made sure the hole was still there, then staged this performance for us."

"So you think Althea told him you and I were going to be here? Even though she said Charles hates her?"

"I wouldn't trust a word Althea said." He was walking back toward the ladder, but this time he was holding Cassie's hand, as though he was afraid he'd lose her in the big attic.

"What makes you dislike Althea?"

"I don't dislike her. In fact, I quite enjoy her company. If she were forty or fifty years younger I would have asked her to marry me after our first dinner together."

"You're certainly free with your marriage proposals," Cassie said tightly.

"I've only asked one woman to marry me."

"Two. Lillian and Skylar."

Jeff opened the trapdoor to the stairs and looked down into the linen closet. The light was still on and the door closed. Turning, he started down the ladder. "When all this is done, you and I are going to have a long talk. I am not and never have been interested in Skylar Beaumont. I told you that I got rooked into being a cover for her so her father had a reason to—" He paused on the stairs. "Cassie, baby, there are some things that I'm never going to be able to tell you, and you'll have to realize that. My job isn't something I can talk about to anyone. Well, except Dad, that is."

As he disappeared down the ladder, Cassie raised her eyes skyward for a second, then she started down the ladder. "Okay, tell me," she said. "What does your dear father have to do with this?"

"Let's just say that if he'd been born a few years earlier, he'd be the prototype for James Bond." Jeff waited for her to get to the floor, then he put the ladder up. He put his finger to his lips, then opened the linen closet door and cautiously looked out. "All clear," he said as he took her hand and they walked out.

The idea of the CIA, a dead body, and a dear, sweet man being a James Bond clone was more than Cassie wanted to contemplate. When they passed her bedroom, she halted. "I'll see you later. Back in Williamsburg."

Jeff took her hand. "No, you don't leave my sight. Faulkener's room is at the end of the corridor. Just a few steps more."

Reluctantly, Cassie followed him. She shook her legs and her silk trousers unfurled, and she did her best to brush dirt and cobwebs off her garment. "Where is everyone?" The huge hall was empty.

"I was told that Charles doesn't allow the servants to wander about freely. Althea said he thinks he's a king, so he makes them sneak about to do their work. As for the other guests, they were outside all day that Saturday. Except for you and me. We were having sex in my bedroom."

"Which means that the killer was roaming around free," she said. They'd reached the door to Charles's bedroom and she looked at it nervously. "Remember that the killer was somewhere. And so was Ruth, your wife. She came into the room and put something under the floorboard. Have you looked there, yet? After all, you did spend last night in that room with Skylar."

"I slept on the couch," he said as he tried the doorknob. It was locked.

Cassie turned to go back down the hall. "Too bad. We can't get in."

Jeff caught her arm and pulled her back. He reached into his trouser pocket and pulled out a little cloth case. When he opened it, she saw several small tools.

"I've seen those on TV! It's a housebreaker's kit." She watched him bend forward and put one of the tools inside the door lock. "Really, Jeff, this is going too far. I think we should call the police."

"And tell them what? That a man who loves drama may have set himself up to look as though his throat was slit so we could spy on him through a hole in a wall? We can't do anything until we find out if he's actually dead."

"And if he is, you'll call the police?"

"Maybe," Jeff said, then stood up as he opened the door.

Cassie had no intention of entering the room, but Jeff pulled her inside and shut the door behind her.

"Stay here and I'll look around," he said quietly. "And don't you dare leave."

Cassie waited. There was a deep cabinet to her right, so all she could see of the room was the wall to her left and a small table at the end. To her eyes, the bedroom wasn't real—more like a stage set. It was all done in a deep, dark red, like for an opera. The walls were covered in dark damask and hung with half a dozen portraits set in heavily carved, gilded frames. Cassie turned to her left a bit to look at the paintings and saw that they were famous movie stars of the 1930s and 1940s that had been rendered to look as though they were fifteenth-century aristocrats. There were Douglas Fairbanks and Mary Pickford, Clark Gable and Rudolph Valentino. On the table were silver-framed photos of more celebrities, each of them signed with gushes of love to Charles.

It seemed that it was a long time since Jeff had left her by the cabinet and she hadn't heard a sound from him. She had the odd idea that he'd left her alone in the room.

"Jeff?" she whispered.

"Stay there," came his hoarse reply.

His tone told her everything. "He's dead, isn't he?"

"Completely," Jeff said as he came to stand in front of her.

"Now can we call the police?"

"No." He put his hands on Cassie's shoulders. "This isn't a police matter. This old guy wasn't as good at investments as people thought he was."

When Cassie began to tremble, Jeff pulled her into his arms and stroked her back. "Ssshhh, be quiet," he said. "It's going to be all right. I sent a text message to Dad and he'll take care of it. I want you to pack your bags and get out of here."

All Cassie could do was nod in agreement. Spies and murderers weren't something that she wanted anything to do with.

"Okay," he said, "for right now I want you to wait here while I go check that your room is all right."

"You want me to stay here? In this room? Alone?"

"Right now I think it's the safest place. I don't think the murderer will come back here and risk getting caught. I'll only be five minutes. Stay here by the door and you won't have to see anything. Okay?"

Again, Cassie just nodded.

Jeff gave her a quick kiss on the forehead, then he slipped out the door and left the room.

The first three minutes he was gone seemed like hours. Cassie stood on one foot, then the other, then back again. She kept looking at the doorknob, hoping it would turn, but also fearful that if it did turn, it would be the murderer.

After five minutes she suddenly remembered the letters in the clock in Charles's bedroom. Althea had told her there were diamonds under the floorboards and letters in a clock in Charles's bedroom. "They're love letters and important to no one but me," Althea had written. "If Charles finds them he'll destroy them, so I want them in my possession before it's too late." The last words made Cassie remember that Althea was old and wouldn't be on earth much longer.

Soon ten minutes came and went, but Jeff still hadn't returned. It was when Cassie heard a clock chime the hour that she decided she had to get those letters for Althea. She was sure that if she told Jeff she needed to get them, he'd drag her from the room.

"I can do this," Cassie whispered, then put her hand up to the side of her face and stepped around the big cabinet that blocked her view of the body on the bed.

She walked swiftly past the bed, keeping her hand up and her face turned. At the far end of the room was a short, fat cabinet and on top of it were three old clocks, each one looking like it should be in a museum. "Great," she mumbled as she picked up a clock encased in mahogany. She saw no drawer or any place where letters could be hidden. The second one was ceramic, covered with pictures of shepherdesses holding crooks. She found nothing in it.

The third clock was brass and too heavy to pick up. The front of it had nothing, so she moved to the side of the cabinet to look at it. Unfortunately, when she did, she was in direct eyesight of the body on the bed.

For a moment she was mesmerized; she couldn't help staring at it. There was Charles in an absurd velvet bathrobe over dark green, satin pajamas, fully dressed as though for a Noël Coward play, splayed across the bed. He was perfect except for the gash across his throat and the blood that had soaked the bed around him.

Cassie put her hand to her mouth to keep from screaming. Her heart was pounding and her body was shaking. Who would want to kill that old man after all these years?

The sound of voices in the hallway, just outside the door, made her snap back to the present. She looked back at the clock and remembered why she'd come there. On the side of the clock was what looked to be a smooth place, as though it was worn out from having been pushed hundreds of time. She pulled her sleeve over her finger so she wouldn't leave any prints, and pushed.

A little drawer popped open and in it was a single piece of folded paper. She grabbed the paper, pushed the drawer shut, then scurried back to where she'd been standing when Jeff left her.

A second later, he slipped into the room, closing the door behind him.

"What took you so long?" Cassie shot at him.

"I had to make a couple of calls. Cassie," he said slowly, putting his hands on her shoulders, "you can't leave now. It's too dangerous. It's going to be a while before they can get here and I'm to keep you with me."

"Who is 'they'? And where is the danger for *me*?"

"They are the people I work for, the ones you refuse to believe in. And the danger to you is that you know Althea. We've been able to protect her so far, but they fear that you're now acting as her eyes and legs."

"Why was Charles killed?"

"Because his luck ran out."

She looked at him questioningly.

"When he was a young man, he made money through investments, but he spent more than he made. When whatever he invested in lost money, he began to buy and sell things."

"Like what?"

"It's changed over the years from legal to illegal, and in the last ten years to dangerous items, such as arms."

"Yeow!" Cassie said.

"Exactly. We've had a man working on him for the last three years, but we've not been able to catch him in the act. For all that he seems harmless, he was a wily old man. His one weakness was these re-creations of that murder. He was obsessed with it." Jeff looked at Cassie. "Althea didn't give you some task to do for her, did she?"

Cassie started to say no, but she wasn't a practiced liar.

"What have you done?" Jeff said, looking at her hard.

"I saw a man with his throat cut, remember? It's upset me."

"Sorry," Jeff said softly. "Come on, let's get out of this room. Let's go to my room and wait there."

"And get whatever's under the floorboard," she said as she hurried after him, but he didn't answer.

His bedroom—the one he shared with Skylar—was twice the size of the one she'd been given, but it was decorated in the same slick 1930s style. She sat down on a pale green slipper chair. "So now we just sit here and wait?" She was looking at the bed and thinking about Althea and Hinton being under it and seeing Ruth raise a floorboard. It had to be on one side of the bed. There was a big Aubusson rug that covered most of the floor but left the edges bare.

Jeff sat on the side of the bed and started typing out text messages on a BlackBerry. After a while, he looked up and saw where Cassie was looking. "Go on," he said. "Look for it."

"You aren't curious?" she asked.

"Not in the least. I can't imagine that a murder that took place over sixty years ago has anything to do with what happened today. And today is my concern now."

"It's for Althea," Cassie said, but Jeff smiled at her in a way that let her know that he knew it was her own curiosity.

She went on her hands and knees beside the bedside table. Jeff swiveled around to put his feet up on the bed to give her room to maneuver.

Cassie felt along the floor, searching the beautiful wide pine planks. They were probably made from trees cut down when the house was built, she thought. She searched, running her hands across every joint, but she couldn't find even one loose board, certainly not one that she could lift with her fingernails as Althea had written that Ruth Landau did.

She sat back on her heels. "I can't find it," she said. "Do you think that Charles found it and had the board nailed down?"

When Jeff didn't answer, she turned to look at him. He was sitting on the bed, his hands poised over the BlackBerry keyboard, but they weren't moving. Instead, his eyes were staring at her, and they had an odd, glazed look.

There are some things that are as ancient as time, and knowing when a man desires you is one of those. It took Cassie a moment to think about what had caused that look on Jeff's face. She thought of how she'd just been on her hands and knees with her backside in the air.

She had to work to hide her smile. Althea had said that Cassie had been a fool when she lived in Jeff's house. She'd made no effort to turn him on sexually. Instead, Cassie had dressed in heavy clothes that were much too big for her, and she'd done her best to play down the sexual aspect of their nonrelationship. At the moment, now that she was seeing Jeff's face—and the beads of sweat on his forehead—she couldn't remember why she'd done that. Why hadn't she done what Skylar did and parade before Jeff in next to nothing?

"Are you all right?" Cassie asked, feigning innocence. "You look like you've seen a ghost."

"What the hell have you done to yourself?"

"Nothing much. Althea sent me to a personal trainer who was a sadist. The man nearly killed me, but it worked." Blinking her eyelashes, she turned a bit and put her hand on her backside. "Firmed this up rather a lot, don't you think?"

"Cassie," Jeff said in a hoarse voice. "When we get out of here—"

"Yes?" she asked, still blinking at him.

He didn't answer but got off the bed, went to the wardrobe, and pulled out his suitcase. He pulled the lining out and there was an entire set of household tools neatly fitted into the back. He took out a screwdriver and went to the floorboards. Three minutes later, he had pried a board up and exposed an empty place beneath it.

"Sixty years of waxing the floor probably sealed it," he said, then took his BlackBerry and went to the far side of the room to sit in a big armchair.

Cassie looked into the space in the floor and saw nothing but dust and some dead bugs. She was reluctant to put her hand inside the space. She turned on the lamp on the bedside table, picked it up, removed the shade, and shined it into the hole. She thought she saw something under the dirt.

Jeff had left his screwdriver on the table so she used it to stir the dust about. In the bottom was a little red envelope that she recognized right away. It was the kind of envelope that held a safe-deposit key. She got tissues from the box on the table and withdrew the envelope.

When she glanced at Jeff she saw that he was watching her intently. So much for not being interested, she thought. She wiped the hanging dirt off the envelope, then opened it. As she'd thought, inside was the key to a safe-deposit box, impressed with a number. The envelope was stamped with HINTON BANK, HINTON, TEXAS.

"What have you found?" Jeff asked.

She went to him, sat on the arm of the chair, and showed it to him.

"Useless," he said, handing it back to her.

"Why do you think that?"

"Unless the rent is paid on a safe-deposit box, it's opened. Who could have paid the rent on this for sixty-plus years?"

"I don't know," she said, feeling disappointed. "Does that thing hook to the Internet?" She nodded at his BlackBerry.

"I could program a satellite with this one."

"Oh, right, how could I forget? You're a big-deal CIA agent." She got up from the chair. "You think I have time to take a shower before your people arrive?"

"Sure." He nodded toward the open door to the bathroom. "Just leave the door open so I can make sure no one tries to harm you."

"Funny. I was thinking of going to my own room where I have my own clothes."

"I rather like that thing you have on. Beats your usual sweats."

"Althea does have good taste, doesn't she? Look, I really would like to take a shower."

He looked at her in speculation, as though he knew she was lying. "I take it you brought your laptop and it has a wireless connection."

She couldn't hide her smile. Since he'd found her in that cabin, hiding in the closet, he no longer assumed that her motives were what they appeared to be. "Yes and yes."

"All right," he said, "what do you want me to look up?"

She sat back on the arm of the chair. "Hinton, Texas."

He typed in the name and came up with nothing. "Doesn't exist."

"Hmm," Cassie said, getting up and walking across the room. "I bet Hinton was born there and took the name of his hometown for his stage name. It's my guess that after he was arrested for murder, they changed the name of the town."

"Makes sense," Jeff said, looking down at the tiny keyboard again.

"All those old-time stars changed their names. You know what Althea's real name is?"

"I have no idea."

"Susie Pickens."

Cassie sat down on the end of the bed. "Really," she said and felt deflated. It was a long way from Susie Pickens to Althea Fairmont. "What about her life story about her mother and how she stole everything from Althea?"

"A lie," Jeff said, not looking up from the keyboard. "She was born to a nice, middle-class family in a small town outside L.A. Her father was a banker. When Susie was four she decided she was going to be a movie star and bullied her poor mother into taking her to the sets."

"But what about her mother spending all her money?" Cassie asked, feeling as though a childhood illusion was being shattered.

"You've met Althea. Do you think she'd let anyone take what was hers?"

"But she was a child."

Jeff looked up at her. "As far as I can tell, Althea was never a child."

"Oh," Cassie said, sighing, and thinking of all Althea had told her. But the story of being a misfit was still the same. "But what about—" She didn't say any more because they heard the unmistakable sound of a helicopter outside.

"Dad," Jeff said, jumping up.

"He couldn't get here from Virginia that fast," Cassie said. "Unless the CIA now has an atomic transporter."

Jeff didn't laugh. "No, I have a suspicious father. He didn't trust Althea with this weekend so he drove to Delray. He's never been far away."

Cassie didn't move off the bed. "No one is who I thought they were," she said. "You, your father, Althea. The next thing you'll tell me is that Elsbeth is a junior agent."

Jeff was looking out the window, and when he didn't say anything, Cassie looked at him. "Does your five-year-old daughter know what you do for a living? I mean, really do, not the bridges that you don't build."

"Actually, I'm a teacher," he said.

She started to ask him more questions but halted when he reached behind the headboard and withdrew a shoulder holster and a gun. "A teacher?" she asked, and her voice squeaked. "Just a teacher?"

Jeff checked the gun to see if it was loaded, then he strapped on the holster. "After Lillian was murdered, I—"

"Murdered?" Cassie asked in a high-pitched voice.

"Yeah, murdered," Jeff said, anger in his voice. "Murdered because of me. I was involved in something big, and when I turned in the criminals, their friends decided to teach me a lesson by murdering my wife."

Cassie put her hand to her throat. "What happened to the men?" she whispered.

"They're all dead now. Every one of them. Would you get my jacket out of the closet?"

"Your gray one?"

"Yeah," he said with a half smile. "The one you gave me for Christmas last year."

She got the jacket out and held it for a moment. "I didn't mean for it to be used to cover a gun."

"Listen, Cass, I want you to stay here and wait for me. Don't let anyone in other than Dad or me. Got that? Not even if some guy tells you he's from the FBI, don't open that door. Got it?"

"Sure," she said, "but, really, couldn't I go to my room and change my clothes?"

Jeff looked her up and down. "Yeah. I don't want the guys seeing you in that."

"I thought you liked this."

"I do, for me, that is. But I've seen paint that was looser than that thing. Ah," he said as he heard three knocks on the door. "Dad."

Quickly, Jeff opened the door and there stood his father. But he didn't look like the semi-invalid Cassie knew. This man wasn't the one who grew purple potatoes and spent the days playing with his granddaughter. This man had his hand on a gun under his leather jacket and his eyes searched the room before he entered and shut the door behind him. It was a gesture she'd seen him make a thousand times, but until now, she'd never understood the significance of it.

When Thomas saw Cassie, he gave her a quick up-and-down look to ascertain that she was all right. "I knew this would happen," Thomas said. "Damn Althea! It was my gut instinct that she was up to something. What did you find in Faulkener's room?" he asked Jeff.

"Nothing. I didn't touch anything. I'll let you guys do that."

He turned to Cassie. "Did you find anything?"

"She was with me," Jeff began, but stopped when Cassie reached inside her bra, pulled out a piece of paper, and handed it to Thomas.

Jeff looked at her, aghast. "Why didn't you give *me* that?"

"You don't trust me, I don't trust you," Cassie said sweetly.

Thomas chuckled. "I told you you were wrong in not telling her you were madly in love with her," he said to his son.

"Give me a break," Jeff said and took the paper from his father's hand. He scanned it quickly, then handed it back to his father. "This is what they wanted. It's an updated list of Faulkener's contacts. It's my guess that his murderer is on this list."

Once he had the paper, the energy seemed to leave Thomas. He walked across the room to sit down in the big armchair, then looked up at Cassie. "I must say, my dear, that you look magnificent. Doesn't she, Jefferson?"

"Too good," Jeff muttered as he began to toss his clothes in his suitcase. "I want to get out of this place. I've had enough of Althea's games.

When we get home, I'm going to recommend that she be moved somewhere else."

"She'll never agree," Thomas said, then patted the arm of the chair for Cassie to sit by him. Smiling, she did so. "I want to hear every word of what you've done since my son ran you off with his constant neglect of you."

Jeff groaned but he made no comment.

"Thanks to Althea, I had a great time in Fort Lauderdale. I met some very nice people," Cassie said.

"And spent some time in a gymnasium, I see."

Cassie leaned toward him. "*He* asked me if I'd changed my hair."

"But then he's not very smart when it comes to women."

"Not at all," Cassie said, smiling. "How is your heart?"

"His heart is fine," Jeff said. "Nothing wrong with him but a few old bullet wounds."

"Is that true?" Cassie asked Thomas.

"'Fraid so, but there are a number of them. Some of them are too close to important vessels, so they can't be removed."

Leaning over him, she kissed his forehead. "I'm sorry that all this has caused so much trouble."

"It wasn't your fault. It's just Althea's love of drama that sent you here. And matchmaking, of course." He looked up at her. "Has it worked?"

"Not in the least," Cassie said as she stood up. "Since the house is now filled with . . . whomever is here, is it all right if I put on some other clothes?"

"On one condition," Thomas said. "You must promise me that you won't put on blue jeans. How I do hate those awful things."

"Althea sent me a wardrobe that includes beautiful trousers that are as perfect today as they would have been in the 1940s."

"Good," Thomas said. "Change and you can go back to Williamsburg with us."

Cassie turned away so neither man could see her face. Like father, like son, she thought. Both of them assumed that she was now going to return with them. No doubt they thought she'd move back into the house with them and everything would be just as it was.

"How's Elsbeth?" Cassie asked. Outside she could hear a siren in the distance. It looked as though the police had been called at last.

"Fine," Thomas said. "She went to the Bahamas with Dana and Roger. Did Jeff tell you about Dana?"

"Not a word, " Cassie said.

"It seems that Dana got up the gumption to tell her husband that it was either the boat or her. Wisely, Roger chose his wife."

"He didn't tell me anything about them," Cassie said, sending Jeff an angry look. "All he's done is dump guilt on me for abandoning his dirty socks."

"I never—" Jeff began, then shrugged and fastened his suitcase. "We can talk about all this later, but now I want you to get packed. I'll give you twenty minutes, then we're out of this place. I've had enough of it all."

"Sure," Cassie said as she went to the door. "I'll be ready."

Jeff escorted her to her room and left her at the door. "Twenty minutes," he said, as though she hadn't heard him.

As soon as Cassie was inside the room, she started running. She took a three-minute shower, barely dried off, then pulled on a pair of slacks and a knit shirt. She got her cell phone off the dresser and called Althea while she was packing.

The second Althea answered, Cassie started talking fast. There was none of the "Slow down, I can't understand you" that most people would have said. For all that Althea was as old as some mountains, her mind was still razor sharp.

"You found the key," Althea said with a great sigh of relief.

"So you knew what was in there?"

"Let's say that I suspected. No, I hoped."

"The envelope is stamped with the name 'Hinton, Texas,' which doesn't seem to exist any longer."

"No, they changed the name of the town during Hinton's trial."

"That's just what I told Jeff," Cassie said, holding the phone to her shoulder and quickly folding clothes.

"So what are you going to do now, dear?" Althea asked.

"I don't know. Thomas and Jeff say they're going to take me back to Williamsburg. They seem to think I've now come to my senses and everything will be just as it was."

"Men do hate to have their comfort disturbed."

"Comfort," Cassie said. "That's what I am." She paused. "I've heard some bad things about you."

"I'm sure every word is true."

"Did you have something to do with getting Charles killed?"

"No. But I knew he was in danger and I knew the inside of that clock was his secret hiding place. He had no idea I knew of it. Was there something in there?"

"Love letters from Hinton to you."

Althea paused only a second before laughing. "Sorry about that. What did you find?"

"A list of people. Jeff said Charles's murderer is probably on the list."

"Good job!" Althea said.

"When I get back, we'll talk about this," Cassie said.

"And I'm sure I'll tell you the absolute truth about everything," Althea said, then laughed in a way that made Cassie smile.

"I'm beginning to see why the CIA keeps you under lock and key."

"You don't know the half of it, dear. Now tell me what it is you plan to do with that key."

"Nothing," Cassie said. "I thought I'd give it to you. Jeff has no interest in it. Only you and I seem to be interested in who killed Florence Myers."

Althea sighed. "Now that Charles is gone, I'm the only one who does care about Hinton, but then he is my daughter's father."

All Cassie could do was laugh as she sat down on the bed. "So tell me, Miss Spy of 1941, what do you have in mind that I do with this key?"

"It so happens that I have a friend who owns a small airplane—not a jet, mind you, but big enough—and he owes me a few favors. Well, more than a few, but that's another story. I wonder if you might be willing to take a little trip."

"Let me guess," Cassie said. "To Hinton, Texas."

"You are a clever girl. Do you think you can escape both Thomas and Jefferson?"

"Not if escaping them means that I have the entire CIA trying to find me."

"They were looking for you when you were in Fort Lauderdale, but they didn't find you, did they? You must learn to trust me, my dear. If there's one thing I know it's how to evade and escape. Now, be quiet and listen and I'll tell you exactly what you must do. By the way, how did Jeff like the pink pajamas?"

Cassie laughed in a way that told Althea everything.

"You're welcome," she said. "Now, dear, get pen and paper and write down what I tell you."

"Will any of it be the truth?"

"Enough of it that you'll be able to find what I want you to. Did I tell you that two of my great-granddaughters are Elsbeth's age? Four and six years old. I'm sure they'd make delightful playmates for Elsbeth. You do plan to see her again, don't you?"

"All right," Cassie said with a sigh. "Tell me what you want me to do."

20

CASSIE DID EXACTLY as Althea told her to do. First, she packed her smallest case with as much as she could, including three sets of clean underwear and a nightgown. The rest of her clothes went into her big suitcases and she put them outside her door. Just as Althea said there would be, a man she'd never seen before was standing outside and waiting for her—or making sure she wouldn't escape. Cassie told him she had one more thing to do and acted as though it was an embarrassing "feminine problem." As Althea said he would, he picked up her cases and took them down the hall. As soon as he left, Cassie slipped out of the room, her small case over her shoulder, her car keys in her hand, and ran down the back stairs—which were just where Althea said they were.

Through all of it, Cassie marveled at what kind of life Althea had had that she knew so much about federal agents that she knew just what they would do. And the bigger question was, Why hadn't they changed their tactics in the last fifty years?

It had been easy for Cassie to find her car parked with the others in back of the garage. Althea had bought a MINI Cooper in Fort Lauderdale, payed cash for it, and had placed it in someone else's name. It was hidden out of sight from the house. The only car that Charles allowed in front of the house was a silver Mercedes.

One of the guests saw Cassie as she ran around the side of the house to her car. He had been playing one of the people who'd been riding when Florence Myers was murdered, and Cassie didn't remember his name. She feared that he'd sound the alarm and give her away, but he gave her a look of envy, then raised his hand in farewell. It looked as though all the guests would be there for a while as they answered questions about Charles's murder.

Her little car started right away, and she sped down a narrow dirt road that led out the back of the estate. The front driveway had a helicopter, three police cars, and an ambulance on it, but the back was the service entrance and empty.

She'd written down Althea's directions about how to get to the local airport, and although she got lost a few times she was there in forty-five minutes and the plane was waiting for her. Standing in front of it was a man with red hair and a beard, and when he saw Cassie's car, he waved.

She smiled back at him and felt that she had just pulled off a major coup. She had escaped Jeff, Thomas, and a small herd of police. She was sure that later there'd be lectures and recriminations, even penalties, but at the moment it felt wonderful to be free of all of them. And that house, she thought. It was good to be out of that house where so much bad had happened. The image of Charles Faulkener on the bed was still in her head, and the sunshine felt good.

"Just on time," the man said. "Exactly like Althea said you would be. I'm Bruno." He held out his hand to shake hers.

"Cassie," she said, shaking his hand and grinning at him. All she could think was that she'd made it. She was sorry she was going to miss the look of shock on Jeff's face when he found her gone, but it couldn't be helped.

"Get on board," Bruno said. "I'll get you two started in just a minute." Turning away, he walked toward the little building at one side of the runway.

"Two?" Cassie said aloud, then thought that Althea had probably bummed a ride for her on a prescheduled flight.

She climbed the stairs onto the plane and when she stepped through the door, she halted. Jeff sat there, a magazine in his hand, a paper bag on the seat beside him.

Cassie couldn't move, just stood there, staring at him. He didn't look up but picked up the bag. "I bought some bagels and doughnuts," he said. "But I guess that now that you're a fitness fanatic you don't eat doughnuts. And I got you some milk. I hope it's still cold, but it's been a while since I got it. It took you longer than I expected to get here."

He looked up at her. "If you don't come inside the plane, we can't leave."

All Cassie's good feelings of having escaped left her. She took a seat across the narrow aisle from him, sat down heavily, then took the bag and opened it. She pulled out a custard-filled doughnut slathered in chocolate icing, and a bottle of milk.

Bruno got on the plane, shut the door, and sat down in the pilot's seat. "You two okay?"

"Fine," Jeff said. "Just great. How about some doughnuts, Bruno?"

"Don't mind if I do."

Cassie ate in silence, staring straight ahead. Jeff went back to reading his magazine. A half hour into the flight, she turned to him. "How did you find out?"

"Are you speaking to me?" he asked.

"Get off it! How did you find out that I left?"

"Easy. I've lived with you, remember?"

Cassie glanced at the pilot and saw that he was concentrating on flying the plane, and besides, it was too noisy for him to hear. "What is that supposed to mean? You've never 'lived' with me."

"Enough to know you. And I've certainly found out a lot about you in the last few months. I couldn't see that a woman who'd hide in a cabinet in some man's house while he sat there and watched TV would docilely wait for the police. Especially since she might fear that they'd take away her precious key. After the way you dug around on the floor looking for that thing I knew you'd do whatever you could to find out about it."

"I didn't think you were looking at what I was *doing* when I was 'digging around' as you call it."

Jeff smiled at her. "I was looking at a lot of things."

Cassie took a bagel out of the bag. "Althea told you where I was, didn't she?"

"She told Thomas, but, truthfully, I think she wanted to tell. She didn't want you to go to Hinton alone."

"And of course you think that I can't do anything on my own. No doubt you think Florence Myers's murderer is still there. He's probably a hundred and twelve by now and just waiting for someone to go to a bank that doesn't exist in a town that doesn't exist and open a safe-deposit box that's empty."

"Actually," Jeff said as he looked inside the bag, "Hinton has been renamed Fairmont."

"Fairmont?" Cassie asked, eyes wide, then leaned back in her seat and smiled. "Why am I not surprised?"

"Having met Althea, I'm not surprised either, but we did miss it. It's a tiny place, with just a couple of stores, a church, and a bunch of farms. The Hinton Bank is now the Bank of Fairmont and it's a savings and loan. They deal mostly in farm equipment, but they still have the safe-deposit boxes in the back."

Cassie looked at him. "Are you telling me that the rent on that box has been paid for all these years?"

"Yes. After Hinton died, all his effects were given to Althea. Ruth wanted nothing to do with him. Some of the clothes Althea lent me for this weekend belonged to him. In his papers was the bill for the box, but no key. She set up an account at the bank that gets enough interest to pay the rent for the box. It's just sat there for over sixty years, paying itself from the account."

"Waiting for the key to be found," Cassie said.

"Yeah," Jeff said. "After the murder, Faulkener was pretty much in a rage at Althea and wouldn't let her back in the house, so she couldn't get the key."

"In all these years, surely she could have found some young actor to go to one of Charles's mystery weekends and dig up the floorboard."

"I don't think she cared," Jeff said. "She's led a very busy life, so maybe she didn't think about whatever had been put under Faulkener's bedroom floor."

"What sparked her interest now?"

"I don't know. Probably boredom. Or maybe it's the years. Charles Faulkener is older than Althea."

"Not that I believe you, but why were you sent to the weekend?"

"Leo has been assigned to Charles's case for years and—"

"Leo is a CIA agent too," she said, more a statement than a question. What she'd seen of the man was beginning to make sense. "Tell me, was there any robbery of Althea's jewels?"

Jeff grinned. "No. Sorry. I made up the whole story. But you helped us catch a robber—and murderer. I didn't like your methods, but you did it."

Cassie nodded. She was almost becoming used to everything she'd been told being a lie. "Okay, go on."

"Leo knew that Faulkener had recently been diagnosed with cancer and that this would be his last chance to find out the truth about the murder. He always said that the key to finding out what happened lay in Althea and what she knew. He'd been heard to say that all he cared about was living long enough to outlive Althea Fairmont."

"Why did he hate her so very much?" Cassie asked.

"She told him he couldn't act," Jeff said.

Cassie smiled. "Ah, now I see."

"Anyway, Charles agreed to tell what he knew if Althea would tell what she knew. Leo was the liaison between Althea and Charles. I think you already figured out that Roger Craig was Althea's attorney. . . ." He raised his eyebrows in question, and Cassie nodded.

"Althea got all the gossip from Roger so she knew about . . . well, about us, so she said she'd only tell what she knew if I would go on the mystery weekend and play Hinton."

"And this was before she met me," Cassie said, then turned in her seat. "Who shot at her that day?"

"No one. She sent her staff away, then fired into the air. I guess she figured it was time to meet you and Dana."

Cassie leaned back in the seat and thought about how what had happened in the last year had been choreographed by Althea. "Was she really a spy?"

"Big-time. She spied through every war we had. She was brilliant at getting secrets from anyone. That woman has—"

Cassie raised her hand to stop him. "I don't think I want to hear. Whatever she did in her personal life, she's still one of the greatest movie stars of all time. She was brilliant on the screen."

"And even more brilliant off of it."

Cassie bit into her bagel. "I wonder who killed poor Charles?"

"We have him in custody."

"Already?"

"Already," Jeff said. "He was on the list you found and he was easy to identify once we had his name. Remember the young men who carried your suitcases to your room?"

"He was one of them?"

"Yes," Jeff said. "Of course he was just a hit man. His shoes fit the prints we saw in the attic. He led us to a warehouse full of—" He gave Cassie a quick look. "Charles Faulkener was not a nice man."

Cassie nodded. Her instincts about him had been right. She closed her eyes for a moment. The noise of the propeller plane roared around them and they'd had to nearly shout to be heard. In spite of what she'd said, she was glad that Jeff was with her. Seeing Charles Faulkener with his throat cut had upset her a lot, and she didn't relish being alone.

The little plane landed on a long, straight dirt road. Bruno turned off the engine, opened the door, and pulled down the steps. "Sorry, folks, but this is as close as I can get."

At the foot of the stairs, Cassie looked around. All she could see for what looked like miles was flat farmland. There wasn't a building in sight. "Where's the town?" she asked Bruno.

"That way," he said, pointing toward what looked like nothing. "A couple of miles. You shoulda had a car meet you here."

"No time to arrange it," Jeff said as he gave the man several fifty-dollar bills. "Thanks a lot. We'll take it from here."

He grabbed his duffel bag, slung the strap over his shoulder, Cassie got her case, and they walked to the edge of the field, then waved as Bruno took off in the plane. The silence after he left let her hear every insect buzzing. In the far distance was the sound of a tractor.

"So now what?" Jeff asked.

"You do have a sense of humor," Cassie said. "Why didn't you get your agency to send a helicopter for us or at least a car?"

"And fill out all those expense papers? No thanks. I have no idea how I'd explain a trip to look inside an old safe-deposit box. And Florence Myers is of no interest to the government, so they won't pay."

"So I guess we walk," Cassie said.

"Looks like it."

They set off down the hot, dusty road in silence. "I'd like you to tell me about Lillian," Cassie said after a while.

Jeff hesitated, but after a few minutes, he began to open up. He told Cassie how they'd met when they were very young, and how they'd known from the first moment that they'd get married someday.

She thought back to that day so long ago. "I remember how much you loved her." She took a breath. "You were doing security work then."

"Just something my father asked me to do. He was helping out a friend of his who was there that weekend, but Dad had been wounded and—" He smiled at Cassie's look. "Dad was a field agent. Don't let his love of gardening fool you. He loved being in the thick of it. If guns fired, Dad was there."

"Your poor mother," Cassie said softly.

"Yeah. We're hard on wives," Jeff said with a grimace, then smiled. "Did you know that your mother met my father once and made a pass at him?"

Cassie's mouth dropped open in astonishment. "*My* mother? Margaret Madden?"

Jeff chuckled. "Yeah, your mother. You didn't get here by the stork dropping you down a chimney, you know."

Cassie stopped walking and her eyes widened. "Wait a minute. Did they— I mean—"

Jeff looked at her a moment, then smiled and started walking again. "Naw. Never. You're not my sister, if that's your fear."

"Might as well be," she said under her breath.

"Cassie," Jeff said, frustration in his tone, "I think we should get something straight between us."

"And what is that?" she asked.

Jeff took his bag off his shoulder and set it on the dusty road, then he reached for her, pulled her into his arms, and kissed her. At first his lips touched hers lightly, as though he meant to release her quickly, but he had eighteen months of pent-up desire in him and the object of that desire was in his arms. His kiss deepened, and he pulled her closer.

As for Cassie, she was at last kissing the man she loved. She leaned into him, trying to get as close as she could.

Later, she wondered what would have happened if a beat-up old pickup carrying four teenage boys hadn't come tearing down the road. They blew the horn and hung out of the cab and out of the back and yelled as they flew past, dust and dirt flying.

Cassie and Jeff broke away from each other, laughing and coughing at the same time.

"I guess we're getting close to town," Jeff said as he picked up his case out of the dirt. "Listen, Cass—" he began.

But she cut him off. "I know, you think I'm a child and—"

"You?" he said. "You a kid? Kids don't take on responsibility the way you do. Kids can't be as good a mother as you are. Kids aren't as un-selfish as you have been in taking on Althea's problems and trying to solve them."

"Since when have you felt this way?"

"Since you left and I had time to nearly go crazy with missing you," he said softly. "Look, about that—" He nodded toward where they'd just been. "I want to wait. I want us to get all of this done before we go any further. And I think I owe you a courting."

Cassie smiled because he sounded just like his father. "Are you talk-ing candlelit dinners? Trips to amusement parks where you win me prizes? Dates? Just plain, ol'-fashioned dates?"

Jeff laughed. "I guess we haven't had much of that, have we?"

"Try none. Look!" she said and pointed. "It's a store. I'll put money on it that they have Nehi cola."

"We can only hope. Race you."

They arrived on the front porch of the little wooden store out of breath and thirsty. On the porch was an old white cooler that was filled with ice and several flavors of Nehi cola. Cassie pulled out a peach one and Jeff took grape.

"Traditionalist," she said, and he laughed, then went inside the store to pay.

There was a gray-haired man behind the wooden counter. "I didn't hear you drive up," he said, then smiled, "so I guess it was you on that plane that landed out in the field."

"Ah, small towns," Jeff said. "I almost forgot what they're like."

The man rang up the colas on the cash register along with two bags of Fritos that Jeff tossed onto the counter. "So why are you here in Fairmont?"

Before Jeff could answer, Cassie said, "We're writing a book about small towns that have interesting histories. We heard that this place used to be called Hinton and that you changed the name because of a murder. Do you know anything about this?"

"If you know all that, then there ain't much for me to tell, is there?" the man said.

Cassie smiled. "Sorry, but there was something about you that made me think you were a good storyteller. Excuse me." She looked at Jeff, who had his head down. "Did you get me some of those burnt peanuts? I love those things."

"I reckon I can tell a story a good as anybody else," the man said. "Trouble is that today people don't have time to listen."

"Try us," Cassie said.

21

"RATS!" JEFF SAID, looking inside the motel room. "Two beds."

"Don't even pretend to regret it," Cassie said. "You had your chance in Williamsburg. Now I'm going to hold out for that courting you promised."

In the three hours since the plane landed, they'd done a lot. With the help of the man who owned the little store, they'd called a local dealer and rented a small car, then checked into a motel. But before that, they'd listened to a story that told them not much more than they already knew—but everything had been twisted over the years.

Proudly, the man running the store said he was much too young to know all the details firsthand, but his grandmother had told him some things. Some movie star back in the 1920s had stolen the name of the town for his own, then he'd killed half a dozen people. In a moral furor, the residents had changed the name of the town to Fairmont.

"After Althea Fairmont," Cassie said.

"I never heard that," the man said. "My granny told me it was an old Irish name that meant 'beautiful mountain.'"

Neither Cassie nor Jeff replied to that. They'd just looked at each other, marveling at how history could be distorted.

Now they were in the only motel within a hundred miles. Most of the rooms had permanent residents, and washing hung across the porch, but they were told that this room was kept for travelers.

"You two stayin' long?" the man at the desk asked. "Here on business? Plannin' to see the sights? Plannin' on lookin' at land for sale? I gotta cousin that sells real estate and he's got two farms for sale right now. Fairmont's a great place to raise kids. We got a bus that takes the kids to school. Only takes 'em an hour to get there. Fine school too."

"Thanks," Jeff said as he took the key from the man but didn't answer any of his questions.

In the room, Jeff put his bag on the end of one bed and looked around. There was dark, cheap paneling on the walls and three pictures of scenery. Both of the beds sagged in the middle and the spreads were faded and thin from being washed hundreds of times.

"I can't imagine why Hinton wanted to get out of this place," Jeff said sarcastically.

"The story has certainly become distorted over the years," Cassie said, looking at him. "Why do you think Hinton is so reviled here? They even have the dates wrong. The trial wasn't in the 1920s but the 1940s." She sat down on the end of the bed and looked at the stained carpet.

Jeff sat down beside her. "Are you sure you want to look into this?" he asked quietly. "All this is connected to Althea, and you say that you don't want to hear about the things that she's been involved with in her life, but I can tell you that she's a woman who loves excitement. She's run from bullets and hidden from known killers. Her movies have taken her all over the world and she put herself in danger everywhere she went. I'm afraid you'll hear things about her that you won't like."

"Did all the excitement in her life accomplish anything?"

"During World War Two, she brought back knowledge from Germany that some of our people think won the war for us."

"Then it was all worth it, wasn't it? No matter what trivia we find out here, Althea's life has been important." He was sitting close to her and she could feel the warmth of him.

"Cassie," Jeff said softly, "I want to apologize for all the things I did to you when you lived with me."

"You never did anything," she said, then gave a bit of a grin. "That was the problem."

"Yeah?" he said with a serious look. "If that was the problem, I could remedy that now." He moved as though he was going to kiss her again, but Cassie stood up.

"I don't know about you, but I'm starving. Do you think this town has a restaurant?"

"If they do, I'm sure it's either barbecue or Tex-Mex."

"Darn! And I was so in the mood for sushi."

Jeff laughed. "You want the bathroom first?"

"Oh, yeah," she said as she grabbed her bag.

The Tex-Mex restaurant was in the middle of downtown Fairmont. There were five stores, two of them empty, and the bank was across the street from the restaurant. They checked the opening hours painted on the door and planned to be there at nine the next morning. When they entered the restaurant, everyone stopped talking and looked at them, and Cassie felt certain that all of them knew they'd landed in a plane and had been asking questions about the town's history. She stayed close behind Jeff as he went to a table, nodding at the other customers as he walked. The waitress gave them stained menus, and soon they had heaping plates full of enchiladas, tacos, and chalupas in front of them.

Just as they finished eating, a tall, gangly kid with an enormous cowboy hat straddled one of the chrome and aluminum chairs at their table. "I hear you two are lookin' for information about this town."

"Yes, we are," Jeff said. "You know anything?"

"Naw, but my granny does. She used to know the murderer."

"Hinton Landau?" Cassie asked.

"I don't know what his name was, but I heard he killed a lot of people. I think they should have left the town named after him. Maybe with some publicity we could get some tourists in this place. You two wanta buy a truck?"

"No, thank you," Jeff said. "We're just passing through. You think we could talk to your grandmother tomorrow?"

"Sure," the boy said. "Anytime. She don't do nothin' all day."

"We'd like to take her a gift," Cassie said. "What would she like?"

"A new game for her PlayStation."

"She would like that or you would?" Cassie asked.

"Both of us," the boy said as he got up from the table.

"How do we find you?" Jeff asked as the boy walked away.

"Ask anybody for Eric," he said over his shoulder as he left the little restaurant.

"Why do I feel like we've just been set up for something?" Cassie asked quietly. There were people at two of the other five tables and they were listening to every word that she and Jeff said.

"Me too," Jeff answered. "Are you finished?"

"Yeah," she said, watching him. He didn't seem to want her to say anything else that could be overheard.

He paid the bill, and they headed outside. It was growing dark and their motel was within walking distance.

"Do you think all these stories are wrong out of ignorance or because we're being lied to?" Cassie asked.

"I don't know, but I suspect lies. But then, that's my business." Reaching out, he took her hand and pulled her into a dark passage between a couple of buildings.

"Jeff! I don't think this is the time to— Oh," she said as he pulled his BlackBerry out of his pocket.

"I got the kid's license number off his truck and I want to send it to Dad to check out," he said as he quickly typed in the numbers and a brief message. When he finished, he smiled at her. "Let's go back to our palace. It's been a long day for both of us."

Cassie agreed. They'd had beer with their food and all the events of the day were at last hitting her. All she wanted to do was go to bed and sleep for about twelve hours.

As soon as they got back to the motel, Jeff climbed onto one of the beds and began punching at the keyboard on his little machine.

"I'm going to take a shower now," she said, and when Jeff didn't respond, she said, "And I'm going to put on my nightgown." No response. "The one Althea sent. It's transparent."

"Mmmm," was all Jeff said, his eyes and fingers on the machine.

With a sigh, Cassie went into the bathroom. When she emerged thirty minutes later, Jeff didn't seem to have moved. She was tempted to ask him what he was doing, but she wasn't sure she wanted to know. She climbed into the other bed and was asleep instantly.

When she awoke the next morning, she turned over to see Jeff still sitting on the bed, fully dressed, and still typing on his little keyboard. If he weren't wearing clean clothes and had wet hair, she would have thought he'd been at it all night.

"Find out anything?" she asked, her voice husky from sleep.

"You don't snore," he said, not looking up. "Which I am very glad to know."

"Me too, and my boyfriend will be glad to hear it."

"If he doesn't already know it, he isn't much of a boyfriend, is he?"

Cassie laughed. "Would you please tell me what you're doing?"

"Just getting some information," he said as he turned off the BlackBerry and tossed it on the bed. "It's already eight, so you have one hour to get ready for the bank. We can eat breakfast at the same place we had dinner."

"Then what?" Cassie asked as she rummaged in her bag for clean clothes. When Jeff didn't answer her, she looked up at him. His face was white.

"I thought you were kidding about transparent."

"I never kid about transparent," she said as she turned her back on him and went to the bathroom. She smiled while she dressed.

"My goodness," said the lady at the bank, "this is an old one."

"Is there any problem with it?" Jeff asked.

"None. The rent's been paid on it since"—she looked at the paper—"1926." She looked back up at Jeff. "The bank opened in 1925."

Neither Jeff nor Cassie said anything in answer to her silent questions.

"I don't see any problem with this if you have the key, but I think I should check with the manager. Would you wait here for me?"

"Of course," Jeff said.

The woman went into an office that had a glass window and they watched as she talked to an older man who kept glancing at Jeff and Cassie.

"He's looking at us as though we'd given them a note saying 'Hand over all your money.'"

"Small towns are suspicious," Jeff said. "A safe-deposit box untouched for over eighty years. Did you see who the box was registered under?"

"No," she said, turning her back on the manager's inquiring looks. "I tried, but she kept the name hidden."

"If I know Althea, she had the box put under her name. She likes to see her name on things."

"If I were as good an actress as she is, I would too," Cassie snapped. "I don't see why you have to belittle her at every opportunity. She's done some—"

"Everything's fine," the teller said, smiling at them. "If you'll follow me, I'll show you to the boxes."

As they followed in silence, Cassie made a gesture of around her neck, then her wrists. At breakfast she'd told Jeff that she hoped the box was stuffed with jewels. "Maybe the ones that were stolen from Althea are in the box."

"I told you that no jewels were ever stolen from Althea," Jeff said. "Any jewels that were given to her, she had copied in zircons, then she sold the real ones. The woman has millions."

"As far as I can tell, Althea never tells anyone the whole truth, so we don't know what's in the box. I'm hoping for jewels."

So now she was letting him know that she was hoping that the box was full of jewels.

The teller used her key, and Cassie used the one she'd found under the floorboard to open the safe-deposit door. The teller pulled the long, narrow, metal box out and set it on the table. She seemed reluctant to leave the room, but Cassie and Jeff didn't move until she was gone.

Slowly, they opened the box. The only thing inside it was a folded piece of paper. Before withdrawing it, Jeff looked about the room, and when he saw the overhead security camera, he blocked its view with his body. He withdrew the paper, put it inside his shirt, closed the box, and put it back.

He and Cassie left the room. In the main room of the bank, she waited by the door as Jeff told the teller that the box would no longer be needed. Whatever was left in the account was to be sent to Althea Fairmont. Later, Jeff told Cassie that the way the teller nodded at the name made him sure that it was Althea's name on the account.

Jeff went to Cassie and they left the bank. "Come on," he said, nodding toward a huge oak tree about fifty yards away.

They sat down on the grass under the tree and Jeff slowly pulled the paper out from inside his shirt and unfolded it.

It was a marriage license, dated 1926, for Lester Myers and Florence Turner.

"Florence Myers," Cassie said.

"Look at the birth dates. He was eighteen and she was . . ." He looked at Cassie. "She was just fourteen years old when they got married."

"I'd put money on it that they got married because they had to," Cassie said. "Fourteen and pregnant, no doubt."

"And I'll bet that Lester Myers became Hinton Landau," Jeff said.

"Do you think he ever divorced Florence?"

"If he did, then he'd have to admit he married her in the first place."

Cassie leaned back against the tree. "Okay, so let's put this story together. Lester Myers—"

"Who was living in Hinton, Texas," Jeff said.

"Right. Lester Myers knocked up the very young Florence Turner and they had to get married."

"I don't know the dates, but I would imagine that right after the marriage young Lester—"

"Who, as we know, was very handsome, fled Texas and went to Hollywood," Cassie said.

"Where he became a movie star," Jeff said. "And in Hollywood, he married Ruth."

"Ah," Cassie said. "Wasn't Ruth from Texas too? I wonder if she was from Hinton?"

Jeff nodded. "That would make sense. Ruth sees that Lester—who by that time had renamed himself Hinton—is now in films, so she goes to Hollywood and what? Threatens to tell the world that he had impregnated and married a fourteen-year-old?"

"That knowledge ruined Jerry Lee Lewis's career in the 1950s. I can't imagine the scandal in the 1920s. My guess is that Ruth blackmailed Hinton into pretending to be married to her."

"Not a very nice thought," Cassie said. "But it makes sense. But wasn't she worried that Lester-Hinton's real wife would find out? And what about the baby Florence was about to have? What happened to it?"

"Good questions. I suggest you take the car and go to the nearest library and see what you can find out," Jeff said. "You can look up the records of births and deaths."

Cassie narrowed her eyes at him. "I guess you mean that I'm to go spend the day in a library while you do what?"

Jeff didn't answer immediately but seemed to search for an answer.

"You're going to that boy's grandmother, aren't you?"

"Maybe," Jeff said with a smile.

"What did you find out on that machine you spent most of the night typing on?" Her eyes widened. "What is that boy's name? Jeff! You'd better tell me."

"Or what?"

"I'll go back to Fort Lauderdale and stay there."

"You're cruel, you know that? Okay. The kid we met in the restaurant is named Eric Turner."

"Florence's maiden name. And how do you know that?"

"After you went to sleep last night, I went to the front desk and shared a couple of beers with the desk clerk. That kid has been in trouble since he was twelve. Everything from shoplifting to 'borrowing cars.' Everyone in town says it's just a matter of time before he commits a real crime and gets sent to jail."

"I guess he's a descendant of Florence's child."

"That's my guess."

Cassie was quiet for a moment. "That poor girl. Pregnant and married at fourteen. A shotgun wedding with no love, then her new husband runs off to Hollywood, changes his name, and denies that he's married. Do you think Florence read about his so-called marriage to Ruth in a movie magazine?"

"Probably. What I wonder is if she knew Ruth. You wouldn't know Ruth's maiden name, would you?"

"No, but I bet Althea does," Cassie said, smiling.

Jeff had his phone out of his pocket before she finished the sentence. He called, asked Althea just the one question, then hung up.

"I think I can guess," Cassie said. "Her name was Ruth Turner."

"Right on, baby," Jeff said, then kissed her cheek as she stood up.

"You think Ruth was Florence's sister?"

"Yes, I do," Jeff said. "And what's more, I think Ruth killed her sister when Florence showed up in Hollywood."

Cassie got up. "Althea said that just before the murder, the studio had fired Hinton. Now I can see why. He impregnated a fourteen-year-old girl, married her, left her, then years later he was living with her sister and posing as being married."

"That would be a scandal today, but in 1941 . . . Wow! And don't forget that he was in love with Althea," Jeff said.

"I think Charles Faulkener found out about all of it and that's why he brought poor ol' Florence to his house that weekend."

Jeff gave a low whistle. "A truly nasty man. No doubt he wanted to show Althea the true nature of the man she was in love with."

"And to get her back for saying he couldn't act."

"But the only person who suffered was poor Florence," Jeff said.

"What about Hinton? His life was ruined. He was tried for the murder and acquitted, but that was the end of his life." She looked at Jeff. "Althea said that she thought Hinton was protecting Ruth, and I think she was right."

"Me too, but I'd like to find out a bit more. I have no reason why, but . . ." Jeff shrugged.

"You want to do it for Althea, don't you? What do you know that I don't?"

"Nothing," Jeff said. "But Dad said he thought that Hinton was the real love of Althea's life. When she lost him she lost a lot. I know she's never told her daughter who her father is."

"Old World chivalry," Cassie said. "If she told her daughter that Hinton was her father—"

"Althea's daughter would look him up and see that he stood trial for murder. Who wants to find out their father was a murderer?"

"Hinton wasn't a murderer, just a bigamist," Cassie said.

"This kid Eric's grandmother lives in a little house about a mile and a half down this road. You wouldn't mind walking, would you?"

"I'd love to," she said.

"Good, then we'll take the path down by the river. If that's all right with you, that is."

She looked into his eyes and saw that there was more that he wanted than just stretching his legs. It looked as though he had something to say to her. "Yes, it's all right," she said softly.

They strolled down a dirt road and soon came to the river, the reason the town had been established in the first place. They turned left and started down a well-worn path, Cassie in the front.

"A man named Edward Hinton settled this area first," Jeff said.

"Did you find that out from your 'sources'?" she asked.

"Yeah," Jeff said slowly.

She turned to look at him. "Find out anything else?"

"Not much. At least not much about this town. I think it's a one-scandal town. But I found out something about my life."

"And what is that?" she asked.

"That I love you."

Cassie kept walking and tried to calm her pounding heart. "I've heard that before. In fact, you've said it to me several times. The first time was when I baked that mocha cheesecake."

"The one with the rum in it?"

"Yes, that one."

Jeff laughed. "This is a different kind of love." He was quiet for a moment. "Did you know that Lillian really liked you?"

"Did she?" Cassie asked. "I was insanely jealous of her."

"She knew. I told her how you'd been following me all week and—"

"Please don't remind me that you knew that." Cassie's voice showed her embarrassment.

"It was my business to know who was where and doing what."

"You sound like you worked for the CIA even then."

"Not on that job, but Dad got me into a training program when I was a teenager."

"And your father couldn't be there that weekend because he'd been shot," Cassie said softly.

"Yeah," he said. "That was the third time he'd been shot. You can't imagine what it's like growing up and seeing your dad get shot on a regular basis."

"James Bond's son," Cassie said. "Yet you went into the same business."

Jeff shrugged. "I wanted to protect him."

"And you have," she said, smiling. "You gave him Elsbeth and a home and love. And he's still alive, so you did what you wanted to."

"I never looked at it like that, but maybe you're right." He moved to walk beside her, taking her arm in his. "You're good for me, Cassie. You're good for all of us. I didn't realize how important you were until after you were gone." For a moment he closed his eyes. "Dad and Elsbeth have bawled me out every day since you left."

"Good!" Cassie said. "You deserved it. I thought I'd die when you told us you'd 'met someone.' It was horrible."

"Skylar," Jeff said. "Who knew she'd take everything so seriously? Sometimes I think she really wanted me to marry her. And she drove Roger nearly crazy too."

"Roger? Oh, yeah, he and Skylar were friends."

"He had to work with her dad, yes."

Cassie stopped walking. "Are you telling me that Roger is also a CIA agent?" When Jeff said nothing, she nodded. "Of course you can't tell me that."

"Cassie, I've told you much, much more than you should know, but I need to stop you from trying to figure out so much." He smiled. "I can hardly wait to tell Leo that you saw through his cover. And that you figured out about Roger." His eyes were begging her to understand.

"I don't think Dana knows what Roger does," she said quietly.

"No, Dana knows nothing."

"But she feels it," Cassie said. "When I first met her, I couldn't stand her. She seemed brittle and angry. And now I know she's angry. She may not know what secrets her husband has, but she knows he has them." She looked at Jeff. "And you! You, your dad, and even Elsbeth are covered in secrets."

"You make it sound like smallpox."

"I think it might be worse."

He squeezed her arm. "Okay, so no more secrets. From now on, I'll tell you everything that I can."

For a few minutes they walked together in silence. "So what do you teach?" she asked.

"I can't tell you."

She looked at him.

"No, really, I can't tell you. In fact, the United States government doesn't have a CIA school near Williamsburg, Virginia."

Cassie couldn't help laughing. Everyone in Williamsburg knew of the nearby training school. "Okay, so you're back to being a structural engineer."

"Guess so," he said, laughing with her.

"All right, enough of your problems, let me tell you the mess I'm in with my mother," she said, then told him about her impromptu mention of opening a small nursery, then told him how her mother wanted to take it over. Since she hadn't had a lot of time to really think about the idea of opening a business, she was tentative about it, but not so Jeff. Immediately, he loved the idea.

"Dad is bored to death," Jeff said. "Until you came into our lives, I think he was thinking about going on another mission into danger. You settled him. But since you've been gone, everything has fallen apart. Starting a business might resettle him. And it would certainly get him off my back. He's always telling me what a loser he thinks I am when it comes to women."

"Really?" Cassie asked, laughing. "Tell me every word he's said."

"That I'm stupid and a fool and not worthy of you."

"I like it. Tell me more."

"Not until you say you'll marry me," Jeff said.

Cassie stopped laughing and stood still as she looked at him.

"Okay, this is as good a place as any," he said, looking around them. They were in a beautiful area, with the shallow river meandering in its bed, tall willows hovering over them, and giant rocks beside the water.

Jeff reached into his trouser's pocket and pulled out a little blue velvet box and opened it to reveal a diamond solitaire. "I bought this right after you left and I've carried it with me every day since. Just having it gave me hope." While Cassie was staring at the ring, he went onto one knee. "Will you marry me, Cassie?"

She stood there, blinking at him, unable to react.

"Will you?" Jeff urged.

She smiled at him. "Yes," was all she could say.

He took her left hand and slid the ring onto it, then he stood up and kissed her. "I'm sorry I put you through so much pain," he said softly, his hand caressing her cheek as he smoothed her hair back. "If I treated you as though you were a child, I'm sorry for it. I had to think of you as a kid and therefore untouchable or I wouldn't have been able to keep my hands off of you."

"I didn't want you to keep your hands off of me."

"I was afraid—I'm still afraid—because of what happened to Lillian. But these last months have shown me that I need you. My whole family needs you. And loves you. I love you, Cassie. I want to spend the rest of my life with you."

"And what about secrets?" she asked, her arms around him.

"I'll keep as few of them as possible," he said, making her laugh, then he moved away from her, took her hand, and they began walking again. They were tightly holding hands, Cassie feeling the ring on her finger. She hadn't assimilated it all yet. She'd had six months of missing what she'd come to think of as her family, and now they were going to be given back to her. Soon, she'd have Elsbeth back. If Dana hasn't stolen her, she thought.

There was so much in Cassie's mind that she wanted to quieten it, wanted to think of something else. "Tell me about Althea," Cassie said. "I want to know what she did."

Jeff squeezed her hand. "You want to know your enemy," he said, smiling.

Cassie smiled back. "She is going to be my neighbor."

"You should ask Dad about her, as he knows much more than I do, but I can give you a brief Althea history. Let's see, I think she started in the 1930s. She tried to help calm Spain down, but it didn't work. World War Two still broke out.

"In the early 1940s, she was in Germany with Hitler and Unity Mitford, and reporting back to us. Later, she was able to get information to the French Resistance. She told the U.S. government what she heard about the concentration camps, but no one believed her.

"In the late 1940s, she was a friend to Eva Perón, Churchill, and Gandhi, and, oh, yes, in 1946, she wore the first bikini at a private party of socialites and some top government people."

Cassie laughed. "I can imagine that well. I think I'll look in her attic to see if I can find a photo of her in that suit."

"You have realized, haven't you, that she wants you to write her autobiography."

"You mean her biography?"

"I didn't make a grammatical error. You know Althea, she'll take full credit for it. No cowriter will be given credit for *her* book."

"She had this in mind from the first?"

"I think so," Jeff said. "Part of the reason she's had to be protected was because she said she was going to write her memoirs. She could indict some people who are still alive."

"I guess she found out I was an avid fan of hers from Roger's gossip."

"And she tested you by opening up her attic and finding out that you're a diligent worker whose only crime has been to try on some of her old costumes."

"Those were nice pictures Brent took, weren't they?"

"I hated them," Jeff said, and Cassie laughed.

"Unless you plan to go into business with your mother," Jeff said, looking at Cassie out of the corner of his eye.

"I've decided to tell her no."

"You aren't saying you're going to stand up to your mother, are you?" Jeff was teasing her.

"I think I am. There's something about seeing a murder victim, and seeing how quickly life can be over, that my fear of my mother has left me. If I open a nursery, it will be the way *I* want it to be, and where *I* want it to be."

"I was thinking about—" Jeff laughed at her look. "Okay, no advice from me."

"Unless I ask for it," Cassie said.

"Agreed."

"Okay, so where were we on Althea? If I'm to write her, uh, autobiography then I should know if it'll be worth my time."

"In the 1950s she was involved in Truman's peace treaty with Japan, then she went to Russia to study."

"Study what?"

"She said it was Russian history, but our records say she mostly drank vodka and listened, then reported everything back to the U.S."

"Am I going to be given access to your records?"

Jeff gave her a look.

"Okay, but maybe I could be given a bit of information."

"Maybe a bit," Jeff said, smiling.

"Did no one in Russia suspect what she was up to?"

"If they did, she talked them out of it. And it was about this time that she gave some money to a man whose hamburgers she liked."

"What?"

"She invested in what became McDonald's."

"Oh."

Jeff smiled. "In the 1960s she was—"

"Let me guess. Friends with the Kennedys."

"Good friends, and heaven only knows what she did for JFK."

"And the 1970s?"

"That's still classified. I can't tell you the specifics, but I can assure you that she was busy."

"With things other than making three movies a year?"

"I think that you'll find that most of those movies are set in foreign countries." Jeff raised her hand and kissed it. "You think this would be interesting enough for you to write about?"

"Has anyone thought about the fact that I have no idea how to write a book?"

Jeff shrugged. "Dad's done some writing. You assemble what Althea tells you, go through that stuff in her attic, and Dad will help you put it all together. It'll keep him occupied."

"And me. So you can do whatever it is that you do all day and not have to worry that I'm going to run off with the next-door neighbor's gorgeous gardener."

"More or less," Jeff said, grinning, then he pointed toward a pretty little house nearly hidden under three huge willow trees. "There it is." The house was set far enough from the river to not worry about floods, but close enough to enjoy the sound and the view.

"Come on," Jeff said. "She's expecting us."

22

CASSIE'S FIRST THOUGHT when she saw the old woman was, What a marvelous thing plastic surgery is. The woman was younger than Althea but looked fifty years older. She was heavy, walked with a limp, and her face showed her years spent in the Texas sun. Her gray hair was pulled back into a bun, and her clothes were worn and faded.

The house was small, but very clean and welcoming. Cassie recognized the scent of old-fashioned spice cake in the air. The furniture was old and frayed, but comfortable-looking. Set around the house were what had to be hundreds of photographs in interesting frames. She could imagine that for every holiday "Granny" was given picture frames, and from the looks of them, her relatives competed to see who could come up with the most unusual frames.

Mrs. Turner went to the kitchen and poured out three glasses of heavily sugared iced tea. Jeff held out one of the chairs to the kitchen table, and she sat down.

"Now what is it you two want to know?" she asked, looking from one to the other as Jeff and Cassie seated themselves at the table. Jeff took the marriage certificate out of his pocket and put it on the table in front of her.

She glanced at it, then looked up about the house. Cassie knew what she wanted and soon located her glasses.

Nodding at Cassie in thanks, Mrs. Turner put on her reading glasses and spent some minutes looking at the certificate, then she put it down and took off her glasses. "This takes me back. Where did you find this?"

Jeff told her about the safe-deposit box that had been rented for over eighty years.

"I guess it was that movie star Lester was so mad about, the one that paid his bills," she said.

"Althea Fairmont," Cassie said.

Mrs. Turner smiled, her face crinkling into a thousand wrinkles. "Can you believe that the fools named the town after a movie star? They were in a hangin' mood because the town had the same name as a movie star they thought had killed a woman, so what did they do but rename it after another one? Did you ever hear of anything so stupid?"

Cassie and Jeff laughed. "I hear you put it around that it was named after a beautiful mountain," Jeff said.

"That's an advantage of living so long," she said. "Most of them died long ago, so I started telling the babies that our town was named after something other than a woman who acted in pictures. In my day, we didn't let women like her into the good parlor."

"But Lester became an actor."

"Not a very good one," Mrs. Turner said. "It was more that women loved him. Today you'd say that they were hot for him. A real heart-throb."

"It got him in a lot of trouble," Cassie said.

"That it did," Mrs. Turner said, laughing and showing that she had three teeth missing on the bottom. "But it was that young Florence that snagged him. Poor kid."

"Which one?" Jeff asked.

"Why Lester, of course. I was only about eight years old, but he was real nice to me. He used to let me go fishing with him. One time he told me that I was the only female he knew who didn't try to kiss him."

"But you wanted to," Cassie said, smiling.

"Oh, heavens, did I!" she said, laughing. "I was so in love with him that all I could think about was him."

"I know about being young and in love," Cassie said, glancing at Jeff. "It hurts. Especially when the older person treats you like you're a kid."

Mrs. Turner chuckled. "But I see you got your 'older man.'" She nodded toward Cassie's shiny new ring.

"That I did," Cassie said, smiling. "So all the women in town were in love with Lester Myers but Florence got him. What was she like?"

"She was my husband's cousin and family, but that didn't keep me from seeing her for what she was. I know that paper says she was only fourteen, but she was a lot older than that. She started fooling around with boys when she was twelve. By the time she was fourteen, she was more experienced than a lot of married women."

"And what about Ruth?" Jeff asked.

Mrs. Turner looked at him in surprise. "It seems to me that you already know all the story."

"Just the basics, nothing else. How were Ruth and Florence related?"

"Half sisters. Same mother but different fathers. Ruth's father was married to her mother, but he died when she was little. Her mother had to take in washing to support them, but she also did a little other business on the side—if you know what I mean."

"Yes," Cassie said.

"Nobody knew who Florence's father was."

"Did Ruth want Lester too?" Jeff asked.

"We all did," Mrs. Turner said. "There was something about Les that attracted women. He was beautiful from the time he was born, that's true, but there was more to it than that. When he was around, women put on their best clothes, and looked at him with big, round eyes."

Jeff drank some of his tea. "So the two women, Ruth and Florence, were both after him?"

"Florence went after him so that the whole town knew about it, but Ruth was quieter. She used to bake pies for his family. But pies don't win a young man's heart."

"Hear! Hear!" Cassie said with feeling. "That's something I know well. Six months in a gym and silk charmeuse work much better."

Jeff laughed and Mrs. Turner's eyes twinkled. "I think I should be listening to a story, rather than telling one."

"No, please," Jeff said, smiling. "We want to hear all of it."

"I think that paper of yours tells it all. It was Les's mother who wanted him to go to Hollywood. She read movie magazines and knew all the gossip, and she said her beautiful son was wasted in this two-bit Texas town. She said that as soon as Les graduated from high school, he was going to Hollywood and become a movie star. She had a little beauty shop in the front room of her house and she saved everything she made for about four years and she planned to give it to her son. She was very proud of him. Too proud, maybe, considering what happened."

"That's just it," Jeff said, "we don't think Hinton, uh, Lester, killed anyone."

"Of course he didn't," she said as she stood up. "Anybody that ever knew him knew he couldn't kill anybody, certainly not a woman. You want some more tea?"

Jeff held out his glass, but Cassie shook her head.

"What do you think happened?" Cassie asked.

"I think Ruth decided that Les being married to Florence was just a little hitch in her plans. She'd decided that she was going to go to Hollywood with Les, so that's what she did."

"But it was Florence who married him," Cassie said, backtracking. "Did she seduce him?"

"Who knows?" Mrs. Turner said. "She came up pregnant just before Les graduated from high school, and my husband's father said he was going to kill Les if he didn't marry the girl."

"But married or not, he left for Hollywood right after that," Jeff said.

Mrs. Turner gave a one-sided smile. "Florence thought that if Les went to Hollywood she'd go with him as his wife, but Les's mother had other ideas. She had to let the marriage go through because back then girls who were pregnant and single . . ." She shrugged. "It's different from today. Anyway, Les's mother took everything into her own hands. The night Les and Florence were married, his mother sneaked her son onto a train heading west. She told Les she'd take care of his wife and child and when he was famous he could send for them."

"But he didn't send for them," Cassie said. "Instead, Ruth went after him."

"She did. Soon after the wedding, she raided her mother's cookie jar and bought herself a ticket to Hollywood."

"And blackmailed Lester, who was Hinton, by then," Jeff said, "into pretending he was married to her."

"Exactly," Mrs. Turner said. "But to be fair to Ruth, she managed Les's career. He was a sweet boy, and if it had been up to him, he would have worked for pennies, but Ruth was a terror. She oversaw all his contracts. She was the reason he was ever made the star of any picture."

"You'd think that someone from this town would have exposed it all," Cassie said. "They saw the movie magazines, so they knew what had happened."

"People can be real dumb," Mrs. Turner said. "But the truth was that Lester wasn't famous for years after he left home. He only had bit parts, and he was never in any magazines. He only got to be famous when he started making pictures with Althea Fairmont. Have you seen any of those old pictures?"

"Every one of them," Cassie said. "Those two were electric on the screen."

"They were," Mrs. Turner said. "That was back in the days when they showed real passion in the movies. Now they don't smolder and yearn. Now they take off their clothes and read each other's tattoos."

Both Cassie and Jeff laughed. "Why didn't Florence go to Hollywood right after she had the baby?"

"Because Ruth paid her to stay away. I was a kid but I heard what was said. Lester's mother told Florence that if she went out to Hollywood, Les would divorce her, and she'd have to come back to Hinton and take in washing like her mother did. But if she stayed here in Texas and kept her mouth shut, Ruth would see that she had money."

"I doubt if Florence liked that idea," Jeff said.

"Not at all," Mrs. Turner said, "but she held to it until her mother died. Then Florence got an invitation to a party."

"At Charles Faulkener's house."

"Right," Mrs. Turner said. "He paid for her upkeep in a little house for a few months before she saw Ruth and Lester again. Mr. Faulkener made her lose weight and dye her hair platinum."

"And when she did see them, she was killed," Jeff said.

"Who do you think did it?" Cassie asked.

"Ruth. No doubt about it in my mind at all. Ruth loathed Florence. Hated her all her life. Florence was pretty and easy with people, and went after whatever she wanted. Ruth was big and clumsy and she wanted only one thing in life."

"Lester Myers," Cassie said.

"That's right."

"But she let him take the rap for the murder," Jeff said. "When the chips were down, she let him hang."

Mrs. Turner shrugged. "Who knows what happened? Ruth came back here right after the murder and she never left again. She bought that big brick house on the corner by the bank and lived there the rest of her life. As far as I know, she never so much as got on a train again."

"What did she do with her life?" Cassie asked.

"She went to church a lot." Mrs. Turner's old eyes twinkled. "A lot of people said it was guilt."

"And poor Hinton-Lester died just three years later," Cassie said.

"Do you know anything about that?" Jeff asked.

"Nothing. I know that Ruth pulled the curtains to her house and didn't come out for a year. She had her groceries delivered. When she did come out, she was an old woman, but she never spoke of her sister or Les. If she'd said a word, it would have been all over town."

"When did she die?" Cassie asked.

"A long time ago. She didn't live but about five years after Les passed away, but she aged a lot in those years. It's my guess it was caused by guilt and grief."

"Do you know what happened to her estate?" Jeff asked.

Mrs. Turner smiled. "You mean all that money she was supposed to have stolen from her rich husband? Oh, yes, we heard about that even out here in Texas. But if someone stole it, it either wasn't very much, or someone other than Ruth got it. Her house was auctioned off, and all the money went to pay off her debts." She looked at Cassie. "The gossip magazines used to hint that Les and Mrs. Fairmont were in love off-screen. Were they?"

"Oh, yes," Cassie said. "Madly in love. Althea had a daughter with Hinton."

"Then she's related to my grandbabies."

"Oh, yeah, about that," Jeff said. "What happened to Florence's baby?"

"She dumped it onto her mother, then when her mother died, my mother got the child to raise." Mrs. Turner smiled. "I'm happy to say that the girl took after her daddy and not her mother. She was as pretty as a flower and as sweet tempered as well. She went to Texas State and married a man who was a preacher. They had three kids and seemed to be as happy as could be."

"I'm glad," Cassie said. "It's good to hear that someone involved in this awful story was happy."

"Just them," Mrs. Turner said. "One of those three kids took after Florence and came back here to wait out her time."

"And what happened to that child?"

Mrs. Turner's eyes darkened. "I'd rather not say what that girl did, but she was too much like Florence. I raised one of her kids."

"Then it was lucky you were here," Cassie said, smiling.

Mrs. Turner sighed. "Maybe so, maybe not."

"What's wrong?" Cassie asked softly.

"The times may change, but people don't. I have a granddaughter— or she seems like mine, but she's descended from Les's child—and she's a throwback to him. She's pretty and sweet tempered, and very smart. But . . ."

Cassie put her hand over the old woman's. "What's happened?"

"She's about to have a baby." Mrs. Turner shook her head in wonder. "Here it is in the time of free abortion, but the girl is a pro-lifer. She said she couldn't bear to kill her own baby, so she's having it. I wanted her to go to college, but she's planning to raise the baby by herself. The boy that fathered it is long gone."

"She doesn't have to give up after she has the baby. She could put it up for adoption," Cassie said.

"We've all told her that, and she agrees, but she wants the baby to be in her family, not given away to strangers."

Suddenly, Cassie sat up straight in her chair. "How smart is this girl? Honestly?"

"She took some college tests and made it in the top two percent in the nation," Mrs. Turner said proudly.

Cassie looked at Jeff and smiled. "I have an idea how to solve it all."

Jeff looked at her with interest. "How?"

"Give me your phone. I need to call Althea."

"She still alive?" Mrs. Turner asked. "She must be over a hundred now."

"She's alive and imprisoned in a huge house and she needs help setting up a library for budding young actors. She will be thrilled to help a descendant of her beloved Hinton's. And there's a fabulous university in Williamsburg that—" Cassie waited for the name.

"Lisa," Mrs. Turner said.

Cassie started punching buttons on Jeff's phone. "Lisa can go to school there, earn money working for Althea, and as for the baby—"

Jeff grinned. "We know a couple who will take the baby. They're not blood relatives, but they're good people. Lisa could meet them. They want a child more than they want life."

"Yes," Cassie said, smiling. "And I'm sure that Roger will shell out for the college expenses. He can afford it, now that he's given up his boat."

Jeff laughed. "I'm going to miss that boat that I never went on," he said.

Cassie stopped punching buttons. "You never went on the boat? But Elsbeth told me all about your last trip and the fish you caught."

"I've never been fishing in my life," Jeff said, looking down at his iced tea glass.

Cassie could only stare at the top of his head. "Are you telling me that you had your five-year-old daughter tell lies?"

"Yes and no," Jeff said, his voice full of apology. "I just told her not to mention that we hadn't gone on a boat and she made up the rest of it. She's a great storyteller, isn't she?"

Cassie narrowed her eyes at him. "There are going to be some *big* changes made in your house—my house. Do you understand me?"

"I look forward to it," Jeff said, grinning. "Now call Althea and get this settled so we can go home and get married."

Mrs. Turner laughed at them. Jeff was grinning, and Cassie was frowning at him. "The world never changes," she said.